The Widow Brigade

(A novel set in the realm of Dhea Loral)

Janice,
Thanks for helping me craft this
story. Folks love it! And I have you
and the rest of the East St. Paul group
to thank!

Douglas Van Dyke Jr.

"Well-behaved women seldom make history."

- Laurel Thatcher Ulrich

My thanks to the folks at the Minnesota Speculative Fiction Writers Meetup group, particularly members from the East St Paul chapter. Their feedback helped me develop Duli's story much better than I could have achieved on my own.

Prologue

Duli enjoyed receiving a kiss gentler than might be expected from the dwarf warrior, Geordan Greencutter. She never wanted that touch to end, but duty tugged her husband away. He drew back, his eyes never leaving hers, his hand trailing one last touch through her sandy-brown hair. She held her pose steady. Duli knew he was relishing an image of her to sustain him on his journey.

Geordan began dressing for the road, lit by a dying hearthfire. She watched lover turn to warrior. His movements echoed in their stone warren, deep under Dhea Loral's surface world. Metal armor covered a brawny chest. An axe with a notched blade sat comfortably in his belt. He tucked a helm featuring the symbols of Nandorrin, God of Fire, under one arm.

His attire contrasted Duli's nakedness, as she lay partially covered in furs upon their bed. Duli looked away from her husband for only a moment, throwing a glance at an item resting against the wall. "I wish you would take your musket. It would make me feel safer."

Geordan sighed and shook his head. He collected the gear close to his musket, yet left the weapon where it rested. He hefted his pack, never turning his back to his loved one. "It wouldn't be proper for the journey. I won't be alone."

"I know the tales about leaving a gun behind."

Geordan gave her a comforting smile. "What do they say?"

In the face of his easy attitude, Duli began to feel that her fears were silly. Perhaps she was worrying too much. She lowered her eyes, "Well, you usually take it with you…"

"Not always…"

"…but you aren't allowed to take it on forays that have a good chance of ambush or capture. Are you being honest with me? How grim is this journey?"

He waited until she looked back up at him. Even though her countenance was beset with worry, Geordan's eyes clearly held her in awe. She didn't know what had attracted him to her so, but he always let her know that Duli was his light in the dark.

"We've had border clashes with the Tariykan Empire, but this isn't a matter worth worrying. My company is going to a peace talk. It isn't proper to walk in there with muskets."

Duli nodded. "I guess I'm just worried for you. I gave up my old life to start one here by your side. You are my home; not these tunnels. If you ever meet your death before me, I hope the gods take my life soon after."

Geordan stood by the door, offering a confident, reassuring visage. "I would feel the same way. You are my world. Try not to worry."

The door closed and he was gone. Duli reclined alone on their bed, trying not to dwell on her fears. The dwarf woman set her mind on the bright future they would have. Her thoughts wandered to when they would try for a baby and what names they would pick. Sleep came peacefully.

CHAPTER 1

Duli walked among the other dwarves living in the subterranean city Tok-Maurron, bartering away the leather goods she crafted in favor of household needs. A new noise drowned out the low, constant echo of voices characteristic of Lower City's large cavern. A pause settled over the crowded marketplace as a series of horn blasts sounded. The cadence of notes carried a clear message: a company of warriors had returned to the clan. The news lifted Duli's spirits. As far as she knew, her husband's company was the only one that had been out. Other dwarves reacted with equal excitement, voices echoing louder across the cavern.

She wasted no more time with her neighbors. It had been eighteen days, almost two full weeks, since he departed for the human country of Tariyka. The chamber they shared felt lonely with his presence gone. She wanted to greet him properly.

Her sturdy, dwarven frame weaved through the crowds as she made for Nandorrin's Halls, a warren full of working-class families. To get there from the market, she had a long run down the gentle, terraced slope of the gargantuan cavern of Lower City toward the bright glow of Hearthfire that gave the city and warrens warmth. She raced through the smoky haze permeating the merchant section, past decorative pillars supporting the cavern roof. Smokeless lamps and a fair amount of luminous plants on walls and in gardens lit her path. Dwarves needed only small amounts of light to see in the dark. It wasn't a lack of sight but a confusing movement in the crowds which caused Duli to stumble into an old friend.

"Pardon me, Sargas!" She told the older dwarf, twice her age, "I shouldn't be running like that." She put out a hand to steady him.

The hunched-back dwarf, shorter than Duli, swiveled his good eye up to look at her. The other eye glinted milky white.

"Nay worries, but don't fuss over me! A hundred and five years doesn't make me an invalid prone to falling on my rump."

Duli relaxed her grip upon noticing Sargas' drinking buddies nearby. They enjoyed some mirth about the collision over ale at Deepmug's.

She tried to turn the situation away from her embarrassment by complimenting him. "A century under your belt and not a gray whisker to show for it."

Before Sargas "Gun Hand" Bristlebeard replied, one of his friends spoke. "How would you tell? His beard is under so much black powder, if he lit a pipe his face would blow up!"

The aging warrior pointed up at his blind eye. "My face already blew up once," His grin stretched the burn marks marring the growth of beard on that side. "Made me pretty!"

Laughter ensued as he turned back to Duli. "I'm going up to greet the boys. I assume you were heading home to get things ready for your fellow?"

Duli blushed, which wouldn't have been noticed on most dwarves except she had been forced to get rid of her beard in order to live with Geordan in Tok-Maurron. Since Duli was born non-clan, and her beard removed because of it, she ranked among the lowest class of anyone in the city. Her old friend could plainly see the red glow about her smooth cheeks as she answered, "It's proper that I have a cozy fire and warm food waiting for him."

"Well, I won't cause you to tarry…"

Sargas barely spoke the words and she went on the move again. Duli's sand-colored hair bobbed loosely just past her shoulders. She did have a braided tail, longer than the rest of her hair, which peeked out from under the back. Some strands bounced into the silver, hoop earrings she wore; a parting gift from her family when leaving her home city. Duli hoped the run wouldn't mess her hair up too much. Generally, once the horn sounded the arrival, there was little time to get ready before Geordan arrived in their chamber.

Duli thrust open the door of their abode, dumping her purchases from Lower City on a stone table cut out of the wall. She spoke a command, causing the smokeless sconces on the walls to light up. It was a simple miracle offered by the priests, allowing many similar sconces and gems to light up the underground city. Duli strode over and fed more wood into the starving fire. The extensive air flues weren't enough to warm the distant warrens; unlike Lower City, which stayed warm due to the forges and heat from dwarf bodies. She paused, taking stock of the larder. Lack of fresh food limited her options. Duli settled for a pot of leftovers sitting near the hearth; a mix of meat and vegetables from the previous evening. It wasn't uncommon to re-cook something the next day, even the day after. Duli hoped some sauce and a chunk of bread might cover up any old taste from the mix.

As the food heated up, she set aside the clutter accumulating in the underground home. Duli grabbed a large wooden frame, supporting a stretched skin, and shoved it into a back corner. Her hands cleaned off the scraper before tossing it and a skinning knife onto a shelf. It surprised her to realize she still wore her self-crafted tool harness. It wouldn't be good for her husband to get jabbed by part of her hatchet or the handle of the big knife when they hugged. Duli undid the harness and tossed it over by the skin-frame.

It further mortified her to realize she still wore her leather buckskins from the trip to the surface that morning. She favored the comfortable outfit while trapping animals, but didn't want to greet her returning husband wearing it. Duli sat down on the edge of the bed, tugging everything off at once. She labored to get into a decent dress and bodice. It was a homely outfit that could be ripped off easily later if he came home in the mood to ravage her. She hoped he was in that mood today! Even if he wasn't, she looked forward to warming herself against him under their blankets this night.

"Sandstone! Nay fresh bread, only these hard biscuits!" With a flurry of motion, she stirred the pot before grabbing some coins and rushing back towards Lower City.

The leather crafter was so distracted she didn't notice the excitement level of the huge cavern had changed to an angry mood. Her first hint of something out of the ordinary struck when she laid eyes upon a friend. Like Duli, Shauna Horgar had seen fifty winters; unlike Duli, her braided beard marked her as native to Tok-Maurron. Shauna had been married for twelve years compared to Duli's three, and had been a friend of hers since arriving in the city.

Duli would have waved a quick greeting, had not Shauna been in the process of going ashen in the face while talking to a member of Geordan's company. Duli couldn't hear the conversation, but she saw Shauna go limp in the arms of another friend. Shauna's husband had been with Geordan.

Several heated words carried through the marketplace, Duli began paying attention to the scattered voices.

"...will be war now! Tariyka will pay with blood!"

"We went to talk and they set an ambush! The humans didn't catch many of us. We rallied and pushed back..."

Duli stood in shock, listening to the outraged cries of her husband's kin. Dwarves were normally a stoic race; their emotions hid behind low brows and thick beards. Anger was the one emotion that could be brought most readily to the surface. From Shauna's open reaction, Duli knew the woman had received the worst news any wife could ever hear. There were already too many widows in Tok-Maurron from small melees with human-dominated Tariyka. She had been hoping Geordan would bring back news of an agreement that would end the bad blood between their cultures.

She didn't waste time in Lower City. Someone called her name, but Duli did not heed it. She would get the news from her husband soon enough. Geordan would probably come home with all manner of worries on his mind. Duli traded for the bread and ran home amidst the growing clamor, and crowds, in the cavern. Grizzled veterans who had once chased monsters from the mountains were calling out to their kin that the king needed to take action.

Duli arrived in her chamber to discover Geordan had not yet returned. She had been worried she would miss him. "Probably talking to a general or noble; more time to prepare for his return."

Satisfied that the pot was hot enough, she moved it further down the spit so as to not overdo it. After all, there was no telling when he would arrive. Duli lost track of the time as she put away clothes, cleaned the table and straightened the bed. Chores kept her so busy that she paid little attention to the dying hearthfire. Duli paused to check on the food again; worried why Geordan was taking so long.

A creak came from the door as it swung open. She put on her welcoming smile and turned around. Sargas "Gun Hand" Bristlebeard stood halfway inside the open portal. Duli realized she had never properly closed the door. Sargas paused there, but his eye avoided looking at Duli. He spoke while watching the floor; his voice pitched barely above a whisper. "I don't mean to intrude; the door was open. Just came to get Geordan's musket and powder."

She took no offense at his apparent gloom. Instead, Duli remained cheerful, hoping for some news about her husband. She pointed to the musket. The polished barrel reflected the care Duli devoted to it while her husband was away. The powder barrel and a bag of lead shot sat nearby.

Duli smiled as she dropped a few lines to inquire about her husband. "Haven't seen him yet. I can help you carry it to him."

The older dwarf's one good eye darted in surprise. He glanced to either side at the preparations on the table and the kettle of food, before turning his gaze upon her content face.

"You haven't heard?" He wasn't directing it at her as much as musing out loud.

Out of respect for the news of the fighting, and knowing that at the very least Shauna's husband had died, Duli returned to a stoic dwarven countenance.

"I know the talks went badly. I heard the humans were aiming to catch some of our men unaware. Someone said we gave them a beating for it."

The older dwarf, veteran of many fights before an exploding musket barrel took one eye, stared at Duli. His feet shuffled a step. Although she could tell he was having trouble saying something, she respectfully waited for his words.

"Duli," he might have paused to swallow, although such action would have been hidden under his bristly beard, "I heard from the others, Geordan was killed in the ambush…"

Duli's mind tumbled. As Sargas continued, she put up a wall to protect her feelings.

"You *heard? Heard* from who?"

The veteran paused at the interruption and glared with his good eye. "People who were there."

"Then you didn't see a body!" Duli's tone became less respectful by the moment. Sargas had no reason to be dishonest with her, but she preferred to think he had erred rather than face the truth. "Nandorrin's hammer! He could be out there lost or something. We should go find him!" Duli worried about her husband being alive and needing their help in the wild. If Geordan had died, she would have felt it in her gut.

In response to her outburst, the veteran showed offense to her insinuation of falsehood. Gun Hand straightened to his full height, though his hunched back still made him shorter than the woman he faced. His voice came across as a respected male of the dwarven patriarchy, addressing an upstart, bottom-caste female. "They brought the body with them! If you have any doubts, you can go up to the Stonebrow Vault and look for yourself! Geordan was a good friend of mine, and other friends of his were there to see him fall. His soul rests in Dorvanon."

His tone set Duli back on her heels. She wanted to denounce his words, but she could form none of her own. Dwarven women were used to hardships, and Duli had made sacrifices of her own. She gave up her previous life to live with Geordan in his clan. Since then, he had made all her burdens seem trivial. If she accepted his death, the world would be an unbearable place.

In the uneasy silence, her fists clenched with nervous energy.

Gun Hand wasted no more words with her. As Master-at-Arms of the clan, he was the one tasked with caring for their arsenal. All the guns were clan property first and foremost. She watched in mute frustration as he walked over to grab Geordan's musket. The gun displayed designs reflecting the dwarven beliefs. The flintlock hammer depicted Nandorrin, God of Fire, raising his smith's hammer to strike. Along the stock were eleven notches carved into the durable wood. Duli had never given thought to the fact that they represented enemies Geordan had killed with the musket. He had faced Tariykans in past skirmishes along a disputed border. Duli refused to believe he was a notch for some boasting Tariykan.

Duli could not bring herself to speak as Sargas snatched up the gun, powder barrel, and bag of lead shot. She wanted to admonish him for taking her husband's things. Her heart ached to snap at the dwarf and tell him that Geordan would be back to claim his belongings later. Sargas had no right to take her husband's gun and pass it on to some young fool. Even as he walked out, refusing any more eye contact, she could not bring her mouth to voice the words she wanted to say. Duli stood there, brow furrowed, eyes glaring, fists clenched, unwilling to give in to despair. Despair was for those who lost their husbands. Duli had no plans to become a widow.

Her body remained so tense that she felt as if many of her muscles were pulled taut. She finally lost strength and dropped to a sitting position on the edge of the two-person bed. Duli whispered to herself that it wasn't true. Her voice, pitched so low that little air actually came out from her moving lips, begged for Geordan to walk in the door.

Another dwarf ran up to her doorway, daring to peek inside. Her closest friend, Glaura Greencutter, was married to a cousin of Geordan. She had befriended Duli the first day the leather crafter arrived here from her home city. Glaura's eyes sought Duli's from within reddish-brown hair and beard swept down to her beltline.

Duli turned her eyes upon this latest intruder. She didn't want anyone coming to her door unless it was her husband.

"Oh, Duli, I heard…" Glaura started to say before Duli interrupted her.

"You heard wrong!" Duli spat with more anger than intended. Her tone caused Glaura to shrink back into the hall a bit. "Geordan is fine. I'm cooking a meal for him. When he gets home, I'm going to give him a big kiss and show how much I love him!"

Her voice cracked, betraying the pain building inside. Glaura got past the frightful moment and stepped into the chamber. Duli knew her friend wasn't about to leave her alone.

Glaura spoke regarding her own husband, "Tormero told me what happened. He helped bring the body down from the surface."

Before she even finished, Duli defiantly shook her head.

"I'm telling you he is alive. He has fought Tariykans before and beaten them. Humans are stupid. They can't catch Geordan!"

Glaura sat down on the bed next to Duli. The beardless dwarf looked away from her friend. Glaura slowly managed to get her arms around Duli, despite the adamant woman flinching from any such comfort.

"I know he's alive!" Her voice cracked. "He'll be here any moment. I'll ask him if he saw any amazing new creatures on his journeys, like I always do."

Glaura held Duli close as her green eyes began to water. There were no words in the dwarf language for crying or tears. Males got somber, while females suffered "sorrows". Glaura held her friend close, yet Duli could see she turned her eyes away out of respect. It wasn't polite to witness a dwarf in the midst of sorrows.

"We are just starting to plan on children." Duli made every effort to make the words sound firm, even as her voice lacked strength. "I hope to talk him into naming a boy after my father. You will still offer us that old cradle, when it's time?"

Duli could not hold her faith any longer. She surrendered her denial while in her friend's comforting arms. The sorrows ran freely down her cheeks.

CHAPTER 2

Two days passed before the bodies of those slain in the Tariykan ambush were placed in Staprel Gom, hallowed hall of dwarf gods, for mourning. The emotions stirred from the surprise attack drew almost every dwarf of the clan to pay their respects in this holiest of places. Mourners crowded the hall, as the air hummed with muttered curses aimed at the humans responsible. Guards turned away foreign ambassadors and merchants who would normally enjoy a walk through this portion of the city. The sight of the fallen was reserved for native families. The dead lay on slabs before the patron deities they most worshipped, thin shrouds covering their fatal wounds.

Duli moved through her husband's kinsmen in a haze of her own creation. She saw and heard her fellow dwarves, but her mind wandered a world apart. Duli felt alone in a clan that was not her own.

The light of her life existed no more. She had barely eaten in the last two days, yet her stomach felt no hunger. The few bites Duli forced down that morning settled uncomfortably in her belly, defying digestion.

One of the first altars she passed belonged to Taekbol, God of the Underworld. Like many others below the surface world, Duli had once held this god in her highest esteem. She knelt before his altar and tried to find words for prayer.

"Taekbol, God of my beginnings, watcher over my youth," Duli projected her thoughts to the statue before her. *"I'm afraid I've forgotten the proper way to open a prayer for you. My mother always told me to start by praising the generosity of the gods...but I can't feel any thankfulness at this time. I feel..."*

Duli paused, clearing a lump in her throat. *"...forsaken."*

She was at a loss in how to proceed. Her mind explored all her worries.

"The fire of my life is extinguished, yet my body remains. How am I to live on as an empty shell? Half-finished crafts, leather scraps, my livelihood, sit waiting to be completed. My traps on the surface go unchecked, yet I have no heart for it. How can I be creative and

industrious when my spirit is so weary from loss? What difference would my craft offer my coin purse? A female crafter, non-clan, bereft of her husband, is little more than a vagabond."

"*Night becomes a timeless eternity when underground. Sleep remains elusive, only to arrive alongside terrible dreams. I wander outside my home to the great clock in Lower City, only to realize I have spent long hours of the night watching the hearthfire dwindle.*"

In that reflective moment, she finally knew what prayer she sought. "*I wish to be reunited with my husband.*" The sorrows wet her eyes. "*I pray for death.*"

Duli dabbed her eyes with the dark-gray headwrap worn about her shoulders. The molber wool headwraps were the mantles of mourning worn by all the widows. The soft fabric, made from sheep native to the Molberus range, covered their hair, shoulders, and draped past beards. For Duli, the touch of that wool against her beardless cheeks served only to remind her of the sacrifices she made to be with a man who could no longer be with her.

She rose up and turned to view the throng of dwarves. Traditionalists composed the majority of her race; adhering to customs long after they were outdated. The loss of her beard was one such example. It was a custom born from the Godswars, when even dwarven clans warred among themselves. Females, so often ignored in dwarven society, sometimes became saboteurs against rivals. The success of those women resulted in clans removing the beards of non-clan females that sought to stay in their cities. The removal of a beard left a distinctive mark that could not be hidden in dwarven society, warranting extra attention from guards. The war faded into ancient history; the custom still persevered.

For that reason, Duli's appearance had been slighted. She accepted the sacrifice in order to make her home by Geordan's side. His death left Duli bereft of her bright future. In her heart, she felt no compulsion to call Tok-Maurron her home. Duli's home was Geordan, and soon he would be entombed in stone.

Duli moved further into Staprel Gom. She came upon Geordan's resting slab, positioned before the god Nandorrin. The God of Fire was revered by smiths and those who made war using the black powder of the guns.

Guffan Stonebrow, a general related to the king, approached her. He didn't ask Duli how she felt. The general apparently felt the best way to talk to her was to tell her how good of a soldier Geordan was.

"He was a dependable gun to have at your side," Guffan slurred his words. His thick fist waved a half-empty mug in emphasis. "I could count on him nay matter what came at us. Now he guards the gates to Dorvanon! He'll serve the gods with as much devotion as he gave to the clan. If only our gods could walk this world again, as they did before the Godswars. They would cast down the humans. We'll go after the Tariykans for you, Duli. We'll bring

11

them justice in a hail of shot. I don't even know why those foolish humans bother wearing armor; our guns'll tear right through it!"

Duli nodded, more for his sake than hers. He stumbled off to drink some more. Like the general, her thoughts cursed the humans, but Guffan's threats seemed hollow. How many fallen humans would it take to bring her love back from the dead?

Duli failed to understand the attitudes of the men. For the most part, they said little to her whenever they did speak. The males were too busy drinking toasts to those fallen. They reminisced about the dead, laughed about past deeds and lifted mugs in last respects. The women were all too often invisible to them.

A gnarled male shambled towards her while leaning on his cane. When Duli saw the pinched face hidden amongst a scraggly mat of white hair, her heart felt a wave of dread. In that visage, she could see the prison destined to become her future. Popguv Rockhand honestly felt he was helping the "poor" women, while putting them in a position the women considered a form of slavery.

Popguv reached out to her shoulder, giving her an arthritic squeeze with his hand to offer comfort. "A sad day this be, but the Mennurdan Guild is there for you. We'll be happy to finish your training and thus help you provide for yourself."

His attitude turned Duli's stomach. She forced a polite tone when she replied. "Geordan never had to teach me anything. I mastered my craft."

The words didn't seem to get through Popguv's maze of hair. "Of course, I'm sure your leatherwork must have made your family happy. The guild is here to help you learn true mastery. The Stonebrows and their kin set very high standards." His tone made it seem that no matter how good Duli considered her craftsmanship, it was amateurish compared to anything their males could teach. "Don't forget we are here for you. We do hate to see it when women try to craft without the enlightenment we offer. The Mennurdan Guild will always be happy to take you in."

Duli knew he genuinely thought he offered her a favor. Popguv took much pride in what he and his masters could teach; he couldn't fathom how a woman could survive without male guidance. As he continued on, moving towards the next widow, he missed the shudder that ran through her body. Duli's future narrowed. She could try to earn a living on her own despite the prejudice the males showed towards solitary females, or she could join the Mennurdan Guild in order to sell more. In the guild, she would be giving up profits as well as her freedom. Worst of all, her pride in her craft would be slowly dismantled by disapproving, narrow-minded males.

The women in Staprel Gom observed the mourning time vastly different from the men. They were more attuned to the loss that the widows felt. They approached Duli with comforting words unsaturated by ale or promises of vengeance.

Duli observed some things lacking amongst her conversation with her friends. Her best friend Glaura tried to bring her comfort. Glaura had her heart in the right place, but not the effort. Duli heard her falter over words and suffer through awkward pauses. The new widow was grateful for her friend, but on this occasion Glaura only reminded Duli of her past words to other widows. The leather crafter remembered how she had always felt unsure what to say when her friends lost their husbands. Glaura's uncertainty seemed to mirror her past attempts to console others. Duli knew no words could give her comfort, though she appreciated her friend's efforts.

Glaura ended the conversation by offering to stop by her chambers later and perhaps sharing a drink. Duli absently nodded.

Her friends tried to bring her comfort. None of them really understood the hole in her soul. Some even dared to wish for good things to come to her. Duli felt that nothing good would ever outweigh her sorrow.

The tone was different when greeted by older widows. They touched hands with Duli or hugged her. Many offered an open door anytime if she needed to talk to someone. They didn't offer false promises or tell her how things would get better. Duli felt the most comfort in their presence, even when few words were expressed.

Duli was now part of a sisterhood, born from the common feeling of sorrow that bound their emotions. They looked into her eyes and shared their loss. Duli was in their shoes now. With new understanding, Duli could see the shadow of pain hidden in their hearts. Some had lost husbands, some had lost sons, and more than a few of them had lost both.

Duli wondered where they got the strength to endure such loss. How did these women persevere? How did they pick up their shattered lives? When does the pain ever become tolerable?

Duli felt the need to find someone with whom she could relate the most. Glaura, despite their friendship, lacked the ability to understand her pain. Instead, Duli found herself standing close to Shauna Horgar. She remembered seeing Shauna across the marketplace the day the news hit her. Her husband, Bolgor, died alongside Geordan. Her pain was as fresh as Duli's.

Shauna's fair hair and golden eyes, (both a rare and attractive attribute to dwarves), were nearly covered by the same molber wool headwrap Duli wore. She stonily held her outward composure well despite the pain, as expected of dwarves. Even as they spoke, their eyes were on another recent widow who fared worse at hiding her feelings.

"That is Katy Dornan," Shauna stated. "She works in the back of Deepmug's preparing food."

Duli noted the young widow named Katy suffering from "the shakes". It was a condition of one who couldn't hold back the signs of their inner pain. Their shoulders would shake, even as the sorrows ran unchecked from eyes to beard.

Duli listened to Shauna's words. "She is maybe forty? Perhaps a year or two older? So young, barely past her childhood, though same as my age when I married. I can look back on twelve years beside a wonderful husband. Katy was only married three months ago."

The two of them watched as Katy's sorrows distracted the male dwarves toasting the fallen. The dwarf warriors called on her to quiet her emotions out of respect for the dead. A few of the widows, women who had lost their husbands a long time ago, went to Katy's side and promptly led her out of Staprel Gom. They threw dagger-sharp looks at the backs of the uncaring men.

It left a sour taste in Duli's mouth. She whispered her disgust to Shauna. "Why do men-folk feel embarrassed to be witness to our suffering? Can we not mourn in whichever way we see fit? I have lost the joy of my life, as Katy has. Do I not have the right to give in to the sorrows if the pain overburdens me?"

Shauna reached up to readjust her headwrap. It lifted high enough for Duli to see the six braided sections of her beard. Shauna leaned closer. "It is a male world. If you aren't the one serving their meals or spreading your legs for them, you're of nay use."

"Geordan made me feel equal. He made me feel loved."

"As was Bolgor special to me," Shauna nodded, "But this is a land of fathers and sons. They care not for our opinions. We are not their equals."

Duli and Shauna stood in silence for a moment. Duli's hand came up, dabbing the headwrap against the moisture at the corners of her green eyes. Even with a friend standing next to her, she felt utterly alone.

Shauna confided, "If Bolgor's death didn't end all my happiness, then it surely ended when Popguv came over and assured me an apprenticeship in his guild."

The mention of the guild leader and what he represented submerged Duli's heart deeper into depression. "He already approached me," Duli mumbled, just barely loud enough for Shauna to hear. "What are you going to do?"

"What choice is left to me?" With no eyes upon them, Shauna took that moment to raise the edge of her headwrap. The woman spit upon a statue of Kelor, God of Luck. It was a reaction from someone who felt that the Lord of Fortunes had spit upon her. The fair-haired widow continued without missing a beat. "I will lessen myself by placing my craft at their disposal. They will teach me to do things their way. My own designs will be ridiculed, for I do not follow custom. When I finally make traditional items the way they tell me to, they will boast over my craft as if it was *their* sweat and not *mine*. The only other choice is to become impoverished making rogue creations without the guiding hand of a male. The men shun the works of a woman trying to survive on her own."

"I face the same prospects." Duli tried to swallow her emotions past the lump in her throat. "I have nay need of a male mentor. Geordan didn't skin animals or craft leather until *I* showed him how."

She recalled her pride when the masters of her home clan had bestowed the rank of master upon her work. Duli did not want to humble herself to a guild of overbearing males. Green eyes looked towards the exit of Staprel Gom, where Katy had been led out only minutes earlier.

Duli declared, "I won't go to that guild. I can sell my wares to the women."

Fair-haired Shauna glanced at her. "But it's the men who control the coins. Most women spend only what their husbands or fathers grant to them."

Duli closed her eyes. She felt Shauna's arm reach around to offer a slight hug.

"Don't mind my words, Duli," Shauna whispered. "It might be possible to make a decent living that way. Maybe I'll get stubborn and turn my back on Popguv as well. I just can't decide how to face a future without my love."

Duli nodded. "Same here."

She reopened her eyes and returned Shauna's hug. "I think I'll be going back to my hall. I've had enough mourning in public. Time for me to be alone."

Once goodbyes were exchanged, she walked through the tunnels of the underground city. Few dwarves or outsiders were around. Once Duli had descended as far as Lower City, it seemed as if she was in a ghost town. Listening to her footsteps echo as she walked, she felt alone with her thoughts.

Tok-Maurron would never be her home. She briefly entertained the thought of returning to her family's halls, but discarded the idea. It was too far over the mountains, and she wasn't even sure where, having only traveled the route once. She couldn't go alone, and a merchant caravan wouldn't take a female crafter. It might be possible if she joined the Mennurdan Guild and finished an apprenticeship, but that could take decades. She would not give in to Popguv at all. Even if she made it back, she might be forced to remain beardless, a 'used' wife no good for remarrying, and be a burden to her family. She simply couldn't return.

Duli's solitary shadow made its way into Nandorrin's Halls, her feet dragged as if resisting her fate. A future without Geordan was an unacceptable destiny. A life alone under the patriarchal customs of Tok-Maurron and Clan Stonebrow would be hell.

Her thoughts turned towards a solution taboo to any dwarven god. If living was hell, then she had nothing to lose by dying. If Geordan was waiting for her at the gates of Dorvanon, she would not make him wait long.

Duli made up her mind and her pace quickened with new purpose. She had to act before she changed her mind. It was up to her to take her own life.

CHAPTER 3

Duli felt like their chambers were the crypt that housed Geordan's spirit. The main entry room felt cold and lifeless. Every little movement Duli made echoed loudly in her ears. "Is your spirit here, watching me?" Silence answered her. "Can you see into my mind and know my plans?"

Doubts crept into Duli's mind. She shook her head as if to spin them away. If she thought too much on what she was doing, she probably wouldn't go through with it.

She hardly paid attention to closing her door as she reached up and tore the wool wrap from her head. Duli paused to consider it. Many of the older widows had worn such a garment for the deaths of parents, sons and husbands. Duli hadn't been in Tok-Maurron long enough to need one until today. She didn't intend to be alive long enough to have need of it again. Her short legs stomped across the room. She heaved the fabric into the hot embers of the hearth, watching it catch fire immediately.

"Burn! Burn alongside my future!"

Her green eyes turned back to the main chamber. The room served as their kitchen, dining area, living space, and bedroom. The only other chambers connected to the room were small dugouts piled with items for storage and Duli's leather crafts.

She looked over the unfinished items. Duli saw a thick belt measured to fit Glaura's husband, Tormero, and regretted not completing it. She was tempted to spend a few hours getting it done, but in her heart she knew she would just be delaying her decision. A leather pouch meant for another friend occupied one corner. It was supposed to have been finished yesterday.

Duli could only sigh. She told herself not to fret about it. Geordan had left unfinished tasks behind. The world went on without him; it could go on without her.

Rational thought made her weak, turning aside her decision. Duli thrust those thoughts aside and let emotions overwhelm her mind. She sat down on a stool near the bed. Duli covered her eyes and let the sorrows roll down her bare cheeks. She didn't even want to look at the bed. In the two nights since Geordan's death, Duli had tossed and turned on her half of the bed. It just didn't seem right to intrude upon the empty half. The whole room was too dark, too cold and too quiet for her liking.

Duli stood and caught a glimpse of her face in a small, steel mirror. She thought she looked at a stranger. Duli picked the mirror up and sat in the stool again. She stared at the wet lines on her cheeks.

"Not so old, and yet not so young anymore. I feel as if the last couple days added twenty years."

At fifty winters, Duli wasn't old by any dwarf standard. The number didn't bother her at all. It was the sorrow-enhanced age of her face that depressed her.

She continued to talk out loud. "You told me I was beautiful and I believed it. How am I to ever be beautiful again? I have nay cause to smile. A person has to smile before they can be beautiful." The widow frowned at herself. "I'll try to make myself beautiful one last time, only because I'm going to see you soon."

She let the steel mirror fall over.

Duli decided to tug off the clothes she wore to Staprel Gom. Naked, she began climbing into the storage recesses at the back of the main chamber.

"It has to be in the chest back here. Why did I pile so many things around it?"

Stored treasures were flung outward as she exposed the lid of the chest. She finally got to it and yanked it open. Once she saw her prize, she took greater care to remove it. The silver and gold colors of the fabric reflected the firelight, colors typical of dwarf wedding gowns.

She held it reverently against her as she remembered the ceremony. It had been held in Tok-Maurron only days after her arrival. Duli hardly knew anyone from the city back then. Geordan's cousin Tormero offered his wife to help Duli with her outfit. Glaura and Duli had been best friends ever since.

The grin brought on by the recollections died as Duli dwelled on thoughts of her friend. She never really gave Glaura a goodbye of any kind. Their last conversation had been awkward. It was the first moment Duli stopped to think about someone who would suffer the sorrows upon hearing of her death. Glaura had been her closest confidant; Duli wondered how she would take the news. Would Glaura be the one to find Duli's body?

Duli shook those thoughts from her mind. She closed her musings like a trap, refusing to give them any more thought. If she stopped to dwell on those consequences, she likely wouldn't be able to carry out her suicide.

The wedding gown was a maze of soft cloth mixed with steel plates, typical of dwarven fashion. To the sturdy folk, a groom and bride's attire would only look beautiful if it was partly made up like armor. The metal pieces included shoulder guards that seemed to build up Duli's upper arms, and metal cups supporting her ample bosom. It looked and felt comfortable despite the steel portions. Duli struggled with all the buttons and ties.

"Did this shrink while in storage? I don't recall it being quite this tight."

Duli turned around, looking over her dress once finished. She actually didn't know how one would begin to take it off. It had only been worn for her wedding day. When that day had ended, Geordan had carefully removed the outfit for her with all the skill and patience of a dwarven craftsman. She supposed it was not her concern anymore.

She rubbed a palm across her chin. The day after their wedding, as custom dictated for women not of the clan, Duli and her husband returned to Staprel Gom. The priests performed the ceremony which rid Duli of all facial hair permanently. She hadn't felt a thing. The braids of her beard fell away at their touch, leaving her neck exposed. Geordan had held her hand the entire time, comforting her. He hadn't showed any sign of being annoyed with her in the days that followed, when she had some unexpected emotional turmoil over the loss of her beard.

Duli reached over her shoulders to undo the braid in her hair. She pulled the silk ribbon out, letting her hair fall free. Her thick fingers ran along the edge of the smooth silk. All the silk either came from Tariyka, Jhuto or the Republic of Lar. Since Tariyka did not openly trade with the dwarves, all the silk that came from there was taken from their soldiers. Geordan had brought her this ribbon after a patrol along the disputed border with Tariyka, about the same time as he had carved two more notches into his musket.

The widow ran a comb through her hair. Once she finished brushing, it was time to redo her braid. Her hands reached under the shorter hair, grabbing the base of the long tail in the center of the back. She worked the long strands into the braid, inserting the ribbon to hold everything in place. It had been a fashionable style in her old clan, but hadn't seemed to catch on in Tok-Maurron.

Her mind kept thinking about the horrors of what she contemplated. Duli tried to turn her thoughts back to her reasons. She had lost any interest in crafting. Food just settled in her gut. Sleep was unattainable. Geordan's loss ripped at the core of her heart. Her future offered her the choice of the demeaning Mennurdan Guild or possible poverty as a husband-less crafter.

Duli held on to her despair. Without it she would be unlikely to act. As her drive to kill herself rekindled, she sought about finding a means. There was really only one method she could bear to attempt. She grabbed her long dagger. After pacing the room again, she went to the foot of her bed. Duli kneeled on the rug at the end. She was momentarily overcome by the sorrows again. She wiped at her eyes and cheeks.

How was she going to do this? She wanted to die, but she didn't want to suffer. A slow death would not do at all, but how could she accomplish a fast one? A vital strike to the heart?

Duli turned the dagger over in her hands several times. She looked down at her wedding dress. The metal cups over her ample chest wouldn't make that route easy. She felt under the metal and came to the conclusion there was barely enough room there to do the trick. A spot existed, just under the junction of the ribs, where she could drive the dagger home.

Doubts assailed again. What if she couldn't push the dagger hard enough, or missed her heart? An image welled up of her lying hurt and bleeding on the floor, too weak to finish the job easily. She began to wonder if she would have to throw herself forward as she stabbed, using her weight to help deepen the strike. Duli shook away her thoughts. Every time she tried to visualize what she was about to do, it made her sick.

"Just do it, Duli," she whispered, "Quick and hard, and you'll be with him in Dorvanon."

She guided the point of her dagger under the bottom of the rib junction. She took in a deep breath...

"Duli! What're you doing?!"

Her green eyes went wide as she almost half-jumped in fright. Duli's gaze swung towards the door. Even as she did, the tip of the dagger nicked her as her body jerked.

Glaura Greencutter stood partway in Duli's open door. Despite the reddish-brown beard, Duli saw the open-mouthed surprise on her friend. She hadn't bothered to completely close the door when she wrestled off her headwrap! The bottle in Glaura's hand reminded Duli the older woman had offered to stop by and chat over a drink later. In dealing with all her emotions, she had forgotten Glaura's words.

Caught by surprise, she couldn't hide her intent with the dagger. Duli tried to put authority in her voice, failing miserably, as she commanded Glaura. "None of your concern! Leave me be!"

"Why do you have that dagger…"

"I said go!" Duli's words were fast and clipped. They came out as fast as the hurried breaths she was taking. "You won't understand. Just go, and don't come back. I don't want you to see…"

"See you dead?" Glaura almost shrieked. "Put that dagger down!"

Glaura moved towards her. Duli didn't want her best friend putting a stop to her decision. If she didn't go through with it now, who knows how long her miserable life might drag on? On the other hand, she couldn't commit her fatal stab while her best friend watched.

Duli let Glaura see her regain a tight grip on the handle. She pushed the tip against her bare skin, wincing as the blade drew blood.

"Don't come close; I'll do it!" Duli was relieved that Glaura stopped halfway across the floor. "Don't make me go do this while you watch. Just leave me be!"

"I am not leaving you like that!" Glaura alternated looks between Duli's eyes and the tip of the dagger.

Duli felt a trickle of blood staining the wedding dress.

Glaura continued, "I couldn't live with myself if I walked out that door while you…"

"Well at least you can live!" Duli's anger bubbled up. "You can go back to a husband, and children! I don't have that! I'll never have children…"

Duli's voice failed her as the sorrows wet her eyes. "Nay children…my own…"

Her words came sporadically. In her emotional state, with her rapid breathing, Duli's ramblings only expressed portions of sentences. Glaura ventured a few steps closer. Duli registered the motion and refocused on holding her dagger in place. She only made the cut worse by an unintentional twist. She winced, but Glaura had stopped again.

Her friend's tone became stern admonishment, surprising Duli. "And is this what Geordan would truly want for you? He didn't choose to end his life, yet here you are throwing yours away! You have a chance to live. I'm sure Geordan wouldn't approve of what you are doing now. Look at yourself from his eyes."

Duli had no easy response. She stubbornly shook her head. "Just go. Please, Glaura. You don't know what I'm going through."

When Duli chanced a glance at Glaura, she noticed her friend had moved a few steps closer again. She readjusted her sweaty grip on the weapon. Duli knew she should just get up the courage to throw herself on the dagger. She couldn't muster up the will.

Glaura whispered. "Geordan wouldn't want you to do this. You know it. Don't be foolish. You still have a future, Duli. You have a life."

Duli's hands shook. More than anything, the widow wanted to just shove the blade in. She wanted to end it. Her heart wouldn't allow it.

Duli's trembling hands dropped the dagger.

Her body collapsed as her emotions threatened to burst from her chest. Glaura was at her side in an instant. Her friend supported her as the sorrows ran free; the shakes following a moment later. Duli wept openly. Her best friend held her close as Duli let the torrent of loss escape from wherever she had bottled it up.

She vented the loudest scream of her entire life.

Glaura said nothing, for which Duli was grateful. She leaned into her friend. The feel of Glaura's reddish brown beard tickled Duli's bare cheeks. If her friend minded the shower of sorrows, she didn't voice any complaints. Glaura left her side once, briefly, both to remove the dagger and close the door lest anyone investigating the scream find Duli in that state.

The words Duli spoke to her husband before his fateful trip came back to haunt her. *"If you ever meet your death before me, I hope the gods take my life soon after."*

Duli had to trust in the same gods she felt like forsaking. She couldn't take her own life. Hopefully, they would take it before long. All that was left for her was to live…happy or sad, healthy or not…just live. For now, she had no choice but life.

CHAPTER 4

It had been five days, exactly half a week, since Duli's suicide attempt. During that time, Glaura seemed more attentive to her than usual. Her friend continued to be concerned for Duli. Duli could see that fear in Glaura's eyes again on this emotional day.

"I'll just spend the day wandering the city. Maybe I'll poke my nose outside for a bit." Duli said when they parted.

Glaura offered, "I don't really need to be here helping them. I could walk with you."

The concern in her friend's eyes clashed with the comical style in which her beard was set. Half of Glaura's beard flowed down, while the other half hung in a tangled braid. The results were always unexpected when Glaura allowed her children to style her beard; however, it brought a smile to others to see Waural and Feena's attempts at fashion.

Duli shook her head. "Nay. The sooner that stuff is gone the sooner I can come back home. For now, a little time alone is what I need. If it will put your mind at ease, perhaps I can meet you for dinner."

Glaura nodded, "Sure. Still, if you need anything, you know where I'll be."

Duli didn't plan on returning to her own chambers until Geordan's relatives were finished removing his belongings. She suffered enough emotional turmoil deciding what to keep and what to discard. She stored a number of oddities for herself. The rest should be passed on to his extended family or simply removed from Duli's sight. Glaura, her husband Tormero, and the rest of Geordan's cousins were taking care of the items Duli left aside.

She started making her way around Lower City. Out of habit, she took her first steps towards Hearthden. The women congregating in that market often supplied a good source of rumors and touched on many entertaining subjects. Duli came to her senses and stopped short of the women's craft stalls. She wondered if Glaura told anyone of her suicide attempt. If so, the topic undoubtedly swept through the attentive ears of the females like any good scandal. Even if word hadn't gotten around, she didn't feel up to fending off questions regarding her loss.

Duli turned away, allowing her feet to lead elsewhere. She went by the popular drinking establishment Deepmug's. Even in the late morning, many chairs around the stone-carved building were occupied. Drinkers downed their tankards while watching the dance of luminescent bugs; the insects' lights bobbing against the backdrop of the high cavern ceiling. Duli pondered stopping for a drink or two.

The approach of Popguv Rockhand interrupted her pleasant distraction. The aged guild master displayed an honest smile at seeing her. Duli couldn't match his positive outlook. Popguv remained blissfully ignorant of the feelings held by those widows who came to work for him. Popguv believed he took in poor widows under his wing, but to Duli and the other women he was an end to all the pride they had felt in their crafts.

"Ah, Duli! I had hoped to see you again soon!" Popguv waved a gnarled hand. "I'm eager to see how well you know your way around a workbench. I have a master leatherworker who is eager to get started with your training. We want to support your abilities so you may be able to craft on the same level as Tok-Maurron."

Despite a lifetime growing up in a stoic race, it took some effort for Duli to keep her temper in check. "Thank you for your offer. I won't be requiring the efforts of your artisans."

"But…"

Duli tried to sidestep around Popguv as she talked. "I earned the title of master back home. I'll manage my craft well."

She could tell by the look on his face that he didn't comprehend how his generous offer could be ignored. Popguv continued to speak.

"With Geordan nay longer guiding you, you may miss some of the intricacies of our customs, our designs. We would like to finish what he started."

At that remark, she turned stern eyes towards him. "Geordan gave me only respect for my talents. I taught him; he didn't teach me. Perhaps I could teach your masters a few new tricks if they wish to learn."

Popguv betrayed his shock. "You mean, you don't know anything about our native animals and our styles? You'll never make a living without the knowledge we can provide. We should head over to the guild so that we might start right away."

Duli just seemed to be digging a deeper hole for herself. Popguv did not understand there were different ways of doing things. She had rightfully earned her station.

Duli turned away. She no longer cared for a drink if Popguv would be present to nag her. Duli only offered a few words over her shoulder as she walked away from Deepmug's. "Your offer will not be needed. I'm doing fine on my own; as I have the past three years I've lived here. If your masters want to learn a few new tricks from my lands, they are welcome at my door."

Duli didn't mention that she hadn't even tried to make or sell anything since Geordan's death, but that was beside the point. The conversation with Popguv became a milestone for her. She felt pride in turning down the Mennurdan Guild. Maybe she wouldn't be able to sell as many goods but at least she would be her own boss. Whether she succeeded or failed, it would be by her own efforts.

*   *   *   *   *

Sargas "Gun Hand" Bristlebeard examined the musket with a sigh. The flintlock hammer of this weapon modeled an image of the god Nandorrin striking with his famed hammer. Runes decorating the barrel reflected the dwarf codes of living. His fingers slid down the woodwork, following the designs honoring the dwarf gods. The barrel was an older one, constructed of bronze. Although steel was available in recent decades, it hadn't always been that way. In the dark millennium following the Godswars, copper was more readily available from their mines. They procured tin through caravans from a distant part of the mountains, allowing them to combine both into bronze. Many warriors of the clan carried their aged bronze muskets with pride.

As with most of the guns Sargas cared for on behalf of the clan, he recalled the history of who wielded them. In this case, the good friend who last used it was dead. Often times the musket would pass down to a worthy son. Geordan Greencutter had left no son behind. All he had left was a widow who seemed to scorn Sargas for bringing her the news of his death.

Gun Hand rubbed a thumb over eleven notches carved into the stock. Geordan had certainly punished a few Tariykans in border skirmishes before the ambush. Sargas' good eye looked over the image depicted on one side of the stock: a scene of the gates of Dorvanon.

"See you on the other side of the gates," He whispered, even though his friend could not hear.

The retired warrior placed the musket on his work bench. It looked to be in good condition. Regardless of the shine on the exterior, Sargas had the duty of thoroughly inspecting and cleaning any musket that came into his care.

As soon as he tried to straighten his crooked back, he noticed he was no longer alone. Duli stood at the doorway. Sargas couldn't recall any female visitors ever coming to the Armory. A beardless, non-clan female shouldn't even be near the black powder. Sargas didn't plan to enforce old traditions. He knew Duli wouldn't mean any harm. He was curious as to why she visited, given the nature of their last conversation.

Duli glanced at the musket on the table. Her gaze seemed to shy away from Sargas.

Gun Hand spoke, "This is unexpected. I wouldn't normally think you would walk up here."

"I'm not interrupting? I'll be brief."

Sargas gestured for her to enter the room. She stepped in rather timidly, as far as dwarves go, and she spent a quiet moment collecting her thoughts.

"I wanted to thank you, for delivering the news to me." Duli said. "I'm hope you understand my wild behavior afterwards. You deserve better credit than I offered."

It was easier for dwarves to say "thank you" rather than "I'm sorry." Sargas accepted the apology for what it was. "Geordan was a good man, warrior and friend. I was thinking of him a moment before you stepped in."

When Duli did nothing more than nod, Sargas added, "Tariyka sure kicked at a beehive. We knew we might not be able to trust them when they offered to negotiate the border. Setting up peaceful talks and then using it as an ambush…well, if that isn't evil I don't know what is."

Duli looked over the stacks of muskets lining the Armory. "I'd take a musket to them myself if I could. I hate them." She turned to stare directly into his good eye. "Why was it that Geordan wasn't able to take his musket?"

Sargas was set back on his heels by the question. "We knew there would be a risk. The Tariykans still fight their battles with large swords and thick armor. Our muskets blast holes right through it. If they learned the secrets of the gun and the powder, they could turn that against us."

Duli shifted her stance, "That wasn't what I asked."

Gun Hand returned her stare. "Dwarves don't take our guns on patrols where we might not be coming back. We can't let the muskets fall into their hands. We anticipated that if something wasn't right with the talks, the guns and men might be lost."

At seeing the hurt look on her expression, he added. "We didn't think they were going to attack our men. If we did, we wouldn't have sent them at all. Believe me, Duli, when I say I thought we were being too cautious making those warriors leave them behind."

Duli seemed to realize she was giving a heated glare towards Sargas. She turned her eyes to the side. "I didn't mean to sound so bitter."

"Well, you've got the right to be. Just aim it at the Tariykans."

Duli nodded. "Anyways, that was all I came to say. I'm glad you gave me the news, since nay others did."

26

Sargas fully expected Duli to leave. She turned partway towards the door, yet she lingered. It was as if she had something else she wanted to say. Sargas had been a close friend to Geordan for many years. If Duli had something gnawing at her, he hoped she would state it so their friendship could go on without worries.

He decided to come up with a small distraction, hoping she might open up. "Duli, while you're here, can you help my half-blind eye to spot my work hammer? I set it down earlier and can't find it."

Duli nodded. As she went about scanning over the workbenches and the racks of weapons, she pointed towards Sargas' belt. "You have a hammer right there."

"Bah!" He scoffed. His right arm reached down to pat the warhammer hanging at his waist. "This here is a pride of my youth. I killed orcs with it, a few ogres...think I toppled a giant or two. It would *lessen* the value of this weapon to use it for menial tasks."

Sargas' good eye looked away to the corner of the room. "Now it just hangs here. Sometimes I feel as useless as it does."

Duli came around a pile of weapon hafts, holding his work hammer. Sargas offered a smile and a nod. Still trying to bribe her out of what was on her mind, he offered her a drink.

"Since you helped me with that, maybe you can help me with some of this mead. There are humans from some northern isle that prefer this to ale. I thought I'd try some."

"Don't think I ever tried it, but I'm willing. I stopped by Deepmug's for a drink..."

Duli paused a little too long before she finished her statement, "...but, I didn't get the chance to wet my whistle."

By the third mug, Duli relaxed enough for Sargas to find out why she had been hesitant to leave the Armory. "His family is in my chambers now. They are taking out all his things. It was too hard on my heart to stay and watch. I prefer to get out and walk the halls a bit."

Sargas nodded his understanding. The veteran warrior waved his empty mug towards the gun sitting closest to him. "Well, as you came in, I was getting ready to disassemble and clean Geordan's musket."

Duli's eyes narrowed as she looked at it. "Why? It's in good shape. I cleaned it while he was gone."

"Because...what?! *You* cleaned it?"

Gun Hand stared right at Duli. She seemed unaware of his scrutiny. He kept staring as she chatted.

"I often cleaned his gun. I felt..." Duli hit another pause. The sandy-haired woman took on a lower tone. "...that with a well-kept musket, he would always come back to me."

The news surprised Sargas. Women of the clan were not allowed to have guns. Women who weren't clan, such as Duli, shouldn't even have any access to them at all. Of course, she shouldn't be in the Armory either, but Sargas wasn't planning to be the one to tell her that.

Sargas shook off his surprise. "It's my job to give each gun a thorough appraisal before it goes back into the ready supplies. I have to take them apart, check if everything looks good. It's probably a little more work than what you did."

Duli set her mug down and rose from the barrel she had used as a seat. "I'll leave you to your work. Just looking at Geordan's gun is like looking at a part of him left in this world."

"Aye," Sargas agreed.

As she turned to leave, he called out. "Where do you plan on walking next?"

Duli half-turned and shrugged. Sargas remembered she was trying to keep busy and distracted while Geordan's family removed all his things. The aging warrior got an idea. It went against clan custom, but he wasn't worried.

"How much did he show you? Do you know how they work?"

Duli glanced at the muskets in the room. "Oh, just a general idea, I guess. Occasionally I've seen people loading their guns."

"So you cleaned it, but he didn't teach you how it worked? How to fire it?"

When Duli shook her head, Sargas put down his mead and started grabbing some ammunition. Gun Hand planned for something that might be a little fun, as well as a good distraction for both of them.

CHAPTER 5

Sargas and Duli entered the great training hall of the Armory, a short walk from Sargas' workroom. Elevated rows of benches occupied the near end of the room. The chamber stretched out a far distance, stopping at a wall covered with sand. A number of wood-and-straw targets, humanoid shaped and riddled with holes, were propped at various distances. Young men of the clan learned how to load and fire their guns in this hall. Sometimes warriors gathered here to gamble wages on their shooting skills.

Sargas held Geordan's gun so that Duli could get a good look at it. "We have lots of variety in the way our brothers like to design their weapons, but the principle is the same for all."

While one hand supported the barrel, the other motioned to the figure of Nandorrin swinging his hammer. Sargas' finger lifted the face plate where the hammer would strike. Underneath this plate was a pan, as well as a hole leading into the barrel.

"This is where the action begins. When loaded, you have a small amount of black powder sitting in the flash pan here, right next to the touch-hole. This plate, or frizzen, would be seated to cover this pan. In a firing position, the hammer would be cocked back…Nandorrin would be poised to strike."

Sargas reseated the frizzen over the pan. His good eye glanced at the widow, noting her green eyes focused on his manipulations of the gun. He cocked the hammer back, allowing Duli to hear two distinct clicks.

"Now, let's assume this gun is already loaded…you always treat a gun as if it is loaded. Never point the barrel towards a friend. Keep the open end pointed down at the 'soft wall'."

He watched Duli as she glanced between the barrel and the end of the cavern padded with sand. "A hazard of having these weapons underground. The shot may bounce off a solid rock and come flying back at you." Sargas pointed at the sandy wall. "That's why one end of this chamber is filled with soft sand. As long as your aim isn't horrible, nay shot will come bouncing back."

Duli's eyes widened, "I didn't know those things could bounce around at you. Why don't they bounce off Tariykan armor?"

Sargas answered, "Well, they could deflect off if your angle is bad enough. Any square hit on their armor will punch right through it. It's really useless for them to wear it against our guns. It may help them when we get close and go at it with blades and hammers, but at a distance, our guns do more damage than their bows.

"Anyways, on to the firing mechanism. You look down the barrel, line up your target…"

The aged warrior brought the butt of the gun against his shoulder as he looked down at one of the humanoid figures. "As I pull the trigger, watch the hammer."

Sargas squeezed the trigger. The hammer of the gun came forward, driving a piece of flint in Nandorrin's hammer against the frizzen. Duli jumped as sparks came off the pan. Sargas held the musket out so that she could get a good look at the hammer mechanism.

"See how the hammer and flint shoved the face plate back? The flint sends sparks into the pan, igniting the powder that should be sitting there. The sparks burn down that touch hole and ignite the powder you have at the bottom of the barrel. The black powder inside the base blows up, sending the shot down the barrel and right at the enemy."

"And boom," Duli spoke, "Dead Tariykan."

"Oh aye, the boom." Sargas smiled. "A big noise, a puff of smoke, and another dead human who won't be hunting us in our lands anymore."

"You didn't just bring me here to tell me that." Duli pointed to the powder horn Sargas had grabbed from his workshop. "I figured you were going to show me."

"Ah, of course. I'm not young enough that I go around teasing women anymore." Duli smiled at his words. Sargas turned Geordan's gun muzzle-up and set the butt on the ground. "Let's get started on showing you how we work our dwarven magic."

He held the gun up with one hand, grabbing the powderhorn with the other. "First, be careful doing this part if you've been firing a few rounds. Sometimes the powder in the barrel didn't burn so well. You might pour some new powder in only to see a second blast come out of the barrel." He almost chuckled as he saw Duli's eyes go wide. "When you pour more powder in, keep your fingers from moving directly above the barrel, for just that reason."

Duli commented. "I guess I never realized how dangerous these things could be. If I'd know about these things before, I would have done more worrying every time Geordan traveled."

Gun Hand thought to himself, *"Which is one reason we don't let the women around the guns."* But he kept the thought silent as he continued his demonstration. Sargas figured he did more help than harm by distracting Duli from her worries with a simple lesson in guns.

"A musket demands a lot of respect. It's a weapon after all, just as dangerous as a blade." The retired warrior pointed to the burn marks on the side of his face. "Sometimes even more so."

He tipped the horn over the barrel. "If I was competing for accuracy, making a wager, I would use a measuring cup to determine how much powder to put in. In the heat of a battle, you just have to eyeball it."

Her eyes were intent on his hands as he poured a small amount of powder. When he pulled the horn away, she asked, "That's all you use?"

"Doesn't take much."

Sargas grabbed a single piece of shot from his pouch. The lead ball measured as thick around as Duli's thumb. "This hits a human hard enough to knock him down," he bragged.

He dropped the ball down the barrel, keeping his fingers away from the edge of the hole. Sargas reached under the barrel and pulled out a long, slender rod housed in the wooden stock.

"The ramrod," he showed Duli. "You use this to seat the shot firmly against the powder in the bottom."

As he shoved the ramrod down the barrel, giving it a few pumps of his arm, Duli gestured to it. "Do you need to do that? Doesn't the shot roll to the bottom?"

Sargas shrugged, "Maybe and maybe nay. When you've fired a few rounds, the inside of the barrel can get a little dirty. The shot may stick halfway down. 'Sides, if you don't properly compress the ball down against the powder, all sorts of things might happen. You lose distance, accuracy…might cause the gun to backfire and risk injury."

Duli watched as Sargas struggled a moment with returning the ramrod into the hole under the barrel. "Looks like a bow would fire a lot faster."

Sargas nodded. "It does, but their arrows don't go past our armor too easily. On the other hand, muskets will punch through any armor crafted…unless magic was used. Very few Tariykans wear magical armor. They stand a better chance against us toe-to-toe in melee, rather than testing our weapons at a distance."

Sargas picked the gun butt off the floor, cradling the weapon on his left arm. "Now that the ball is loaded, you need to tend to the firing mechanism."

Gun Hand brought the hammer back one click. He pushed the frizzen forward, revealing the pan and touchhole underneath. "You heard that click from the hammer?"

Duli nodded. Sargas explained. "That is called 'half-cock'. A gun is not supposed to allow the hammer to go forward at half-cock." Sargas already had the gun pointed downrange when he squeezed the trigger. The hammer didn't move. "See? Nay musket should go off in this position, even if you pull the trigger."

He once again grabbed the powderhorn, hanging from his neck. "For wagers, I'd use a different powder that is a finer grade in the pan. In battle, it's faster and easier to just use the powderhorn again. You just sprinkle a small bit."

Duli leaned closer to watch as he shook a small amount of grains into the pan. Sargas allowed her to take a good look, then snapped the frizzen back into place. "Now, we're ready for business."

Sargas switched places with Duli, while still keeping the gun pointed safely down the range. He began to hand the gun to her. Her shock was clear on her bare cheeks.

"You're going to let *me* fire it?"

"Sure. It's something every dwarf should do once in their lifetime."

Sargas handed it to her gently, taking care to guide her fingers to the right places. He helped her bring the butt of the gun up to her shoulder, settling it in the right spot. The aged warrior warned her it would kick a bit when fired. He never removed his hands from the gun. Sargas wanted to make sure Duli didn't do anything impulsive that might cause an accident.

"Now, pick out a target on the range." Duli aimed for one of the wood-and-straw figures. "Keep the gun in place, but reach up with your right palm and pull the hammer to the next click."

Duli nervously brought a hand up to do as he asked. Her hand stayed uncertainly on the hammer after she heard the click. Sargas encouraged her. "That's right. The hammer will stay in place. Bring your hand back near the trigger, be aware that a little pressure on the trigger will fire it. Keep your finger off it for a moment."

Sargas told her about the marks on the top of the gun. "Line them up so that the nub on the end of the barrel is squarely between the notches in the back. Do you see the bright cloth pinned on the target's chest?"

"Aye."

"That's what we aim at. It's the heart of your enemy."

"It's small."

Sargas grinned. "Humans may be two feet taller than us, but their hearts aren't any bigger. Just aim for it."

He could tell Duli was shifting the musket a lot. "It's harder to line these up than I would have guessed."

"Well, even your breathing will move it around. See what happens when you let your breath out, and hold it out for a bit."

Duli tried it. "That was better."

"Fine. I've taught you the nitty-gritty; the rest is up to you. When you are ready, put your finger on that trigger. Steady your gun with your breath out; put pressure on the trigger without taking the gun off the target."

Sargas kept his hands lightly touching the musket, but he turned his good eye to see the target. Duli took two long breaths. She moved her finger to the trigger. He waited as she allowed herself to get the feel of the gun. He could feel the barrel twitching, though not as badly as before. He heard Duli slowly blow out a breath.

A moment or two passed when Sargas didn't hear her breathe back in. By the way her finger flexed, he assumed she was making her shot. Silence was broken as the hammer snapped sparks down the face plate. The pan ignited with a puff of smoke and flame. A fraction of a heartbeat later, the barrel belched a cloud of smoke. Sargas felt the gun jab Duli's shoulder backward. She didn't fall, but it moved her back a half-step.

Sargas watched as a puff of dirt came from the soft wall, high and to the right of the target figure.

Duli blinked her eyes, looking down the cavern with her mouth partly open. The smoke from the blast hung heavy around them. "Did I hit it?"

Sargas rumbled with laughter, "You mean you didn't see it?"

She blushed. "I…might have blinked."

The old, stooped dwarf tried not to show too much amusement at Duli's expense. A number of people blinked when starting out. "You missed, but came close. A decent shot for a first timer."

Duli allowed Sargas to take Geordan's musket from her hands. He noticed how she seemed to look at it longingly. Sargas assumed Duli didn't want to part with it any more than she wanted to part with Geordan's other mementos. Before she could say goodbyes or anything, he spoke.

"Now that I showed you how to load it, let's see if you remember."

Her green eyes brightened as she looked into his. "You are going to let me try again?"

"Isn't that how the phrase goes?" Sargas set the butt of the musket against the ground. "See one, do one, teach one."

He handed her the powderhorn, keeping a good eye on her safety as he helped her reload. As she reloaded, Sargas noted how her mood had brightened. Duli seemed to lose track of why she wandered from her chambers. With a proud heart, Sargas helped her find a distraction.

*   *   *   *   *

Duli returned to her quarters late that day. She didn't dwell on how open the main chamber looked without Geordan's old belongings taking up space. Duli's mood had improved, but if she dwelt on thoughts of her husband for too long she would drown in the sorrows.

She bit into a meager meal before heading straight to bed.

That night, she dreamed of firing a musket at Tariykan invaders. They kept coming, but she worked to keep her home safe. Geordan depended on her. The Tariykans soon faded from the dream. Duli found herself in Geordan's arms, both thankful to be together. She kept trying to hug him tighter with each passing second.

In a dreary haze, she awoke. Her hands reached across the bed, fumbling through a maze of fur blankets to cuddle against her man. After finding lump after lump that wasn't him, Duli struggled to open her eyes wider. The dream had been so sweet. She just wanted to brush against him and fall back to her dreams while Geordan's handsome body warmed her.

Awareness stabbed through her sleepy musings with the intensity of a dark door being thrown aside to let in the sun. Geordan was dead. There was no one sharing her bed.

Duli's reality came crashing back down on her. She longed to return to the irretrievable dream. She could still recall how happy Geordan looked…even as the dream was fading away. Her fists curled around the bumps in the fur covers, trying to hold a memory.

Unashamed, she broke down and let the sorrows take her. Teardrops trickled upon the covers. The shakes came later, accompanied by a futile pounding of a pillow. Duli stopped short of wailing out loud. No self-respecting dwarf wanted their kinsmen to see their emotions in such a state. As long as she was alone in her room, Duli allowed her other feelings to vent silently into the stale, cavernous air.

"Gods take me soon," she whispered. "Don't let me linger in misery."

CHAPTER 6

Duli passed Shauna as she walked through Lower City. Her fair-haired friend glanced at the sizeable pack on Duli's back. It once contained all Duli's possessions on her journey from her homeland to Tok-Maurron. Now, everyone recognized it as the bag of her craft.

Shauna hailed her, "Going up to check your traps?"

Duli nodded grimly, "Aye, though I don't expect to find anything worth keeping. With Geordan's passing, it's been too long since I've checked them. Scavengers have likely destroyed anything by now."

"I heard how you turned Popguv down." There was a spark in Shauna's eyes, "I wish I'd been there to see it."

"He was certainly dazed at my reaction. Now I have to see if I can keep my words. I can't afford to waste any more time letting my traps lie dormant up there. Unless I want to end up coinless or indebted to the Mennurdan Guild I need to work extra hard." At the mention of the guild, Shauna winced. Duli realized Shauna's path took her in the direction of the guild.

"Is that where you're headed?"

Shauna gave a sad sigh, "I have nay choice. So far my experience in there has been humiliating, but there is nay other way for me."

"Surely you have a choice. Strike out on your own. Find your own success without those males treating you like a child."

The woman turned away from Duli, "I wish I had your confidence."

Duli watched her friend trudge away, noting the hesitation in every footstep.

When she arrived on the surface, the cold wind of the mountains blasted her bare cheeks. It was a sensation she had learned to live with these past three years in Tok-Maurron.

The new year was blossoming, but the grip of winter had not faded away. Humans called it the planting season, but dwarves referred to it as the waking season.

A shiver ran over Duli's shoulders as she exclaimed, "Brrrr! That wind is cold enough to put icicles on a forge." She spoke to Geordan's soul as if he could hear. "I can't believe you marched out in this weather to meet the humans."

Duli turned to look at the landscape of the Molberus range. Having stayed underground for so many days, she had to lift a hand to shield her eyes. Her gaze swept across the season's first flowers on the lower southern hills, patches of mud near the underground entry, and the ever-snow-capped peaks towering to the north. The northern mountains loomed tall enough to make the Molberus mountains seem like foothills.

As Duli walked along the muddy ground, she muttered to herself. "Now that would have been a painful way to end it, if I'd chosen. Not a single dwarf has been able to get over those mountains. Can't even tunnel under them without coming across one danger or another, never reaching the other side. That leaves us stuck between them and the Tariykans."

She turned her gaze southward at the sound of hoof beats. A contingent of dwarf warriors mounted on molber rams rode out of Tok-Maurron. Guffan Stonebrow, a relative of the king, was leading his men towards the Tariykan border. The warriors riding forth had been open about their purpose during their heavy drinking at Deepmug's, so Duli had heard about their goal. They were supposed to be looking for signs that Tariyka was sending armies to expand their borderline. Everyone knew Guffan was really out to repay the blood lost. They rode their rams with a grim purpose, muskets hanging by their saddles.

Duli felt a twinge of envy. She wanted to go with them. It was harder to decide whether she wanted to go for vengeance or death. They wouldn't have granted her the opportunity had she asked.

The sandy-haired widow trudged animal paths to the closest trap. Normally Duli could find a number of fine catches, despite standing directly over Tok-Maurron. One advantage of a subterranean city was the abundance of wildlife that roamed the surface. In days past, Duli might be overheard by others singing a song as she walked. The dwarf woman grew up appreciating the open sky. The fragrance of the early seasonal blooms would normally lighten her emotions. This day seemed to be a change to the wilderness, but it was in Duli's heart.

Her loss was still too recent. Walking through the mountain woods only distracted her mind with thoughts of the past. Duli walked past a spot where Geordan had taken her for a memorable picnic, back when these mountains were new to her. The weight of her pack reminded her that she wasn't as young as she used to be. She began to wonder if all her glory years were behind her. Duli's future continued to lurk behind a haze of uncertainty.

A noise jerked her into the present. Something else was out there, moving in the trees. Her only hand weapons were actually tools: a long dagger and a hatchet on her belt. She carried an old crossbow, which she raised in the direction of the noise. The aged weapon was more for self-defense than hunting.

She scanned the woods. The tree cover was sparse enough that she could spot any threat within range of her crossbow. Duli heard bird calls, the wind in the leaves, a squirrel hopping along a branch and her own breathing. There was another sound. It seemed like something moving branches as it went about its business. From all Duli could sense, it was probably some distance away. Likely just some animal moving around, yet doubtful to be anything that would stalk dwarves with such noise. Determining that she was in no immediate danger, Duli lowered her crossbow and kept walking.

Duli glanced around hoping to catch sight of whatever made the noises. There was nothing amiss. The emptiness of the terrain, if not for the bird calls, could make her feel she was the last person alive. As far as her heart was concerned, she was alone in the world.

She picked her footing carefully around an old rockslide. Only a few steps away, the ground dropped into a small wash. During the rain or the waking season thaw a creek flowed past this spot on its way to become a grand river. It was a good spot to leave a trap.

Duli moved slowly, not wanting to disturb anything getting a drink at that moment. She cradled her crossbow close as she edged towards the lip of rock. She didn't expect to see much of anything left in her trap, but the God of Luck might finally favor her by leaving a deer to shoot. Cautiously, the widow peered into the green dell.

A thin creek of water trickled down to form a small pool. Her eyes sought movement—there was none. Duli held still in her perched position for several breaths. She glanced into the trees and the dark areas beneath overhangs for any sign of resting creatures. As she squatted on the top of the rockslide, she noticed her trap had been visited. She couldn't make out much detail from her vantage point. There was definitely a fur body lying where her trap was placed. She saw patches of blood and scattered tufts in the grass. She cursed under her breath. Something had chewed apart portions of her kill. She would have to remove the body from her trap, without much hope of a decent pelt.

Duli descended the slide. As she closed the distance to her trap, one thing became clear: there was more than one dead animal in the dell. The partially torn body in the trap was that of a wolf. The tufts of fur scattered around the grass weren't just from the wolf; they were the bodies of pups. Duli's trap had killed their mother, then some creature had come along and caught the rest of them. The dwarf crafter began to look around for signs of the wolf's mate. She saw nothing. It was that moment where some unexpected feelings took the wind from her gut.

Emotions stirred, stemming from her recent loss. A male wolf might be left out there without its mate, bereft of its litter as well. Her trap had destroyed a family. It was something Duli would never let into her feelings before. It was her lifestyle. Dwarves depended on her craft. Fur and leather kept the clan warm. Duli caught many animals and had learned to bury them without trepidation about handling a bloody corpse. Today, it felt like her world had shifted. The sense of loss from her loved one began to cause feelings of guilt over the slaughter by the creek. Duli's mind was telling her she was feeling foolish even as the sorrows began to pour from her eyes. Even the pose of the wolf mother added to her guilt. Its head had been rolled at an unnatural angle, staring in the direction Duli approached. The canine mouth hung open. It gave Duli the impression of a harsh question that would never be sounded out loud.

The creek ran along unspoiled by the dried blood. Duli knelt by it and splashed the cold water against her face. She wanted to wash herself clean of the unexpected emotions that kept assailing her senses. She had been strong once. Duli recalled days when she had the backbone to stand up to anything. The death of an animal had never gripped her with such dreadful feelings before. Her unwarranted empathy towards the dead wolf was very un-dwarflike.

Duli remained squatting on her heels beside the creek, taking time to collect her wits. Her calloused hands ran through her hair. She readjusted her braided tail. Her mind sought any distraction that would strengthen her will enough to handle the corpse.

A cloud passed across the sun, dropping a shadow across the dell. A cold wind accompanied it down the creek. It gave Duli a slight shiver. She dismissed the wind as nothing more than the toothless gnawing of a receding winter.

The head of the dead wolf moved.

Duli's green eyes widened in shock. She stared at the dead eyes, the open mouth, the dried blood. It wasn't moving now, but surely it had! Duli couldn't have imagined it!

Her breath caught in her throat as she froze in that awkward stance. She was silent as her ears were picking up the rapid pace of her heart. The grip on her crossbow tightened until her knuckles paled. Duli's gaze locked with the unwavering eyes of the dead wolf. She was afraid to blink, lest the wolf move again and she miss it. The shadow of the cloud had yet to pass. The high sides of the dell left it dimmed as if the sun had gone below the horizon. Her mind knew the dead wolf couldn't move. The wolf's mind could not survive the damage done to its body, although it wasn't unknown for an evil spirit to animate a dead corpse. Even as the thought came to her, she began to fear that a malicious spirit had come to torment her.

Duli watched with disbelief, and mounting horror, as the head moved again. This time, a barely perceptible noise uttered from its throat.

The dwarf widow tried to scramble backwards but only succeeded in falling on her rear. A clumsy contact with the crossbow sent the bolt zipping into the trees. Her mind filled with such fear that she dared not look away. Her gut wanted her to get up and run for home. Instead, her irrational mind caused her to crab-crawl backwards. Duli couldn't take her eyes off the quivering wolf head. Her unguided scrabbling caused her to back into a tree. With a yelp, she threw her crossbow-laden arm up before her face to protect from any threat.

"Dear gods…oh spirits!...Let not your cruel jests fall upon me!" Duli yelled in panic. "Forgive me of any crimes that have turned you against me!"

Duli's instincts screamed at her to grab a new bolt and reload. Her reasoning argued that if the dead wolf could somehow rise, a crossbow would not harm it. She should be running, but fright froze her in place.

It occurred to Duli why a spirit would stalk her. "I know I asked to be sent to my husband; I still wish it! Can I not die peacefully in my sleep? Must I suffer in fear before my demise?"

Her breath came in quick gasps. Although the wolf had not stood, nor even showed signs of approaching, its head still lolled about as if it was trying to bite at her. It reminded her of scary tales told in the late hours at Deepmug's, when warriors would claim that they saw the dead walk. Now, Duli was witness to that fear. She stayed mindful of the fact that in those stories someone usually ended up dying.

"Please have mercy," she repeated a few times, gasping in whispers. "Please have mercy."

Duli was approaching the edge of her sanity when the situation changed. A small head popped up from underneath the wolf. This new creature, a wolf pup, had been hiding next to its mother's body.

Duli's fear turned to disbelief. Disbelief faded into embarrassment. The wolf pup made a small noise. It was only a little whine, but it mimicked the sound Duli heard coming from the corpse earlier. The leather worker waited for her heart to return to normal as the wolf pup abandoned the corpse and dove for cover in some rocks. A moment later, it peeked out towards her from the edge of the rocks. The dark nose turned her direction and sniffed, as blue eyes looked back at hers.

"You gave me the scare of a thousand demons, you know that?" Duli shook her head as she spoke. Her tone of voice was soft, for she did not mean to return the scare the pup had given her.

Perhaps because Duli was making no sudden moves, the pup got up the courage to circle behind a tree that was slightly closer. Its furry head and ears poked out to sniff the air again. The clouds passed on, leaving the dell bathed in full daylight.

Duli sat forward, taking a few deep breaths. "I was expecting the gods' own vengeance to strike me down because of you. I predict you'll be a fine hunter someday—you have a talent for scaring prey half to death."

Duli cracked a smile at her own foolishness. The smile disappeared a moment later as she thought about her last words.

The dwarf tried to estimate the age of the wolf. She knew next to nothing about how wolves lived, only how to trap them and use their skins. The pup was probably too young to hunt by itself. It and its litter mates seemed old enough to follow mom out of the den, but young enough that they depended on her. Duli looked at the small teeth when the pup gave out some kind of call. It was a mournful call, as if hoping that its mother or father would return to protect it. The teeth didn't seem threatening enough to kill any decent animals.

Without a family, this pup would not survive. It was too young to know how to hunt prey. Even if it found more wolves, Duli suspected that it might be driven off or eaten.

This young pup had every right to blame it on Duli. Duli had killed its mother, and was responsible in some way for the death of the rest of the litter. Although such was the way of trappers and their prey, it wasn't easy for her to stare into the reality of it after her recent loss.

The strong and unpredictable emotions she had felt ever since Geordan's death began to tie in with this wolf pup. Her hopes of a family were dashed. The pup was without its own family. Some unwanted sympathy welled up inside her heart. It caused her to attempt something she admitted wasn't the smartest thing to do, but she did it anyway.

It took a few knee scrapes, some muddy leggings, a choice array of curses, collisions with some bushes and some offerings of bait, but Duli finally caught the wolf pup. She smuggled it back to Nandorrin's Halls.

CHAPTER 7

"Don't whine at me and walk off. It's milk! You must have had milk from your mother." Duli sighed, throwing her hands up in futility. "Come over here and sniff it again, you'll like it."

The wolf pup glanced over at the woman. Duli sat on her heels next to a bowl of goat's milk. The pup's blue eyes seemed to convey that it didn't understand. It returned to sniffing around Duli's bed.

"I'm going to be upset if you mark that bed as yours. Don't make me get up and drag you back to the bowl again."

Ignorant of Duli's words, the wolf pup began to assume a squat near the bedpost.

"Oh nay! Hsst!" Duli jumped into action. The male pup was beginning to catch on to the meaning of those words. She caught the lupine furball as it tried to scurry into hiding.

She lectured it as she carried it back to the bowl. "I think I better get you used to a sandbox, at least until I can walk you outside to do that kind of business."

The wolf twisted in her hands. It even attempted to nip her to no avail.

A knock at the door startled the dwarf and her reluctant pet. Duli began to worry who it might be and how she would explain the wolf. She hugged him closer as his eyes locked on the origin of the knocking sound.

Glaura's voice called from the other side. "Duli? Let me in for a second. I was hoping you might come with me down to the Hearthden and see what the women have on display."

Duli tried to think of a reply. Any other day she would be glad to stroll down to the Hearthden and glance over the crafts of the other women. Right now, her attention was focused on the pup that was now dependant on her. She tried to sort some responses in her mind. Duli couldn't think of any explanation that would excuse her from a conversation with her friend. If Glaura stuck around, she would eventually figure that Duli had something to hide. She decided that the best thing to do might be to remain silent. Hopefully Glaura would think that she wasn't home.

"Fine, play games with me." Glaura huffed, "I know you are in there, you were talking to yourself as I walked by."

Duli finally broke her silence. "It's just a bad time right at this moment. I'll maybe meet you down there in, uh, half a candle."

The wolf pup decided to pick that moment to reply to the unknown voice on the other side of the door. It let out a yip. Duli moved a hand to cover its mouth.

"What was that?"

Duli thought quickly, "Just the hiccups. Ate too much food and too little drink. Always makes me hiccup like that."

There was a moment of uncomfortable silence between Duli and the woman on the other side of the door. Her hand tried to keep the wolf shushed. Duli hoped that Glaura would leave things at that and go. She was not so lucky.

"Duli, let me come in for a moment."

"It isn't a good time…"

"Why isn't it?" Glaura asked. "You aren't…you don't have a knife to your chest again do you?"

Duli's worries began to rise. Glaura suspected something amiss and seemed to be jumping to the conclusion that Duli might be entertaining suicide again. She had to calm her friend before Glaura made any dumb decisions.

"Glaura, stop worrying for me, I was halfway into slumber when you…AAYEE!"

The leather crafter had to shake her finger loose from the pup's teeth. Wolves had an incredibly strong jaw.

Of course, that sound helped Glaura get the wrong idea about her friend's secretiveness. "Duli! Let me in, now!"

She was sucking on her finger, trying to juggle the wriggling pup in one arm. "I'm fine. Just go. We'll meet up later."

Glaura's words were hammering the door in a rush. "You're not fine. Gods, Duli, are you at it again? Just let me come in and talk to you. Please open up."

Duli and Glaura began shouting back and forth at the closed door. Glaura's tone became increasingly filled with panic, while Duli's frustration didn't help calm matters. The pup began to yip again. Duli tried to cover the noise, but it only served to make Glaura think that her friend was in pain.

"That's it!" The voice in the hallway declared, "If you don't open up your door right now, I'm going to find help to take it off its hinges."

The last thing Duli wanted was for others to find her wolf and start spreading tales. She relented to her stubborn friend. "Alright! Fine! I'm opening the door. You better keep silent about this!"

Duli held the wolf in the arm opposite Glaura as she flung the door open. The widow's friend stormed in, reddish-brown hair hanging in uneven lengths once again, as they always did when Glaura's kids helped her with their own styles. She was quick to close the door as Glaura's eyes swept the room for anything suspicious. Her eyes rested upon Duli last.

"Keep what silent? I'm wondering if you lost your mind, woman…Taekbol's whiskers! What in the…?"

Glaura's mouth dropped open as she stared at the furry form wriggling in Duli's arms. She pointed a stern finger at it. "Duli, that pelt still has a live animal inside it."

"Aye. This one is alive. I intend to keep it that way."

Glaura seemed a loss for words, until she sniffed the air of the chamber. "Your room smells like he marked his territory."

Duli walked over to the bowl. She turned back to Glaura as the wolf in her arms strained to look around as well. "This little guy has been trying to leave his mark in spots. I plan to find a sandbox or something until I can work out a solution."

"Where did you get it? Did it wander into the halls somehow?"

Duli's gaze lowered. "Its mother and all its littermates died. Poor baby was alone."

"You can't just take a wild animal as a pet." Glaura stood before Duli, but distanced herself due to the pup. "A small, unruly wolf tends to turn into a big, unruly wolf."

"I killed its mother. She died in my trap. The rest of the pups died too."

Glaura stared at her in silence, expecting more. When nothing else was forthcoming, she said, "You've killed lots of animals in your traps. Why was this different?"

"Because this wolf lost his whole family because of me. He's just as lonely as I am."

Glaura closed her eyes, giving a slight shake of her head. Duli ignored her friend as she tried to get the wolf to drink again. She set it down by the bowl and attempted to push its nose in close.

She heard her friend sigh. "This isn't for the wolf, it's for you. You aren't thinking straight. You just seek a replacement for Geordan."

Duli set her fists against her hips. "I can't replace Geordan! No animal can give me what he has over these many years. I have to help this wolf! I have taken from him his family, just as mine was taken from me. I have to make amends."

The wolf tried to nip her hand again. Duli was getting frustrated over its refusal to drink the milk. She was ignoring the other woman, until Glaura spoke in a softer tone.

"Is that how you are trying to feed it?"

Duli turned a glare on her friend. "It's milk," was all she stated.

"I meant the bowl. I don't think it knows how to use it."

"How else am I supposed to feed it?"

Glaura seemed to have an idea. "Try offering it a nipple."

Duli was sure her eyes nearly fell out of her head. She slapped a free hand over her breast. The leather crafter was trying to think of a response as Glaura chuckled at her reaction.

"I didn't mean it had to be a real nipple. Try pouring some milk on a finger. Here…"

With Glaura's guidance, Duli tried a new trick. She poured some milk from a mug over her finger. The wolf pup looked at the dripping milk. Soon the pup moved closer for a sniff. Eventually, the wolf started licking and suckling Duli's finger. The milk kept dripping from the mug, only to run down her finger into the wolf's mouth. She watched the pup feed while trying to suppress some surprisingly strong emotions. She really began to visualize the wolf as her child. He was feeding from her, suckling like it would from his real mom. A bond began to link them.

Duli wanted to thank Glaura, but she was afraid to show the emotions on her beardless face. She continued to pour the milk as she asked, "How did you know this would work?"

"Motherly instinct," the mother of two replied. "Though we need to get him drinking from the bowl."

"Aye, his teeth keep nipping me."

Glaura kneeled on the floor to get a closer look. She stayed a good distance away, fearing that the pup would take fright if she seemed to interfere. "Try to get your finger closer to the bowl. Inside it would be best."

Duli allowed the drops to run down her finger as she used one knee to nudge the bowl closer. The pup's blue eyes were half-closed as he enjoyed the milk. Duli brought her finger downward, touching the surface of the milk. The pup followed, eagerly lapping the milk from her finger, but also catching some from the bowl.

"That's good," Glaura observed. "Take your time. When you are ready, stop pouring the milk over your finger, but leave your finger touching the milk in the bowl."

The pup noted that the flow of milk over the finger had ceased. It was now lapping at the milk close to the finger. Duli felt its tongue flick against her skin. When the wolf readjusted its head for more efficient drinking Duli slid her finger away. The wolf pup was too busy lapping up the bowl's milk to notice.

She was glad that the wolf was finally doing what she had been trying to teach him, yet in her heart Duli missed that brief contact when he was suckling at her finger. Her thumb rubbed along her finger, feeling the wetness but not in a hurry to dry it off. Duli knew it was foolish, but she felt like she had become a mother.

They watched in silence as the pup drank. Duli was tempted to reach out and pet its fur, but she held back. Now that he had found sustenance, she didn't want to interrupt the process. Glaura was watching Duli as much as she was watching the pup, and Duli noticed. The widow assumed her friend was trying to figure if she was crazy or not. She ran her fingers back down her sandy braid as she pretended not to notice her friend's scrutiny.

"He won't eat meat yet?"

"Nay, I tried," Duli replied. She made a slight gesture in the direction of the wolf's mouth. "He has the teeth for ripping into some meat, but he hasn't shown interest."

Glaura nodded. "Maybe he's just too young. It could be that he just needs another trick to get him started."

*   *   *   *   *

It was in the late hours of the day when Duli made a simple meal. All her time spent chasing and playing with the wolf had exhausted her. A sandbox had been set up in one corner, although the pup had yet to adapt to it. Duli's efforts for the day included a leather leash which was left unfinished. She left the leash hanging over a table. It would do her no good until she tried to find a buckle of some sort. She had managed to persuade her tired bones to fry up some strips of meat. They sizzled beside a boiling pot of roots.

The pup was beginning to take an interest in everything she did. Duli swore more than once as her feet nearly tripped over the furry bundle. He was shadowing her every move. The pup was beginning to understand that its welfare was under the control of this alpha female. Duli ignored him as best as she could while trying to step around his tail. She piled up a plate with her supper. Those small, blue eyes kept track of every movement of the food; that tiny nose kept sniffing the air. Duli set her meal on the stone table without a glance at the pup. She didn't want him begging for food while she ate. The pup would have to learn that she would separate their meals.

Duli grabbed a shallow bowl for the wolf's portions. She wondered if he would show any interest in it, since he finally seemed to accept the milk from a bowl. Duli brushed her hair out of her eyes as she cut some strips into smaller portions for the pup. Some roots were mixed in with the rest, just in case the wolf took a liking to them. Those eager blue eyes continued to stare.

45

Duli set the bowl next to the table. She sat down, pulled a mug of ale closer and watched the pup from the corner of her eyes. The wolf alternated sniffing and glancing between its portions and the dwarf. It cocked its ears to one side, as if questioning something. Duli said nothing as she continued to watch the wolf discreetly.

It turned its attention back to the bowl. Without a sound, those tiny paws padded over to investigate. The pup stuck its nose close and sniffed the food. Duli was sure it would take a bite. It definitely showed interest. To her dismay, the wolf let out a whine and backed off. It sat down, looking up at her as if it expected something more.

"It's food! Eat it or settle for milk." Duli growled. "I know you want it, just take it or do without. Stop begging!"

The pup jumped back from the tone of her voice. It began to pace and whine. Duli stared at it for a minute before she said anything else. When she spoke again, she was calm and confidant.

"I'll leave it there, and you'll eat it. I know you will. You know that's meat and you'll eventually learn to take a bite." Duli grabbed some meat from her own plate. "If you expect me to drape meat bits over a nipple, you are mistaken."

Duli pointedly ignored the wolf as she ate. He whined again. That plea fell on deaf ears. Duli felt the pup rub against her leg, and she nudged it angrily towards the bowl. She believed her message was clear. She didn't want to talk to the pup and have him feel that he could pull at her for attention.

She wasn't able to finish all her food. The antics of the pup were getting under her skin. In a huff, she stood up from the table and made her way to the hearth. She was preparing to skim the leftovers from her plate into the fire, yet she was interrupted by the furry form scuttling around her legs. She knew those irresistible blue eyes were staring at her without even looking down.

"Stop setting your camp at my feet!"

Duli glowered at the pup. Glancing back at her food, she decided to have one last piece before burning the rest. Duli popped it into her mouth. She began to lecture the wolf. "Don't act interested…and turn your nose up…food is food…I algh, haakk!"

Duli just about doubled over as the stringy morsel got stuck at her windpipe. She tried to swallow it. Despite a few attempts, the chunk wasn't going down. It preferred to push against her airway. The pup's ears perked up. It got out of the way, making yipping noises as it sensed Duli's distress. The sorrows stung her eyes as she tried to dislodge the meat. Her breath came out in wheezes. In the back of her mind, she found it an odd twist of fate that she had wanted to take her own life. Her instincts were prompting her to fight to survive. Duli was getting so weak that she stumbled. One last effort of her lungs heaved the chunk out of the way.

Her sorrow-struck eyes barely made out the small piece of meat as it landed on the floor. It was such a small thing to have caused her so much suffering. Her limbs were weak and uncoordinated from the lack of air. She leaned back against the side of the hearth for support. Her breathing was slowly returning to normal, despite a few more coughing spasms to clear her throat.

The wolf pup was calming down now that it sensed the dwarf was better. It ran over to sniff the salivated glob of meat that rested on the floor. Duli watched in surprise as the pup eagerly gulped it down. Its tail started wagging as it turned eyes toward her.

Duli had recovered from her near-death experience. She was breathing easy as she stared at the pup incredulously. It had eaten the food she had touched! She reached over to the cracked bowl of leftovers she had spilled by the hearth. She took a small piece in between her fingers and held it out for the pup to sniff.

The pup did nothing more than touch it with his nose before sitting back and whining again. Duli brought the meat to her lips. She didn't put it in her mouth, but she gave it a lick and held it out. The wolf glanced back and forth between her face and the proffered nibble. Duli withdrew the piece and plopped it in her mouth. She stared at the wolf. The pup was watching her, waiting for her next move. Duli slowly started chewing the meat, working it into a softer form. The pup definitely took interest. It focused on her moving jaw as if waiting for a prize to pop back out. Duli grabbed the softened piece out of her mouth and held it before the lupine muzzle. The wolf eagerly snatched it up. Duli could see the contentment in its eyes. Leaning against the hearth as she was, it was easy for the wolf to scoot closer and lay against her leg. It turned its head to glance at the rest of the meat, and then looked back to her green eyes.

"Oh, so I have to chew your food for you, is that it?"

Those angelic blue eyes offered no response.

She inserted another portion of meat in her mouth, chewed it, and handed it to the pup. It gulped the morsel down and then licked the remainder of the juices from Duli's fingers. They repeated this several more times. The wolf pup had no problems taking the meat as long as Duli chewed it first. For all her trouble, she was rewarded with a lick to the face.

"Is this what pups and their mothers do to nurture their family bonds?" she asked. The wolf answered with the same phrase it had for most everything: *yip!*

They stayed next to the hearth, leaning against each other, while Duli continued to feed the pup. Sometimes she would tease him by dangling the morsel just out of reach. He always captured the treat. Duli pet his soft fur with her other hand as they shared their first real meal together.

*   *   *   *   *

Duli shed her clothes as she walked around the bed. The hour was late. She threw on an oversized shirt that was once Geordan's. She held the fabric to her bare cheeks, smelling the pipesmoke and ale that reminded her of him. She noticed that the pup was playing with a leather string foraged from some of her crafts. It rolled about on the molber wool shirt she had worn that evening.

"Good night, wolf." She stopped to laugh. The pup looked comical: rolled on its back, string draped over its nose as it paused to listen to her voice. "Maybe tomorrow I will think up a proper name for you."

Duli glanced to the wall, at the lamp created by the priests to light the rooms of Tok-Maurron. She spoke the word which commanded the miraculous device to cease its illumination. The only light left in the chamber came from the hearth embers. She collapsed onto her bed and snuggled under a padded fur blanket. Her eyes began to surrender to the evening hours.

A thud hit the bed, followed immediately by a scrabbling sound of claws as the wolf bounced back to the floor.

"What the…?"

Duli peered over the edge of the bed. It was elevated on a wooden frame, too high for the pup to easily jump. She peered over the edge and saw the pup whimpering at her under those innocent blue eyes.

"Nay! You are not sharing the bed with me!"

Duli settled her head down, but kept her eyes towards the side. As she predicted, the pup's form came flying back up, catching precariously by its claws, before dropping back to the floor.

The dwarf got up and scolded the pup. Looking for options, she decided to pull her molber shirt and the piece of string against the edge of the bed. She set the pup down on the makeshift mattress, and firmly pushed him to lie down. "Stay!"

He settled there with no argument, though he let loose a few whimpers as Duli climbed back into bed. He made no further attempts to jump up with Duli. She got comfortable again and stared into the hearth.

"I was almost with you tonight, Geordan," Duli whispered into the dark. In her mind, she could almost see the otherworldly gates of Dorvanon in the hearth. "The gods finally were willing to take me, yet I fought it."

Silence reigned for a few minutes. "I'd like to die a million deaths to be with you again, but dying scares me. I can't even die the one death needed to be at your side."

Almost without thinking, her hand slipped over the edge of the bed and began stroking the pup's fur. Duli continued to whisper to the night, "Hopefully it will happen sometime soon, my love. I hope they take me in the night."

The wolf stretched and rolled under her comforting touch. "Until then, at least I am not as lonely as I was before."

CHAPTER 8

The Hearthden thrived with women plying their wares or congregating to gossip. The huge fire sunken into one wall helped keep Lower City a comfortably warm temperature year-round. The early planting season of the surface world had witnessed Duli smuggling a wolf pup into the city, now the summer sun warmed the nearby hills. Changes on the surface as the months passed went unnoticed by those who spent day after day near the glow of Hearthden's furnace.

Duli moved among the tables with Glaura and her children, sharing in the conversations with other females of the clan. The male dwarves ruled the city of Tok-Maurron, but the females claimed control over Hearthden. Hearthden gave them the strongest gathering of their voices in this otherwise patriarchal society. Stalls and tables were set out for women to sell goods, so that their men could relax at the pub or fight battles against humans. The men rarely ventured here for any period of time. Any man who entered the Hearthden soon found himself the target of the women's humor.

Waurel and Feena, Glaura's two young children, raced around Duli's legs as the widow haggled a deal with an elder named Fosha Spindlebur.

"…but I simply must have these. How about this: I'll make you a better carrying bag than the one you have now. It will have a shoulder strap and I'll give it more space than that worn bag of yours."

The older dwarf woman paused to glance between the knitted molber wool shirts in Duli's hands and the bag she used to carry her wares to the stall. At one hundred and fifteen years, Fosha often was sought by other women for advice. "Hmm, I think I could part with them for that. I'd like to see that bag before the week is out."

Duli heard Glaura calling to her, but she finished setting up her trade with Fosha. "I'll have one put together in nay time at all. You know you can depend on me."

Duli accepted the wool shirts from Spindlebur. It was common for Duli to barter for goods instead of using coins. She still stubbornly refused the assistance of the Mennurdan

Guild, despite Popguv making the occasional inquiries to see if she was alright. Rumors circulated among males that her work quality suffered in the months since the loss of her husband. It lacked truth, since Geordan never guided her talents in any way; however, the men had decided to spend their coins elsewhere. Even Duli's female customers were constrained by how their husbands wanted money spent. A few coins still managed to flow to her purse. For the most part, Duli had become adept at using a barter system instead. She traded goods for goods, without the involvement of coins and thus getting around the husbands' consents.

Duli turned towards Glaura's voice, "What are you squealing my name for?"

Glaura stood at the sweetest-smelling craft stall in the Hearthden. "I was not *squealing* your name! You're making me sound like a pig!"

"Well, after the way you swallowed noonmeal earlier…"

Duli allowed that comment to trail off as the merchant next to Glaura laughed. Leli Gorm's goods catered to women more than men. She used sheep milk to make soaps and lotions, throwing in different herbs as needed. Although she was a few years older than Duli, the skin of her hands made her seem a decade younger. She attributed her young looks to her trade.

Glaura savored the aroma from a bar of soap. "Come over here and smell this before I wash your mouth out with it."

Duli joined in while Leli watched. The craftswoman offered, "I'll give you a deal if the two of you will be willing to take three of those off my hands."

"I have plenty, but thanks," Duli replied. "Maybe Glaura will buy all three from you. She seems to like buying a lot of soap."

"You try keeping these two kids clean for…now where did they go? Waurel! Feena! Get back in my sight!"

As the mother of two was distracted, Leli turned a conspirator's look towards Duli. Leli made a loud comment for the amusement of the other women. "At least she gives me good business. A lot of those men seem to make a bar last a whole year."

The women of the Hearthden shared some mirth over that comment. A few had some stories to share along those lines. In the middle of it all, Fosha quietly called Duli back over to her stall. The wise woman had a look of concern on her face.

Mindful of Duli's privacy, she spoke in low tones. "And how has your business fared these past few months since Geordan's passing? Are you well?"

Duli offered a smile from her beardless face. Some might tell Fosha to mind her own business, but she understood how the old woman fretted to look after the younger ones.

Fosha acted like a caring grandma to all, with just the right amount of spitfire at the most interesting moments.

Duli patted the elder's hand. "I do well enough to get by. I like having my freedom. I've seen how poor Shauna has acted since joining that awful guild."

Duli didn't add that she had taken an extra job beyond her trapping and crafting. Sargas had been so impressed with her knowledge of cleaning muskets, that he paid her to assist him. They kept it secret, due to the clan's customs toward women. Duli cleaned muskets, assembled and disassembled them, ran errands for him, and helped him keep his shop a bit more organized than before her arrival. That last bit seemed to infuriate him, but despite some words of warning he never actually stopped her from improving the shop.

The older woman sighed, a reaction to Shauna's name. "I know what you mean. She had a fire in her eyes once, but it has been dulled ever since venturing into Popguv's domain. Her craft gives her nay joy anymore. The only pride she has taken seems to stem from some of the musket stocks she makes."

"Why?" Duli asked with raised eyebrows.

Bolgor, and thus Shauna, carried a reputation for excellent work and inspiring designs on crossbows and musket stocks. (Crossbows were still commonplace among the clan, as a hunting weapon for women or as a silent weapon for scouts.) Since Bolgor's death, Shauna had succumbed to working under the Mennurdan Guild to make a living. Despite the guild offering to 'complete' the training of widows and female orphans, a woman never seemed to master her craft under their eye as long as she remained confined to her gender.

Fosha explained, "Have you seen her work? She started putting designs on the stocks that paint the humans in a rather *uncomplimentary* manner. The words she engraves on them have shown that she has a better knowledge of insults than I have experienced in my many years. The warriors love them. Many of those young men going off to fight procure a gun displaying her designs. The sacred runes of our ancestors, the image of Dorvanon or the gods…just add Shauna's creative curses, proudly displayed along the woodwork, and young warriors have a weapon that inspires pride."

Duli kept most of her thoughts hidden from her expression. She responded, "Shauna sounds like she's eager for a lot of Tariykans to die by her handiwork."

The elder commented, even as Glaura returned with her two unruly kids in tow. "I think Shauna would go fight the war if she could. Turn your back on her near a musket, and she'll be firing lead loads towards Tariyka."

Duli took special note of those words. A shadow of an idea was starting to creep into her head. Before she could give it serious thought, her attention followed the conversation that was picked up by the other women.

Leli commented, "How big is Tariyka? We've fought with them all summer. Considering how many of our young men have died, certainly the Tariykans have to be bleeding their country into the ground."

Fosha answered, "I hear it's a vast territory. They seem to own everything south of the mountains. Herothe, where have you been?"

Their attention turned to a woman running back to her stall. Duli knew her well. Herothe Darkhair also followed the craft of leather. The dark-haired woman had a few details that set her apart from Duli. She didn't trap for her own leather. Often she bought skins from Duli. Her work focused on saddles and reins needed for the ram riders and work animals. She also made several useful items to sell to the other women of Hearthden.

The woman answered even as she started packing away the contents of her stall. "I heard my man's company is back. They had a tussle with those humans at the base of the hills. Good thing my husband and those other priests were with them. I'm worried that some are reported dead, but others were saved who would have died trying to get back home."

Since the ending of the Godwars, the gods were banned from interfering directly in mortal affairs. The gods could only channel their powers through men of faith. Dwarven priests could bring forth a number of miracles to cure disease or heal grievous wounds. Unfortunately for the warriors of Tok-Maurron, the Tariykans believed in their own gods, and had their own miracle workers. Duli knew that Herothe's husband, Nandorrin, was a priest of the God of Fire,.

Leli had her head tipped forward, in silent prayer for those who lost their families. She lifted her head and turned back towards them. "Every time my husband leaves, I worry if I will get that dreaded news. I can't understand why the Tariykans have to be so greedy for land. If only the humans would learn to tunnel and create some vast cities under the sheltering earth."

Duli took notice of Glaura at her side, trying to settle her kids. She leaned over to her friend and whispered. "Count your blessings that Tormero is a gemcutter. You don't have to worry about him getting himself killed along the border."

Glaura's reddish-brown hair bobbed as she nodded. A whisper returned, "I thank the gods every day. I can't imagine trying to raise these two alone."

Duli became aware of a male skulking his way into Hearthden. She didn't know his name, but he looked as if he had been out traveling in the surface world for days. Garments wet from rain adorned his muscular frame; he left mud tracks from his boots. The dwarf warrior snuck over to Fosha's side. Even the men knew that Fosha Spindlebur was well-known and respected among the other women. Duli couldn't hear the words, but she saw Fosha's lips tighten. It was a sure sign that some bad news was being passed to her ears. The elder woman sent the visiting dwarf away; the warrior seemed eager to slip back out of the female-dominated Hearthden with as little notice as he had entered.

"Duli," Fosha looked at her with eyes devoid of any visible emotion. Her tone suggested that her request should be obeyed without question. "Watch over our wares, please."

Without waiting for an answer, Fosha stepped over to Herothe. The elder interrupted the dark-haired leather worker, taking one of her arms and guiding her away from the market. Duli followed them with her eyes, aware that Leli also watched the departing pair. Herothe seemed reluctant to leave her things behind. When they were out of earshot of the others, Fosha braced Herothe against a wall and whispered into her ear. Duli watched with growing understanding, and sympathy, as Herothe's legs lost strength. The other leather crafter began to suffer from the shakes. Herothe leaned on Fosha as the elder helped her walk to her warren.

Leli had grown quiet. She understood the news passed to Herothe. "If I ever get word of my husband like that…"

The soap seller looked over to Duli. "I would do even more than Shauna. Nay dwarf here will stop me from taking my own war to Tariyka."

Duli nodded. "I would be lying if I said I never felt the same way."

Glaura excused herself and her children. She had the sudden urge to get them home and spend some time with Tormero.

After several minutes passed, the conversations began anew around Hearthden, though it became short-lived. The gossip quenched once again with the arrival of a male dwarf with crooked fingers and scraggly white hair. He nodded politely to the women as he passed, while they all tried to suppress their feelings about him. The elderly dwarf looked at the unmanned stall.

"Is Herothe Darkhair around? Anyone know where I can find her?"

Duli tried to meet his gaze without showing her revulsion. "She went somewhere to be alone, Popguv. Someone just told her about her husband."

The head of the Mennurdan Guild seemed unaware that half the women were staring at him, half were pointedly ignoring him, and none were participating in the small talk commonly found in Hearthden.

"Ah, I just wanted to reassure her that we have a place for her …"

"I'll tell her." Duli interrupted. She barely kept her voice calm as her insides turned in disgust. "She knows where to find you."

Popguv nodded and shambled out of Hearthden. Duli stared at his back as he left. She idly wondered if Herothe would sell her self-respect and join the guild.

Duli worked hard helping Sargas "Gun Hand" repair some misfiring muskets, when Clan-Sire Boreval Stonebrow walked into the Armory. Duli was so intent on tinkering with a hammer spring, that she almost didn't look to see who had arrived. Once she did, she turned her eyes back down to her work immediately. She pretended to be concentrating on her work while noticing that Boreval paused in his steps to glare at her.

Boreval enjoyed a close relation to King Harvagot Stonebrow. He claimed a spot among the king's inner circle of advisors and counseled in military matters. His bald head managed to sport a long black and gray beard that nearly swept along the floor. Boreval reputedly wielded a two-handed mace in combat, though Duli had only seen him use it as a walking cane. He entered the Armory with it in hand. His thick fingers enveloped the top knob of the weapon, while the metal cap on the handle's base would echo a ringing noise down the stone floor wherever he went. Boreval's presence didn't bode well with Duli, since he was notoriously tradition-minded. This Clan-Sire upheld the beliefs of shaving non-clan women beardless. He praised the Mennurdan Guild for giving widowed women something useful to do. His family continued to craft muskets from bronze, despite the availability of steel, for tradition's sake.

As she fiddled with the bronze flintlock, Duli could feel Boreval's eyes boring into her.

"Master-At-Arms!" Boreval barked. "What is she doing here?"

Sargas Bristlebeard acted indifferent, not even sparing a glance at Boreval, when he spoke. "Replacing a worn spring on that hammer. I'm sure if you asked her to show you how, she'd be willing to explain it herself."

His answer grabbed Boreval's gall enough to turn the Clan-Sire away from Duli. "You know that isn't what I meant. Why is a beardless, non-clan female given access to our muskets?"

Sargas huffed and met Boreval's stare. "You know the reasons for her being beardless shouldn't even apply these days. Dwarves got worse things to worry about; the Tariykans are a good example."

The Clan-Sire started to say something, but Sargas talked right over him. "She cleaned and cared for Geordan's gun. A damn fine job she did! She's working for me because I could use a hand, and she gives it a good effort."

The king's advisor shook his head. "She doesn't belong in the Armory at all. A woman shouldn't be allowed near a musket. All they can do is make and raise babies; they even make a mess of doing that craft."

Duli did her best not to show her rising anger. Throwing words at Boreval would only make the situation worse. She kept her eyes on her repairs.

"Gun Hand" stepped closer to the Clan-Sire, drawing his attention. The old dwarf tinkerer pointed at Duli to accentuate his words. "I am keeping an eye on her, trust me."

Boreval adopted a cool, superior expression as he calmly insulted the aging warrior. "As far as I can tell, you only have one eye to spare. I'd rather it be focused on your work."

Sargas' eye glared back. "If I thought she was a danger to the clan, she wouldn't be here. You should check her work before you question my judgment."

The traditionalist didn't bother listening to Sargas' words. He simply stated, "We'll have more words about this in private, perhaps in the company of the king."

Boreval turned and walked straight over to Duli. She set down her work and turned to face him. His words were unexpected. "This saved me some time. As it so happens, I was looking for you."

Her green eyes widened. "Looking for me? Whatever for?"

Duli had been prepared to let loose some inciting words since it seemed her secondary craft at the Armory was about to end. Instead, she found herself put on the defensive for something else entirely.

Boreval sneered, "That bandit of yours is running loose in Lower City."

Duli groaned. It wasn't the first time the young wolf had somehow gotten out of her chambers.

Before she could say a thing, the Clan-Sire continued. "He followed his nose to Deepmug's and stole away with a sizeable piece of sausage. This isn't the first time he showed up at Deepmug's from what I hear. How many times does that critter get out and terrorize our kin? I hear he's traveled all over the city."

Duli's wolf got into the habit of escaping, only to show up later with all manner of items taken from Tok-Maurron's inhabitants. The wolf's bed somehow began to accumulate stolen pipes, a mug, someone's coat, a colorful baby rattle and even some leather bags Duli had made and sold to other people.

Duli lost all her anger in the face of the crimes her wolf committed. "I'm sorry. I'll try to find out how he is getting out. I swear I lock the door every time. I'll go down to Deepmug's and pay for what he took."

"Aye you will, right now. That bandit is a nuisance and will get shot if it continues!" Boreval turned towards Sargas. "I came to tell you that Guffan's raiding party returned, bringing forth all manner of useful items from a Tariykan keep. They brought a few wagons of things, but they are delayed down at the lower watch house due to muddy roads. I want you to go tally up what they brought and organize some hands to store it...*after* you throw this non-clan female out of Stonebrow Vault."

Boreval left. Sargas packed up a few things to take with him to the lower watch house. "I apologize, Duli, but I can't go against Boreval. If he says you can't work here, then his word is as good as the clan's. I wish he could see how much you have worked to help keep our muskets operating smoothly."

Duli tried to force a smile. She still held a musket her hands. Sargas hadn't asked her to stop, so she finished the job. "I'm glad for the time I've spent here, my friend. It gave me some spare coins, and it made me feel..."

After a pause, she found her words. "I'm so lonely and sad without Geordan. At least, working on these muskets, I felt as if I could get back at the Tariykans. I hoped to be a pain in the human's saddle region as long as I lived."

Sargas nodded. The aging warrior seemed ready to leave. "I will miss your work here. Curse Boreval for that, and for making me get down to the lower watch in the mud. I may be down there the entire day trying to inventory Guffan's haul. Wouldn't be the first time this year I've had to sleep down there."

The hunched old warrior walked over to her. "Duli, go ahead and finish what you're doing. Lock up when you're done and don't let anyone see you leave. I'll pay you when I get done with this chore."

Sargas left Duli alone in the Armory. She relished the privacy. For some reason she felt as if the sorrows might come upon her, even though she scolded herself that nothing was lost. Boreval Stonebrow would see to it that she didn't go near the Armory again. Duli still had her leather crafting to keep her busy. She told herself that the loss of privileges with the muskets would be nothing of note. By clan rules, she shouldn't be there in the first place. Nevertheless, the rude removal of her access to the guns...to her husband's gun...with no regard for her efforts on behalf of the clan was a stinging blow to her pride.

Duli finished her work and stood by the Armory door. She cast a forlorn glance back at the rows of muskets and other weapons. "I wonder if the Tariykan women suffer as we do." She mused in the quiet room. "Are they allowed to be masters of their craft? Are they allowed to use weapons to defend their home?"

Duli walked over to a case and grabbed the sword that lay within. It was a captured Tariykan blade. "Are those human women allowed to wield this steel against their enemies? Or are they shielded behind the scorn of their men?"

She replaced the blade in its resting spot. "Are we doomed to live long, unhappy lives at the mercy of senseless clods? Shauna would fight the Tariykans herself if given the choice. I would gratefully throw myself at their best warriors. My gun's voice would thunder a song of vengeance to repay them for Geordan's death."

Duli walked over to the rack of muskets. Geordan's gun remained there, displaying eleven notches from the men he had killed. Duli lifted it in her arms, cradling it reverently. "I would kill as many as I could…but only if they would kill me too. I can't commit my own body to the act. One try was enough. If the gods would still bless me, they would let me fight to avenge you…and let me die to join you."

In that moment, a dangerous thought entered Duli's head. She thought of the Tariykans, the muskets, the disrespect she and Shauna endured. A course of action came to her mind. It wasn't something that would get her into danger, but it would defy the clan laws. Even Sargas would be in an uproar, but only if he found out. Duli knew he would be out of the city for the rest of the day. That left plenty of time for her to have one last bit of fun before Boreval would shut her out of the Armory forever.

"If I am to be punished as a criminal, at least I should have the pleasure of committing the crime."

Duli glanced at the bag full of goods purchased in Hearthden. She didn't return Geordan's musket to the rack. Instead, she proceeded to grab a powderhorn and a bag of shot. She stuffed the musket and all the ammunition into her bag. The barrel stuck out, but she used the molber wool shirts to wrap it up. Anyone would see she had something covered up, but no one would expect it to be a musket.

The widow took Sargas' spare set of keys, then locked the Armory behind her as she snuck off with her husband's gun.

CHAPTER 9

"Get in there you little bandit!" Duli's roar caused the wolf to run into the chambers with its tail between its legs. Her feet tromped against the solid floor a moment later, threatening to kick his behind if he slowed at all. The angry tone coming from her mouth could stampede a whole pack. "You have got to stop stealing from the clan. I can still turn you into a coat any time I like!"

Duli closed the door behind her as the wolf crept over to its bed. She noted the piece of sausage from Deepmug's, along with another child's toy.

"Let's find out how you are getting in and out of here."

Duli began a thorough search of the chambers. She knew he wasn't getting through the door, because the latch remained in place. Hard rock formed most of the walls and the parts that weren't had stones fitted in place. Duli doubted he could claw a tunnel through that. She was passing close to the bed when a draft of air caught her attention. It reminded her of something hidden from view. The dwarf woman got on her belly, scanning the wall under her bed.

One of the many ventilation shafts that moved air through Tok-Maurron opened up under the wooden frame. Geordan and Duli had moved the bed into that spot to take full advantage of the heat coming from the deep furnaces. The opening had no cover over it. The wolf could squeeze through and get anywhere in Tok-Maurron.

"Ahh, now you're little secret is out."

Her green eyes studied the support posts of the bed, judging them to be too narrow to block the opening even if she moved them in place. She paced her chambers before an idea came to her. She grabbed a stoneware cooking board. Before long, Duli had used the board to block the hole, allowing only a thin crack of air to pass. She shoved the bed so that one leg pinned the stoneware board to the opening.

"There. That will do until I can manage to lay my hands on some kind of grate."

Duli went to her bag. She pulled out the musket and admired it in the glow of the priest-made sconce on the wall. Her hands went to the side of the barrel, pivoting the spike bayonet that was tucked alongside it. The long metal spike added another foot to the weapon when extended. She ran her hands lovingly over the decorated wooden portions. Her eyes fell on the design of the gates of Dorvanon on the side of the stock. The sorrows tried to come to her eyes, but she pushed them back.

"Welcome back," she whispered to the gun. "It feels like you belong here."

The musket, powderhorn and bag of shot were transferred to the pack she used for checking traps on the surface. The old, large pack could conceal the gun easily, as well as large traps. Duli used a pelt to help cover the barrel from anyone close enough to look into her pack.

When finished, she resumed every appearance of a trapper going to check her traps. No one would realize she was carrying a gun and ammunition unless they ruffled through her pack. She turned a stern glance at the wolf.

"*You* stay here. I'll be back soon."

*   *   *   *   *

The two dwarf women walked through the warm, tree-filtered sunlight along the ridges of the Molberus range. Duli actually huffed a bit as she hopped over a downed tree. Her pack began to shift dangerously, but she set it right with a quick toss of her shoulders. She spoke to her companion, "Must have been a good storm. Leaves and branches all over the ground."

Shauna Horgar grinned through her six-braid beard as she matched pace. The fair-haired dwarf pointed at a twisted branch hanging from one damaged tree. "When the wind gods favored by the elves wreak such damage on the surface, it makes one appreciate having underground gods who offer their shelter within a solid foundation."

Duli nodded, even though it had been months since she offered anything more than curses to those same gods. "Agreed, but I still appreciate having access to this windy world. I often look upon the birds in the air. Look how much freedom they have. Imagine how far their wings must take them."

"Are you thinking of spreading your wings?" Shauna asked with just a trace of disappointment in her tone. "Are you thinking of blowing away, perhaps to your clan's home?"

"Not at all," Duli reassured her friend. "Those gates are closed and are long gone. I was more or less wondering about if you were thinking of spreading your wings at all."

"Ah-HA!" The woodworker exclaimed. "So now we are getting to the point of *why* you asked me to join you outside today."

"Well, maybe." The sun highlighted the sandy hue of Duli's hair as she tromped through the wild grass. "I was worried the Mennurdan Guild had caged you in."

Duli threw a quick glance at her friend. Shauna's face had gone impassive, hiding all emotion. The fact that her friend had gone from a jovial mood to a guarded one was a statement in itself of the woman's feelings on the subject. Duli turned her head to watch where she was going, awaiting an answer that wasn't willing to face daylight.

Duli asked, "What is the Mennurdan Guild like?"

Shauna let loose an audible sigh. The woman reached up and idly twirled one of the six braids of her beard. Her answer drew forth in a slow manner; as if agonizingly pulled from the source.

"This guild is like a new, terrible marriage. It's a husband that makes me work all day, under the scorn of how wrongly I perform simple chores. He takes credit for any of my efforts he approves. He grows fat on money made off my toil, then hands me a pittance. He shows me off to others as if he made me, while striving all day to unmake me. He offers me a home by filling me with the dread of anything outside his doors. In short, he teaches me how to remove half my brain in order that I might wipe my ass with it."

The two women went on in silence for several heartbeats. Duli waited for more words. When she was sure no more were coming, she put a hand on Shauna's shoulder.

The leather crafter said, "There are worse things than that…one time I wiped my ass with poison ivy."

Shauna snorted in laughter. Duli valued bringing a jovial mood to her friend after such a straight admission.

Her friend managed to squeak, "Well if your reasons for bringing me out here involved putting a smile on my face…it worked."

They passed within sight of one of Duli's traps. Duli turned her head towards it, whipping the long, single braid that grew out from under her shoulder-length hair. As soon as Duli was satisfied the trap was untouched, still baited by a piece of meat, she continued walking. That short glimpse to the side made Duli aware that her friend watched her, perhaps trying to see into her motives for the walk. She pretended not to notice her friend's subtle glances.

Shauna finally asked, "How have you managed since Geordan's death?"

"And since shunning the guild?"

Shauna nodded.

Duli had counted on Shauna asking such a question. "I appreciate still having my freedom. I won't misguide you…fewer coins fill my purse these days. This summer has taught me how to narrow my goods to the essentials. I trade more than sell, but it still is enough to provide me comfort. I survive."

Duli glanced back at her friend. Shauna missed the eye contact, intent upon whatever thoughts were on her mind. She continued, "Has pressure from the males and the guild hurt me? Only in my coin purse. They tried to strangle it, but it still breathes. Once I got past the early problems, and emotions stemming from my loss, I found out that I could do pretty well on my own. My spirit stays free."

She turned towards the fair-haired widow. "I suggest that you do the same. Break away. Fly free."

The other woman said nothing right away. She offered a glance to the birds riding the air currents in the vast sky. Duli wondered if Shauna looked upon those flyers with the same appreciation of the freedom that Duli held. After a few moments, her friend seemed to shake off any such private fantasy.

"I wouldn't know how," she began. "My situation has a few big differences from yours. You harvest your materials. Bolgor and I paid others for it. Even now, the guild provides it. I would have to cut down and collect my own wood."

Shauna sighed before continuing. "I would lose most of my customers. My foremost work has been the musket stocks. The men appreciate the work I put into all the details. They won't use stocks crafted from a female that lacks male guidance. I also craft many objects used by the various sects in Staprel Gom. Those fools are even more pompous than the clan warriors. I would lose their business too. I can't do it, Duli."

Duli walked a few more steps before realizing that her friend was not following. She turned her green eyes on Shauna, witnessing how the other woman had turned her gaze to the south. Ridges descended to foothills, then rolling gullies, eventually fading into a mostly flat expanse of plains belonging to their warring neighbors. The human lands of Tariyka lay beyond the hazy horizon.

"Damn them," Shauna whispered, just barely loud enough for Duli to catch her words. "Damn them all."

When Shauna turned in the direction they had been walking, the two women once again went along side-by-side. Duli shared her friend's sentiments. She thought this would be a good time to lead a conversation which might reveal whether or not she would show Shauna the forbidden item hidden in her pack.

"Since Geordan was taken, I have hated three things. The gods were one of the first ones I cursed. Aside from them, I also bit my tongue every time I dealt with the thoughtless males of the city."

Duli clambered over a downed tree, glancing up the hill towards where her next trap sat. "Most of all, my hatred has focused on the Tariykans. There was a time when I wouldn't have wished anyone ill. That part of me died with my love. Every time I see the men return from a successful raid, I feel somewhat better…and yet, it is never enough."

Shauna picked up the cue as Duli silently glanced at her. The fair-haired dwarf admitted, "My anger burns up my insides. The work I do on the musket stocks is my secret joy. Every gun I help craft throws shot into the humans. I guess…that is the most satisfying thing that gets me through every degrading day at the guild."

"I would go fight them if I could," Duli ventured. She noted the interest in her friend's expression. "Of course, I would hope to die in the process. Death would only deliver me to my love in Dorvanon. Before they send me, I would gladly take as many of their lives as the gods allow. Do you feel the same way?"

Her friend didn't hesitate. Shauna drew forth the axe hanging at her belt, a relic from her warrior husband. "Aye. I would take a war to the throne room of their lord if I could…not minding that it would be a one-way journey."

Shauna dropped the axe back into a holder on her belt. Her golden eyes regarded Duli. "At least I can help make those muskets. How do you survive day to day with such feelings? And I don't mean your craft. How do you deal with those vengeful feelings every day?"

"Here it is," Duli thought, *"Time to find out if I am doing her a favor, or showing her my folly."*

"I have been working another job, one that was supposed to stay unspoken." Duli noted that she had Shauna's complete attention. "I helped ol' Sargas with cleaning and repairing muskets."

A gasp issued from her friend. "How? That isn't allowed for women!"

"I guess he got soft one day. He knew I still had an emotional attachment to Geordan's gun, and he learned that I cared for it. I started helping him more and more. I actually earned some coins doing some of that work. He needed an assistant, and I took good care of everything."

Duli smiled. "That was my contribution to this war. Some of those uppity males were using guns that I had fixed or cleaned to go after Tariykans. I felt I was doing my part."

Shauna was digesting the fact that Gun Hand broke a timeless tradition. "I'm happy for you. I won't say a word; it should remain unspoken."

"Too late," Duli sighed. "Boreval found out."

"Boreval Stonebrow? Ugh. I imagine he might have popped vessels all over his face at such news."

Duli couldn't help but giggle. "That's exactly how it looked. I've seen few men so upset."

The leather crafter led the way to a dip between ridges, where there was a heavily wooded spot and one of her baited traps. Duli figured the trees would provide nice cover for them.

"Well, that is why it is nay longer unspoken. I'm discovered. Boreval already made it clear he is throwing me out of the Armory. Sargas is forced to obey him."

Shauna shook her head before spitting on the ground. "It would offend the kin if I were to wish Boreval ends up as one of the casualties in this war."

Duli heard how her friend had phrased her words, but understood her real meaning. She simply agreed, "It would."

They stepped into the edge of the small wood. Duli knew they were a few dozen steps from her trap, but she paused as soon as they were hidden in the branches. She halted Shauna.

Duli lowered her pack to the ground as she asked. "Have you ever really handled the muskets? Have you gotten your fingers on the trigger of one?"

Shauna tugged at one of her beard braids. "I've had my hands on them…rarely. I mostly design my stocks around a brass mold they gave me. Sometimes, I'm able to hold one to reexamine my handiwork."

She frowned, only half-paying attention as Duli dipped her hands into the large pack. Shauna's face betrayed no emotion, but her voice rumbled with malcontent as she continued. "That may be a thing of the past. Popguv is turning my focus towards furniture…"

Her voice went silent as Duli slowly pulled the barrel out of her pack. Shauna's golden eyes flashed between Geordan's musket and Duli's smile. She half-reached for the gun, as if trying to disprove that a non-clan dwarf woman was actually standing there holding it.

Her voice came slowly. "If you are caught with that…when Boreval learns of it…"

"He won't," Duli insisted, watching the range of emotions that her friend was trying to hide. "Sargas is out of the Armory for the day and I have the key. It will be safely back and cleaned spotless before he finds it."

"Why did you take it?"

"I thought you might enjoy holding it, maybe even see how it is loaded and fired."

Duli caught the glint of greed in Shauna's features, like a miner striking gold. Shauna tried to keep her face impassive, but her fingers were already twitching in anticipation of touching the weapon. Those golden eyes of hers darted about in all directions, in case any patrols were in sight. Little could be seen due to the trees.

Shauna whispered, as if the clan city in the rocks beneath their feet might hear her words. "You stole shot and powder too?"

"Might as well do all if doing part," Duli said. "Boreval would see fit to treat me as a criminal, I might as well live up to his expectations."

Before Shauna could say more, Duli placed the musket in her possession. "Take this into your arms. Think of putting it to use against the Tariykans. Dream for the moment."

Shauna's eyes wandered over the engravings in the stock and barrel. One of her fingers touched the hammer, tracing the figure of Nandorrin. Without hesitation, she pulled the hammer back until it was cocked. Keeping her thumb on the hammer, she pulled the trigger in order to slowly relax the hammer forward against the flash pan. The woodworker brought it up to her shoulder, looking down the barrel.

"I would love to give the humans a surprise taste of this."

Duli retrieved the powderhorn and a solitary lead shot. She helped Shauna through the motions of loading the barrel. Her friend poured in the powder and rammed the lead ball into place. Duli considered priming the pan with powder, but decided against it. She didn't want the musket to go off by accident.

A sudden sound came from the trees around them. A branch had moved by no will of the wind. Duli and Shauna turned to glance at the source. They saw nothing.

"Maybe just a small animal?" Shauna ventured.

"Probably," Duli agreed, her eyes scanning the wood. "I have a trap just past those trees there."

"Might it be a patrol?"

"They make a lot more noise. We'd hear them if they tried to move through that with their rams." Duli regarded the musket clenched in Shauna's hands. "You carry that for now. We'll find a nice spot and I'll give you the powder for the pan. For now, it is safer to walk without anything sitting under the frizzen. Just keep the gun pointed up."

They heard another branch move. Both women turned towards the sound. Duli took the lead, guiding her friend. "Maybe we'll be trying your aim on some wild game…"

Duli got a glimpse of the area where her trap had been set. She didn't spot the metal teeth at first; it was disguised by a layer of leaves. The trap remained hungry for prey.

The sight that interrupted Duli's comments to Shauna included sudden movement to the side. A pair of humans! Duli had never seen one before, now two of them were charging at her and her friend with Tariykan-style swords raised for the kill.

CHAPTER 10

Duli's heart nearly stopped when she saw the two armed Tariykans charging them. In the shock of the moment, she forgot her longing for death even if it was presented by a human's sword. Her first glimpse of them made her realize how different their two races were.

Dwarf warriors prided themselves on their long beards. The two humans had remarkably little facial hair. Their bared swords were thin blades in comparison to the heavy dwarven axes. Duli doubted that such a flimsy blade could deflect a stout attack. The humans were sparsely armored compared to her clan. They wore metal chest straps and skirts over leather clothes, with nothing covering the arms or legs. A glimpse of their protection reminded Duli how Sargas described guns shooting right through Tariykan armor.

The humans didn't seem to be a physical threat despite their taller stature. What dwarves lacked in height they made up for it in their wide, stout build. The muscles on the arms of the two men seemed smaller than Duli's.

Despite any apparent disadvantages of the Tariykans, they remained two armed and armored men, attacking with surprise against two women who had not seen combat. Duli glanced at the unprimed, forbidden musket briefly, with the realization of her folly. Without powder in the flash pan, the musket was useless. Shauna carried the musket, Duli carried the powder, but the closeness of the enemy left no time to finish loading. If they lost their lives, the enemy would have Geordan's musket as a prize.

Both dwarven women jumped aside as the humans closed. Duli went right, Shauna went left, leaving a sizeable gap between them. One sword barely missed Duli. She found herself trying to grab her dagger as the human turned his stance. Another swipe went in her direction, nearly marring her. Duli came to realize that whatever the humans lacked in strength or heavy weapons, they made up for it in speed and agility. The human was quick to recover from his two misses. Each swing had been delivered and recovered in a heartbeat.

Shauna also began to respect their speed. Her opponent stayed close to her, despite all her scrambling. She held the musket before her. His blade swung down, leaving a mark on it. Shauna wasn't so concerned about marring the musket as she was just trying to stay alive. She made the mistake of grabbing it on one end with both hands and swinging. Her strike was slow enough that the Tariykan easily avoided it and struck while the gun was to the side. His blade whisked past in a blur. The first blood of the fight splashed the ground.

Duli barely got out her long dagger and hatchet as the human continued to harass her. The trapper moved between a few trees, hoping to make it more difficult for the man to swing. He kept up his balanced stance just out of easy striking range. The Tariykan seemed to be considering his next move.

Her green eyes swung to find her friend. She saw Shauna reeling from a cut on her arm. The fair-haired dwarf seemed in danger of losing her grip on the weapon. It occurred to Duli that Shauna probably hadn't paid attention to the spike on the side of the barrel, and she would probably need any and all advantages.

"Folding spike on the…"

That was all Duli could manage before reacting to her opponent. The Tariykan struck fast as she was distracted. Her reflexes happened to get her hatchet in the way of his uppercut swing. The two weapons made incidental contact, neither doing any real damage. The move did succeed in backing Duli a step. Her opponent hadn't even completed the sword's arc when he launched forward into a kick. His foot sent her stumbling backwards. She no longer had the benefit of trees on both sides.

Shauna kept a good grip on the musket despite the sting in her arm. The action kept her too occupied to see how deep the cut was, but at least she still had some arm strength. The Tariykan switched the grip on his sword while slowly circling her. Shauna got the feeling that he was sizing her up for a finishing move.

Her right hand dropped to grab her husband's axe from the belt. He quick-stepped forward as she moved. Her wounded left arm lifted the musket well enough to block a hit. She backed up as she went, denying him a second strike. A moment later, she stepped forward and lashed out with the heavy axe. This time the human had to back up.

They stared at each other for a moment. He had his sword poised for use, while she had her axe held high and bearing the musket between them.

Duli kept on the move as the human blade shadowed her. She kept both of her own weapons ready to parry; however, she admitted to herself that any such attempt would be more likely to lose her arm than do any good.

As the Tariykan kept pressing her back, she glanced behind her as she retreated. By the time she focused once again on the man, he made use of his longer legs. The invader swept a foot across the grass. It caught Duli behind her own foot as she continued to back up. She offered up a grunt as she fell.

Shauna and her enemy both advanced at the same time. Her swing was limited by a lack of confidence. The axe blade came nowhere near hitting him. His attack was not hindered in the same way. The Tariykan made an obvious move with his sword, drawing Shauna's blocking musket up high. Quick as a blink, he spun a kick that jolted her wounded arm.

Geordan's musket dropped to the ground.

Shauna gripped the axe with both hands, holding it up straight before her. The Tariykan almost smiled. Shauna's position was totally defensive, offering no threat of a strike. Her mind grappled with the decision of trying to back him up with some swings, or wait for his move and react.

Duli started rolling. The human rushed her, trying to strike her during her vulnerability. She had to reverse her roll to avoid dismemberment. As he recovered his stance, she made a desperate move. Duli threw her hatchet at his torso.

The Tariykan moved to deflect it with his sword but missed. Duli's hatchet hit him in the stomach. Duli paid little attention to the results of her hasty attack. She glimpsed the hatchet bouncing away. There was no grunt of pain from the man, and no obvious blood. With how poor her throw had been, she probably hit him with the blunt end or struck armor. Her only weapon was the dagger clenched in her right hand. There was no time to mull over the danger as the human recovered from his shock.

Shauna and the other Tariykan made their move at the same time. They made more contact with their arms than their weapons. As they tangled, the Tariykan snapped a free hand into a jab towards Shauna's shoulder. The female dwarf lost some feeling in her hand momentarily. The axe went flying from her grip. In return, her other arm elbowed him in the gut with all the strength inherent in her race. Shauna kept them tangled. Her hands grabbed his arms, clutching and tearing at his sleeves. They began to struggle for possession of his sword.

Duli could swear she felt the human's breath on the back of her neck. Still in a roll, she threw herself over a patch of overgrown grass, hoping the gods hadn't completely abandoned her.

The sound of a spring snapping the steel jaws shut came from just behind her. The Tariykan gave out a howl of pain. Duli looked back upon her handiwork. The jaws of her trap held his lower leg. The anchor chain, spiked into the ground, pulled taut. This particular trap had been made strong enough to hold anything short of a bear's strength. Duli reached over, got her fingers on his dropped sword, and yanked it away while the human screamed in pain.

She glanced around to check on Shauna. The fair-haired woman was grappling with the taller human. Duli noted the musket laying in the grass, halfway between her and the struggle. Throwing aside the Tariykan's sword, she crawled over to the musket. All she had to do was flip the spoon-like frizzen back, pour a dash of powder from her horn onto the flash pan, shut it, cock it and fire.

Even as she got her hands on the weapon, it appeared she might be too late. The Tariykan used his martial skills to fling Shauna to the ground. She landed in a pile of her own limbs. The human raised his sword to deliver a quick blow.

A flash of gray fur launched out of the trees. Duli's young wolf landed jaws-first on the Tariykan's sword arm. The wolf's weight dragged him down. Duli was witness to the most bloodcurdling screams coming from both men at the same moment. The one in her trap tried to pull free of the jagged teeth with no luck. The other attempted to pull the wolf off, even as the animal started jerking around to rend the arm.

"How did he get loose again?" Duli thought.

She watched in amazement as the wolf's wriggling body began to tear apart the man's flesh. It suddenly occurred to her that she better get the musket primed and ready. She tried to keep her hands from shaking as she threw back the metal frizzen. She pulled the horn to her lips, popped the stopper with her teeth, and threw a hefty dash of powder down. Half of it missed the pan entirely due to her haste. She didn't even attempt to properly recap the horn, allowing it to fall to the ground. Her fingers were snapping the plate back as her thumb pulled the hammer all the way back.

With hammer at the ready, she glanced back to the Tariykan caught in her trap. Duli's trick put a halt to his aggression. The injured human was trying to staunch the flow of blood coming from his leg. She turned back to face the struggle between wolf and man. There was no safe angle at which to shoot. The two combatants staggered in irregular movements.

Duli called out to her friend, "Shauna, move away."

Shauna put space between herself and the frenzied fight. The woodworker reclaimed her axe while Duli dropped to one knee. She brought Geordan's gun up to her shoulder. There was a brief memory of all the times she had looked down those sights after cleaning the gun. In the Armory, she used to fantasize that the wooden cut-outs were real men. Imaginary enemies were always there when she tested the muskets. She used to wonder how things would be if she had actually stood in defense of her people. Now, Duli tried to keep the heart of a human centered down the barrel.

The Tariykan facing the wolf turned to throw his weight into a tree. The canine tugged and tore at the arm. Its efforts ceased when the human rammed his weight to pin the wolf against a tree. A yelp was heard as the wolf dropped from the arm. It recovered just as quickly, growling and skulking around the man.

It was the moment Duli needed to fire her shot. She had the Tariykan lined up. Her finger began squeezing the trigger. The trapped human behind her shouted warnings to his comrade. The second man turned to stare directly at Duli's green eyes. The musket kicked backward as the shot released. The explosive noise in the barrel echoed like thunder across that portion of the mountains. Duli inwardly cursed herself for blinking again, but her eyes opened to the truth. Smoke from the powder lingered in front of her eyes for a breath. The cloud passed away, revealing her target on the ground, rolling in pain. Those struggles became less and less as the grass beneath him turned red.

Duli watched with a mixture of relief, pride and shock as the human surrendered to death. The wolf jumped away at the musket's boom, but it rushed back in and attacked the helpless human. By the time Duli had the presence of mind to call it off, the human became a mangled corpse.

Shauna's good hand clamped over her wounded arm as she walked over to Duli. "What about the other one?"

Duli swung the barrel in line with the remaining Tariykan. The man offered no threat. His leg remained caught within her trap. Her green eyes sighted down the smoking barrel, only to realize the emptiness of the gesture. The musket wouldn't do her much good until reloaded.

She kept her attention on him as she dropped the butt to the ground and reached for the powderhorn. He simply stared back at the two dwarves. Rage burned in those eyes, barely concealed behind his pain. Duli went through the reloading procedure as Shauna stood guard with her axe. The wolf began to skulk towards the wounded man, offering a growl. Duli called it to her side before it could attack the human.

"Scouts perhaps?" The beardless dwarf mused. "The males have been attacking human settlements all summer. Maybe the Tariykans are looking for our warrens."

Shauna cast a side glance at the musket as Duli rammed a lead shot down the barrel. "You should go. The sound of that musket will draw attention here."

She shook her head as she proceeded to prime the pan. "All the more reason why I'm not leaving. He is wounded, you are wounded...there may be more near."

"I wasn't referring to Tariykan attention," the fair-haired dwarf nodded towards the gun. "The clan may find you with that forbidden weapon. What might they do to you then?"

Duli shrugged. "Hopefully, they come to their senses when they see I shot one." Her words were all bluster, even Shauna knew it. Duli pointed the loaded musket at the Tariykan as she went on, "The dwarves will see that the other one was dropped by lead when they find you here. As for this one..."

She stared down the human, then watched with disbelieving eyes as the human assumed the position she chose for her own suicide. He carefully placed the dagger under the joining of the ribcage. Her eyes were transfixed as the warrior sought out some inner focus.

Duli watched as he did what she couldn't find the courage to do to herself. He stabbed the dagger into his breast, falling forward as he did so onto the handle. The two women watched as his body succumbed to spasms. It was morbid to watch, just like how she would have died if she had done the same, yet she could not pull her eyes away.

Shauna was shocked. "He took his own life. How could he commit such an act?"

She could only express admiration that the human had done something she lacked the will to accomplish. "What courage," Duli whispered, too low for Shauna to hear.

Both women were still discussing the two Tariykans as a number of dwarves led by Horace Smokebore arrived on molber rams. Duli and Shauna watched him dismount with growing anxiety gnawing at their guts. While the rest of the patrol looked over the human bodies, Horace kept his gaze locked on Duli. His scolding visage stared down at the beardless woman.

"We heard a musket blast. This be it?"

His eyes held the answer, but he listened for Duli to confirm it. She raised the gun up for him to examine or take. "Aye, I fired that shot."

Horace's arm snapped out, tearing the weapon from her grasp. Duli could see his face flushing with anger. He never took his eyes off Duli as he held the gun before him.

"Where did you two get this?"

"Shauna didn't know I had it until we were outside."

Duli felt the wolf moving past her. The raised hackles sent a signal to Duli the wolf considered the dwarf warrior an enemy.

Horace interrupted Duli's words in order to motion at the wolf. "Call that monster off before I order it shot."

She restrained her pet before he could do any damage. Once she forced the wolf to heel at her feet, Duli noted that Horace's angry expression never veered from her. She tried to speak with conviction, but the words were choked up in her throat. "This is my husband's gun."

The dwarven patrol leader huffed so hard that it sent a rolling wave down to the tip of his long beard. "Your husband is dead. An honorable passing. Thank the gates of Dorvanon that he wasn't around to see you disgrace his clan as you have. We'll see how the council will deal with the both of you."

CHAPTER 11

Duli sat still as stone in the rounded chamber, but on the inside her nerves were running wild. A couple of dozen dwarves shared the room with her, most of them sitting on a raised area that allowed them a good view of all the proceedings. Duli occupied a hard stone bench alone. She resisted the urge to look up from the bare floor. Earlier, she noted every member of the clan staring in her direction. Some pulled at their long beards while contemplating how much they would love to dole out their own awful punishment to the leatherworker. It imparted an urge to tug at her own beard, just to busy herself with any action, but her facial hair was long gone.

The patriarchs of the tribe…Clan-Sires, high priests, guild leaders, and noteworthy elders…weighed the testimonies given to them in the privacy of another chamber. Quiet stares and smoldering anger focused on her as all those present waited for the return of the council. She didn't know which reception she would prefer: the venomous hush or verbal sparring with those angered by her action.

Her eyes lifted enough to glance at those whose reputations had been endangered by her actions. Shauna sat the closest. The dwarf clerics had channeled the miracles of the gods in order to heal her arm. The fair-haired woodworker had full use of her limb, despite the cut suffered the day before. Duli hoped her own admissions would take much of the brunt of judgment off Shauna's shoulders. The council's scorn seemed to focus mostly on the beardless female. Regardless of Duli's guilt, Shauna would likely face consequences.

Duli found it harder to meet Sargas Bristlebeard's good eye. He stared at her when her gaze lowered, but when she looked his way he turned aside. She listened to those present when they blamed the stolen musket on Gun Hand's incompetence. No matter how much Duli argued that all blame should be hers, there were those who pointed accusing fingers at the old warrior. Boreval, a member of the council, made his displeasure known regarding Sargas' blundering choice to let a non-clan female have access to the Armory. Gun Hand served the clan well for more decades than Duli had been alive. His accusers shamed his honor under the pretense Duli used her womanly wiles on him to steal that gun. It hurt her to see the way the younger dwarves tore into the veteran's pride.

She didn't waste any time looking over the audience surrounding her on the higher seats. There were a number of male dwarves she didn't know and wouldn't care to know. Sprinkled between those sets of narrowed eyes and tight lips were a few familiar faces. Horace Smokebore testified before the council how he had caught Duli outside the clan tunnels with the forbidden weapon in hand. On a softer note, Duli felt the gaze of Fosha Spindlebur pass over her often. Fosha's husband was among the Clan-Sires judging Duli's actions. The elder woman had a position which often compelled her to stand before the council and advocate on behalf of the clan women. Her words mostly fell on ignorant ears. Fosha was neither allowed nor compelled to say anything of the matter at hand, but she attended the trial to observe the results. Duli knew that whatever judgment fell, it would be the subject of conversation around the Hearthden the next day.

She shifted her position slightly. Even such a small motion caused her clothes to scream noise to the far edges of the chamber. Duli returned to imitating a statue once again. She preferred to trade silence for comfort.

The sandy-haired woman contemplated her fate, wondering what punishments the male elders would deem necessary.

Perhaps death? The females of old who infiltrated enemy clans were served that sentence innumerable times. Duli did indeed steal a musket, and had almost delivered it into the hands of the enemy. Death would hold no terrible fate for her. Such an outcome would achieve her dream: reuniting her with Geordan. Even as she considered it, she realized the comparison to those old crimes were a stretch. Death would probably not be their decision. Duli would actually have preferred such punishment, yet she was sure it was not in her future.

The next most likely outcome would be exile. Duli thought it probable that Geordan's clan would think it best to kick her out the door since she no longer had family ties to them. She would be forced to find her own survival out in the mountains.

"Perhaps that would be best for us all," Duli thought, *"They will be free of a beardless non-clan, and it would force me to make the trip to reunite with my relatives."*

Tok-Maurron was no home for her. If this clan chose to exile her, she would simply be making the journey to her ancestral clan. She would have to face wild beasts, monster tribes, lack of shelter, all with no good sense of direction. The more Duli considered the trip, the less she feared it. She could use her own traps to catch meat. Duli had plenty of skins and fur blankets for comfort. If she died on the trail, it would only hurry her soul to Geordan's side. If she got back to her clan, they would reverse the spell on her skin, allowing her to grow a beautiful beard again. As she contemplated this likely outcome, she became more at ease with the idea of facing it.

Her thoughts scattered as the guards announced the return of the council. The elders filed into the room. As each man took their place on the chairs facing Duli, not a single one looked directly at her. The last one to enter was King Harvagot Stonebrow. The Grand Sire didn't meet eyes with anyone at all. He moved as if distanced from the proceedings, casually taking his seat. The image formed in her mind that it would be a dishonor on the king's part to offer any words defending the beardless woman's actions.

Boreval Stonebrow took a stand at the forefront of the seated elders. He had a parchment in one hand. His face was grim as he glanced over the decree penned in the council's chambers. Duli did not mind this arrogant male addressing her. In her estimation, there was nothing he could say that would make her loathe him any less.

"Shauna Horgar."

The fair-haired widow stood to receive her sentence. She did well adopting a typical stoic expression so favored by the dwarves.

Boreval stared through her. "You may have been an accidental observer, but this council questions how much you tried to participate in Duli's ill-advised actions. You will be watched. We will be noting your friendships and associations to make sure that you won't have any future involvement in such a crime. The eyes of the clan will be upon you, but that is not all. Some discipline must be handed out for whatever participation you had in Duli's motives. Some tax advisors for our lord and king will examine your holdings, profits under the Mennurdan Guild, and any possessions of value in your warren. They will determine a sufficient tax."

"Sufficient for what?" She asked in a small voice.

Boreval squinted at her. He held his silence long enough for Shauna to start getting uncomfortable. "Sufficient to keep your nose in your work for some time. Your free time has proven dangerous to the good of the clan."

He motioned for her to sit, which she did, but then he added, "Oh, and you will not be crafting any more musket stocks. Popguv has plenty of table and chair requests to keep you busy for awhile."

Duli watched as Shauna threw a muted glance at Popguv. The expression on Popguv's face indicated he must have argued to spare the woman some of her pain by pointing out her continued usefulness to the guild. As the leather crafter looked between Shauna and Popguv, it was apparent Shauna was upset about her change in craft.

Duli watched with silent sadness as her friend ducked her head in meek submission. Shauna had no choice but to obey. It galled Duli to recall Boreval's words that Shauna's friendships and conversations were going to be the subject of the clan guards' interest.

Boreval turned to the next accused. "Sargas Bristlebeard."

The aging veteran rose as tall as he could. Due to his hunched back and bad eye, his stance lacked strength. He kept his eye away from Duli.

"It is with disappointment this clan endured your lack of good judgment. We entrusted our most valuable weapon to you, a weapon, which nay other civilization outside of the mountain clans has been able to reproduce. Your carelessness could have cost many lives in our future. You know the old traditions and why we mark the non-clan women with the removal of their beards."

Boreval's hand gestured at Duli's smooth cheeks.

"Such an obvious lack of sense will not be overlooked. The council still observes and respects the service offered to us these past decades. We will not remove you from your duties maintaining the guns; however, you will nay longer be in charge of the Armory. You will hand in all keys, Sargas, and will nay longer work unsupervised."

Mumblings were heard in the audience as the crowd discussed the punishment amongst themselves. Sargas stepped back in shock. He almost tripped over his seat as his good eye passed over the council. He even beseeched the king with his gaze, but King Harvagot pointedly ignored eye contact. Duli felt like hanging her own head in shame. Both her friends suffered the loss of their life's work because of her. Guilt tore at her gut.

Sargas managed to ask a question. "What experienced master will I be serving?"

Anyone could recognize the sarcasm in his voice. Folks genuinely believed that no one knew the inner workings of those muskets like Gun Hand.

Boreval shrugged his nonchalance. "The council will attend to that decision next. Someone with more loyalty to the clan and respect for our traditions will be selected. Hand me the keys."

Duli could only imagine the bile forming in the back of Gun Hand's throat. Sargas took the few steps needed to stand just below Boreval's podium. The hunched dwarf reached up as far as he could with the keys. Boreval, making clear his disgust in order to further insult the old veteran, adopted a weary sigh to his voice as he leaned over in order to reach them. Sargas returned to his seat. His head hung low in wounded pride. Duli ached as if she had plunged a dagger into her friends.

"Duli, stand before the council." Boreval sneered.

The omission of her husband's surname was not unexpected. It was Tok-Maurron clan tradition that non-clan females, even ones married into the clan, were not given the privilege of a surname. Duli hardly cared to dwell on their old customs anymore. She threw the omission from her memory as she stood before the council.

Duli realized that she was hanging her head just like Sargas. She vowed not to face her sentencing in that same manner. Duli picked up her gaze and stared Boreval Stonebrow straight in the eyes. From her proximity to him, she noted the sheen of sweat on his bald head. It would not have surprised her if he had worked himself into a rage during the council's closed doors.

Boreval gave a tug at his black and gray beard while he returned Duli's stare. Their eyes stayed locked for several breaths. Duli figured Boreval held all the cards in his hand, but he wanted to see Duli back down before he unloaded his accusations upon her.

Duli was melting under that pressure, but she knew the longer they waited the more the council would be angry with Boreval. In the end, she decided on a bold statement to finish the staredown in a way that would put the king's relation to shame.

"Well, we know I'm guilty. I did a stupid thing. Now condemn me so these people can get on with their drinking!"

The staunch traditionalist snorted her direction. "At least you have the guts to admit you were wrong, maybe you should learn the humility that comes with such mistakes."

Boreval took a deep breath in order to deliver such humility upon her. "Perhaps you do not understand us as well as you should, having been reared from a clan hidden deeper in the mountains. Maybe your people have grown soft hiding behind neighbors who face daily conflict with the humans and other invaders. Our elders recall that our people endured much during the Godwars and the dark years since."

"Why is it our custom to shave the beards of non-clan females? The rest of us know this answer by heart. Our clan was often victim of traitorous females whose allegiances held to dishonorable clans. Have we not suffered enough sabotage and stolen goods by disreputable women masking themselves as visitors or beloved brides? We thought such events were a fragment of our past, but perhaps it was a blessing that Duli showed us we are still vulnerable to a manipulative face."

Duli's blood began to boil. It infuriated her that Boreval dared link her action to the saboteurs of the Godswars era. Her anger got the better of her as she spoke out in protest.

"How dare you compare me to those shameful tramps! I did not plan anything malicious upon the tribe…"

Boreval interrupted. His stern tone reminded her it would be best not to raise her anger. "It is for that reason alone that you weren't shot where you stood outside the clan walls, with stolen musket in hand. We accept that you meant nay harm, yet harm was brought upon us due to your faulty female reasoning. We nearly suffered at your hands by almost losing our greatest weapon to Tariykan scouts."

Duli was rankled to her core, but she kept silent.

Boreval went on, playing to the crowd of onlookers. "Most normal females know that they aren't qualified to lay hands on a weapon. Their flights of fancy are better served with a needle and thread."

The scorned leatherworker threw a side glance towards Fosha Spindlebur. She noted how the respected woman was staring tight-lipped back at Boreval. Duli had no doubt that some of Boreval's words would be echoed in the Hearthden the next day. She turned back to see the Clan-Sire's eyes staring right at her.

"You seem to have trouble holding your words behind those lips," he remarked. "If your tongue hasn't tired of flirting with old gunsmiths and gossiping around the women's stalls, then please feel free to offer us a sound reason why we shouldn't pass judgment on you now."

Duli's fists were clenched and shaking. A part of her knew silence would likely be a safe thing at that moment. On the other hand, if she was about to be sentenced to death or exile, then she might as well tell Boreval her true feelings.

She gave a long, intentional look back at Fosha. She wanted to make sure that the elder woman was paying attention, and that Duli wanted her words carried on to the Hearthden. Fosha's eyes were fixed on her.

Duli's sandy hair and singular braided tail whipped about as she turned her scowl back on Boreval. "Bless the gods for breathing life to us all, male and female alike. You insinuate that the gods must be half-blind, carelessly making women worth little more than the scrapings of your shoes. If I had been one of your sons, stole a musket out of my eagerness and managed to kill two Tariykans sneaking up on our fair city, then I would be branded a hero. You would raise a drink to me in pride of my accomplishment.

"Males are quick to proclaim mastery over any domain. Usually you spend all day at Deepmug's doing so, while the women do the hard work of cleaning your clothes, raising your children, and cooking meals that may go cold and uneaten during your drunken stupor!

"If you even thought of giving us a decent chance, you'd realize that we could fight every bit as well as you. Our women deserve better than their lot. Right now we can only hope our fathers don't sell our marriage to buffoons that will ignore us. We toil as your slaves when we could be doing our fair share of killing humans. We don't need the Mennurdan Guild to praise us for outdated designs when we could be pioneering our own styles."

Popguv sat with the council, his mouth opened in shock upon hearing Duli's opinions. Boreval quickly quelled any further outburst from Duli. He directed his words at the men of the council.

"Now you all see the rotten core of this apple! Duli's crazy talk is most unbefitting of a woman of the clan. Allow this non-clan temptress free access to your ears and what will be the results? We'll likely have men locked in the tavern, our guns in the hands of the Tariykans, and the rest of the city falling apart from poor craftsmanship."

The speaker returned his attention to Duli. She tried to measure the reactions of the council as he spoke. It was hard to read, given the aptitude at which dwarves block emotions from their faces. Unfortunately for Duli, she saw several Clan-Sires nodding in agreement with the Stonebrow kinsman.

She listened as he went down the list of her failures. "She set aside her duty to the clan for personal gain. Her careless regard for our guarded weapons put her adopted kinsmen in danger. Her words spit upon our culture. Such a breach of our trust and lack of respect brand her for what she is."

He turned his dark, squinted eyes to stare through Duli. "I brand her beardless!"

Boreval's insult only added to the previous insult remaining from Duli's heritage. The term "beardless" referred to a dwarf who had no honor. She already had been forced to endure the removal of her beard from clan priests. Boreval Stonebrow's accusation resonated through the chamber like a slap added upon the past physical injury.

Popguv, acting on Duli's behalf, interceded. "Proceed with reading the judgment. I think we've heard enough."

Boreval glanced back at the aging guild master in annoyance. The Stonebrow kinsman once again glanced at the decree in his hands. When he looked up, Duli still managed to lock eyes with him. She knew he could read the anger bottled inside her as easily as he could the penned marks on the parchment.

"Death or exile, I don't care. Just give it to me. I'm ready." Duli thought, keeping her chin up and eyes proud.

He allowed the words to escape slowly. "Seclusion. The council hereby imposes solitary confinement."

Duli felt a second slap in the face. She would not be joining her husband in death, or her family in her old clan.

"For two years," Boreval decreed, "you will be restricted from leaving your personal chambers except at certain times. Once every three days you may briefly leave Nandorrin's Halls, only to carry out needed purchases in Lower City…under guard of course."

Duli's legs almost lost their strength. The clan planned to lock her up in her chambers for two years! Her ears couldn't believe it. She glanced at Popguv's concerned expression, allowing realization to flood into her thinking. The aging guildmaster probably guided the council to make a decision other than Duli's death or banishment. Two years even seemed like a light sentence for a dwarf, but Duli knew there would be more conditions beyond that time. Even as she considered what two years would mean, she began to fathom how constricting the sentence would be on her purse.

Her voice shook as she interrupted Boreval. "What about my craft? I trap for hides on the surface. Without a supply of skins…"

Boreval became incensed over the interruption, "The surface is absolutely off limits to you until your sentence is over. After your time is up, you will still be watched."

Duli had been prepared for anything but this. She tried arguing with a dry throat. "How can I survive two years with nay wages?"

His fist slammed a stone podium, interrupting Duli's voice and all other whisperings in the chamber. Boreval practically roared back a reply. His beard shook as spit flew from the corners of his mouth.

"I have nay sympathy for females that don't heed as instructed!" His shaking fist pointed out Popguv. "The Mennurdan Guild was formed to help untrained widows like you achieve some measure of preservation. Time spent in the Mennurdan Guild is the only extra time granted outside your chambers during your sentence!"

Popguv tried to offer her a consoling look but Duli saw only his pity. The thought of giving up her ideals in order to have money for food threatened to bring the sorrows to her eyes. Duli would never again have self-respect if she humbled herself by passing through the door of the chauvinist guild.

Boreval finished. "Such is the judgment of this council and it is final! Duli is hereby sentenced to seclusion in her chambers. She may have nay visitors while inside her quarters. She may not leave her chambers except under guard and under scheduled visits to Lower City. Only the Mennurdan Guild will be an exception. There will be nay visits to the Armory, nay converting women to foolishness, nay stealing of weapons, and her eyes will certainly not be allowed to look upon sunlight for two years!"

He slapped the podium for emphasis once again, sealing Duli's fate.

CHAPTER 12

"If you want it done, get the muskets out of the lockroom; otherwise, it ain't getting done!"

It angered Sargas to have to make such a request from the Armory foreman. The aging warrior had been the heart and sweat of the Armory before Duli stole the musket. Now, he only served up a sweat cleaning and repairing the muskets under the scornful eye of a superior.

Boreval Stonebrow casually swiveled around to face him. "Oh, my mistake. Sometimes I forget that you can't be trusted with the security of these guns." The foreman pulled out a key and walked over to the lockroom. "Take them and let me know when the hammers are fixed so I can put them back safe."

Every calm word Boreval uttered ground against Sargas' wounded pride. The words were crafted in such a smooth, soft manner, as if to goad the veteran into anger. His gut reaction wanted to throw the impudent taskmaster out the door. Hitting a Clan-Sire would certainly bring about worse punishments than old "Gun Hand" wanted to face. Sargas tolerated it rather than be taken from the job he loved.

His one eye stared into Boreval's back as the Clan-Sire sorted through the keys. "Before you came along, I'll have you know I kept the guns in shape, got my work done well before it needed to be, without the struggle of having to make your lazy butt open the door for me several times a day. Two years of this treatment and you couldn't at least learn how to take care of these guns yourself! You never lift a finger to wipe the dust off a barrel."

Boreval stepped aside as the door opened. He refused to dirty himself to even pull the guns out of the lockroom. His eyes looked down on the hunched veteran. "I don't need to fix them. That is your expertise. I'm here to make sure they don't walk over to Tariyka."

Gun Hand grumbled as he went by the smug foreman. He knew Boreval boasted about how well *he* took care of the clan's guns. Just because Sargas didn't go as often to Deepmug's it didn't mean that word never reached his ears.

He took the muskets that were tagged for repair. His good eye scowled as he noted one particular gun. One of Boreval's friends failed to keep his powder dry on long trips, resulting in a few misfires. Of course, Boreval blamed Sargas' ineptitude. They claimed the hammer wasn't striking the flash pan hard enough for a decent spark. The foreman used many similar words over two years to slowly erode the clan's respect in the gunsmith.

Sargas set down the muskets on a worktable as he heard another dwarf enter. The new arrival and Boreval whispered words in a private conversation. The foreman used an agitated tone, though Sargas couldn't make out all the words. When he looked up, Boreval was locking up the lockroom. Something clearly upset the Clan-Sire; he handled everything he touched in a rough manner.

"Something wrong?"

Boreval cast an irritated glance at the one-eyed dwarf. "Duli is stirring up the women again! Her two years are up. She should be enjoying time back on the surface and returning to trapping animals. Instead, she enjoys spreading discontent among the clan."

Over the years that Sargas had put up with Boreval's soft, innocent barbs, he learned to make a few of his own. Sargas inquired, "What is she doing to rile a Clan-Sire? She isn't thinking about delivering a load of daggers to the Tariykans this time?"

He earned a scowl from the foreman. The Stonebrow dwarf shouted his response. "She has some influence on a number of the widows. Right now, several of them are gathered for some sort of weapon exercise down in Hearthden! They should be selling their wool and sharing their gossip, not brandishing weapons around Lower City!"

The veteran gunsmith withheld his emotions. No one in Tok-Maurron could elicit more revulsion from Boreval than Duli. She had become a thorn in his side.

The Armory master was about to storm out the door on his way to Lower City when he paused. He pointed to the muskets Sargas was repairing. "I see four muskets there. When I get back, they all better still be on that table."

"Boreval." Gun Hand's call stopped the Clan-Sire just as he was making his exit.

"Sometimes I use a different table," he continued, speaking in as even a tone as he could muster.

The angered Clan-Sire just sneered and walked out. It gave Sargas some entertainment to poke fun at his supervisor.

*   *   *   *   *

Glaura Greencutter rushed through the crowd of people in Lower City. Her path appeared more unimpeded than before the war with the Tariykans. Lower City was noticeably quieter than it had once been. There fewer people to sell or buy, standing amidst the occasional empty market stalls. Glaura missed the days when one could meet any of a number of neighbors and kin chatting among the bustling aisles. She recalled how hard it had been to keep track of her own rambunctious children in the multitude of legs.

Years of fighting had taken their toll on Tok-Maurron. Males went to war and never came back. Some families had uprooted and moved to safer clanholds deeper within the mountains. A few merchants who joined the fight now had disabilities that hindered their movement, forcing their wives to sell their crafts. Where once the women only held dominance in the stalls of Hearthden, now they had been driven to contribute in places around the city. The moods of the people likewise led to stark conversations. Glaura continued past sparse avenues, too distracted by other matters to dwell on the quiet emptiness of the city.

One notable exception remained to the subdued tones that ruled much of Lower City. Glaura looked ahead to the Hearthden, her destination, as angry battle cries echoed over the women's domain. The huge cavern would have been close to the silence of a tomb, if not for the presence of several shrill voices echoing off the rock.

She saw Duli at the head of the screaming riot. Her friend led a spectacle that Glaura considered foolishness.

Roughly two score of women were lined up in neat rows. Each of them brandished some kind of weapon. A few axes, spears and maces were cutting deadly paths through the air. More often than not, the items held by the women were actually some domestic tools which played the part of a real weapon. The women followed Duli's commands, swinging to and fro as if enemies surrounded them. At a shout, they would try to turn as one and strike in the same direction. While they may have lacked complete unison, their faces revealed the strong emotions which hardened their resolve.

Other women in the Hearthden were going about their business with disapproving glances at the display. Trades continued and coins changed hands despite the commotion.

As Glaura continued making her way towards Duli, she couldn't help but notice the familiar faces among those practicing war. Fosha Spindlebur stood to one side of the group, observing the techniques of those closest to her. Fosha had long been a voice of the women among the Clan-Sires. She devoted her efforts towards compromises and discussions amongst the clan…until the death of her husband and both sons to the savagery of war. These days she stood alongside Duli, promoting the idea that the women might be needed to defend Tok-Maurron someday.

Leli Gorm stood nearby as well. Leli had once joked that the men rarely visited her cart, due to the rarity at which they used her soaps to wash. The two years of conflict shifted her business to other focuses. The woman made lots of healing poultices and liniments which the warriors bought to soothe injuries. She had always been an easy one to approach for conversation, until the tragedy that struck her family. Leli's husband had come back from fighting Tariykans unscathed but suffered some kind of disease. The proud dwarf warrior was too stubborn to admit the extent of his infirmity, and did well to hide it. Their young child caught the disease and died. By the time Leli decided to get help from the clerics, it was too late. In his delirium, her husband stumbled out of the city and managed to fall off a cliff. These days Leli spent less time selling at her cart and more time participating in mock warfare.

Another friend of Glaura's, Shauna Horgar, was among the ranks of women. The fair-haired dwarf was swinging her late husband's battleaxe in tune with the others. Whenever her duties at the Mennurdan Guild were completed, she could be found training with the others. Their activities disturbed Popguv, but he had no claim on any of the widows when they were outside the guildhall.

They were all widows. Fosha and Duli had set the rules for who could and could not join them. Both felt certain that the Tariykans would be at the city's doorstep…Duli had already killed two on the surface! As more and more of the males were lost, they organized the widows to be able to help defend their home. Duli's requirements were that no volunteers would be accepted but childless widows. She feared they might be the forefront of protecting the other women from invaders, and didn't want anyone with family ties to die in the process. The membership was further narrowed by the breach of culture they represented. Males and females alike mocked them. Some who would have been allowed under Duli's rules were not interested in her 'foolishness'. Duli was too stubborn and rebellious to pay any heed to what others thought.

Glaura strode right up to her friend. "Duli. Duli! Pay attention to me!"

Duli turned an irritated look her way. Glaura almost stopped breathing as she locked stares with those green eyes. The past two years had left Duli more moody. She was prone to snap at the most innocent comments. Glaura was still her best friend, sneaking supplies to her during her two year confinement. Even with Glaura's help, it was unknown how Duli had supported herself in all that time. Not once had the sandy-haired female ever stepped foot inside the Mennurdan Guild. Somehow she made a living, though the effects of the past two years were obvious. Duli kept her sturdy look, but the lean years had taken away some of the plumpness around her middle. The lack of sunlight left her face pale.

Duli stayed calm as she spoke, "I'm busy. I'll see you later."

Duli turned away, but Glaura stayed persistent. "Duli, I'm not here for chatter. I came to warn you."

Her friend started to turn back to her, though a distraction jerked her head back towards the ranks of widows.

"Katy, keep your spear tip up!"

Duli's words were directed at Katy Dornan. She wielded a boar spear, trying not to stab her fellows. The younger widow looked to Duli for direction.

"You're not stabbing a boar or a dwarf," Duli shouted. "Men are more than a head taller than you. Aim higher to stab at their hearts."

The subject exasperated Glaura. "This is why I loathe bringing my children around the Hearthden anymore."

Those green eyes flicked her direction before returning to the ranks of widows. "Why? There is nay shame here."

"Just a bunch of women who seek to tear apart our clan family from the inside."

Duli was shaking her head. "This clan holds outdated ideas. Sooner or later we'll find ourselves closer to the fighting than you realize. There is nay harm in being prepared. If you don't have a reason for being here other then to scold me, I will continue training here without interruption."

Glaura lost patience. "Duli, you're almost out of time. They'll be here any moment."

"Who?"

Glaura didn't have to reply. Even as she spoke, noise on the steps of Lower City drew the attention of the Hearthden.

"Boreval Stonebrow. He gathered some of his kin. They are on their way down here to break up your gathering."

The many eyes of the Hearthden viewed the approaching warriors. Glaura counted only half as many males as there were widows. It alarmed her to see the men carrying their muskets.

She turned back to Duli, who observed the approaching men with a surprisingly casual attitude. Glaura implored, "Sandstone! Duli, they brought guns. You better cease this fool's course."

Duli gave her an amused smirk, "They aren't going to use guns on us. Boreval is just trying to put on a show to scare us."

"It's working on me, and I'm not the one misbehaving!"

Her friend ignored her, turning instead to Leli. "Leli, keep the women training. Just keep giving commands to them. Fosha and I will have a few words with Boreval, but I don't want it to seem like they can interrupt us. Just carry on and don't stop."

Duli and Fosha traded glances. Neither said anything, but Glaura got the impression that they looked forward to confronting the armed men. The two women turned their backs to the approaching Clan-Sire. Glaura knew she couldn't talk sense into her friend. The mother of two put some distance between herself and the rebellious widows. She didn't want a front seat to the confrontation.

Boreval marched his kin right over to the ranks of screaming women. He stopped just behind the ringleaders, but he kept his face towards the rest. The Clan-Sire looked ready to vent rage at Duli, but he aimed his words at her followers first.

"You will stop now. This is disruptive to the marketplace and insults our customs and forefathers. Go back to your home and craft, where you can contribute to the war effort."

His stern words shocked a few of the widows out of their poses. Centuries of tradition that had been ingrained in the minds of the women made it hard to ignore the commands of a Clan-Sire. They cast eyes back and forth, and in those nervous gazes were the first seeds of doubt.

Hesitation lasted only a moment. Leli performed as she had been told. Steeling her own nerve against the thought of any repercussions, she bellowed a command from her gut.

"Right circle, thrust!"

Glaura watched as the widows went into their trained motions. The movement wasn't as uniform as the previous attempts. Some widows responded slowly, yet each one snapped to complete the order. Weapons stabbed to the right; voices shouted as if the dwarven women were really stabbing human foes. The noise of the two-score women drowned out any echoes of Boreval's words.

Glaura watched the Stonebrow sire's eyes go wide for only a moment, before redness flushed his bearded cheeks. Flanked and backed by battle-hardened friends and family, the sight of him and these decorated warriors should have been enough to disperse the women by any tone of voice he put forth. The Clan-Sire fumed the whole walk down to the Hearthden, and now his mood was visibly turning worse.

He inhaled to shout something else, but Duli's soft-spoken tone interrupted him. She turned to him as if just noticing him standing there. The sandy-haired widow had the audacity to act as if she were a host greeting a guest.

"I'm glad you could join us Boreval!" The smile on her lips did not match the tone of her eyes. "We're so proud at how the new ranks of volunteers are doing. We'll have those Tariykan's turning tail yet."

Her words proved to be a jarring interruption from whatever Boreval planned to say. Instead, he sputtered nonsense for a moment as he collected his wits. Glaura found it impossible to melt further into the row of merchant carts as Duli continued to incite him.

Other women crafters in Hearthden started considering whether they should stash their valuables before a brawl broke out.

"Oh, they don't look as impressive as they could if their weapons matched, but as soon as they all have muskets it will be a splendid sight." Duli's cheery demeanor only acted as a barb to aggravate the males even further than Glaura thought possible.

Boreval finally blew up at Duli. "Muskets are for warriors, not for baby-makers! You've apparently paid too lean a price for mishandling our guns, Duli! Our weapons are too good to trust to wenches who should be busy using their teats to feed baby dwarves…preferably capable *male* babies."

In Boreval's anger, he failed to realize most of his audience included the few hundred female inhabitants of Hearthden. Faces went red from embarrassment or anger; young children found hands clapped over their ears before they could hear any worse comments.

The Clan-Sire stepped closer to the ranks of widows. They were losing concentration on the stances they held since Leli's last command. With a start, their drill master realized that she and the others were paying too much attention to Boreval, instead of performing the maneuvers. Leli Gorm shouted another command. Widows turned and stabbed the air, issuing more piercing cries.

Glaura glanced around the Hearthden. She noted many women staring with contempt at the participants of the scene below. She knew a lot of them were upset over Duli and Fosha's actions, but now a number of them fumed over Boreval's comments. Glaura happened to see Popguv lingering back in the crowd, watching the situation with interest.

"We have an army," Boreval insisted to the foremost row of women. "They have been gifted since birth to fight. Go back to your duties. The army doesn't need you."

Fosha Spindlebur broke into his speech, "Your words hold nay truth!"

The Clan-Sire wheeled around to face the respected female elder. Fosha didn't pause between words as she continued to speak. Boreval was slow to get a word in as Fosha addressed him and all of Hearthden.

"The army is in shambles compared to what it was years ago. Most of our promising young men…sons, fathers, husbands, my own included…lay dead."

"And you should honor their memory…" Boreval began, but Duli cut him short. The two women stood on opposite sides of the Clan-Sire, making him turn this way and that if he was to address both of them.

"I honor my husband by doing what he died doing!" Duli proclaimed. "I'm readying myself to defend my home against the humans. Women throughout this hall have lost someone dear to them in this war. Those who take up arms and train with me already lost their future. They've nay man to comfort them, nay children to raise, and all of it was stripped of them by the humans. The only sacrifice they have left is their own lives, gladly offered to spare the rest of these women from the same grief."

Boreval had fists balled as he took a quick step towards Duli. He didn't quite touch her, for it would be very dishonorable, but he tried to make her give ground in fright. "We should have just exiled you…"

All of Hearthden heard a menacing growl came from the shadows. Boreval's aggressive movement had brought forth the ire of Duli's sole family member. The almost three-year-old wolf now weighed over a hundred pounds. Glaura wasn't even sure how Duli had money for her own food during seclusion, though the wolf seemed to have no problems at all. Bandit skulked around an abandoned cart, displaying all the grace and muscle of a healthy predator. Hiss golden eyes and rumbling snarl focused on the Clan-Sire. Some of the male warriors tightened their grip on weapons as they retreated from his advance. In stark contrast, Boreval froze where he stood. His voice returned to a calm level as he spoke to Duli.

"Call off that cur or we'll shoot it." Boreval noted that Duli seemed to be casually considering his request. Bandit stalked ever closer. "I mean it. You won't even be able to use what's left of his pelt by the time we're done with him."

Duli decided not to push her luck. She used a firm voice on her pet wolf. Bandit did as she instructed, though obviously reluctant to back down from a threat to his master. The wolf skulked behind Duli while keeping its eyes on Boreval. Even after he sat his haunches down, he still looked as if he could jump to the fore at the smallest aggression.

Fosha resumed pestering the Clan-Sire as Bandit was restrained. "Months go by as our warriors proclaim fewer and fewer victories. From what I hear, we nay longer raid them; all our patrols do is hassle their advance into the mountains. We take in refugees who speak of other clans wiped out by Tariykans. How far will they push us? We have to train ourselves to be ready for the worst."

Boreval angrily stomped a few steps away from both women. Standing among his armed kin, he turned back and tried to give the widows an ultimatum. "Disperse now. Go back to your homes and we won't have to use force."

Glaura and the other craftswomen of the Hearthden drew a breath in shock. Boreval Stonebrow dismissed their culture even as he tried to enforce it. The same customs that forbade women from fighting also created restrictions to keep a male from physically imposing himself on a female.

Duli turned towards the ranks of widows. "Weapons down, but stand on your ground! If the men want to remove us, let them do the work!"

Glaura watched in amazement as the widows set aside their implements of war. Shauna tucked her axe into her belt. Katy dropped her boar spear on the ground. All the widows stood at an attentive pose. Fists on their hips, they awaited any male that was bold enough to try carrying them from the spot. The male warriors were uneasy about the situation. Some glanced at Boreval hoping he would come to a different solution to this showdown.

Fosha softened her voice only slightly as she looked across the ranks of men. "If the Tariykans will be stopped, as Boreval says, then what does it really matter that we trained needlessly? On the other hand, if the humans try to wipe this clan out as they have others, wouldn't you want an extra weapon defending your children and loved ones? Let us do as we will."

Boreval looked as if he was about to go through with his threat, when one of his kin stepped up and whispered to him. Guffan Stonebrow had led many parties against the Tariykans. As the general whispered into the Clan-Sire's ear, Boreval began to look back over the crowd in the Hearthden. Glaura couldn't hear what was said, but she could give a good guess as she also looked around.

The Hearthden had a few hundred women inhabiting it, witnessing the whole affair. Although the women may disagree with Duli's beliefs, they would be outraged if Boreval's kin laid a hand on the widows. Several angry murmurs were heard. Guffan had also noted the disappearance of several "runners" who were likely going to inform some of the other Clan-Sires about the situation in the Hearthden. Boreval began to understand that anyone who came at the call of the runners would be sympathetic to the group of unresisting women, and not so understanding to the men who would be dragging them out at the time. Quite simply, Boreval's kin were outnumbered. If they made good on their threat, they would be facing judgment from the king.

Glaura could see Boreval's face as it reacted to Guffan's advice. His expression went from the sting of disappointment to the steamed reluctance of one who was forced to play with the hand dealt to him. Boreval turned to face the widows.

"Be it on your heads! Play at war if it pleases you, while the clan suffers from the lack of effort put into your crafts. You will never even see the opportunity to know how inadequate your skills would be in the face of the enemy."

Boreval dismissed his kin. They melted from the Hearthden with all the dignity that toothless dogs could muster. The women heard lots of grumbling coming from their throats. At least a few of his kin hoped Boreval would exercise sense over customs by dragging the women off to the Mennurdan Guild. In their view, the women could use a humbling experience before they got any more foolish notions into their head.

The widows smiled with pride. Boreval's words were mostly ignored as the women simply relished the feeling of victory. In all of their childhood memories, no woman of their clan had ever made a public stance against a Clan-Sire. Duli and Fosha had stared down the great Boreval Stonebrow and refused to give an inch. Even the women who felt shameful of the widows' training acknowledged that they had just witnessed a turnaround of power and customs. Glaura reluctantly admired her friend's spirit, despite her own view of Duli's foolishness.

She watched as Duli barked an order at the women. All of widows retrieved their dropped weapons. As they parried and thrust to the commands, their voices echoed throughout Lower City with an increased sense of strength.

CHAPTER 13

Duli walked toward her chambers in Nandorrin's Halls while Shauna matched steps beside her. Bandit padded along silently in the comfort of their shadows. Even in the dwarven tunnels it was easy to overlook the wolf, so soundless were his movements. Duli always sensed when he was near, though she failed to spot him at times. She paid little attention to his presence as Shauna spoke about the day.

The fair-bearded female referred to Boreval's standoff. "Somehow I knew something like that would happen. I didn't expect he would be dumb enough to try forcing us out in front of the whole Hearthden."

"A couple years ago he would have succeeded," Duli voiced her thoughts aloud. "I guess so much has changed everyone's views. Many of the widows wouldn't consider taking up arms if it wasn't for how badly we've fared in this war. I don't know how many Tariykans have died, but we've lost half the men of the clan."

"More than half...of fighting age."

Duli nodded at her friend's perceptiveness, "Last I knew they drove four other clans out of their ancient homes?"

Shauna paused in her thoughts to recall names and stories, "Aye. I think that's about right. The Steelfoot clan, a week south of us, was attacked from within their own tunnels by some Tariykan magic. Those humans are slowly killing us. Families are retreating deeper into the mountains. I wouldn't have joined the Widow Brigade if I felt things would end peacefully before it came to our doorstep."

"That's because, for you and me, war already visited. We've already struck blows," Duli faced Shauna as they walked. "And what is with this constant 'brigade' nonsense? Leli was making a joke when she came up with that phrase."

Shauna laughed, "It has a good ring to it."

"Forty-seven trained women aren't enough numbers for a brigade."

Shauna's voice resumed a serious undertone as she confidently declared, "We will have to recruit more numbers until we have a brigade."

They reached an intersection where they would be parting paths. Duli stopped to ask her friend, "What of Popguv? He watched the event today. How does he feel?"

Shauna made a face as she thought about the guildmaster. "He's expressed his displeasure at the whole concept of women fighting for the clan. Popguv is as old-fashioned as they come."

Duli unconsciously tugged at her braid while thinking, "I wonder what he might do about it."

"He can't do anything." Shauna threw a glare back down the corridor, toward Lower City. "I'll craft their chairs and carts while working wood in the guild, but they can't tell me what to do during my late hours."

Duli was glad that Shauna's spirit burned like her own. They parted ways with a few well-wishes. Duli strolled to her chambers with Bandit in tow.

She threw open the door briefly enough for the two of them to slip inside. The dwarf knelt down and glanced under the bed, noting a latched grate in place covering the air vent under there. Bandit padded over to his bed. It consisted of ripped blankets, a couple of Duli's old tunics, plus a few gnawed bones. The wolf turned about and settled on the bed before realizing that Duli was staring at him.

"So, my little skulker, how did you get out this time?" His ears perked up. He sniffed the air as she mused out loud, "I clearly recall asking you to stay here while I was out; I threw down the door latch behind me as I left. The vent under the bed is closed. If you didn't dig a tunnel, then how did you find your way out to Lower City?"

Bandit's typical answer to most questions she asked was simple: he stretched out and waited to be scratched.

She let out a sigh. Duli was too tired to go crawling around looking for any more tunnels. Just the act of dropping her butt onto a padded stone bench seemed to relieve her legs of more weight than could be attributed to her torso. There was a weariness in her stance, due to the responsibilities of leadership over forty-seven believers. When Duli set into motion the women's militia, she expected the natural leader to be Fosha. The old woman earned a lot of respect for how she spoke out for women in a male-dominated council. Instead, Fosha threw Duli to the fore. Since Duli was responsible for the deaths of two Tariykan scouts (Shauna's participation was mostly forgotten, which was fine for the fair-haired dwarf), the women looked at the beardless female with awe. The logic followed that if Duli could fight, then she could teach them to fight.

The tired widow began to shed her clothes in preparation for a good night's sleep. Her outer coat caused irritation around her neck. Duli scratched at it before her fingers touched the edge of the scar. The feel of that rough wound, healed but not forgotten, caused her to give pause. She reached over and grabbed the polished steel mirror. Her hard-working hands pivoted the reflection until she could see her collar. One hand moved to draw back the neckline of her tunic. She stared at the ugly, dark scar. Her finger brushed over it, feeling the roughness of her skin.

The scar remained from Duli's second suicide attempt.

The worst part was she never remembered the incident. During her isolation, Duli suffered from loneliness, the seclusion of her sentence and the bleakness of her future. One evening she had taken her fill of drinks from Deepmug's. In her unremembered drunken stupor, she had kicked Bandit out and proceeded to set up a noose over a beam in her chamber. When she woke the next morning, she was laying flat on her back beneath the beam. The noose circled her neck, but the other end had slipped free. The rope-burn scar remained a permanent reminder of her latest failure. It scared Duli to comprehend that she could wake up after a night of drinking maimed from failed suicide attempts.

Since that event, Duli kept away from alcohol. On the few occasions she found herself near Deepmug's, she would sate her thirst with milk. Duli knew that if she ever got up the courage to take her life again, she didn't want alcohol interfering with her success. Unfortunately, she couldn't get up the courage to try again while sober. Her only early route out of life seemed tied to her plans for a women's militia. The Widow Brigade would die defending their besieged mountains…or at least Duli would die if the Tariykans cooperated. In this method, Duli didn't have to try ending her own life. All she had to do was recklessly defend her home until the humans did her that favor. So far, the widows weren't even taken seriously by narrow-minded males.

A knock on the door caused Duli to jump in shock. Bandit's head perked up and swiveled to the door. Duli set aside the mirror as her hands flew to her neckline. She began tightening her collar, hiding her scar, as she called out to her visitor.

"Who knocks?"

"It's Glaura. Have a moment to talk?"

"Aye. I'll get the latch."

Duli satisfied herself that her tunic hid her scar, then crossed the room and admitted her visitor. Glaura was still in her motherly apron, though the kids weren't around.

Duli asked as Glaura entered, "Nay kids? I was hoping you were bringing them for a visit."

She wasn't honest with her words. Despite loving the time spent with Glaura's children, their departure always brought on depression. Once their playful smiles were gone, Duli would dwell on her childlessness.

The beardless dwarf predicted her friend hadn't come for a simple visit. She wasn't surprised her opening question seemed to catch Glaura off guard. Her flustered friend tried to think of a proper response while Bandit loped over and sniffed at her.

"A visit? This late? 'Tis time for the stars to be out above ground and little ones to be sleeping below." Glaura composed herself quickly. "I'm here to express my disbelief at the outrageous behavior today…and a little respect. I wouldn't have believed the great Boreval Stonebrow would back down from a group of women, defiant of his orders."

"I'd say a cavern full of women. All the Hearthden stood with us, even if it was for a moment. I'd still give most of the credit to a group of women who were pushed to the point where they have naught left to lose."

Glaura walked near Bandit. The wolf, accustomed to her touch, invited her to pet him. As her fingers trailed through his coat, she turned her head to address her friend. "Do you truly feel that way? Have you already lost everything?"

Dwarves were well-capable of holding an emotionless face, except to the eyes of other dwarves that knew them well. Duli couldn't hide a flash of pain that most others would miss. "I feel as if I've lost the most important things. All my prized dreams died with Geordan." Duli tried to put some warmth in her expression. "Sometimes I don't know how I've survived the last few years, but you helped keep me strong. I can't thank you enough."

The mother of two cocked her head to the side. "I've always wondered that too."

"What?"

"How have you survived these past few years? You won't work for the Mennurdan Guild, thus men won't accept your craft. You haven't been on the surface to hunt for food or gather hides. You haven't diminished to the waistline of a gnome. Bandit has grown big and strong…"

"Bandit hunts his own food."

At the mention of his name, the wolf rubbed against Glaura, reminding her to keep stroking his fur. She complied unconsciously. As Glaura looked about, Duli noted how her eyes lingered on the many half-finished leather projects lying around. For someone who supposedly couldn't live on her craft, Duli had a large amount of work piled up.

Glaura was awed. "Is your bartering actually working out this well? How are you selling your craft?"

Duli pursed her lips. She wrestled with a decision. "If I told you, you have to keep it a secret. If word leaks out, my buyers will lose respect among the clan. They will be forced to end our arrangement and I will starve."

"You have my word, Duli. I won't tell a soul."

Duli judged her friend's sincerity a moment before nodding her satisfaction. The leathercrafter picked up some of the leather straps and cut sections of hide. "What does this look like?"

Glaura shrugged, "Pieces of a garment?" A moment after she spoke, she realized how rigid some of the leather pieces were. "Pieces of armor!"

Duli nodded. Glaura wore a look of confusion as the implications were felt. The mother of two asked, "Only the males would buy armor, and even then, only from other males. How is it the men are getting this from you?"

Duli started to speak but paused as a new thought came into her head. "Might as well show you all of it."

"All of what?"

While Glaura watched, Duli went to the other side of the bed and retrieved something hidden behind the furs. She beseeched her friend. "Turn away for a second."

When those eyes were averted, Duli ducked into the section of her chambers used for storage. She pulled a frame supporting a hide across the entry. "Alright. Just don't peek, I'll explain the leather."

Duli couldn't see her friend, but since Bandit didn't sound like he was moving, she assumed Glaura was still petting him. The leathercrafter started changing her outfit.

"Glaura, who is doing the most business in leather these past couple years?"

The reply came back after a bit of silent thought, "I suppose those making armor, ram saddles, hilt wrappings for weapons…anything related to the war with Tariyka."

"Exactly," Duli agreed. "Now, do you remember we lost a couple of our more industrious crafters near the start of the fighting?"

Again, there was a bit of silence on the other side of the hanging hide before Glaura answered. "Aye, I vaguely recall it. We've lost many men since then. I still don't see why they would buy from a woman. They would likely have a crafter in another clan make what they need if the other males were too busy."

Duli smiled, although her friend couldn't see it. "You are partly correct. Let's say that our crafters were somehow able to keep up with their demands, they wouldn't need to go elsewhere would they?"

"Of course not."

"Let's take it a step further and suggest that some clans closer to the fighting would be ordering supplies from us. After all, they may have lost some crafters or at least some access to hides as battles happened around their warrens."

Glaura was tiring of the questions. "So you are saying we had more demand, and somehow you got involved in it? That is where your coins have come from, but *how*?"

"The crafters here hired me to help."

Duli chanced a glance around the side of the stretched hide. Glaura's face was almost comical. The female was stroking her long beard as she contemplated how Duli could edge herself into trade with the males.

Duli continued, once again ducking behind the hide to arrange her attire. "The males here stood to gain a lot of coin, *if* they could keep up with the demand. This is where I took up the part of convincing them they needed a hand. They tested me, of course. I had to prove to them that I could do the simple tasks they needed. None of them wanted me in charge of anything difficult. Sometimes I just string together pieces, or punch holes, or get raw hides ready for them to use. I do little stuff, but it helps free their time up to concentrate on the 'hard' stuff."

Her friend spoke up. "In secret, of course! If any paying folk found out that a female helped, they wouldn't buy a thing. That is why it has to be kept quiet?"

"Aye," Duli was buckling on her belt. "It must not be known, or they and I will be ruined. I get barely enough coins to pay for what I need. You've helped keep me from starving or settling for the Mennurdan Guild. I truly hope to repay you someday for supporting me."

"Wait a minute. You've been secluded in your room except for escorted trips into Lower City. How did you manage to arrange all this work?"

The leathercrafter chuckled at how some things have an odd way of turning out for the best. "Bandit showed me. There is an air vent under the bed that connects with the system running all through Tok-Maurron. It was tunneled by dwarf craftsmen; I barely fit through some portions, but you can actually walk upright in places. It allowed me secret access to the whole city."

Glaura's laugh could be heard. "Amazing, Duli. And you couldn't pay me just one visit in all that time?"

Duli shrugged, though Glaura couldn't see the motion. "I had to be as secret as possible. Only a handful of crafters knew what I was doing."

"You said you were going to show me all of it." Duli heard the bed sag as Glaura sat on it. "What is the rest of it?"

Duli sighed. It was a moment of truth that would show Glaura that the widows were serious about defending their home. "Most of my work goes back to the male crafters and sold to whomever. Some, but not all, of the rest is used for my own bartering needs. Whatever is left over goes towards my passion."

"What passion?"

"The widows."

Glaura gave a chuckle. "You don't actually think you'll ever be fighting Tariykans? None of you are even prepared…"

Her words were interrupted as Duli stepped out from behind the stretched hide. The miracle-empowered wall sconce lit the smooth, polished, dark leather breastplate Duli wore. There was a slight creak from the shaped, hardened leather pieces strapped around the thighs. Her arms had bracers that were decorated with dwarven curses towards human lineage. Her thick belt held the two weapons that felt comfortable in Duli's hands. On one side was the bronze hatchet she used for many utility purposes. The expensive steel dagger hung from her other hip. The armor was more to deflect blows from any clumsy Tariykan that might normally nick her. Hopefully, she would someday find a human whose skill would allow him to finish her with a skilled blow.

Glaura just stared at the armor for the longest of breaths, unable to find the words to make any comment.

*   *   *   *   *

Guffan Stonebrow should have been enjoying one of his favorite pastimes. The aging general sipped cold ale at Deepmug's. His only worry would normally be keeping the ale and greasy meat pieces from finding their way into his nearly-to-the-floor beard. Instead, his pleasure was soured by the mood of his drinking companion. Boreval Stonebrow was randomly alternating between drinking and waging a verbal tirade against the stubborn widows. His words shifted between too-quiet curses and roaring tirades. The latter would continue until Guffan would remind him that Katy, one such woman, worked with her family just behind the bar.

Guffan's irritation finally led to an outburst of his own. "Why don't you give them what they ask? Send them out so they can get themselves killed and I can get back to drinking."

Boreval sputtered his drink onto the table. As some rogue drops dangled off his well-combed beard, he managed a shocked response. "Are you mad? Let them die uselessly against our foes? Lose good axes and Mennurdan crafters...the other women will cause nay end of trouble if I did that."

Guffan shrugged as both returned to their drinking. As the alcohol flowed, it helped spawn some ideas in the general's head. "You know, it's a bad idea, but maybe it's the right idea."

The Clan-Sire squinted, "A bad idea is never the right idea, especially when it gets dwarves killed."

The general shook his head. "Nay, let's think on this for a moment. I'm not saying send them out to get killed. But, perhaps..."

Guffan's mind was busy formulating alternatives. He forced Boreval to wait as he took a long swallow of the Deepmug ale. As ideas entered his thoughts, he scanned around the room to make sure no one paid undue attention to them.

"They aren't going to stop just because you ask them to stop. They got it stuck in their heads. The best way to get them to put down their weapons is to make them *want* to put down their weapons."

Guffan watched Boreval edge closer. The Clan-Sire inquired, "So what is the cure for their madness?"

The general accentuated his plan by tapping a thick finger against the table. "We send them on a mission...a safe one...with some guardians from one of our top companies. The trick is to send them somewhere that has seen some awful fighting. I want them to have a close up look at war."

Boreval leaned back slightly. The Clan-Sire scratched his bald head as he put his mind on the possibilities. He continued where Guffan had left off. "They'll see some freshly wounded warriors. Their weaker stomachs will probably empty at the sight."

Guffan was about to say more when Boreval spoke again. "In order to go to such an area, there will be a risk."

The general nodded. "Of course. Would that be such a bad thing? Many a young warrior has wet his leggings upon first seeing ranks of Tariykan soldiers. We do want to scare the widows, after all. Let them get a close-up view of some blood and guts."

Boreval hunched over his mug, taking another sip. "I like it. Gods damn me, but I like it. Send them out as proud fools, bring them back as crafters mewling for repentance." He frowned and stared into Guffan's eyes. "But if some end up in a fight with the Tariykans?"

The general shrugged. "I'll do my best to protect them. I'll be honest gold with you. Will it really be such a tragedy if it gets these strange notions out of their heads? One or two might be lost if the worst comes to pass, but in return, dozens more will return to their crafting."

CHAPTER 14

After the encounter with Boreval Stonebrow in the Hearthden just days earlier, Duli would not have expected participating in any undertaking for Tok-Maurron. As she marched among the clan, part of her mind realized that this mission likely had some hidden agenda. She buried such worries while focusing on making the best of this opportunity. The widows were receiving a chance to pursue their goal of defending the mountains, leaving Duli with plenty of other concerns as she tried to lead the women in the presence of veteran clan warriors.

The task laid before them by General Guffan Stonebrow involved accompanying a caravan bearing supplies for the Steelfoot clan. The Steelfoot clan was driven out of their home warrens by Tariykan soldiers and mages. The fleeing dwarves barely stayed a step ahead of the humans' advance. Skirmishes occurred daily as a rearguard of warriors slowed the humans while kinfolk fled deeper into the mountain passes. Tariykans had the advantage of numbers and resources. The dwarf clans knew the terrain of their native land better and had the use of molber rams to carry them places horses couldn't go. The dwarves of Tok-Maurron eagerly set aside clan differences to assist their distant cousins. Duli still found it surprising that either Boreval or King Harvagot Stonebrow approved recruiting the widows for assistance. Perhaps it wasn't surprising given the number of Tok-Maurron warriors escorting the caravan. General Guffan Stonebrow was at the head of a large contingent of dwarf warriors. Hundreds of the able-bodied males of Tok-Maurron were involved in the march. Ram riders were out patrolling in every direction. Duli's band made up a small portion of the army's strength. The "Widow Brigade", all forty-eight female soldiers, were walking closest to the carts loaded with supplies. On the carts were a number of older warriors and some suffering from wounds that prevented them from marching with any speed.

Duli juggled the many new responsibilities thrown at her. The widows' practice involved only small areas inside the clan city. Duli, Leli and Fosha were sometimes running laps around the length of the caravan, making sure that the women were in ideal positions surrounding the wagons. They tried to look fierce and proud, since many eyes of the men were upon them.

One new addition to the women's ranks was Herothe Darkhair. The former leathercrafter, and thus a competitor of Duli, had been taken in by Nandorrin's church following her husband's death. While she wasn't yet considered among the ranks of the widows, she qualified by virtue of the fact that all her family was dead. In those many months since her mourning of her husband, she had trained to be an accomplished healer and priestess in the service of Nandorrin. For this trip, the church knew a healer might be needed to accompany the widows to safety…Herothe presented the most logical choice in an organization composed mostly of men.

The widows were once again armed with whatever weapons had been bequeathed by their departed husbands, or whatever makeshift tools that could serve in a pinch. Duli wore her hatchet and dagger, though she also borrowed a bladestaff. Fosha wanted to bring her husband's mace, but it was too large for her to wield effectively. Fosha settled for a pickaxe, (owned by her oldest before his death), designed more for combat than digging. Leli carried her late husband's single-edged battleaxe. Katy carried her boar-spear, even though she also had a crossbow hanging on her back. Shauna rode on one of the wagons, giving her an elevated position in the event her crossbow expertise was needed. All the other widows had a similar mix of weapons.

The caravan drivers they were supposed to be guarding were armed with muskets. The women were still forbidden to use them. Horace Smokebore was among the famed elite of Tok-Maurron's warriors. He rode in the lead cart, frequently traveling alongside Duli. His demeanor suggested that he expected to protect the widows, instead of the other way around. Her green eyes would occasionally catch him glancing over at the organization of the women. Although he wasn't giving his opinion out loud, Duli got the impression that she needed to move mountains in order to win any respect from him.

She decided not to dwell on the fact that the widows were being used more as a labor force. Duli was simply glad for the chance to prove themselves. She had never been so far outside Tok-Maurron since moving there as a newlywed. Her duties as head of the widows took too much of her concentration to be distracted by the charming mountain vistas.

The column of dwarves marched in the late morning of their fifth day when they heard a distant musket shot. Conversations halted amidst the sudden quiet that descended. Most of the caravan pulled to a stop. Anxious ears listened for any further noises. The din of hundreds of dwarves had been reduced to whispers and creaking leather harnesses. A few graybeards remarked that the shot could have come from a few miles away, echoing down the course of the valley. Veterans began urging the caravan to resume their march. They were moving again by the time another shot echoed in the distance.

Duli felt her heart beating faster at the anxiety building in her bones. Fosha and Leli ran to her to discuss the implications. The three women held a brief council before running around to make a few changes in the widows' positions. The men on the carts kept a cool head. All of those warriors had seen combat before. Duli caught a glance from Horace which suggested the dwarf was amused at the widows' nervousness.

For the next hour, more scattered shots echoed from somewhere far ahead. The caravan continued forward. Duli could not observe the whole Tok-Maurron column, so couldn't see what was going on at the front. She did note that the movements of ram riders on the flanks increased.

Herothe Darkhair appeared beside Duli. "Heard anything?"

Duli glanced at the Nandorrin priest. She noted the former fellow leathercrafter was walking with staff in one hand and a potion held in another. "Nay word yet. I'm thinking of sending a runner up front to see."

Herothe smirked, "I'm sure General Guffan isn't used to female runners coming up during combat and asking him what is going on."

Duli snickered at that thought. "Aye, I'm sure I'll piss in his ale if I do that."

"I'm going to stay closer to the middle of the carts," the priest offered, "Keep this handy on you just in case."

The dark-haired widow slipped a healing draught into Duli's hands. The beardless woman looked at it. The draughts were empowered by the priests' miracles. They had amazing abilities to heal wounds in a short time. Duli didn't want to save herself, but the potion might allow her to help someone else. She pocketed it.

After a few hundred paces listening to distant shots, Duli decided to approach one of the veterans. She strode over to Horace Smokebore's cart. The warrior was an amusing sight if you didn't count him as an enemy. The right side of his beard was darker and charred thinner than his left side. Horace had come upon that appearance by consistently overloading the flash pan of his musket.

"What're you thinking?" Duli asked him, as she craned her neck to look up to his seat. "Could some of those shots be from us?"

Horace frowned as he guided the reins of the rams. "Too far."

Duli began to think he would say no more, but he continued. "We'll be closing in on that soon enough. When you start hearing people screaming from their wounds, then you know we've joined the fight."

She nodded to him. They were silent a few more moments as she kept pace with the cart. Duli muttered some words that she thought he wouldn't hear. "I didn't think Guffan would actually take us into a fight."

There was no masking the eagerness in her voice as she spoke. Duli was looking forward to meeting the Tariykans face-to-face. Maybe this night she would sleep in Dorvanon with her husband.

Somehow, Horace overheard her comment. She was aware of him scrutinizing her. His face remained impassive, but his eyes were weighing her in an unfavorable manner. Duli tried to straighten her back and walk proudly, but Horace scoffed.

"He wouldn't intentionally march this caravan into a fight. The Steelfoot clan must be just ahead, trying to move their families and belongings to safety. I assume the Tariykans have a few small parties out to harass their every move. Those shots are too scattered to be a big fight. It's just a few skirmishers trading shots with their bowmen."

Horace's words sounded right to her ears. Duli didn't find it easy settling for the notion that any combat would likely be kept at a distance from the widows.

Less than an hour later, she wasn't so sure that a fight would miss them. Musket shots were going off closer and with more frequency. The flanking ram riders always seemed to be racing to their destinations. There were odors of smoke and sulfur drifting in the wind. The widows kept eager eyes scanning the uneven ground. There were plenty of trees at this altitude to block visibility. Their anxiety was fueled by the reactions of the veterans in the carts. Dwarves who had fought for years were priming muskets, loosening blades in sheaths, setting axes within easy reach and tightening the gaps between carts.

Fosha and Leli approached Duli. After a brief conversation, Duli sent them to different parts of the caravan. Her last orders were for Leli and Fosha to each gather a personal guard of four widows to follow them everywhere. In this way, each leader would have an escort to keep them safe and react to any threats. Duli hid the fact that she was disregarding her own advice. The last thing Duli wanted was to be saved from a Tariykan arrow. Although she hoped to finally deliver some blood to her husband's murderers, she wished even more to rejoin her love. Against Duli's wishes, one of her friends moved up to join her anyway. As if fearing for her leader's life, Shauna Horgar hopped on the back of Horace's cart with her crossbow in hand.

A ram rider galloped back to Horace. He paid no attention to Duli at all as he traded words with the veteran. "We came across some wounded from the Steelfoot! All are refusing any help walking. We did invite them to come back here and take a rest on the carts. You will come across them soon."

Before the rider could depart, Horace shouted out to him. "Has Tok-Maurron begun to bloody our axes on the foe?"

"As we speak!" the rider exclaimed with a swell of pride.

The rider sped back towards the front, even as word of the fight spread throughout the caravan.

*   *   *   *   *

Duli and the other widows watched with a sober fascination as the wounded dwarves limped into view. The members of the Steelfoot clan looked no different from her own, if one didn't spend much time contemplating their boots. Every boot had smooth steel lining the edges of the sole. Small metal spikes usually adorned the toe end or the heel. Anyone kicked by these dwarves would have a mark to advertise who had bested them.

The warriors of Tok-Maurron either ignored the newcomers or offered brief, respectful nods. Few words were exchanged. The raggedness of the new dwarves' clothes and the abundance of bloody wounds were testament to the difficult road these refugees traveled. The humans hounded them every step from their ancestral home. In return, the dwarves inflicted as much retribution as they could muster while seeing to the safety of their kin. Duli could understand why the dwarves appeared so glum. A dwarf meeting those outside of his kin would prefer to boast on the monsters he had slain. The Steelfoot marched among those who knew they had been fighting a retreating battle. The land of their elders may have been lost to the humans, but no dwarf would beg for help retaking his own home. The wounded had good reason to say little. Unable to defeat the legions of Tariykans, they settled instead for getting a temporary reprieve resting on the supply carts.

As the dwarves staggered past, the widows noted the dripping red bandages and odor that could not be described. The sight of a red, empty eye socket on one caused Katy Dornan to cover her mouth and turn away. Another widow let loose a nearly inaudible gasp at one who carried his weapon with a hand missing two fingers…freshly cut. Duli was likewise open-mouthed, until she realized Horace watched the widows with an amused twinkle in his eyes. Duli resumed the stoic expression characteristic of her race.

The widows merely watched with curious stares at the strangers who limped and bled. Herothe Darkhair was the first female who moved to intercept one staggering on weary legs. She approached him to heal some of his injuries. Instead, he pulled up short as he realized the sex of the person before him.

"Hands off me! I don't need a woman for a crutch." His words softened slightly as he realized the nature of her Nandorrin vestments. "I do not mean to speak so rough to a soul of the fire god. My wounds are small enough. I don't need your help in tending them."

Another member of the Steelfoot clan glanced around the caravan. His eyes widened as he spoke to the wounded dwarf, "Yank my beard if I'm mistaken, they're all women! Look around, you old fool."

Duli and the rest of the widows received their share of stares as the wounded examined them with disbelief.

"Tok-Maurron must be worse off than a drunk with a hole in his tankard," joked one Steelfoot. "If they have women fighting with them."

Horace, ruffled by this statement, promptly responded. "You got it all wrong. These lasses kept getting underfoot back home. We decided to send them all to you to breed and rebuild!"

Duli's bare cheeks immediately reddened. She whirled on Horace, even though she had to look up due to his perch on the cart. "A thankful one you are, Horace! We're here to make sure the Tariykans don't chop your beard and eat your ram! You don't need to thank us."

One of the Steelfoot dwarves swiveled a shocked look from Duli to Horace. "That one is beardless! You would entrust a beardless female to protect you? Has Tok-Maurron lost all sensible customs?"

Horace glared at the offending dwarf, "It wasn't my idea to let her follow us."

Duli started to object, but Horace waved a pointed finger at her and went on without pause. "The only protection you would offer me is the two seconds it would take for a human to step over your corpse."

The closest dwarves nearly jumped when an angry growl answered Horace's words. Even for those from Tok-Maurron, it was easy to miss Bandit's presence until the wolf moved to defend Duli. The Steelfoot dwarves readied their weapons for an attack. Duli and the widows were quick to calm them long enough for a proper introduction. The wounded watched in amazement as Bandit obediently retreated to Duli's side. There were considerable discussions and insults traded between clans, as well as males and females.

Duli thought the situation involving Bandit had calmed down...a thought that was interrupted by the sound of a musket blast.

CHAPTER 15

Duli's eyes instantly sought her lone, remaining family. Bandit was still standing there, unhurt. She followed the wolf's eyes to the origin of the musket blast, spotting the dwarf with the smoking gun. He and everyone near him were raising shouts and pointing fingers to the side.

"Humans!"

Everyone began noticing a few Tariykan scouts bolt from their hiding spots. They were well out of range of most weapons, but several more muskets emptied in their direction. Even Shauna fired a shot with her crossbow, though the bolt fell shy of the mark.

For many of the widows, it was their first glance at a human. They gawked at how fast the long-limbed, almost gangly-looking, creatures could run.

The caravan watched as ram riders chased down the fleeing enemy. Some of the Tariykans turned to fire bows, one threw a dagger. The ram riders dropped most of them with musket shot. The noisy weapons blew holes through the ineffective leather armor the Tariykan scouts wore. The smoke and trees obscured some of the ending, but Duli saw dwarves dismounting with axes in hand to finish the rest.

It was minutes later when Duli and the others realized that it wasn't the ending. Dwarves started to take notice as ram riders began mounting up in a hurry. The flanking riders dug their heels into their rams in their haste to get back to the caravan. Apparently, there was more beyond the trees than some dead scouts. Warnings were shouted. A messenger turned towards the head of the dwarven column, riding his mount so hard that he cared nothing for the belongings bouncing out of his saddlebags. He rode to tell General Guffan Stonebrow of the news.

A major Tariykan force was coming out of the woodlands to the side of Tok-Maurron's long line.

Caravan drivers, wounded Steelfoot clansmen, and widows watched in disbelief as formations of human soldiers appeared in the breaks between trees. Many of the marching footmen had pennants raised from poles on their backs, proclaiming their direct lord or master. The pennants complimented the multi-hued colors of the armor. Blocks of yellows, reds, blues, whites, and more marked the different sections of Tariykan fealty. The armor was built to flare out at the shoulders and hips. The effect made the humans seem much larger than the dwarves. Bright, silk ties wrapped around in patterns that suggested a complicated dance of fabric. The banners and tabards made such a tapestry of color that it was hard to determine the material of the armor underneath. The front lines were dominated by men with polearms. Behind them came archers and finely dressed swordsmen. At a glance, the force coming out of the woods could easily be a match for the dwarven numbers.

Duli stood similarly entranced as some of her widows, leaving her slow to react. It was after she took notice of other dwarves forming hasty lines that her duties came into focus. The dwarven warriors were forming defensive positions between the caravan and the approaching humans. A sizeable gap in the defense existed directly in front of the widows.

The beardless dwarf went into action. She began pulling the widows closest to her into a line of their own. She shouted for Leli and Fosha to get the "brigade" formed up and move them into the gap. Duli missed the worrisome expression passing over Horace's face as he watched the women move toward danger. The widows were all unaware of the silent looks thrown between the male drivers. The veteran males were tempted to abandon their wagons and leap ahead of the women in order to protect them. Duli only took notice of one particular wagon rider that was preparing to join the line.

"Shauna, get back on that cart!"

The fair-haired dwarf met Duli's gaze with surprise. "Don't you need me on the line?"

Duli had half-turned to the others, but she spun back around to answer her friend. With annoyance, the beardless dwarf flipped her solitary braid back over her shoulder. "You're too good a shot with that crossbow. Some will likely get past us. I want you ready to bring them down."

After a good deal of shouting and pushing, Duli's officers had formed the widows into a line and were marching them forward. Veteran warriors on either side of them were surprised when the bodies that were helping to fill their ranks belonged to the "weaker" sex. Kinsmen were more concerned with protecting the women than they were with the wagons of supplies. The Widow Brigade was a small pocket of barely-armed females tucked between ranks of musket-carrying soldiers.

Duli was the most vulnerable of all…by her own choice. She ran back and forth in front of the widows, rallying them to stand tall and make her proud. Much as Duli wanted to spill Tariykan blood, it would not have been a disappointment to her to be one of the first to fall under human bows or magic. Thus, Duli directed the movements of her company from several paces out in front, waving her arms with great flourishes, with the wolf following her every stride.

Every widow along the line, every woman who now faced the reality of their decision to join Duli's and Fosha's company, found some courage in their leader's words.

"Stand proud in the face of dishonorable Tariyka! Mark well the courage in the men to either side of you. They have faced this enemy before and are alive and willing to trade fists again! Remember the other women and children of Tok-Maurron, for you are the shield which keeps the fight from their halls!"

Duli continued to run at the fore of the widows' ranks, with loyal Bandit matching every step. She interceded between every forlorn glance cast by a woman towards the swelling ranks of human warriors. The eyes of the widows were drawn to her as she passed.

"What are you afraid of…death?" she asked.

Some widows actually nodded at this, unaware they were thinking out loud.

"Why fear death?" Duli demanded an answer, yet interrupted before it could be given. "Your husbands, lovers and children await you at the gates of Dorvanon! Your death will bring you to that road. How can the humans take anything from you by killing your body? Some of you may make the journey to Dorvanon this day! Some of you will be reunited with those you love! Make your passing a badge of honor that will make your warrior-husbands proud!"

The brigade stamped their feet on the ground as they cheered their leader. Women brandished weapons in the air and hurled insults at the humans. The males were impressed at the fire burning in the hearts of the widows.

None could hear the silent prayer that Duli added for her own sake as she turned to raise her pole-arm to taunt the Tariykans.

"Gods, if you have any mercy left in your hearts, let me walk the path to Dorvanon this day. I need to be beside my love."

*   *   *   *   *   *

When the dwarves finished forming a line, the call went up to fire a volley at the distant Tariykans. Commanders among the dwarven companies ordered their troops to prime their muskets. Most dwarves had already completed that stage when they first caught sight of the Tariykan scouts. The next shouts called on the dwarves to raise their muzzles at the enemy.

The Tariykans were putting up a slow march towards the caravan. Duli noted the force split itself between melee and missile sections. Armsmen took up the lead, moving behind a wall of shields and bristling pikes. In the back, bowmen were being called to ready their weapons. Duli looked over those far lines for any signs of Tariykan magic-users, but couldn't see enough individual details at that distance.

The air was split as the first volley of muskets opened fire. It was quickly followed by more thunderous rumblings as other companies followed suit. Duli tried to recall Geordan's few stories of battle. He had mentioned that muskets tended to have no greater range than bows. If a sizeable clash of forces were joined, both sides would fire a massive assault of missiles at each other. The individual musket or bow would likely miss its target, but a mass of muskets firing at a mass of bowmen would result in casualties. Geordan had given her the impression that the dwarves would fare better in such a fight. The Tariykan arrows fired faster, only to be deflected by dwarven armor. Muskets, on the other hand, could go right through Tariykan armor. Even as she remembered his words, she recalled Geordan likely never saw a fight this big. Most of her husband's battles involved small parties of Tariykans.

Clouds of dirt and grass clumps flew up in front of the humans as several shots fell short. Duli saw a few armsmen scream or drop out of their line. The few gaps that were left behind were quickly sealed shut by the sheer numbers of men.

A cloud of arrows shot into the sky from the humans. Every widow on the line followed it with their eyes. They were feeling helpless at this stage of the battle. They had few enough crossbows to add to the dwarven fire, but they were still targets in the eyes of the enemy. A few widows took a cautious step or two back as the arrows soared past the height of their arc. Duli shouted for them to hold their ground. As the shafts descended, it became clear that most if not all didn't have the required range. The ground in front of the widows became dotted with feathered sticks. When the cloud was no more, Herothe could be heard asking the females if any had been wounded. None were.

Duli glanced back towards Shauna. The fair-haired dwarf stood with a grim look and a loaded crossbow. She could read her friend's mind, and knew that Shauna was also hoping for the enemy to get a lot closer so the widows could inflict some damage.

The brigade leader looked to the rest of her line and called out to a few individual dwarves. "Herothe, move back from the line so you don't get hit by their next volley! Leli! Some of your warriors stepped back; get them even with the rest of us! Katy, get that spear tip up higher. They are taller than you."

A few ram riders came into view beside the caravan. Duli was surprised to see General Guffan looking over their battlefield. The general was glancing over the dwarven line, pausing as his eyes noticed the position of the widows.

*   *   *   *   *   *

Guffan watched with a worried glance as the Tariykans advanced towards the line of inept females. The general hadn't planned on endangering the widows in such a large conflict. He had hoped to scare them, not leave them in a position where they were as good as a hole in his defense. His thoughts were interrupted as one of the wagon drivers, veteran Horace Smokebore, ran over to him.

"General Guffan, are you seeing how soft your line is?" Horace pointed at the widows as he spoke, making clear his meaning.

Guffan scowled at him, "I see and share your concerns."

"You might want to get them off the field and find someone better to take their place."

The veteran was about to storm off, but the general barked at him to wait. "We are going to move them. Here is what I need you to do…"

*   *   *   *   *   *

Duli had been wondering where the Tariykan spellcasters were, and suddenly she got her answer. Where once there had been some gaps between the archer companies, a few large siege engines appeared as magic conjured them into place. They appeared in an instant, courtesy of those unseen masters of the dark arts.

"Catapults!" swore a veteran nearby.

Duli had heard of the machines from Geordan's stories, but had never seen one. She was aware that humans used them to launch large boulders at city walls. It vexed Duli that they would bring some to the mountains. There were no walls hiding the dwarves here, and their cities were built underground.

Duli's thoughts were interrupted as another round of arrows arced in from the humans. As before, most fell short, but now the Tariykans had a better idea of the range.

Shafts rained closer to the widows' line. One glanced off a metal breastplate on one of the women. Another arrow drew a cry of pain down the line. Herothe ran down to the victim, only to find a shallow flesh wound. Duli was checking the health of those closest to her, shouting above the ensuing round of musket blasts.

She turned to see a few more Tariykans drop to the ground. Duli was about to shout encouragement to her fellows, but was interrupted as the catapults entered the action. She saw the arms of the engines snap forward. Instead of a single large boulder, the catapults let loose nets full of smaller rocks. Warnings were yelled up and down the line as the bearded folk watched the incoming missiles. Duli realized that the rocks were coming down with better accuracy than their arrows. Each piece of stone was large enough to do serious damage to whomever they hit, and the loads were going to cover lots of ground in the way they fanned out in the air.

"Shield yourselves!"

Most widows didn't have shields. Duli raised one arm in front of her head for protection. A number of women winced or closed their eyes. A few raised weapons high on the chance that they might deflect a rock. There was a long moment of silence as everyone waited for the impacts. Duli heard the rapid thumping of boulders raining down. Female cries erupted to either side of her. She gritted her teeth, hoping any rock hitting her would finish her quickly. A bit of mud splashed her face from one rock that bounced past. Even as the noise of crashing rocks abated, it was a couple breaths before she dared lower her arm and look around.

This time there were a few widows on the ground. Herothe was putting the healing prayers of Nandorrin to use on one of the downed women, while others were calling for aid. Duli went looking for someone who could use her healing draught. One such widow was lying on her back, shouting for help while waving her weapon in the air so that someone might spot her easier. As soon as Duli saw the boar-spear, she recognized its injured owner.

"Don't move Katy, I can help you."

Katy Dornan's shoulder had been laid open to the muscle underneath. Duli took great care in lifting her head for a drink.

"Swallow this. Herothe left some healing miracle in here for you."

Through the tear in Katy's leather sleeve, Duli could see the miraculous draught working. Blood stopped leaking, the skin began to close over the area and color returned to Katy's face.

When the drink was finished, another widow dragged Katy closer to the carts in order to let her recover. Duli patrolled her line. Only two widows had been seriously wounded, though a couple others had smaller scrapes. She wondered how many of the widows were gritting their teeth through injuries greater than they would admit. It was dwarven nature to cover up one's pain.

She shouted encouragement to them as Horace Smokebore ran to her. "Duli, call your women back to the wagons."

She wheeled on him as if she was ready to cut him down with her bladestaff. "What? We'll do nay such thing! We're here to fight!"

Horace pointed at the closest wagon, where Shauna sat and watched the exchange. "You're here to protect those supplies so they reach the Steelfoot clan! We are moving the wagons away from those catapults. The widows are to come with us."

"So you say?" Duli scowled at him.

"So General Guffan Stonebrow says," Horace argued back, emphasizing every syllable. Duli glanced at the general, but his attention was on the battle. The veteran continued, "He respects the stand you are making, but your priority is still the safety of the wagons. They aren't safe here. We're moving towards a riverbed over that direction. The widows are to keep the wagons protected."

"But the line? It would leave a gap…"

The veteran was already shaking his head and pointing behind her, "That group is coming up to take your spot. Move off the line and give them room to form up."

She noted that most of the newcomers were formerly ram riders that had dismounted to fight alongside the army. Duli was ready to put up a stubborn argument with him, but she couldn't deny that his words were ringing true. The elders of Tok-Maurron had allowed the widows to take part in this journey. If she refused to listen to a general during a battle, the widows would likely never get another chance. She nodded her agreement.

Horace stormed back to his wagon and took up the reins. Duli looked with a bit of regret at the lines of battle. She had succeeded in coming face-to-face with the hated humans, without a telling blow traded by her or unto her. The scene before her scared her more than she thought it would, yet her concern was that she might survive again, only to face more lonely nights.

"Leli! Fosha!" The two officers ran to her side. "The wagons are being moved to safety. Our orders are to safeguard them as before and make sure they stay safe. Don't argue; I felt the same way as what I see on your faces. Pull the widows back to their earlier wagon assignments and we'll march out of here."

The order was passed to the rest. They grudgingly turned away from the faces of their husbands' murderers. Most were upset that they weren't allowed to charge the humans, though there were those who secretly harbored relief that they would no longer have to stand as targets for those catapults. Some had become more scared than they would ever admit.

They took up their spots on and around the wagons as the caravan turned away from the battle. Behind them, they heard another round of rocks thudding into the dwarves that had taken their positions. Widows looked back with mixed feelings. They moved with heavy feet as the wagons crested a ridge and left behind the view of the battle. The screams of the wounded and the sounds of musket volleys still echoed as they marched away.

CHAPTER 16

Once the Tok-Maurron caravan was hidden in a switchback maze of a dried river basin, the widows took vigilant positions. They were determined to serve as guards in a respectable manner, even though they knew their post was an empty one. The true fighting could be heard in the distance.

Some openly showed pride in their stance that day. They cheered the honor of facing Tariykan humans in battle, despite being pulled away before the fight had been settled. Others could not meet the eyes of their fellows, dwelling on their fears now that they had a peek at war. A few hid behind jests aimed at their unseen foe. Widows insulted the fine, yet useless, battle fashions of the Tariykans. A few secretly sought out Herothe now that the nervous energy had departed them, thus making them aware of bruises that had been dimmed by the blood rush of battle. The Nandorrin priestess treated their wounds. Many passed the afternoon in grim, stony silence. Their secret contemplations remained locked behind guarded expressions.

None of the widows, save Shauna, paid much attention to the absence of their leader. Fosha and Leli were making rounds, checking on everyone. Duli was nowhere to be seen. Shauna asked Leli about her absence; Leli responded that Duli was keeping a watchful eye on the entrance to the river basin. Shauna was tempted to go look for her friend. In the end, she didn't want anyone to think she was leaving her post. So she stayed and waited.

Duli paced circles around parts of the dry ravine. On the outside, she examined how defensible the river basin could be if they had to repel an attack. Her eyes glanced over the smooth boulders on the sides of the basin. Deep inside, she was hungry to get another close-up look at the humans. Such a confrontation would likely end in a death, but kill-or-be-killed, Duli would have accepted either option.

Bandit padded along as a silent shadow. Sometimes he crossed her path, other times he went sniffing animal scents. He always kept his eyes on her. As far as Duli could guess, the wolf thought they were out hunting game. More than once he seemed to indicate some promising scent to track, but Duli wasn't interested in the same prey.

Her hands absently twirled her new bladestaff as she walked. She hadn't had much chance to practice with it before they left. Duli tried to imagine how best to use it against a taller foe. Her heart desired to see the cutting edge dripping in human blood.

Despite her self-distraction, she didn't miss the sight of some dwarves on rams riding down a parallel section of the twisted river basin. She didn't see their faces, just the dust their rams kicked up. The dwarf was certain that they had missed seeing her. Duli's curiosity tugged at her, persuading her to make contact and find news of the battle. The winds no longer carried sounds of gunfire as they had before. Bandit noted her change in attitude and skulked along behind her.

Words barked out from the other side of the rise. "Ho! General!"

It took only a moment for Duli to place the voice. It belonged to the veteran, Horace Smokebore. Duli heard the ram-riders pulling their mounts to a halt. Although her feet carried her towards her husband's clansmen, the rise between dry river channels still blocked visual contact.

"Smokebore, how fares the caravan?" Boomed a voice that could be none other than General Guffan. "Are the goods safe?"

"Not a scratch on any of the wagons. The Steelfoot clan will find their supplies undamaged. Did we beat them bloody humans back?"

"Oh aye! They left the field littered with a good number of dead men, all dressed well for their funeral."

The general lowered his voice on the next question, though Duli still made out the words. "How about the…escorts?" She noted the hesitation as he chose his words. "Are they well?"

Horace snorted, "The women? A few got banged up a bit, but none serious. I imagine they got quite a scare."

Duli paused just before her head would have become visible to the males. Something in their voices made her decide to linger out of sight a bit longer. She leaned closer, but kept her profile under the lip of the ravine. Bandit almost revealed her. The wolf was about to pass her up until she put a hand out in his path. The wolf understood and crouched lower to the ground, waiting.

She heard a response from the general that she would have never expected. Guffan Stonebrow was chuckling over the news. "Indeed, I imagine it was a good scare. One they sorely needed."

Horace seemed surprised as well. "Guffan? Why is that amusing?"

"Tell me, are they pissing their skirts about now?"

"I'd say a number of them got a scare, but others looked like they wanted to return to battle."

"Bah! I'm sure when they reach the safety of the clan warrens they'll have learned their lesson. This went even better than planned." General Guffan was still chuckling.

It was all Duli could do to restrain herself from sticking her head up to watch his face. She continued to duck low against the ravine edge while turning an ear towards the men.

"Planned?" Horace stumbled over words. "By Daerkfyre's beard! You didn't actually intend to throw those women at the enemy did you?"

"Of course not! We intended to give them a scare, not put them in harm's way." Guffan's voice went from arguing his defense back to amusement. "This was as much as I'd hoped. They got their faces smarted, but not hurt. Hopefully it will be enough to teach them a good lesson! I can't wait until we get back to Tok-Maurron and Duli's wenches go back to their crafts."

Duli's knuckles went white on her bladestaff even as her eyes glared in the direction of the voices. Bandit picked up on her anger and began to sniff the air. The wolf was incapable of understanding the focus of her rage.

Duli was only half-listening to Horace speak as she fumed. "You play a dangerous game, Guffan."

"General Guffan Stonebrow!" The ranking dwarf reiterated. "And nay soul will be leaking that news to the Hearthden gossipers, will he?"

Even from her spot, Duli heard Horace spit on the ground. "Of course not. General, even if you have scared a few, what of the rest? They'll be looking forward to the next fight. Quite a few are proud of themselves for standing up to their kin's murderers."

Guffan gave a loud huff. "Then they better appreciate it, because that was their last chance. The only reason they came along is so that they would learn a hard lesson about war. It's a man's game, and they aren't welcome. Boreval allowed me to take them for just that one purpose. Obviously, they were at too much risk today, so for their future good I'm sure the king can pass an edict barring them from any further forays. Once the scared ones run back to their Hearthden stalls and the rest find out they aren't going anywhere, I'll be drinking at Deepmug's to the tune of Widow Brigade falling to pieces."

"Hopefully you're right," Horace shrugged. "It was a cruel thing to do, but maybe it's just what was needed. As far as anyone is concerned, I never knew anything about your plans."

Duli could barely restrain herself from trying to kill Guffan at that moment. She stared at the soil and fumed. Bandit crawled into her field of vision, likely hoping for a clue as to what she intended. The female dwarf simply averted her eyes.

She could hear Horace and Guffan going separate ways now that their talk was concluded. As much as Duli wanted to stare the general in the face and make him realize she had overheard him, another part of her didn't feel like forcing a confrontation. As Duli absently scratched at her neck, she heard Horace call over to the general once more.

"You know, Duli isn't likely to stop stirring up trouble."

Duli listened as the rams pulled to a stop. Guffan shouted back. "As far as I'm concerned, she is too incompetent to do the simplest things. The next time she feels like putting a noose around her neck, I hope she calls me over to tie the knot right."

Even as he said it Duli realized she was scratching the scar around her neck. Her hand snapped away as if it was touching fire. She began to mutter some incoherent obscenities as the men left the area. By the time she steeled herself to say something, they were out of sight. Bandit pranced around her nervously as Duli started cursing and waving the bladestaff around. The shame of the sorrows was upon her cheeks again as she rambled her low opinions of males to the wind. Duli fretted and jabbed her staff into the ground for hundreds of breaths as she vented her anger. Bandit backed off to a respectable distance, tilting his head in confusion.

Finally, Duli came to a dead silent stop. She stared at the ground, appearing calmed except for the flaring of her nostrils with every sharp intake of breath. Bandit took a hesitant step forward.

A moment later Bandit skittered several feet away, for Duli exploded into motion. Screaming a most unholy wail, Duli seized her bladestaff in both hands and raised it high. Having finally decided on a temporary target for her rage, she brought the staff down upon one knee, cracking it in two.

*   *   *   *   *   *

Duli sat on the edge of her large bed six days later, staring at the carelessly upended contents of her packs. The Steelfoot clan had been supplied and decided to merge with the

118

inhabitants of Tok-Maurron. Even now, the underground city bustled with excitement at the swell of numbers. Halls, which had become emptier with each clash with the Tariykans, were seeing an infusion of fresh families and crafters. In the halls outside her warren, voices carried on cheerful conversations despite the fact that those new families had been rooted out of their old homes. Inside Duli's room, the atmosphere was quite different. She wondered if the new numbers meant more work for her or the loss of work agreements with her current business partners. In a greater sense, it really didn't matter to her at that moment. She still brooded over Guffan's revelations.

She didn't care to see friends, nor did she care to properly put her gear away. She just didn't care to do much at all of anything. Duli sat there brooding, with her only movement an involuntary petting of Bandit after the wolf had snuck his head under one dangling hand.

Bandit's head came up when Duli finally spoke. He could not understand the words, but they were not for his ears anyway.

"Geordan, I'm so sorry. If you look upon my life since you left you would likely be disappointed in me. I simply can't hold to anything else if I can't hold you."

Duli got up. She disregarded the pile of junk spread on the floor. Duli took only a bag of coins as she headed for the door. Bandit jumped up to follow. In response, she held a staying hand as she grabbed the door handle.

She looked back at him with the only goodbye she could muster. "I'm sorry I killed your mother, but I know you can take care of yourself now."

Her green eyes had to turn away from him before the sorrows took her again. As she went out the door, she set all the latches into place. She figured it would be redundant. Somehow he had escaped the room before even with them in place.

Duli set forth with a determined stride before her feelings could have the chance to change her heart. Before she could reach Lower City, she bumped into Fosha.

"Oh, Duli! I'm glad I found you. You should hear the news down in the Hearthden! We're heroes!"

She couldn't hide the surprise on her face as she glanced at the century-old elder. "What?"

Fosha was shaking with excitement. "The brigade has been telling their stories and the news spread like a powderkeg going off. All of the sudden the number of tongues that were lashing us are now praising us. They didn't think we were serious before, but now they've been hearing how we stood against the humans in battle. We have a mob of widows wanting to join. You should see the enthusiasm that has swept through those women. I've even had to turn away some married ones who were demanding to carry weapons alongside us."

The elder misread the shock on Duli's face. Duli hadn't told any of the others about Guffan's and Boreval's plans to scare them and then bar them from any future assignments. She didn't feel right to tell them and break their hearts. Duli wanted nothing more to do with any of the misfortune in which she was mired.

With a dry throat, she asked, "How many?"

Fosha smiled and put her hand on Duli's shoulder. "I think at the very least we've just doubled in size. You have to come down there right away. Several of the women want to apologize to you and find out when we can start training them."

Duli was certain that her answer was the slowest she'd ever given to a question, but she managed to reply, "I'll be down shortly. Go down there and keep them occupied."

The elder didn't leave right away as Duli had hoped. Fosha leaned towards her. Although the beard helped hide her emotions, Duli could see the hint of the sorrows in the old matron's eyes. Fosha whispered, "You don't know how long I've waited for such a day, Duli. My whole life I watched the old males treat us like cattle. What we have become today is because of your guidance. We have something we've never had before. We earned some respect."

Fosha gave Duli a fierce hug. Never had Duli seen the elder so emotional. The older woman turned back towards the Hearthden. As soon as Fosha had disappeared, Duli sagged against a wall. She was shaking her head at the insanity she found surrounding her. Fosha couldn't see that they had been played as fools. It didn't matter if every widow in Tok-Maurron flocked to their cause, because the patriarchs held all the power. Duli took a moment to weigh her options.

In the end, she found herself feeling the same way as before. She continued down towards Lower City, though she took a route that would avoid the Hearthden. Duli had not had a drink since waking up to a failed suicide attempt a few years ago. For many months she had known that if she ever drank again, she might act the same way. The leather crafter didn't want to take a chance at screwing up her suicide attempt with a head heavy with ale. On the other hand, her life was about as worthless as it could go and she really wanted that drink. She planned to get drunk enough that she would never live to suffer the hangover. With a mind aimed at drinking herself farewell, she carried a purse full of ale money to Deepmug's.

CHAPTER 17

Duli dragged her feet within earshot of Deepmug's and paused. She could tell by the clamor of voices that the tavern and outer seating areas were busy with celebrating dwarves. The great cavern that housed this section of Lower City echoed with the tales of returning veterans and toasts to the new Steelfoot residents. Duli cursed silently. Of course the tavern would be overflowing with customers! Warriors would be drinking on behalf of friends lost during the battle. Some veterans would be drinking to their continued health. Other dwarves would likely be quick to show the new Steeelfoot clan members where the best drinks and food in all Tok-Maurron could be found. The thought of trying to drink herself into a stupor witnessed by all those males made her knees weak. She immediately cursed her cowardice. All she wanted to do was drink enough ale that she would either die from the alcohol or from whatever method of suicide she managed to find under the haze of its effects. Instead she stood frozen, scared to appear before so many scrutinizing eyes.

"To the hells with them," she declared. "I'm going to be with my husband tonight if I can help it, and they can stand and watch the results of the insults they have piled on my name."

With determined stride, her legs climbed the final few steps to the open square outside Deepmug's.

Deepmug's tavern was carved into a rock face on one side of a courtyard, but the overflowing customers who shared seats and tables in that open cavern made the courtyard a part of Deepmug's. The establishment even had a large serving window carved out of a rock face where folks could order their drinks without wading into the crowded tavern. The open area was lit, and artificially warmed, by several lights created by the holy priests of the city.

Duli navigated over to the serving window. It was crowded, but as soon as folk saw the beardless female face they tended to distance themselves from her. She hopped onto a stool on one end of the serving window. She was served by no less than Loram Deepmug himself, although the elderly brewer looked to be in a foul mood.

"If you've come looking for Katy, that worthless lass isn't here. I've got a mountain of mugs to be washed and food orders to be filled and she's letting me down."

His tone caught her by surprise. "Nay, although I suspect she is with the others down in Hearthden."

Even with the beard, Duli could see Loram's mouth tighten into a hard frown. "Then it's all your fault. Putting ideas into young girl's heads. She probably is off thinking she's some war hero now. Doesn't have time for her duties to the clan anymore."

Duli was in no mood for an argument. Her tone took on a decided edge as she barked back, "Not my problem! I'm here for ale and I expect to see one in my hands soon."

Loram huffed and started to turn away. Before he took a step, he turned an amazed eye back at the beardless widow. "Not your usual goat's milk?"

A twinge of something…perhaps guilt…went through Duli. She clamped down hard on her feelings and reinforced her need to drink until she was dead. "Aye, I'm wanting ale. Give me one with a good kick to it."

As she waited, Duli let her gaze wander around the area. Folks at the window were giving her plenty of space. Some were newly arrived Steelfoot dwarves who saw the non-clan, beardless face and kept away. Others were Tok-Maurron dwarves who knew Duli and likewise wouldn't come within an arm's reach of the troublemaker. It was the Steelfoot clan's reactions that actually bothered Duli more. The women of that clan were not native to Tok-Maurron, yet since the whole clan had joined instead of individuals, they wouldn't have to endure having their beards removed. By all rights, a female Steelfoot had more status than Duli, despite her years of living and crafting in these halls.

Duli's eyes came upon a sight that made her blood boil even more. She noted a table out in the square which was host to three males she despised most. Boreval Stonebrow, Guffan Stonebrow and Horace Smokebore were drinking and laughing together, while a fourth chair went unoccupied at their table. The men hadn't noticed her. Even though she couldn't hear their conversation, she knew they were gloating over their victory. The three men likely didn't know that their little plan had actually boosted the numbers of widows. Then again, what would it matter anyways? The Stonebrow family controlled the city, and if they wanted to keep the women collared it was well within their power to do just that. It burned Duli's ears to know they were probably talking about her and enjoying her defeat.

That explained how she felt: defeated. Geordan's death hadn't killed her spirit, but it brought it close enough. The arrogant male elders finished the job. Duli felt that her life was just a big waste ever since Sargas had given her the news and took her husband's musket.

Loram slammed a tankard next to Duli. He took her coins without a word and walked away. She wondered if his mood would have improved if he had known he was giving her the key to exit his life.

Duli brought her hands up to the metal tankard. She stared at the foam running over the sides. She hadn't realized how much she really missed drinking until that moment.

She thought to herself, "Maybe this is for the best. Dying to a flood of ale has fewer stings than arrows and thrown stones."

Duli shuddered when she thought of those Tariykan catapults. It might have been less scary if they had launched one large boulder that one could dodge. By using a spray of smaller rocks, it was assured that sooner or later Duli would have been hit hard. With her trend of luck, she probably wouldn't have died right away. Duli's mind conjured an image of her laying maimed on the field while an army of Tariykans started killing the wounded dwarves.

She tested the heft of the tankard. Turning it in her hands, she admired the worn symbols of dwarven heritage engraved on the sides.

Her thoughts were interrupted by a shout from the kitchen. Loram was yelling at a family member who was trying to learn Katy's duties. "Two full twists! Can't you remember it straight yet? Two full twists and then toss the spices into the pot."

Duli watched as the replacement helper grabbed a nozzle attached to a leather bag. He turned the nozzle as directed, which sent the spices falling into a cup in his hands. As soon as he stopped twisting it, the flow stopped. Thus measured, he then emptied the cup into whatever was boiling over the stove.

The widow pulled her attention back to her drink. She raised it close enough to her lips that she could almost taste it.

She relished her last moment before total surrender. With just enough drinks, her rational mind would slowly fade away. All she needed was for her judgment to be impaired enough that her mind would carry out her suicide before she could talk herself out of it. Geordan had always said that a few drinks had the effect of making her bolder and more foolish with her choices.

In that instant before she surrendered to her drink, that reasoning portion of her mind suddenly took root on an idea. Without even realizing it, Duli was slowly lowering the tankard. The taste of ale had gotten no farther than the barest caress of her lips before it was slowly pulled away. The rational portion of Duli's brain, which she had wanted to bury under an onslaught of rich ale only a moment before, flared to life. Duli opened her eyes. The ale was filling her vision, but she was looking past it. She was considering if there were any loose ends to the conniving plan that had formed in her mind. A smile slowly crept across her lips.

"Must be your first ale in years! Have you forgotten how to drink it? I'm sure the men could show you." Loram grumbled at her as he moved past her spot.

Duli's green eyes shifted to glance at Boreval's table. She noted one chair still empty. Swinging back to Loram's weary face, she said, "Just wondering if you are going deaf. I asked for three ales, not one."

Even as Loram's eyebrows rose, she added, "As well as my usual goat's milk."

The patron of brewing stared at her. "You did not."

"Well, you heard me now," Duli replied. "How long do I have to wait for them?"

Boreval, Guffan and Horace were laughing their drinks into their beards as Duli approached. She actually caught part of their disrespectful remarks towards women as she approached their table. As soon as Boreval spotted her, his face went back to a traditional stoic countenance. The other two were warned and quickly followed suit.

If it had been any other time, Duli would have had a few choice words to launch right back. Instead, to their surprise, she proudly walked up to their table with a smile on her face.

"How are you this fine evening? You seem to be in as good spirits as I would suspect given our successful mission." Duli hoped her added cheer didn't sound too forced.

"Aye," Guffan managed to utter after a brief surprise. The general noted the tray of drinks Duli carried but was too stunned by her sudden appearance to ask about it. "The humans got beat back and those Steelfoot boys are going to make fine additions. It was a good journey."

Boreval was better adapted to insincerity. He did a good job of trying to mask the condescending undertone of his voice as he slid into the conversation. "I am sorry to hear about the widows' losses. I'm told a few were hurt badly. I'll see to it that…"

Duli spoke quickly to keep him from finishing his sentence. She was sure that he was going to say something to the effect of holding the widows back from any more journeys. She couldn't let him get the upper hand.

"Oh, don't be worried. It wasn't anything beyond the priests' healing. A few got banged up but they're flaunting their wounds like badges of pride!"

Duli could only hope that was true. Knowing that the three men were hoping to see the brigade fall apart, she figured she would add Fosha's news and see them squirm around under that knowledge next.

She happily added, "The other women of the Hearthden are cheering for us. We've got double the volunteers that we used to have! A lot of others are eager to get trained and defend our home."

If she hadn't known to look for it, she might have missed the concerned looks that flitted between Guffan and Boreval. Duli had to work hard to keep from laughing at the reaction in their eyes.

"That is…" Boreval stammered for the proper word. "Unexpected."

Duli didn't have to fake cheerfulness anymore. Regardless of anything else that happened tonight, she had already soured their fun moment. As the men continued to hide their unease, she set the tray of tankards in front of them.

Horace was the first to react. "What's this about?"

Duli changed to an apologetic tone. One hand idly combed through her sandy hair. "In a way, it's an apology. It's also a thanks."

The three males traded bewildered gazes over the fresh supply of ale. Without asking permission, she pulled back the fourth chair and helped herself to a seat. Duli kept chatting before any one of them could break her momentum.

"I realize I've kept a rough edge for as long as we've known each other. I'd rather not be enemies…we have enough to worry about from the humans. I'm also very grateful that you finally gave us a chance to go out and do something for the clans."

"Aye, well…" Boreval started to say. Duli cut him off before he could go far.

She turned and laid a hand on Guffan's arm. As much as she hated the man, she was amused at how he endured the touch while at the same time squirming under the contact. "General Guffan was an inspiration. He relied on us to do our job yet worked to keep us safe when the humans came. He handled them in a way that made them look like newborns."

She wondered if the general's beard was hiding expressions of discomfort. He hated her, yet she heaped praises on him as if he was her hero. Duli couldn't let these men realize that she knew they plotted against her. They fell for it. As long as she spoke in a civil manner and praised them, none of the men wanted to antagonize her.

When Duli could tell that Boreval couldn't restrain himself from talking for much longer, she shifted her focus to him. "The widows appreciate you most of all, Boreval."

"Huh?"

"Indeed! You gave us our chance. And here we were saying such bad things behind your back! You deserve our thanks the most!"

Boreval threw a confused look at Guffan, Guffan to Horace, and Horace simply looked down at the tankards Duli offered.

"You gave us your blessing and allowed us to be true dwarves! Marching out to meet the enemy! Spitting in their faces before watching them go running!" Duli paid Boreval the same discomfort she had visited upon Guffan by laying her hand appreciatively on his arm. "We owe you most of all. I think I'll ask some of the widows to get you something special. Maybe a new padded quilt, a prettier one, between your ram and saddle."

Out of the corner of her eye, she saw Guffan throw a wide-eyed look towards Boreval. The Clan-Sire managed to stutter, "Oh, that would be most unnecessary, I assure you."

"Nonsense," Duli offered him the prettiest smile she could form. "You deserve our thanks!"

She took a moment to dole out the drinks before each man. Staring down at the table as she was, she still cast subtle glances at them while they thought she was preoccupied. Their expressions made her want to laugh until she cried.

Of all of them, Horace had the decency to just accept Duli's gift. He pushed his empty mug out of the way and hoisted her offering. Boreval and Guffan reluctantly followed his lead.

"A toast!" She yelled, raising her drink.

Guffan huffed. "You're toasting while drinking milk?"

Duli rolled eyes towards him. "You know I don't drink anymore; however, I'll be happy to keep the drinks flowing for you men all night!"

Horace perked up at that. "All night?"

Duli smiled at each one in turn. She hoped that none of them could see the scheming going on behind her smile. "All night," she reassured them.

She toasted and they drank. Despite their dislike of Duli, all three men were disarmed by her sweetness and generosity. The beardless woman sipped her milk while prompting them into toast after toast loaded with ale. She asked them war stories and got them more tankards whenever their throats got dry.

Ale was great for impairing judgment. Duli was happy to use it against them, as opposed to herself this night. They talked and they drank, while Duli waited for the right moment. They slurred words and began forgetting details in their stories. The drinks made them treat Duli as if she truly was an old friend of theirs.

During the entire time, Duli kept a level head. The evening reminded her of trying to set out a trap for a cunning animal. She had to slip in unaware, bait it irresistibly and leave no hint of the steel teeth. Her male prey patted themselves on the back as they were taking advantage of her coin purse. They overindulged on the bait. When she finally deemed them to be drunk enough, she set her plan into motion. Boreval was in too much of an alcohol-induced fog to realize the danger when his words sprang the trap.

By morning, his blunder was the gossip that swept through the city.

CHAPTER 18

Sargas "Gun Hand" glanced over a musket barrel with his one good eye. He let loose an unsatisfied grunt as he noted the slight misalignment of the sights. He laid the barrel piece on a work table as he donned his heavy leather gloves. The aging veteran stared down the length of the Armory's training hall floor at one of the straw-and-wood targets. The target was cut in the shape of a human, displaying a yellow cloth patch where the heart could be found. Several holes were grouped to the left of the cloth.

He scowled at muskets that weren't up to his high standards, yet in reality he enjoyed the work and the challenges they offered. He regarded his position as Master-at-Arms the best job in the whole clan. As long as foreman Boreval Stonebrow left him alone, he remained content working on the guns.

This was not destined to be one of Sargas' good days. Boreval walked into the training hall slowly, leaning on his heavy cane more than usual. His black-and-gray beard lacked the careful grooming he normally gave it, and he put a hand to his bald head with a wince. Sargas suspected the rumors he heard regarding the Clan-Sire's previous night's escapades were true.

Sargas said, "Come to help me fix the sights on this barrel, have you? Very nice of you."

Boreval didn't even glance at the barrel. The foreman never helped maintain the muskets in any way. It surprised Sargas how delayed the reaction was from the Stonebrow elder. The Clan-Sire glanced at the hole-filled dummy standing on the target range.

"Bristlebeard, how good is Duli's aim with a musket?"

Sargas straightened as far as his crooked back would allow. In a huff, he removed his leather gloves and threw them on the floor. He continued to stare in silence at Boreval with his one eye until the foreman turned to look at him. The old Master-at-Arms could wear a very intimidating frown when he wanted. The scarred area on one side of his face only lent it more menace.

128

"So the rumors are true?" Sargas spit on the ground. "You're not only the head fool of the Armory, but of the city as well!"

Normally Boreval wasn't one to get intimidated by anyone. Sargas was used to the foreman giving orders and not answering questions. When Boreval spoke, it was as if the stone exterior had been cracked.

"I'm not sure what the rumors are saying. Don't be calling me a fool just because…well, the ale last night made things foggy. I don't really recall what I said, and shouldn't be held accountable for it."

Sargas raised his good eyebrow. "We're dwarves, not humans! We hold ourselves accountable for our actions. You made a foolish choice last night. All of Lower City was eager to discuss every drunken detail of the whole discussion. By the gods! Are you prepared to lose such a bet?"

Boreval huffed and turned his back to the old veteran. In a low voice, he said, "Maybe I made a wager, maybe I didn't. I don't recall."

Despite Sargas' anger, he took some joy retelling the shameful details to Boreval; although he still couldn't keep the ire out of his voice.

"You made a wager pitting Duli against four of Tok-Maurron's best shooters. Here in the training hall of the Armory, Duli will be given a musket. She will compete against the four other dwarves to load and shoot as quickly as possible."

He pointed towards the yellow cloth marking the dummy target's heart. "The first one to shoot five targets wins. There will be twenty-five dummies set up at different distances, so you can't shoot the same one twice."

Sargas held his silence a bit. He was interested to see if Boreval could remember any of the rest on his own.

The Clan-Sire shifted his weight slightly between cane and legs. He refused to look at Sargas when he asked, "I specified that a shot had to hit the heart target. Aye?"

"Aye, and if Duli wins…" Sargas left it unfinished.

When Boreval failed to speak, he ended his statement. "…you agreed to arm the widows with muskets and let them train to use them."

Boreval snorted. "Absurd! Women with muskets!"

Sargas could barely contain himself. "That is what you offered if she won!"

"What if she doesn't win? Four of our pick of shooters will face against her: the elite of the city's warriors. I must have had some good punishment if she lost."

Silence greeted him. Boreval was denied an answer until he turned around to look Sargas in the eye. "From what got to my ears, if she loses, she will be out of your…" Sargas glanced at the bald head, "...hair. Duli agreed to quit the brigade forever. She will devote all her waking hours inside the Mennurdan Guild for the rest of her life."

The Clan-Sire allowed the shadow of a grin to peek through his beard. "Well, that is a nice wager. Duli won't be able to beat our best shooters. She'll tuck her tail into the Mennurdan like a good woman should and I won't have to worry about her again."

Sargas did not share his optimism. He stomped a full circle, growling and cursing.

"What?" Boreval asked, "It isn't as bad as it sounded. I'll be free of that beardless..."

"That isn't what doused me forge!" Sargas growled. "I lost my privileges in the Armory because I let a woman touch a musket. You handed me the sentence." Sargas tried to straighten his back, but had to settle for pointing one wrinkled finger at Boreval. "You're making bets that could result in knowingly giving muskets to a large group of women! Where is your trial?"

The Clan-Sire leveled a cold gaze at Sargas. He held it long enough for Sargas to lose some of his bluster. Boreval pounded his cane against the stone floor, causing a ring that echoed for a long time in the large chamber. "She will not win. She can't best any four muskets of my choosing. You still haven't answered my question."

Sargas snapped, "My senile brain seems to have been addled by our little talk. What question?"

"How good can Duli shoot?"

Sargas grumbled curses under his breath, not caring that Boreval likely heard him. He looked at the yellow heart cloth.

"Almost half the time," Sargas admitted. "She was getting to be a really good aim before her trek outside."

Boreval allowed a smug grin on his face. Sargas imagined that several of the clan's best shooters could do much better, and Boreval was counting on it. Boreval's expression suddenly changed briefly to one of worry.

"She hasn't had her hands on a gun since?"

Sargas planted his two sooty, callused hands on his hips. His stance was enough to let Boreval know that he considered the question to be a serious insult to his clan honor. "Since you always keep the muskets under such tight lock-and-key, it would be your fault if she got her hands on one, wouldn't it?"

The Clan-Sire abruptly turned towards the door. Still somewhat addled by a hangover, he leaned into his cane as he moved to the exit.

Sargas called out, "You didn't leave her any provision to get in some last minute training before the day of the contest?"

Boreval turned in surprise, "Nay, I didn't. She hasn't stopped by to ask has she?"

"I haven't seen her. I was just making sure you weren't as complete a fool as you look."

As much as Sargas liked Duli, despite the hardships her carelessness had dumped on him, he still didn't care for the idea of arming a band of women. Sargas was serious about the guns and feared most women didn't have the touch that Duli had shown around the weapons.

Boreval threw a hard stare back at the veteran. "Fool, you say, but by next week Duli will be sitting at her proper place in the Mennurdan Guild." As Boreval left, he added over his shoulder. "You know, they might have some room at that guild for more male mentors as well."

*   *   *   *   *   *

Sargas Bristlebeard had a number of places to visit for supplies; the first was the pressing mill. Paper was not a cheap commodity. He had little need of it, but Boreval was in charge now. The Clan-Sire had the wealth and the inclination to use paper on all number of new records kept for the Armory.

Sargas entered the outer office just prior to the departure of a few dwarven priests. The representatives of Nandorrin were hauling a small cart stacked with paper back to Staprel Gom. Once the priests were gone, Sargas turned his attention to the only other dwarf there.

"Hope you've been finding your fortune, but if not, Boreval gave me some to pass on to you."

The miller let a smile part his facial growth. "He ran out again? I had nay idea you kept such extensive archives of records."

As the coins changed hands, Sargas sighed, "It's a waste! Shameful waste! Not all of it is for the Armory. A lot of time spent 'overseeing' my work is used on letters to his many relations."

The miller chuckled. "Ah well, business is business for me. It doesn't matter one grain of sand to me what he does with it."

Sargas nodded agreement, "If not for Boreval and the priests, where would you find so much business?"

"Apparently, among the leather crafters! I just got a new customer today that bought several long sheets."

Sargas squinted his good eye. "A leather crafter? I usually see them make signs from hides. Was it one of those Steelfoot folks?"

"Nay," the miller answered. He leaned in close to Sargas as if to part with an important secret. "That troublemaker Duli spent several good coins here."

The corners of Sargas' mouth dipped into a frown. "Duli? Today?"

At the miller's nod, Sargas thought back to the foolish bet Boreval had made. "Did she ever give any indication, before today, that she needed some paper?"

The miller shook his head. "Nay. Just walked in and asked me for some cheap lengths of it."

"What for?" He asked.

"She didn't say," the other dwarf shrugged.

Sargas spent a moment quietly considering any hidden meanings to Duli's purchase. In the end, he didn't pay it much mind. There could be any number of reasons why a person might need some, or maybe she was purchasing for someone else. He dismissed it from his thoughts as he went about his chores.

Sargas' next stop involved a smith from whom he had ordered some musket hammers. He went into Lower City to an area where a number of forges belched smoke into an exit shaft. The place was alive with the sounds of hammers ringing against metal and blowers fanning coals. He moved through the maze of hot metal until he found the face he sought. He heard the dwarf's voice before spotting him in his heavy apron.

"…nay clue, but I'll be hunched over my forge for the better part of two days making that many ball bearings. Wonder why she needs them?"

The smith that had spoken noticed Sargas. "Gun Hand! Come for your supplies?"

Sargas shook hands with the smith, an old friend of his. "Got them ready for me?"

"Finished them yesterday. Good thing you got your order in early, I've got a request that will keep me out of relaxing at Deepmug's for two evenings!"

The smith bade farewell to the dwarf he was chatting with and led Sargas over to a small crate filled with musket hammers. Sargas trusted his old friend; but even so, he scrutinized the work with a professional eye. He looked down the lines of the hammers and fidgeted with the flint clamps. A grunt and a nod were all he offered in praise.

He set the last piece back into the crate as he asked, "Busy with what? I heard something about ball bearings?"

The smith snorted, "Hundreds of them! She didn't even say what they were for."

"She?"

"Duli."

Sargas paused in surprise, his jaw hanging open. "Duli? What did she request? When did she stop by?"

"Less than an hour ago." The smith dabbed the sweat of the forge from his forehead. "She came in and requested me to make hundreds of tiny ball bearings. There was something odd about the way she wanted them."

Sargas' curiosity swelled. He was starting to hear Duli's name in too many places for one day. "What do you mean…odd?"

The smith showed Sargas a pair of calipers sitting nearby. "For one thing, she wanted them rather small. She wanted them about this big."

Gun Hand put his thumbnail up next to the caliper prongs. The circumference of the bearings would allow two or three to fit within the size of his thumbnail.

The smith continued, "What was also odd was that she wanted them 'about' that size. She didn't care if they were a little larger or smaller. Duli even said they didn't have to be perfect spheres but had to be close. What use does a dwarf have for a few hundred ball bearings that aren't a standard size and aren't even smooth?"

Sargas looked at his friend, "She didn't say?"

"I asked her so that I could make sure I was doing the right job on them, but she wouldn't give me any details."

By the time Sargas finished his visits in Lower City, it was time to stop for a tankard at Deepmug's. He intended to relax his mind with a deep amber brew. He made his way through the mild crowds who had gathered for the afternoon. One aspect of an underground city was that any hour of the day was a good time to find the pub open.

He stopped in his tracks as he recognized a familiar person making her way through the crowds. Slung over her back was a scroll case, presumably carrying the lengths of paper purchased from the miller. Duli had just stepped away from the courtyard bar. Loram Deepmug was still hovering at the same opening, counting out the coins in his hands. Sargas thought to go to him and ask what Duli was doing but the leather crafter was headed his way. She was fidgeting with something in her hands. Sargas decided to approach her and get a firsthand look at what it was. He got in a peek before Duli realized she was being watched, then responded by clamping her hands shut.

He adopted a grin and tried to speak casually. "Thought you were stealing a tankard from Deepmug, but that's too small."

Duli offered him a small smile, but she seemed surprised to be caught holding…whatever was in her hand. After a moment of visible hesitation on her features, she offered up her hand to show Sargas. "Not a mug, a measuring spigot."

Sargas looked over the metal nozzle. The narrow tube had a valve bisecting its middle. It was a small item that could have easily stayed hidden in Duli's hand if she had wished.

"It looks too small to measure ale."

Duli nodded in return, "You hook it up to a bag of spices or salts, and regulate how much you want to use. The more you turn it, the more you get."

Sargas furrowed his brow as he tried to figure out why Duli had an interest in that item. He was at a loss for how such a thing might mix with her other strange purchases.

He asked, "What do you need that for?"

As practiced as the dwarven race was at hiding emotions, Sargas could see a reaction in Duli's eyes. She knew he had more than a conversational interest in her purchase. The widow's face went neutral as she pocketed the spigot. For whatever reasons, once it was hiding out of sight, Duli's attitude changed. She once again became the old friend of his who had joked and chatted with him before her offense to the clan landed both of them in hot water.

"Sargas, my friend, I still regret that I got you into trouble. I wouldn't want my worst enemy to have Boreval looking over his work. Come to think of it, I think Boreval is my worst enemy."

Her green eyes stared into his good eye for a moment. Duli absently fingered one of her large, hoop earrings as Sargas waited for her to continue. When she finally found words, they spilled out in an abrupt manner.

"The day will come when I will see Boreval humiliated before the clan. He deserves nay less and I want you there to see it."

Duli turned away, but before she even got two steps he tried to see if she would let slip anything else. Sargas inquired, "And what is the spigot for?"

She threw a glance over her shoulder. Her eyes sparkled with mystery as she replied, "It's just something for adding spice. I'm cooking up something."

She turned away without another word. Sargas watched Duli disappear among the crowds of Lower City. He began to turn his feet back towards the Armory; his thirst for ale forgotten.

"She's cooking up something alright," he muttered, "and Boreval is a fool for making a bet with that one."

CHAPTER 19

Sargas Bristlebeard looked across the twenty-five human-shaped targets standing at irregular positions in the Armory's training range. Some were flat planks carved from wood. Most others were bags of straw hanging from wooden frames, much like scarecrows. Each one had a small, yellow cloth marking the heart.

In less than an hour, either Boreval or Duli would be humiliated before the clan and city. Sargas could predict the shame that would be heaped upon the loser. He wasn't sure whose victory would be more favorable for him. As much as he liked Duli and hated Boreval, the thought of arming a swarm of females went against Sargas' better judgment.

One thing Sargas could not have predicted was the excitement buzzing around the training hall's cavern. All that morning a train of visitors kept intruding upon the hall. There were more Clan-Sires than were normally seen anywhere except in the halls of the king. They traded jokes with sons and kin. Loram Deepmug arrived with a few wheelbarrows loaded with casks and was quickly admitted into the training hall without asking for Sargas' approval. As the time of the wager approached, a crowd of onlookers found seats in the stone-carved benches on the safe end of the room. In recent memory, Gun Hand couldn't remember the hall being so packed with spectators.

Since Duli's trial, women were forbidden to approach the Armory, but that rule seemed to be quietly ignored for this occasion. A few Clan-Sires or their sons brought their wives. Sargas wasn't feeling like bringing up clan rules in the face of the lawmakers. The drinkers paid no heed to the presence of Katy Dornan helping Deepmug pass out drinks and collect coins. If Duli's widows were armed, Katy would be among those coming to him for a musket.

Although Katy may not have raised any eyebrows, the entrance of Fosha Spindlebur and Leli Gorm surely did. Duli's two officers managed to hush the room for several breaths as conversations turned to scandalous whispers. No one argued the women's attendance in the presence of their own wives. Fosha and Leli stopped only for a tankard before setting themselves separate from the others.

Sargas noted Duli's two officers frowning when Popguv Rockhand and a few masters from Mennurdan Guild arrived. They were likely planning to take Duli under their wing when she lost her bet.

Heads turned again when Boreval arrived with his four chosen shooters, and they were followed by Guffan Stonebrow. It was no surprise that one of Boreval's choices was Horace Smokebore. The dark-bearded dwarf said little to those who tried to greet him. The second shooter was Murglor "Half-Foot", a captain of one of Tok-Maurron's most renowned company of fighters. The debilitating injury which gave him the "Half-Foot" nickname kept Murlor from doing much on the ground during battle. Instead he led from the saddle of his ram. Nevertheless, he had gained a reputation from his musket skills after many wages won by him in this same hall.

There were two younger warriors of whom Gun Hand was less familiar. One was a member of the ruling clan, Bundak Stonebrow, while the other just went by the nickname "Headshot". Despite not knowing them well, Sargas knew their skills must be good for Boreval to choose them for his champions. Sargas couldn't help but wonder how Duli could hope to put up a good contest against such fighters. Each had likely fired hundreds more rounds than her.

The crowd kept glancing at the entry, waiting for their missing challenger. Half-Foot indulged in some ale while making side bets on how well he could defeat Duli. One Clan-Sire offered up a bet that Duli wouldn't even show. Sargas knew that bet would be wrong. Just the previous evening, Duli had shown up asking Gun Hand for enough powder to fire several shots. He had the rights to deny her such materials, but she didn't ask for a gun.

"Nay shot," she had told him, "Just the powder if you don't mind."

It was probably against the law, but since Boreval didn't explicitly tell Sargas not to give her powder, he decided to slide this one request past the foreman. The muskets might have been locked up, but black powder could be found around the Armory.

Many dwarves reflected surprise when Duli walked in the training hall door, wearing her surface buckskins. There was a momentary hush, followed by boisterous cheers or jeers from the onlookers. Sargas glanced over some leather bags and straps encircling her frame. They looked new, but only left the Master-at-Arms wondering what they contained. He noted that one of the bags hung upside-down, the bottom end capped with the spice nozzle from Deepmug's.

"Good morning all." Duli said in a deceptively sweet voice. "I hope you will find the entertainment you seek today."

136

Boreval leaned on his mace-cane as he walked over to meet her. "Are you so eager to begin your daytime banishment to the Mennurdan Guild?"

Duli turned her head to look towards Popguv and the masters sitting to each side of him. "Are those the ones who will teach me the difficult art of bending animal hides to my will, in the styles approved by Tok-Maurron?"

Most everyone in the room could feel Duli's sarcasm. Popguv only nodded. Sargas knew the guildmaster was aware that she would be coming to him under the implied pretense of serving a life sentence.

Boreval wasted no time. "Bristlebeard, please provide the musket you picked for Duli."

Sargas reached under a canvas cover and drew it forth. He saw the gleam in Duli's eye as she set her eyes on it. The design was unmistakable for her. The gleam of bronze from the barrel...the flint hammer designed in the image of the god Nandorrin...the scene depicting the gates of Dorvanon on the side of the shoulder stock...the eleven notches cut into the wood next to the barrel.

Boreval narrowed his eyes upon seeing it. He couldn't help shaming Duli. "Isn't that the same gun that caused us to sentence her to isolation? A proper choice, Bristlebeard, for it will send her into isolation from the surface world again."

Duli ignored Boreval. She accepted the musket as if it had always been hers. She lovingly appraised its designs. She whispered her thanks to Sargas, "Two years aren't enough to dim my memory of Geordan's gun. It's the one part of him that still seems alive in the world."

Sargas only nodded back.

"Boreval," she said without looking away from the musket. "Before we begin, remind everyone else of the terms of the bet you made with me."

Sargas grinned at the slight Duli had made in her use of words, throwing the consequences of the bet on Boreval even though she had likely cornered him into making the bet. Sargas gave Duli a powderhorn and a bag of lead shot. Duli absently tied them to her belt as she and Boreval repeated the conditions of their wager to the crowd. Sargas and the four shooters noted that Duli fastened the shot bag and powderhorn to her belt in an out-of-the way position. It would be awkward for her to reach across her body to access them in a timely manner. Sargas held his comments, though Murglor and Bundak were clearly amusing themselves with whispered comments at Duli's inexperience.

They repeated the bet and the wager. A shot had to pierce the yellow heart cloth to be considered a hit, and the first one to accomplish that feat five times won. Only one of Boreval's champions had to outscore Duli for her to lose the bet. As the shooters took their place on marked positions, Duli was given a spot on one end. They assumed a starting position where the butts of the muskets were on the ground and unloaded.

Boreval announced, "As a neutral party, they will commence on your command, Bristlebeard."

Sargas took up a position on one end of the line, closest to Duli. Other dwarves took up positions behind the shooters to call out the shots as they connected. Gun Hand made them wait a couple heartbeats.

"Begin!"

As expected, the five shooters exploded into motion. Murglor was the first to raise his powderhorn to barrel. He reached into his bag of shot for a round only a heartbeat before Horace.

None of the male shooters had noticed that Duli stopped before even grabbing her powderhorn. Sargas stared in wonder as she made it a point to raise her hand to her eyes and squint at the targets. Duli turned her green eyes upon Sargas. Her face gave no indication that she was in a hurry, even though both Horace and Murglor were already using their ramrods to pack the shot to the bottom of their barrels.

"Sargas?"

"Duli?"

As she raised a hand to point at the target silhouettes, the other shooters realized Duli wasn't loading her gun. They all slowed down as they turned their heads. Boreval was no less shocked.

"Aren't the heart targets smaller than they used to be?"

A few chuckles erupted from the crowd. Murglor and Horace continued to load at a very relaxed pace, while Bundak and Headshot stopped altogether. All eyes turned to Duli.

Sargas flicked a finger towards Boreval. "I was asked to change them yesterday."

Duli and everyone else turned eyes towards Boreval. The Clan-Sire kept his face straight as he replied. "It wasn't my doing. With the war spreading and the Tariykans moving into the mountains, the king ordered smaller targets in order that our men will train harder."

Sargas was sure that no one actually believed such an explanation. Boreval wouldn't lie about the king's orders, but that didn't mean that the elder hadn't helped convince the king to make such a decision.

Duli did not look surprised nor dismayed with the target size. She had to have noticed it the moment she first set eyes on the targets, yet she deliberately waited until the contest had started. Her demeanor remained casual, even relaxed, as she looked over to Murglor.

"Well it sure is a small target, are you able to hit it?"

Half-Foot was already loaded and cocked. He and the other shooters were laughing and smiling. Murglor easily and slowly raised his musket, took aim and fired. The shot went through the middle of the cloth.

His caller shouted, "Murglor – One!"

Not to be outdone, Horace also finished loading and fired.

"Horace – One!"

Laughter rang through the cavern as the two shooters slowly went back to reloading. Even Boreval cracked a smile, anticipating an easy win.

Duli locked eyes with her old friend Sargas. She grinned as she asked, "Do you think I can hit that target?"

Sargas stared back in confusion. He knew she had gone through a lot of effort for some purpose, why wasn't she serious? Behind her, Bundak hit his target while Headshot actually missed. The crowd threw its share of playful insults at Headshot's embarrassing opener.

Looking upon Duli with his one good eye, Gun Hand said, "I doubt it, but if you're serious about wanting a gun, I think you better start shooting."

Unconcerned about the action behind her, Duli flashed Sargas a wide smile…a smile unnaturally large for a dwarf. In that one unsettling glance, Duli sent him a message: she had won, all she had to do was throw the cards on the table.

While others joked amongst themselves or watched the other shooters compete, Sargas kept all his attention on Duli.

Duli dropped her hand into a bag at her side, ignoring the powderhorn. She pulled out a small tube of paper, as thick and long as a couple fingers. She brought the tube to her teeth and ripped open the end, black powder staining the side of her lips. Duli stuck the open end into the barrel, emptying the powder. It impressed Sargas. She had a method to use pre-measured loads for the contest without fumbling with a powder horn, even though the paper was an expensive means to do it.

He expected her to grab the lead balls from the bag he had given her next, but she skipped that step. She went straight to pulling the ramrod from beneath the barrel. He was stumped even more a moment later when she glanced at the ramrod, uttered "Hmph", and carelessly threw it over her shoulder.

Sargas thought, *"What is she firing at the targets? Why isn't she ramming it down?"*

Duli grabbed the gun firmly and stamped the butt against the hard floor twice. Gun Hand groaned. She was using gravity to make everything drop to the bottom instead of packing it with the ramrod.

Some of the other lighthearted shooters glanced at her actions as they loaded for their second shots. Duli brought Geordan's gun up to her hip. Normally, the next step would be to reach again for the powderhorn and fill the firing pan. Duli popped open the musket's frizzen underneath the upside-down bag. A quick half-turn twist on the nozzle, and a measured amount of powder dropped into the pan.

Duli snapped the gun up to her shoulder. Since she wasn't messing with the ramrod or eyeballing amounts with the powderhorn, Duli loaded her gun almost twice as fast as the others. Murglor and Horace were both loading their pans with powder, while the other two were still fumbling with their ramrods.

Sargas and most of the crowd turned towards Duli's first target. A larger, echoing boom exploded from her musket. Instead of a hole, they were all shocked to see the entire top half of her wooden target blasted to splinters. The bright cloth disappeared along with the silhouette's chest. Sargas realized how hundreds of small ball bearings, likely tucked into the paper tube atop the powder, fit into Duli's plan.

A curtain of silenced had descended over the room. Even the other shooters paused as they stared at Duli's mangled target. A noticeable delay passed before Duli's amazed spotter croaked out, "Duli – One."

No playfulness existed in the woman's attitude now. She was already dropping the butt to the ground and reaching for the next paper tube. Bundak offered a wide-eyed glance at Boreval, though Boreval's mouth dangled open in amazement. Horace and Murglor resumed their loading and firing with the smooth action of veterans who knew they were dealing with a real challenge. They quickly shot their second targets.

As Sargas watched Duli work, he had to admire her method. She invented a new way of firing the musket, specifically designed for the short range of the training hall. She tore open the next tube, poured in the powder followed by lead mini-shot, stamped the gun on the ground two more times, and was back to loading the pan faster than any dwarf Sargas had ever seen.

"Headshot – One!"

"Bundak – Miss!"

Bundak Stonebrow cursed. If it wasn't for the smaller cloth targets, his shot would have been a hit.

Duli raised her musket. Another echoing blast tore apart the cloth and dismembered the left arm of her target.

"Duli – Two!"

Horace and Murglor were already sweating as they slammed their ramrods down their barrels. Sargas glanced over at Boreval. The Clan-Sire kept his stoic countenance. Fosha and

140

Leli did their best to hide emotions, but Sargas saw Leli's hands clasped hard enough to make the knuckles go white.

By the time Horace and Murglor brought their guns to shoulder level, Duli twisted the nozzle over her pan. Shots and voices went off in quick succession.

Murglor – Three. Horace – Three. Duli – Three. Headshot – Two. Bundak – Two. The last two callers shouted even as Duli's latest shredded silhouette toppled backwards.

Murglor and Horace were desperately trying to reload as fast as Duli. Both were slowed by ramming their shot. Murglor didn't bother to replace the ramrod in its slot under his barrel; he stuck it upright in a bucket near his feet. Sargas noted Horace following the same idea. The veteran leaned his ramrod against a small table. This would make it easier to grab the rod, use it, and just set it down without trying to pull and replace it from its small housing in the musket.

By the time both men were preparing to throw powder in their flashpans, Duli was ahead of them and aiming for her fourth target. The crowd was getting used to the louder bang as her weapon fired. Sargas saw the wood-and-straw target shudder from the hit. By some miracle the silhouette stayed together. For a moment, Boreval thought Duli had suffered her first miss, but the caller declared it a hit. As the musket smoke cleared, everyone could see the yellow cloth peppered with five holes. The silhouette tilted backwards.

Sargas glanced at Boreval. Losing his stoic composure, the elder Stonebrow shouted, "Don't let this non-clan beat you! Load faster!"

Murglor took aim at his target even as Duli grabbed her next paper tube. His hammer sparked the pan. The shot punched a hole just to the side of the cloth. The smaller heart targets Boreval had championed were more of a hindrance to his own shooters. Murglor Half-Foot cursed.

"Horace – Four!"

Headshot and Bundak each scored their third hits. Bundak hit across the range at the silhouette which would have been Duli's next and likely last target. Bundak forced Duli to pick her fifth and final target from ones standing farther away.

Only Horace could threaten Duli, but he was still shoving a shot in the barrel as Duli was stamping her gun against the ground. A second musket butt was heard smacking the hard floor. Sargas turned to see Bundak trying to use Duli's tactic. The one-eyed gunsmith frowned at the young warrior's behavior. Apparently, Bundak barely flung powder and shot into the barrel and thought he could settle them to the bottom as easily as Duli. Although his next target would only be his fourth, it occurred to Sargas the shot could take out another target close to Duli, giving Horace a better chance.

Bundak dumped a messy waste of powder onto his flashpan. He actually got his musket in line before Duli, but Sargas took a step back, anticipating an exploding gun. Bundak's flashpan sparked a bigger explosion than what came out the barrel. The ball of shot came out slow enough for everyone to see it drop to the floor.

Duli raised her gun. Horace couldn't possibly finish loading in time. Her spray of shot shredded the cloth heart and broke the backbone holding up the silhouette. The human-shaped target slowly fell forward at the waist, giving the victor a bow.

"Duli – Five!"

Sargas thought the contest would end with the declaration of Duli's winning shot, but the action never ceased. Horace finished loading and shot his fifth target. Duli continued to load for her next shot, clearly intending to further the embarrassment of Boreval's champions.

Murglor hit his fourth target, followed by Headshot hitting his fourth. Duli picked her sixth target from the ones in front of Bundak, repaying the Stonebrow for taking one of hers. The cloth heart disintegrated as a gaping hole took its place. As Bundak fumbled through loading, Horace blasted his sixth target from one standing in front of Headshot. Murglor claimed his fifth.

One silhouette remained in front of Bundak's position. A quieted crowd watched as three dwarves raced to finish loading. Bundak had his gun up steadying for a shot. Headshot got his gun in line as Duli cocked her hammer all the way back. Both males fired their guns. The crowd cheered as they witnessed a hole punched through the cloth heart. That small victory was diminished a moment later, when Duli's blast ripped apart the upper half of the target.

Silence reigned in the training hall, interrupted only by cracked boards swinging from shattered human look-alikes. Duli had left her mark. Seven of twenty-five targets were broken, hole-riddled, missing limbs, leaning at crazy angles or all of the above.

Duli's stride was calm and confidant as she turned to Boreval. The Clan-Sire stared down the target range as if to deny what he was seeing. As Duli walked into the elder's vision, she half-turned to where Sargas could make out her face better. There was no hiding the grin tugging at the corners of her mouth.

Duli's voice spoke to Fosha, Leli and Katy, even though she kept her eyes steady on Boreval. "Looks like we earned our guns."

As Clan-Sires began muttering behind him, Boreval spoke up before he could be drowned by protests in the crowd. "Nay, Duli. I can't give you a musket."

Duli's eyes flashed in anger. "Our wager stated…"

"I'm sorry, Duli." Boreval stated, though he clearly wasn't, "Blame me for being a fool and betting what wasn't mine to give."

Every female in the room stared at Boreval as if he was vermin. A crazed goblin would have gotten a friendlier reception. The Clan-Sire, upon making his excuse, began to straighten his back and look away from Duli. His stance and head tilt suggested he was above honoring a bet against a non-clan female.

Sargas assumed his own angry stance by planting a fist on each side of his hips. "We are not like those back-stabbing, ambushing humans! If we give our word, we keep it!"

Duli's fists clenched as she hissed at Boreval. "Are you going back on your wager? Is your honor so easily cast aside?"

No one else spoke to defend Duli. Those who were friends of Boreval pretended to turn a deaf ear to what was going on. The Clan-Sire responded, "Honor has nay influence here. I was drunk and bet something that isn't mine to give. If you want to go against our customs, against the laws of our ancestors, then I suggest you make your next wager with the king. I couldn't give you a musket even if I wanted to."

Duli looked from face to face in the hall. Only her friends met her eyes. The Clan-Sires turned away, ignoring the betrayal of clan values. The wives stared angrily at their husbands. Sargas wasn't about to let such a dishonor pass. The gunsmith was opening his mouth to speak but Duli was quicker.

"We all know you can shape clan rules if you wanted to, just as you have in the past. Drinks are never an excuse to undermine the value of a dwarf's word. These witnesses recognize your dishonor; by their silence, they have dirtied themselves in it. You are hereby declared a false tongue!"

Duli showed she had not forgotten the insult Boreval hurled during her trial. "*I brand you*, beardless!"

In her rage, Duli threw down her late husband's gun in disgust. The wooden stock was spared damage only because Boreval's boot was softer than the hard floor. The Clan-Sire held his composure despite the blow to his toes. Nothing more was said as Duli turned from the stoic Stonebrow. Duli marched over to Loram, threw a purse of coins at him in trade for a wheelbarrow carrying one of his casks. She wheeled the drink out of the room. Leli and Fosha followed, both officers throwing angry glares at Boreval.

CHAPTER 20

Glaura Greencutter approached Duli's door with some trepidation. No one had seen the leatherworker since she embarrassed the clan's top muskets two days prior. Glaura had attempted to gain entry already, but was usually turned away by drunken slurs. Glaura had flashbacks of when she had walked in on Duli's attempted suicide. She wasn't sure what she would find, but she wouldn't give in to her fears. She rapped her knuckles on the door of her friend's chambers.

At first no sound was audible except a whimper from the wolf. Glaura's fist hammered the door even louder. "Duli! Duli! I need to see you."

Even with the thick stone walls, the cracks around the door allowed the sound of rustling bedcovers to escape. Bandit let loose a grunt. Glaura continued to address the door. "Duli, talk to me. Please open up this door. You've been holed up in there long enough; I need to know you're alive."

"Immup," Duli murmured. When Glaura continued to shout at her to open the door, she heard Duli clarify. "I said I'm up. Give me a moment."

Duli took her time stumbling to the door. Glaura was ready to push her way into the room as soon as she had a chance; however, an unwelcome surprise greeted her instead. As soon as Duli opened the door, Glaura nearly retched from the stink that filled the air.

Duli's sandy hair was wet from sweat or ale. From the reek of her disheveled clothes, Glaura assumed it was ale. She still wore the same outfit she had at the contest. The long tail of hair Duli always braided was tangled into a greasy mess. Glaura's friend viewed the world through eyes nearly squinted shut. She leaned on the door to find the balance that her legs weren't providing.

"By Nandorrin's forge! What have you been doing?"

"C…c…can a soul drink in peace? Eh-very few hours someone pounds my door."

"When did you start drinking again?" Glaura tried to look past the staggering dwarf.

Duli had trouble speaking and standing at the same time. "After I…um…that stupid wager thing…"

Glaura finally got a good look at the rest of the room. Empty ale mugs, enough to rival any large party, littered the floor. A couple casks were present, all tapped, some broken open. Duli's hatchet stuck out of one broken cask. Most of the floor was sticky from spilled drinks. That wasn't the worst of the floor's concerns: the room stank of urine and upended stomach contents as well. Glaura noted several ruined fur blankets. The stains sat there the full two days while Duli continued to drink. From the smell, the chamber pot likely needed emptying.

Bandit was hardly recognizable from ruined furs. The wolf stretched out on the dirty floor, lacking the strength to hold his head up for any length of time. He whimpered. Glaura covered her mouth as she looked over the wolf's own mess of excrement. Apparently there had been enough ale for the wolf to get as drunk as Duli.

"Duli! How can you live like this? Were you trying to kill yourself from drinking?"

Duli's words came slowly. "It's as good a way as…a good way to face death."

Glaura shook her head in disbelief. She took a deep breath and forced her way through the door. Duli almost fell over trying to keep her out, though Glaura grabbed an arm and led her to a bench.

"What are…? I'm fine. Go, get me some more ale if you're a friend, but go."

Almost too late, Glaura realized that the wolf wouldn't take kindly to someone pushing Duli around. She glanced at Bandit, but the wolf was having too hard a time just focusing on what was going on. His growl almost sounded like just another whine.

Glaura forced Duli to sit down. "It's because I'm a friend that I'm not turning my back on you like this. Not like I have a choice. You're being summoned."

"Summoned?"

"By the king and council. I'm to take you up to Stonebrow Vault."

Duli sighed, "Council? They'll probably put me on trial for something else to get me out of the way."

Duli's balance still suffered. She nearly fell over except that Glaura caught her in time.

Glaura shrugged. "They didn't give me a reason. Nay other wanted to come near the wolf, so they sent me to get you." As she spoke, Bandit tried to make another attempt to stand, only to stumble and fall. "The widows are all busy. They were summoned as well."

"I shouldn't be surprised. Since I lost Geordan, I've just been a plaything for the gods. Why not just put me through another trial? Shoot me or exile me."

"I hope the gods blame your behavior on the drinks. Such words are unwisely spoken." Glaura huffed. "Whatever the council wants, we better get you ready before someone else comes down and sees this mess."

Glaura locked the door shut and proceeded to force Duli out of her soiled clothes. The widow hardly put up a fight, which concerned Glaura. Most dwarves, especially Duli, were not ones for giving up and going along with something they didn't like. She feared her friend's heart broken under the weight of their male-dominated society.

Duli muttered as Glaura struggled. Her words were sometimes lost under her breath, but Glaura was able to make out a few things. "…might as well hang or shoot me. I'll be out from under their beards then. I know the males treat me like I'm a joke…now I'm just an embarrassment to the women. The widows will probably do the honor of killing me."

Glaura stopped and snapped her eyes up to meet Duli's. The widow kept chatting. "I gave them hope when there is none to be found. The men won't listen. Nay matter what we do, they'll take nay notice of us."

Glaura made sure Duli was looking into her eyes. "Do you have any idea what has been going on in the city these past two days? Have you put even one ear outside your door since the contest?"

As Duli shook her head, wincing at the pain of even that small movement, Glaura spoke again.

"Up and down Tok-Maurron, from Nandorrin's Halls to Taekbol's Halls, from the Mines on up to Top Plaza, the women have been revolting. The city has been echoing with their cries of injustice. You can't do business anywhere in the city without passing groups of women chanting or ranting. I thought they were being foolish at first, but every bit of gossip that has been passed around these days validated that they are unnerving the Clan-Sires. It started with the Widow Brigade. Nearly two hundred strong…"

Glaura saw how Duli's eyes widened at that news. Apparently, Duli didn't know they had gained so many new members in the last few days.

"…they marched up to Stonebrow Vault. The whole mob of them got as close to the king's throne as the guards would allow. In the presence of dozens of Clan-Sires, their families and visiting ambassadors from other clans, the whole brigade shaved their beards! They left a mountain of hair on the king's doorstep."

Glaura resumed helping Duli out of her clothes while the brigade leader sat there open-mouthed at Glaura's revelations.

"They camped on the steps of the palace for hours. They chanted 'Injustice! Dishonor!' and sang songs about the legendary traitor Grayknuckle, one of our most

146

despicable tales of dishonor. Fosha and Leli claim the king shares Boreval's dishonor until something is done to remedy the ignored wager."

Duli took some time to digest the news. Her alcohol-addled thoughts apparently hadn't kept pace with Glaura. She asked, "They shaved their beards?"

"Aye, they're all as smooth-cheeked as you now. They…" Glaura thought a moment before she completed her sentence. "…said that since men made all the decisions in the clan, they would rather just mark themselves as a lower caste now rather than let the truth stay hidden under beards."

While Duli sorted her confusion, Glaura snuck up on her with a bucket of water. The widow was doused, sputtering curses as she flailed in protest.

"Hold still! You're getting cleaned and dressed whether you like it or not!"

Duli attempted to throw Glaura out, but the mother of two decided to distract her with the rest of the news.

"That was just the fire-starter, it swept through the rest of the woodpile after that."

"What do you mean?"

Glaura tried looking for some decent clothes while she relayed the tale. "It spread to other women. None of us took Boreval's dishonor lightly. Even some like me, who don't really understand why the widows are so eager to get muskets, got angry. We did our talking and discussions around the Hearthden.

"The wives of the Clan-Sires who attended the shooting match, some of whom were present, were shamed enough to withhold favors from their dishonored husbands. I'm told that you said something in the Armory about the Clan-Sires muddying their own reputations due to their silent assent of Boreval's dishonor? The wives agreed with you. I wish I could have personally seen what happened. According to rumor, they all made a pact. Until their men did something to renounce Boreval or make amends, there would be nay cooking, cleaning, and definitely nay coupling. It even affected Clan-Sires not even present at the contest. The wives of these other husbands likewise didn't want any shame spreading to them. Since the contest, I believe nearly every Clan-Sire has foraged his own meals and slept alone."

Glaura started slipping a new tunic over Duli's head. The widow wasn't cooperating much, but she no longer actively fought her friend. Every part of the tale deepened Duli's shock.

"It wasn't just among the Clan-Sires," Glaura continued, "The same attitude spread to women throughout the clan. I'm glad I didn't have to cut off Tormero from any favors; he was already discussing his anger at what he called Boreval's Folly with his drinking buddies at Deepmug's."

Glaura caught a glance Duli made in her direction. Beneath her own reddish-brown beard she almost blushed at the thought of what she implied to her friend.

"As I was saying, it has spread to a number of couples outside of the Clan-Sires. Thanks to the Tariykans, the women outnumber the men in Tok-Maurron. The Hearthden has been in an uproar. The men were all chased away from the women's craft stalls. Katy quit Deepmug's, declaring she won't serve any man until justice is done. Leli took her in and is trying to care for her. Oh! And all those old veterans who sought out Leli's healing salves...she won't sell to any men unless one of two reasons: either a woman vouches for them, or they must openly yell out Boreval's dishonor."

Duli's eyes would have fallen out if able. She sat there, saying nothing, still swaying a bit from the drinks, as Glaura continued to get her dressed.

"Then there was Shauna's declaration. I'm surprised they didn't lock her up." At Duli's questioning glance, her friend said, "Shauna busted apart every project she was working on in the Mennurdan Guild and stormed out over Popguv's protests. She yelled some comment like she would rather sell wood carvings to forest gnomes than work for men anymore."

Glaura put on Duli's leather shoes. "Your contest started a firestorm in the city. The weight of the women is behind you, at great cost to our race in a time of war. Probably won't end well. There is tension unlike anything I have ever seen here. I know Boreval did you wrong, Duli, but I'm also afraid of how this will end."

A moment of silence stretched for a few breaths, interrupted by a growling noise from Bandit's stomach. The wolf still watched them through bleary eyes.

Duli stared at the floor. "So now the council summoned me?"

"Aye, you and the entire Widow Brigade. The rest are likely waiting for us up there."

Glaura watched as Duli rubbed her knuckles across tired eyes. The widow whispered. "I wonder if they'll hang me or run me out of town. I guess I'm fine with either choice."

"Don't say such things! They can't be too harsh on you or the women will tear the city apart. You can't possibly hope for exile...how could you be so casual about the loss of your home?"

Duli put up a hand and half-shouted. "Geordan was my home!" The beardless dwarf squinted and recoiled. Duli winced at the volume of her own voice. In a lower tone, she said, "That home will never come again. A curse on all of Tariyka for my loss. Tok-Maurron may house me, but it will never earn the comfort of that simple word, 'home'."

Glaura had no reply for such words. A clan was the first thing that defined a dwarf. She looked down, only to be reminded of the sticky, messy floor sucking at her every footstep.

Duli's next words brought her eyes back into contact. "If I'm going to another trial, I'm going as everything I want to be. I'm going to wear my armor."

The widow faced the bed upon which her armor had been discarded. Duli abruptly got to her feet, but just as suddenly started to sway back and forth. Glaura had just enough time to catch her and lower her back onto her seat. She was certain that Duli's hangover was bound to last for the rest of the day.

Her green eyes were spinning as she faced the general direction of the armor. "Bring that over here and help me."

As soon as her friend seemed steady, Glaura left her side to pick up and brush off the crafted armor. Some unsightly chunks had to be removed. Duli insisted she be sentenced while making her finest appearance.

When they were ready to leave, Duli cast a look at poor Bandit. The wolf still lay sprawled on the floor.

"This time, I think you'll finally obey me and stay put."

He replied with a whimper.

CHAPTER 21

Duli tried to keep a steady pace next to Glaura, despite the sensation that Tok-Maurron kept leaning back and forth. The shock of Glaura's news and the uneasy anticipation of being brought before the council helped wake her. Her head still pounded and her thoughts wandered through mud as she numbly allowed Glaura to set the pace. She had very little recollection of anything since the contest. Duli mostly kept her eyes down on the path she walked; it made it easier to take strides without getting dizzy.

There was one fleeting moment when she envisioned herself running. That brief fantasy of ignoring the council's summons and simply escaping to the surface world, facing some uncertain future alone rather than dealing with the people around her, tempted her for the span of a couple breaths. She let the impulse fade and die. She already tried her escape, but the drinks didn't kill her. Another day dawned with her still in Tok-Maurron. On her honor, she would stand and face whatever punishment awaited her.

She barely registered the fact that Lower City seemed virtually abandoned as they walked through it. Not a single business had its doors opened. The large cavern was empty of its natural rumble of conversations. A few guards paced, keeping watch for thieves who would pick that time to go looking for valuables. All of those guards took note of Duli as she passed, following her with their lowered brows.

"Most of the clan must be gathered up there," Glaura said.

The words pulled Duli's attention from her queasy stomach. "What?"

She looked around and studied the lack of people in Lower City. Glaura responded, "Everyone must have followed Widow Brigade up to the Vault when they were summoned. With so many ruckuses these past couple days, I'm guessing people are standing on their neighbor's shoulders to get a look at whatever the council plans to do."

"Oh, that's just lovely," Duli sighed.

They came to a great stair which led towards Top Plaza and the Stonebrow Vault. She managed the steps holding Glaura's arm.

Duli nearly whispered, "Can you do me a favor?"

"Aye."

"If I am facing some severe punishment…" Duli took a long pause before she could manage to get the words out. "Could you try to send Bandit back into the wild? Let him out and try to lead him away from here?"

"Don't say such things! The council can't be too harsh on you or the women might really get nasty."

"Just promise me. I want someone to get him out safe. If some guard does it, they might shoot him if he protests."

Glaura was silent for a breath. "Alright. I promise I'll try. That doesn't mean I'll have much luck. He may decide to come back on his own."

"I know. Try your best, that's all I ask."

As the structures of Stonebrow Vault loomed in the cavern ahead, they could hear and see a multitude of voices.

"By Nandorrin's beard! The whole city is up there alright." Duli lamented.

The large corridor leading towards the royal section of the Vault stood as an immense, hand-carved masterpiece of dwarven culture. On the walls, building fronts and the ceiling, not a single smooth, plain surface existed. Even the Arch, a carved stone gate protecting the palace area, was decorated with bas-reliefs of legendary heroes. Some parapets formed a brief space between the top of the Arch and the ceiling, allowing for dwarven muskets and priests to defend from foes outside.

The street outside the Arch abounded with citizens. Duli and Glaura could see a gathering of dwarves on top of the Arch, looking down into the palace side. She doubted they could squeeze past the thick crowd. It wasn't long before she was spotted. Everyone knew they were waiting on her, and several had been keeping an eye on the approaches. She heard her name announced from several areas. A roar went up as the crowd began shouting at Duli. Many yelled to her, coupling her name with either praises or insults. The insults thundered above all. Glaura yelped as thrown objects hit both of them. Old food bounced off Duli's armor as she raised an arm to shield her face. A couple fights broke out in the crowd as some women attacked the throwers, and not all of the throwers were male.

Duli's concerns about squeezing past the mob were answered in moments. A six-member squad of male guards trotted from out of nowhere and formed a ring around her and Glaura. Parts of the crowd parted while others tried to push inward for a better look. After surrounding the two women, the guards turned towards the Arch and shouted at others to clear the way. The six guards wielded heavy cudgels, threatening anyone blocking their path with a solid whack for the offense. No one wanted to test the guard's willingness to hit kinsmen. A path formed and they ushered Duli through it. They crossed underneath the Arch and into the palace's outer courtyard.

The courtyard displayed considerably more order than the throng of dwarves outside the Arch. Rows of benches accommodated a sea of beards surrounding a raised stage. The king often carried out court judgments or announced grand proclamations to the crowds here. A few thousand sets of dwarven eyes had room to sit and stare at whatever speaker or criminal stood upon that stage.

Upon knowing she would be standing under their scrutiny on that stage, Duli nearly lost control of her stomach. She swallowed back the sensation until it abated. She briefly contemplated her stupidity in making that wager with Boreval, rather than just drinking herself to death in the first place. Every action she took since Geordan's death attracted unwanted attention. She removed a fruit peel from her collar and brushed off other garbage.

The male guards moved to the sides. One of them grunted and nudged Duli forward, a clear sign that she would lead the way. She took a very small step. It was enough for a few spectators in the way to move aside.

The sight before her caused Duli to gasp. Members of the Widow Brigade stood lining the aisle leading to the stage. They extended in single rows on each side, a hundred on the left facing a hundred on the right, shoulder against shoulder. Every set of eyes turned toward Duli. Most kept their faces expressionless, though a few favored her with a nod or a grin.

Every one of them was shaved clean.

Less prominent, but not unnoticeable, were the rows of veteran male warriors surrounding them. Few of the males retained any semblance of stoic indifference. The lowered eyebrows and clenched fists voiced their displeasure to Duli.

Now that Glaura's duty was done, the mother of two stepped aside from the procession. She planned to stay where she could watch the rest of the proceedings from afar.

Duli barely noticed the departure, too intent on the scene before her. She began to walk down the lines of widows. Leli Gorm stood at the near end of the line. Duli almost felt as if she were looking at a stranger. Duli wondered if her own change had been so dramatic when she was shaved to marry Geordan.

Leli interrupted her thoughts by commanding the others, "Widows! Stand at attention!"

They all snapped into a proud stance. Backs became straight, gazes locked together across the aisle, arms dropped by their sides, chests puffed up with pride.

Duli passed in awe of her sisterhood. She only wanted death while facing her husband's enemy, yet these women seemed to stand for something more. She walked with a slow pace. Duli planned to make the most of this moment before she faced the elders. She saw so many new faces, it made it hard to recognize the beardless expressions from old friends.

Shauna Horgar changed in a remarkable way. When bearded, she had always combed her fair hair straight back, but left her beard braided in six tails. Now that her beard was gone, she braided her top hair into six tails. Duli caught a smile from her golden eyes.

Duli easily recognized Katy Dornan. The woman who had quit Deepmug's had always left her beard short due to preparing food. Without her beard, she looked as if she shed ten years from her life. From the look in her eyes, Duli guessed that Katy felt as young as she now looked.

The leather crafter thought of how Popguv might view this show of support. She knew he had to be somewhere in the audience. Half of the women who toiled under his guild were present in the ranks of the brigade.

She passed by several unknown faces before another made her pause. The older, dark-haired dwarf had her hair in a style familiar to Duli. The brigade leader still didn't recognize the woman until she noticed the holy symbols of Nandorrin adorning her clothes. Herothe Darkhair, priestess of the God of Fire, served in her ranks. Duli contemplated how much that act probably insulted the other priests.

Duli found Fosha Spindlebur at the end of the line. The elder made sure to position herself closest to the stage to be witness to whatever transpired there. Duli gave her the slightest of nods, which she returned. Duli felt any words would be a waste of breath. In all likelihood she would no longer be able to serve as their leader. The Clan-Sires would do whatever they wanted to Duli, but at least Fosha would still be there to lead these women.

The stairs leading up to the stage loomed before her like a gallows; and yet, somewhere down the line of widows she had lost her nervousness. The resolve of all those women to stand beside Duli and support her had buoyed her spirit. She tried to swallow back any remaining qualms in order to face her judgment in true dwarf fashion. Duli ascended the stairs.

The council viewed her, but they stared from benches on the other side of the stage. The only figure that awaited her on the stage was the most prominent dwarf in the whole city.

Duli wouldn't have to endure the council; she would answer to the king.

*　　　*　　　*　　　*　　　*

King Harvagot Stonebrow's titles also included Grand-Sire. His clan had been the backbone of Tok-Maurron nobility for centuries. All the Clan-Sires bowed to his views. In dwarven society, a king stood as close to the gods as the head priests. It was believed that all their judgments came from divinity. The kings' seat of power was so secure, that only major indiscretions against the church or conquest from a more powerful clan, likely an outside one, could end the line.

Duli did not know much at all about the Grand-Sire. He kept most of his counsel within the hierarchies of the Clan-Sires. King Harvagot rarely made idle conversation with anyone who wasn't nobility, high-ranked officers, or head priests, though he was known to attend services in every church of the city in turn. He raised two grown children, though the queen died sometime before Duli arrived.

"As my king requests, here I am," she said, kneeling and bowing her head as she did so.

She let slip amusement in her eyes as her gaze happened to catch sight of Boreval. Duli noted that her amiable presentation seemed to sting at the Clan-Sire. His eyes narrowed and his fist clenched around the top of his mace/cane. Apparently, Boreval might have been hoping that Duli would do something foolish before the king.

The king looked down on her, face as stoic as any dwarf would expect, and spoke. "Rise."

Duli stood straight and tall before him. She couldn't stop one of her hands from shaking, so she clasped them behind her back. She kept her gaze locked ahead. Not wanting to appear too arrogant, she avoided looking directly into his eyes by focusing on his beard.

"The first time your name was made known to me was when you stole a gun from the Armory and killed two human scouts outside the warrens. An impressive feat, even though you placed the clan at risk by stealing the musket."

King Harvagot continued, directing his words equally between Duli and the audience. "In many decades of sporadic fighting with the Tariykans, they have never copied our technology and used it against us. Our weapons continue to put their armor to shame. At a distance, we can outfight any Tariykan force with ease."

He leaned towards Duli, dropping his voice slightly. "You understand the mistake you made when you took that gun to the surface?"

Duli nodded her agreement, though she believed her regrets differed from what the king presumed.

"I recall you were allowed to work on the muskets? Sargas spoke little of it. Knowing him, I can only assume you weren't unskilled at handling them?"

At his pause, Duli answered. "I used to help Geordan maintain his gun. I wanted to make sure it was clean and working, so that he would always come home."

Duli barely kept her voice from catching on that last statement. King Harvagot kept silent. Assuming that he waited for more, Duli continued, "Sargas handled Geordan's gun after his death. Gun Hand seemed pleased by my knowledge of muskets. He allowed me to work on the others, and for my part I can say I did not disappoint him with my efforts." A moment later, she admitted, "Just my judgments."

Duli glanced around and spotted Sargas in the audience. The old dwarf said nothing. He sat quietly, arms crossed, waiting to hear what the king would say.

The Grand-Sire turned away from her. He approached one side of the stage and called out to a dwarf sitting nearby. "General Guffan, you were in command that day when Duli's widows faced battle near the Steelfoot clan? Tell me how they conducted themselves."

General Guffan stretched to his full height, a posture that barely got the tip of his beard off the floor. His tone aimed to amuse the clan. "They were quite a raggedy lot. Armor and weapons all mismatched. A little slow to fall into line. Those widows mostly had hand-to-hand weapons but stood there like idiots hoping to make a difference against veteran human warriors."

King Harvagot continued to keep his face neutral, even though a few dwarves were chuckling at Guffan's words. "They did not show disorder when the Tariykans launched attacks at them? Did they follow all your orders or disobey?"

General Guffan paused to remember that day. "Can't say I recall Duli disobeying orders. The widows left when I told them to leave. As far as during the bombardment..." He turned to face those behind him, trying to incite laughter from the crowd, "They were too dumb to run."

Merriment came from those closest to him. Several of those dwarves were longtime friends of the general. They subsided as the king stated, "That is all," and turned back to Duli.

"How did you and your women feel during the battle?"

Duli had to pull her eyes away from the glare she offered Guffan. "Folks may not admit it, but I dare the person to come forward who says he felt nay fear during his first fight. We resolved to stand firm and win." Duli realized she could throw Guffan's amusement back in his face. "It is true; we weren't allowed to have muskets. The only reason offered was, 'That's the way our people have always done it.' Nevertheless, we stood there and endured the humans' best shots."

The brigade leader turned to face the widows. "Widows! Raise your hand if you shed blood during that fight."

Katy Dornan brought her arm up, followed by a few others.

Duli swiveled back to the king, letting her words and eyes express her feelings to the whole assembly. "Nay self-respecting dwarf turns and runs at a little bloodshed. We stood there with the grit to go hand-to-hand with the Tariykans once they got up the courage to walk over to us." Looking into the king's impassive eyes, she stated, "And when asked to leave the line and guard the wagons, we marched in formation and followed orders."

The king was staring hard at Duli, but she couldn't decipher what he hoped to find. She was about to speak again, but he held up a hand to silence her. Moments passed as the king looked her up and down.

"There has been a lot of unrest in the city; not just in the last few days."

The cavern construction amplified even the slightest words on stage. Despite such masterful work, dwarves in the back had trouble hearing the king's low-spoken words.

"Your name has been attached to both praise and insult more than any other citizen in recent history. You've challenged our culture. At a time when several dwarf clans take refuge among us, fleeing collapsed homes, we should be united in every effort against Tariyka. Your women seem to take a different definition of events. By your claims, we must abandon parts of our heritage in order to strengthen ourselves as a race. Such changes can never be reversed once they are embraced."

The Grand-Sire turned his back to Duli, sending a signal that he was not inviting any conversation from her yet. The brow supporting the crown wrinkled slightly. The king turned his head towards the many depictions of dwarven gods on the walls. If the gods chose to talk to him, it happened silently. He spent time lingering on each one.

"Your victory on your wager was nay small task." He turned to face her. "Boreval picked his champions well. You bested our finest warriors. Their shame is your pride. The effort was notable enough, yet you also invented a new way to use our guns. Sargas showed me the remains of your targets. I imagined how such carnage would shake the resolve of any human witnesses."

King Harvagot walked to within a foot of Duli. His visage dominated her vision. His wise eyes held hers captive. "Muskets carry many responsibilities on the shoulders of those who would bear them. First of all, we must never let the secrets of the black powder into the hands of our enemies. The destruction of the muskets is preferable to their capture, even if doing so prevents your escape. The bearer of such weapons also dons the responsibility of the clans' safety. If you carry it, you must be trained and ready to use it to defend others. Armed dwarves step up to any challenge for the good of their city. Death is our companion and one day it will claim us. If a losing battle seems imminent, we leave the guns safely behind and die by swords if required."

The Grand-Sire took her shoulder and turned her to face the line of widows. His words were directed at Duli and her followers. "You dare ask to be the men's equals? Do you have the courage to watch each other bleed into the ground for your cause? Will you hold your ground despite nightmares raining upon you, knowing that if you turn around you will doom those helpless folks who shelter behind you? Can you treat a musket with more reverence than your own life? Can you choose to leave it safely behind when going out to face long odds? Can you be molded into armor without betraying us as the weak link?"

When he finished, the silence ruling the chamber was so absolute that Duli almost hesitated in her reply. "We can and we will."

The old dwarf kept his stern tone. "Will you take an oath to that effect?"

Duli already knew the answer. She happened to catch a glance of Popguv's wrinkled face, watching with wordless shock. If there had been any doubt in her mind, it would have been erased upon seeing the old guildmaster and knowing what he represented to these women. Boreval and Guffan were likewise reacting with concern about the direction the king's words were taking.

"Aye, I'll swear. We all will."

The king strode past Duli. She turned so her gaze could follow him, once again putting the widows behind her. The Grand-Sire called out for a musket. Sargas rose from his seat. Boreval showed more surprise when his assistant revealed a shrouded gun, placed next to the platform. Sargas reverently handed it to the king, who then turned and approached Duli.

She recognized Geordan's gun.

Duli caught the glint of a smile in Sargas' good eye before the aging veteran returned to his seat. A rumble of conversations erupting to the far ends of the cavern broke the silence. Many in Tok-Maurron openly voiced discontent with the king's apparent intentions.

"I will have silence for the oath!" He roared. His tone softened somewhat, from steel to hard stone, as he fixed eyes on Duli. "Place your hands upon this weapon and repeat after me. Let your words ring with truth and conviction over every ear in this hall. Let all your followers who would follow this course repeat the same, but only if they can hold strong their course.

"I swear fealty to Tok-Maurron: its rulers, families and allies."

It was the oath all young men of the city took when given their gun. King Harvagot rarely performed the rite.

Duli repeated, "I swear fealty to Tok-Maurron: its rulers, families and allies."

The widows echoed her, *"I swear fealty to Tok-Maurron: its rulers, families and allies!"*

"I swear to put the concerns of clan, family, and the secrets of the black powder above the concerns for my own life."

"I swear to put the concerns…" Duli repeated the king's words. With each time the widows voiced their part, their words became more in unison and gained strength.

"…above the concerns for my own life," almost two hundred female voices finished.

"I swear to give my honor, strength, love and life to the call of Tok-Maurron."

"I swear to give my honor, strength, love and life to the call of Tok-Maurron!"

"I swear to uphold and defend the freedom and lives of my fellows."

"I swear to uphold and defend the freedom and lives of my fellows!"

"This all I swear and bind my fate to my city, in witness of clan, king and gods."

"This all I swear and bind my fate to my city, in witness of clan, king and gods!"

King Harvagot Stonebrow set one hand on her shoulder. He whispered, "Never find opportunity to shame me for the chance I grant you this day. The clan will be watching your every move. When your warriors meet the Tariykans, you will need to outperform the veterans before they give you any respect. You won't see me being so generous if you cause me embarrassment. Turn, soldier of Tok-Maurron, and take your shot."

As per the normal ritual, Duli turned to face the gathered crowd. The widows were all staring at her with excitement clear in their eyes. Duli raised the musket towards the high ceiling. There was no chance of a ricochet; the musket was only loaded with powder for this rite. She cocked the hammer to full and let loose a thundering announcement with the weapon.

The echo eventually surrendered to scattered applause, disapproving grunts, gossip and muttered curses. Duli looked down upon her widows and gave them a rewarding grin. She brandished Geordan's old gun high above her head with pride.

Her gun.

CHAPTER 22

Duli watched as the last brigade member exited the Armory. Sargas stood beside her, his eye on all the untouched targets sitting on the range.

"I don't think a single one suffered any worse than a grazed finger," he remarked.

Duli offered a slight grin. She recalled when Sargas had taught her how to load and shoot a musket. "Don't tell them that my first shot completely missed. I have to thank you for showing them how to load properly. You make a better teacher than I." Her green eyes glanced over to him. "I don't recall you being as strict with me. You didn't raise your voice at all back then."

Sargas nodded. "Well, back then it was a fun diversion for both of us. I wasn't expecting that you'd ever be going into combat."

Duli nodded and was about to take her leave when he added. "I heard a rumor. How come they aren't going to be practicing on these targets? How did you, of all people, convince Boreval to let all these women take their guns to the surface to train?"

She shrugged her shoulders, "My charm?"

At his amused huff, Duli added, "They will have fewer eyes on them if they practice on the surface. It comes at a cost. Boreval agreed that a few ram riders will be nearby at all times to keep a watch over everything. Actually, I think I put the idea into his head."

She glanced at Sargas. He stared through her with his good eye. "You're up to something again. When did you become so devious?"

Duli gave a tired sigh, "When I had to be."

* * * * *

The Widow Brigade relaxed in a small valley, surrounded by trees. The peaks of the Molberus range rose through a sparse veil of clouds north of them. Several tarp-covered objects sat in much closer vicinity. The widows occasionally glanced at the shrouds, shrugged, and continued their conversations. Under Fosha's orders, none had their guns loaded. They spent a long time milling about, waiting for the unknown, while Fosha and Leli remained tight-lipped.

Duli appeared over one rim of the valley, pulling a small cart. Voices raised in cheer, only to diminish a moment later when the widows saw who accompanied her. The three male dwarves walking in stride with their leader were easily recognizable, in reputation if not personally. Two were Duli's challengers during the wager. Murglor "Half-Foot" limped along using a staff. Horace Smokebore displayed a jovial mood as he cradled a mug in one arm. The third, Soran Spindlebur, was a cousin of Fosha. Despite this close relation, he knew few friends among the widows. Soran had seen warrior days, though now he bore the notoriety of teaching crafts in the Mennurdan Guild. Some of the widows apprenticed under his supervision.

As the females threw smoldering glances at the men, Soran shouted to one of his apprentices. "Fair morn, Shauna! When you finally give up on being able to fire straight I have a number of orders for more chairs."

Shauna Horgar's lips tightened around a restrained reply.

Murglor turned and spoke to Soran, his words carrying down to most of the widows. "What if her chair legs aren't any straighter than her aim?"

At Horace's chuckle, Soran replied, "I have orders for firewood too."

The widows obviously didn't share in the men's mirth. Several glanced at Duli, certain she would admonish the rudeness, but their leader kept a neutral face. Duli led the men to a shaded spot near one end of the line of widows.

Murglor retained respect among the females due to his past reputation. He quickly started losing it as he opened up another round of insults. "Are we going to sit here until they hit something or they give up?"

"Either way, we'll be here at least a day waiting for a shot to hit anything more than a slow-moving hill," commented Horace.

"I say once those pale cheeks show sunburn we can go," added Soran. A couple of women unconsciously rubbed at their shaven chins.

Duli set up the cart near the men as Fosha approached the group. The elder turned to Duli. "Why did you bring Bandit?"

"I didn't," Duli started to say, until she noticed the wolf padding through the grass.

160

The wolf picked his own shady spot near Duli. She sighed and told Fosha, "Two years it took for him to loosen the grate I placed over the room vent! I keep trying to block it with other things, but he is persistent."

Duli managed to find a leather treat for the wolf to chew apart, while Fosha ordered the widows to load their guns. "Once loaded, bring it up to your shoulders like I showed you. I want to be able to see when you are all ready."

The widows did as ordered, suffering a few insulting comments from the men. One female happened to fumble her powder horn, spilling too much into the grass.

"Now she has a plan!" Horace exclaimed, "Dump piles of powder into the grass and ignite it when the humans walk by it!"

Another widow accidentally dropped several balls of shot.

Soran laughed, "A Tariykan has a better chance of walking into their shot by stepping on it rather than them firing it."

Katy became so nervous listening to their banter, she almost forgot the ramrod shoved into her barrel. She sheepishly lowered the weapon from her shoulder and pulled it free. The movement didn't go unnoticed.

"Nay, put that back in!" Murglor instructed, "If the rod happens to spin sideways in midair, it will have a better chance of hitting the target."

The widows' ears were burning red, yet not one word came to their defense from any of their officers. Most of the widows had the muskets cradled against their shoulders as Shauna turned a glare towards the men. "Who asked you to come here and use us for your entertainment?"

To her surprise, and the shock of the entire line of muskets, Horace pointed at Duli. "She did! Even offered us drinks."

A couple hundred sets of eyes swiveled upon their leader. If Duli felt the attention, she didn't let it stop her from unpacking the cart. The widows saw her break out a cask, then proceed to fill the men's mugs.

Shauna was only offered the back view of Duli's head as the latter responded, "Is there a problem?"

The fair-haired dwarf huffed, "I'll say there is. I thought we moved out of the Armory to avoid ridicule as we practiced."

Duli casually filled each mug to the brim. Shauna was forced to keep stoic silence as her leader and friend refused to rush a response. When Duli turned around, she marched with a determined stride towards the end of the widows' line.

"Boreval insisted that you be watched when on the surface. These are only three men. In the Armory, you would be ridiculed by many more that pass by."

Duli shifted slightly, making sure she was visible to all. Bandit padded over to her side, settling on the grass with his leather toy.

She continued, talking past Shauna. "Most of you were not at the first battle that gave us scars. The dwarf men may ridicule you but the humans are aiming to kill you. If you can't load and shoot a gun under the pressure of your clan's taunts, what will it take to get you to stand bravely when arrows and rocks are raining on you?

"When we fight them up close, hand-to-hand, we will be on even ground. Our advantage lies in making sure we inflict the most damage with our armor-rending weapons before that gap closes. You will be loading and firing even as the enemy retaliates. Expect magical tricks from their wizards. Expect some form of attacks to come at you while you're frantically trying to load for your next shot. Learn to endure."

Duli stepped behind the line of widows, Bandit following once again.

"By the way, you should thank these men for designing your targets."

"What?" Shauna blurted.

As one, the widows turned to face the shrouded shapes. Duli gave a signal, followed by Leli yanking a rope tied to the tarps. As each became uncovered, the women found themselves reading a deluge of insults painted on the human silhouettes.

"Fill dwarven bellies, not human ones"

"Females are a waste of good powder"

"Use meat, not shot, and aim for the stew pot"

"Beardless dwarves aim here"

Neither Duli nor any of her officers even had to give the order to fire. Shauna's musket snapped to eye level. The fair-haired dwarf yelled, "Rip them to pieces," as she fired a round into a target. A chorus of musket blasts followed.

The women reloaded and fired on their own, as insults streamed from the three male drinkers on the hill. At times Fosha and Leli looked to Duli to question if the men should be rebuked, or what orders they should give to the women firing the volleys.

Duli remained silent, a hint of a smile on her lips.

*   *   *   *   *

A few weeks later, the widows were gathered in the same valley. The daily ritual was the same. Duli led three men into the valley and served drinks while the women worked on marching and shooting skills, as well as cleaning and care of the muskets. Although they

162

didn't always have the same men watching over them, this day it was the three who had seen them on their first day: Horace, Murglor, and Soran.

"Where are the targets?" Katy asked, looking at the empty meadow.

Murglor overheard the comment and shouted out, "You're all getting too cocky with pieces of wood that can't move. Ever see a human charging across a field?"

"Or shoot a fast-moving deer for dinner?" Horace added.

At the edge of her vision, Duli noted Shauna staring in her direction. She finished pouring a mug for Soran before turning towards her warriors. Duli and Bandit walked down to the row of women. "Are you ready for a tougher challenge?"

At some mumbled replies, Duli barked loud enough to startle the wolf. "I said, do you want a challenge?"

"Aye!" The brigade responded.

"Alright Fosha, start it up!"

Off to the side, Fosha and Leli sent a pair of molber rams into motion. The rams were harnessed to a rope, which traveled through a gear system. On the field in front of the widows, they saw the rope rise up as it went taut. A rumbling noise came from behind a barricade. Moments later, a wagon rolled out with a large, circular target mounted on it. The target was marked with rings, and in the center was tied a yellow cloth.

The wagon had a sign painted on it, saying: *Crafted like a musket – meant to be untouched by women*

Once again, Shauna didn't wait for anyone else. She gave her own command to fire as she put a hole through the target. The rest of the muskets tried to line up with the moving wagon and echoed her.

As the hole-riddled wagon stopped at the end of the line, one of the widows grumbled as she lowered her smoking musket. As she rubbed her shoulder, Horace got to his feet with a roar. "Haven't you learned to seat a musket properly by now? Put it in the wrong place and it will break your collar bone!"

Duli watched as the veteran stomped down and grabbed the musket from the widow. "You have to set it against your shoulder properly, like so…"

As Horace proceeded to instruct the woman, Duli hid a grin.

* * * * *

Glaura only had a vague idea of where the outdoor training range was, but she could tell she was getting close once she heard scattered gunfire. She relied on Tormero's directions, since he witnessed some of the widows' training. Glaura spotted a hill where Duli mingled with some other dwarves. Smoke from expended muskets rose from the other side.

Bandit noticed her first. The wolf padded over in greeting, sniffing her offered hands and accepting petting. Bandit never gave her problems; it knew her closeness to Duli. The wolf paced her as she walked up the hill and waited for Duli's attention.

"Glaura! What a surprise!"

Duli gave her a hug. Behind Duli, Glaura watched as the widows mingled in the valley. Some were firing at targets under Horace's supervision. A few others were getting musket tips from a ram rider. Sargas observed the rest as he chatted with Herothe Darkhair.

"Did you bring the kids with you?" Duli smiled, "I haven't seen them in too long!"

Glaura shook her head. "Nay, Tormero is watching them. They would like a visit from 'Aunt Duli,' but you know how I feel about muskets. I don't want little Feena getting ideas at her age."

"Well, come with me and have a drink."

Duli poured ale for her, though Duli continued to drink water. Glaura asked, "How is the training going?"

"Very well, I'd say. Their aim is good. It's hard to find anything verbal to shake their concentration. The men here have taught much about the muskets."

"I find that surprising."

Duli nodded, "Well, they weren't so friendly at first. As they watched the widows train and get better, they couldn't help but impart some of their own advice. At one point, they just seemed to take over teaching the women a few things about shooting."

The brigade leader gave a conspiring wink, "I didn't really know a whole lot about guns, so I'm glad Horace and the others started giving us some respect and some lessons."

Glaura looked over the ranks of women and guns. "How did you get these veterans out here to help?"

Duli smirked, "Boreval ordered it." The widow's attention was pulled in another direction. "Ooh, pardon me. I have to prepare something."

Glaura looked back to see what distracted Duli. She noticed a patrol of ram riders approaching in the distance. The standard of General Guffan Stonebrow waved from atop one of the riders.

Duli was in the valley, organizing her widows into a long line. Even the priestess Herothe ran into place and hefted a musket. Fosha and Leli were exceptions, running over to

164

a pair of rams hooked by rope to a gear system. Horace, Sargas, and the few other men went back to the ale on the hill.

Glaura overheard Horace commenting to Sargas, "I think Katy is finally listening to my advice. She holds the musket with more confidence."

Sargas responded, "They shoot better than most of the younger warriors."

As the ram rider patrol was nearly to the hill, Glaura heard Duli give the command to fire.

"Empty those muskets! Put a shot into the ground or the sky, but make sure you're musket is unloaded."

A cloud of smoke came up from the valley as the guns fired. General Guffan's riders pulled to a stop alongside the other males.

"Musket butts on the ground. Be in a position to load but don't start yet." Duli glanced up the hill. "Good day, General. How are you?"

General Guffan snorted, "I'll be better if I know these muskets won't fall into the hands of the first humans they meet. Have they learned to shoot yet?"

"We were just about to try something new. Stay and watch."

Duli turned to address the line of widows. "When I start counting, but not before, I want you to load as fast as you can. By the time I count thirty, we're going to set loose the wagon. When that happens, you better be ready to put a hole in the center. Everyone understand?"

They nodded their heads. Duli started counting, "One. Two. Three…"

The widows raised leather bags to their barrels, using the nozzles at the ends to drop pre-measured amounts into the gun. They had Duli and Herothe to thank for fitting hundreds of leather bags in a similar fashion to what Duli had used in her shooting contest. The bags caused less fuss than messing with powder horns. Lead shot was dropped in shortly after. Glaura watched the widows reload at a fast pace.

"Fifteen. Sixteen…"

Up and down the line, ramrods packed the deadly loads into place. Musket butts were swinging upwards as the faster widows prepared to prime the pans with twists from the powder bags.

"Twenty-four. Twenty-five…Release the wagon! Go! Go!"

Shauna was once again the first shooter in line. As the wagon bounded out early, the fair-haired dwarf snapped the hammer back to full cock. She brought it up to her shoulder and fired. Not a single widow had been too slow to meet the rolling target. General Guffan and the other males watched as smoke blossomed down the entire length of muskets.

Glaura held her hands over her ears until the shooting ceased. She examined the target as the wagon slowed to a stop. The center of the target was one rough hole. The bright cloth no longer existed.

Duli looked up to the general in apology, "I'm still working on them. Some missed by a bit."

Glaura knew Duli well enough to know when she was masking her humor. The general's stunned remark was simply, "Decent shooting."

Guffan turned his riders away to continue their patrol, while Duli turned over the training to her officers. Glaura watched her friend walk up the hill.

They were out of earshot of the other males when Glaura said, "I didn't think Boreval was the kind of person to lend you some trainers."

Duli winked, "Not knowingly."

* * * * *

A couple days later, the widows were continuing their training in the valley. A few anxious ram riders rode up with news. Several groups of Tariykan scouts had been spotted near Tok-Maurron. The widows were told to get their muskets and themselves into the city for safety. Boreval made sure the widows couldn't train on the surface when he heard about the invaders. Another week went by as Duli resumed training in the Armory and Lower City. She noted how the widows were continuously distracted and on edge. Every day brought reports of skirmishes on the surface. They all wondered when they would be called upon to fight.

CHAPTER 23

Duli walked in front of the ranks of widows standing idle in Lower City. They occupied an open space not far from Hearthden. Most stood in line for practice, but a few stragglers still approached. She overheard one conversation as Katy rushed to her spot with a flushed look about her face.

Shauna spoke to her, "What happened? You look like you got steamed instead of the food."

"Loram, curse his brew!" Katy muttered, loud enough for most to hear. "He didn't want me to come down here. Says I should be getting food and drink ready for the fighting men who will be coming back from the surface. Says I got nay business wasting time with a musket. Well, guess what I told him? I said, 'Loram, I'm going to be fighting sooner or later, and you better have food and drink ready for me once I get back!' That set a fire to his beard."

Shauna let out a hearty laugh, along with the other widows. "I wish I was there to see that!"

Leli and Fosha stood apart, waiting to give out orders. Herothe Darkhair, priestess of Nandorrin who had recently been promoted to officer, arrived at their side. As Duli rejoined them, Leli leaned over and confided to her fellow officers, "I can't help but wonder when or if we'll get our chance."

Fosha replied, "I wouldn't worry about it. Whether or not we face them in battle, we've already accomplished much. Where once stood widows who would be trying to flee these halls if invaded, now we have warriors waiting to take aim with their muskets."

Duli looked upon the widows. She still couldn't believe how the course of her life swept her in a direction she would never have thought possible. Aware of the lingering silence as the last of the dwarves entered formation, Duli spoke to her officers.

"Let's continue their melee training. We'll have them pair up…"

Duli's voice halted as an alarm gong went off. As large as the cavern was that housed Lower City, the noise of the alarm originated in a distant antechamber. Its echoes rang with feverish intensity, quickly drowning out all other noise in Lower City as other dwarves paused to listen. It left uncertain questions on every dwarf's tongue.

Fosha glanced to one side. "That's coming from the entry to the mines."

Duli tried to look that direction, but there was no direct line of sight to it. Merchant carts, stone structures and the mass of people blocked her view.

Herothe spoke, "They may have run into a pocket of bad air or an underground orc lair. Somehow, the intensity of that ringing is worse than I've ever heard."

Fosha confirmed it, "I've never heard the alarm ring so forcefully and urgently."

Duli turned to the other officers. "Make sure everyone is here, but keep them formed up and ready for anything. I'll go see what's happening."

Duli rushed through throngs of dwarves lingering about uncertainly. Behind her, she heard Fosha calling out orders to the brigade. Farther along, she heard mothers calling their children near or others questioning the source of the alarm. The urgent hammering of the gong was matched by Duli's steps as she raced closer. She followed the curve of Lower City's cavern wall until coming through a narrowed portion, into a smaller though still large cavern.

A mass of confusion greeted Duli. A clamor of dwarves swarmed around the tunnel leading to the mines beneath Tok-Maurron. This portion of Lower City remained smoky, from the numerous forges and other devices used to work the ore from the mines. She saw a few miners, identified by their telltale gray outfits. They staggered from the cavern, suffering from wounds, supported by their fellows. The redness of spilled blood stood out against their soot-stained clothing. Two dwarves bore a companion on a makeshift stretcher. The wounded dwarf had an arrow in him!

A voice cried out, catching her attention. "Humans are in the mines! We're being invaded from below!"

Duli's mind reeled with confusion, *"Below? How could they attack us from our mines?"*

She saw a few armed dwarves taking up posts where the tunnel entered Lower City, but they were a scant number compared to the crafters and families running about. More wounded miners limped out of the tunnel.

Duli turned abruptly, colliding with Leli. Leli started to explain, "I thought…"

"Get the brigade over here, fast!" Duli shouted, "Tell Herothe to run ahead of the rest; she has some wounded folks who need her!"

Leli turned and sprinted away. It would take her a few minutes to run the brigade over from Hearthden. From Duli's spot, all one could see of Hearthden was a flickering glow against the cavern wall caused by the large hearthfire. Too many structures and dwarves obstructed the path. Duli turned back to the mine entry. She shouldered past a few onlookers. Once at a merchant stall, she paused. She scanned the crowd, looking for any familiar faces. With a shock, she noticed a miner leading someone unexpected out of the mines.

Glaura was limping, blood in her side. The wound didn't seem bad; regardless, it caused Duli to forget to breathe for a moment. She ran to join her friend. Glaura was lost in sorrows, the wetness from her eyes rolling onto her beard. She didn't even respond when Duli slipped under her arm and took over for the other miner. Duli ushered her friend to a low table at one of the stalls. She swept clean the table in one pass of her arm.

Laying her friend down, Duli kept a hand in hers and asked, "Glaura? Speak to me. What happened?"

"They just appeared. There were...odd words hanging in the air. Cursed magic!" Sobs choked her as Duli stood by her side. "The humans stepped from the shadows...they..."

Glaura lost her focus again, shifting back towards wracking sobs. Duli glanced at the wound on her side. It looked as if it wasn't deep. Duli glanced over her shoulder. She couldn't see far, but she yelled out for Herothe anyway.

The brigade leader readjusted her grip on her friend's hand, reassuring Glaura with her presence. "What were you doing in the mines?"

Glaura took sharp breaths as she spoke, pausing often. "We visited Tormero's appraising room. Down in the mines...showing our children some raw gems...we were there, when...Oh gods, why?! The humans drew swords...my babies!"

Duli tried to make sense of the words as Glaura spoke partly to her and partly to the gods. The awful meaning dawned on Duli. Glaura wouldn't have limped out of the mines without her kids unless...

"Glaura, I'll have the widows here soon. We can go down there. If they are alive..."

Glaura shook her head, "Nay. I saw, Duli...I *saw*."

Duli didn't have to ask what Glaura saw. It was apparent in the way her friend gave herself over to the sorrows at that moment. Duli's heart went out to Glaura. She had only suffered the loss of her husband; Glaura watched her entire family die.

"Duli!?"

"Herothe! Over here!"

The Nandorrin priestess was by her side an instant later. "What happened?"

Duli showed Herothe the wound. "Humans in the mines. They attacked the miners." Duli leaned over and whispered the rest into Herothe's ear. The other widow soon understood that Glaura's sorrows were for the wounds in her heart, not the body.

The priestess pulled out a bag stuffed with healing elixirs. She glanced back at Duli. "I can handle this. The brigade is asking for you over by the mines."

Duli looked upon Glaura once more, though her friend was lost in her own sadness. She wanted to say something, yet she remembered how the reassurances of her friends did little for her in the days following Geordan's death. Unable to voice something proper, she simply offered one last squeeze of the hand before turning body and mind towards the commotion around the mines.

A stray thought entered Duli's mind unbidden. Waurel had celebrated his tenth birthday a couple months prior; Feena had celebrated her eighth. Unable to afford getting soft at the moment, Duli squelched her sadness with anger. Geordan's killers may be long gone, but these other humans remained within reach.

Duli ran around members of the Widow Brigade as she entered the large tunnel. Dust and soot hung heavy in the air, as it always did around the mines. She could feel the heat emanating from nearby forges. Wounded miners were still staggering out of the lower, branching tunnels. Frantic voices echoed from below. To one side, an aged miner was looking over a map, Sargas "Gun Hand" and General Guffan stood by him. Duli approached and got little more than a glance from any of them.

"…this branch of tunnels right here. They used some kind of magic, popped out of thin air. The spell likely followed the smaller air pipes we have running to the surface. We can only hope it was a one-way teleport spell." The miner traced the branch of tunnels to three parallel passageways. "These three are connected. Humans have been reported swarming up from all three. The rest of the shafts and tunnels seem free of danger at the moment."

General Guffan motioned to some pipes which fed past Duli and into the lower tunnels. "Can we drop the stone blocks and turn off the air flue?"

"Like if we'd hit a pocket of bad air or an orc tunnel?" The miner shook his head. "Considering their positions, they've already passed the distant blocks. One option is to drop this set of blocks and seal the tunnels here."

He pointed to a spot where several tunnels branched together. "Unfortunately, that would also cut off these other areas. We still have folks down those other branches. They would be separated from the air and trapped with the humans. The small surface pipes wouldn't be enough to circulate good air by themselves."

"Like the Steelfoot clan," Duli mused, a bit too loudly.

Sargas looked up, "What?"

She replied, "I think Shauna told me about it. She said something about the Steelfoot clan being invaded from their own tunnels when they lost their home."

"Aye," Guffan gruffly interrupted, "But none of us are losing our home today."

The general turned his attention back to the map. "If only we can delay them a bit. We'll throw something in their path to slow them until the other miners get out. Once we collapse the stone and shut off the air flow, time will slaughter them."

The miner motioned at the tunnels, "How do you hope to slow them? I have some explosives but not enough handy to drop a tunnel on them."

More wounded walked by, telling others of the 'swarms of humans' below.

"We'll send some muskets down there." Guffan replied. The general glanced up. He accidentally met Duli's eyes, yet quickly turned away. Guffan looked to the few armed guards nearby.

Duli noted his gaze and became indignant. "You've got only a dozen armed males." She turned to indicate Widow Brigade, lined up in formation outside the large tunnel. "We're ready and standing right here. Send us in; we'll handle it."

The miner scoffed, "Get back to your crafts, girl, let the men handle this."

With Guffan saying nothing, and Sargas trading glances between Duli and Guffan, Duli put herself square in the miner's vision.

"How many miners are down there?" Duli asked.

"Just over a hundred, maybe…"

The widow turned back and yelled to her officer. "Fosha, how many widows stand here?"

Fosha replied, "Two-hundred-and-sixty-seven stand ready to defend Tok-Maurron!"

Guffan seemed ready to spout another one of his rude jokes, but Sargas spoke up. "And you'll need every one of them to ensure the safety of all those miners. There are too many humans down there. A dozen aren't enough to hold back those humans; certainly not when divided among three passages."

The miner angrily replied, "I forget, Sargas, are you blind in one eye or both? These are women! They don't know which end of the gun goes toward the enemy!"

Guffan began to pace. Sargas glared at the miner but spoke to the general. "You won't be able to get enough guns down here before the humans get through the drop-block. For the gods' sake, use what you have in front of you."

General Guffan faced Duli. His eyes measured her for the span of a couple breaths before speaking. "I'll give you what you want. I'm sending you down there."

The miner started to protest. Guffan cut him off, "I've seen them shoot." The general continued before Duli could say anything. "Never thought the day would come I'd be asking you for such a task. Don't fail me."

Duli nodded to the general. She couldn't mask the enthusiasm in her eyes. She turned towards the fretting miner. "Have some of your miners ready to guide us where we need to stand. We'll give those humans a good fight."

Despite shaking his head at the madness he witnessed, the miner turned to grab two others. Duli gathered Fosha and Leli around the map. She addressed her officers, dimly aware of Sargas standing nearby watching them all with undisguised admiration.

"We'll be splitting up and taking the women down three passageways. These miners will show us where we need to go. We don't have to press the humans, just hold them back long enough for the others to escape. Once that is done, we slowly pull back and get everyone through the drop-block before they use it."

Fosha glanced back into the larger cavern forming Lower City. "Herothe should be along soon. For now, the wounded here are keeping her busy."

"Understandable," Duli nodded. "Fosha, you'll take the right side, Leli the left, I'll anchor the middle. If we get any wounded, we have to try to drag them to safety. Once the block seals the mines, death will claim anyone caught down there."

Most of Lower City had their eyes on the widows in the well-lit mine entry, scrutinizing them as they made ready for the fight. General Guffan watched even as he sent runners into the rest of the city to summon reinforcements. Sargas Bristlebeard gave a few last-minute words of advice to some of the women he helped train during his time with them. The dozen armed guards and all the dwarves working the forges stared as the widows loaded their muskets.

Duli stared beyond the staggering survivors exiting the mines. She sent her thoughts to the unseen humans below. *"You've come to my doorstep, but I've made myself ready. I'm eager to pay you back for every day spent apart from my beloved. Is there one among you who can give me what I want in return? Do you have a sword arm among you to send me to Dorvanon?"*

"Widow Brigade, ready!" Fosha yelled.

Lines assembled, muskets lifted into easy-to-carry positions, nervous hands readjusted shot pouches and a few eager widows stamped their boots as they awaited commands.

"For Tok-Maurron!" Duli shouted.

The leathercrafter-turned-leader led the brigade in the wake of the guiding miners' footsteps. They soon disappeared from the eyes of those in Lower City. The widows charged downward into smaller tunnel networks. They ran through a continuous veil of black soot. Smokeless miracle-lamps were set far apart, though some miners moved with oil lamps. The widows passed several stunned faces: wounded dwarves surprised by human invaders, finding their would-be rescuers to be beardless women.

As they ran, they thundered past a larger chamber. A miner pointed to a set of large pipes along one wall. "Those are the air flues. Once we cut them off, nay air will get to the mines." His arm turned to indicate a massive set of gears and chains on the far wall. "That is the drop-block! Once we see humans, we'll seal the tunnel. Don't be caught on the wrong side."

Duli and the rest of the widows glanced at the imposing chunk of mountain suspended over their path as they ran underneath. None proved to be shy as they passed into the narrower mines. All two-hundred-and-sixty-seven widows eagerly took their place at the forefront of Tok-Maurron's defenses.

CHAPTER 24

The miners led the widows through a maze of tunnels. Sometimes they descended ladders or mechanical lifts. Miracle-empowered sconces lit the way at regular intervals; a non-smoking, ever-burning gift from the priests. They passed many wounded, confirming their proper course deeper under the Molberus range. They asked the survivors about the distance to the humans. To the relief of the miners guiding them, they arrived at the three-passage split before the enemy.

The officers and widows traded glances as they separated down the passages. All knew some faces wouldn't be seen alive again. As planned, Fosha went right and Leli turned left, leaving Duli to spearhead the center defense. A momentary surprise greeted them as three more wounded miners stumbled into their path.

"Humans just ahead! Two lamed souls are trying to hold them while we get out."

The miners passed by, amazement in their eyes as they recognized the widows. Duli ignored them as she turned to her guide. "Where is the best place to set up and defend?"

The miner glanced down the hall. "I think right here in this hall. If you take that next turn, the tunnel becomes narrow and winding. They will be within sword range even before you can lift your muskets. From here, you have room to take shots and reload."

Duli considered the path between her and where the three passages joined. The entire length was composed of straight veins with minor turns. If forced to retreat, they had a few long tunnels they could defend behind them.

She turned back to the miner, "Go see to the safety of your people. Tell us when it's clear to retreat."

"Gods watch over you," he replied.

He promptly departed. As Duli looked back, she noted the many beardless faces looking to her. Despite the stoic visages, Duli could sense their emotions. Some hid their apprehension, others held an eagerness to prove themselves and get revenge. Over all of this, they looked to her for guidance. Duli, who still thought of herself a leather crafter, felt unqualified to be taking charge of so many lives. Yet, her own actions settled the weight of that yoke on her shoulders. She wasn't sure what to say, but a memory came to her mind. Sargas told her many tales about warfare as they fixed jammed muskets and cleaned barrels. One of those stories came back to her, inspiring her on the proper tactics for these tunnels.

"What is this mess?" She chided those closest, "All standing about, filling wall-to-wall and fighting to look over the front folks? Are you asking for a spellcaster's fire to smite through all at once?"

She grabbed the closest two, which included Shauna, and pushed them shoulder-to-shoulder against the right hand wall. "Get in pairs, like this. Touch shoulders and the right wall. Be ready and loaded."

Duli glanced at the far corner for any sign of the humans. Seeing none, she turned back to the widows. "There is barely room to fight here, much less have four dwarves squeezing wall-to-wall. The first two will fire as soon as they see a target. When that happens, they will drop left and run back to the far end of the line to reload. Everyone else takes two steps forward, taking the spot of the pair that was in front of you. The next two will fire when ready and drop back to be replaced by the next two. I believe we have enough in the line for about forty pairs. This way, we'll always have two loaded muskets aimed down this passage."

Duli moved down the line, making sure the widows in the back knew the strategy. All the widows had already loaded. A few fidgeted with their gear, but for the most part they smoothly picked partners and stood against the wall. As Duli watched the battle line take shape, she vowed to thank Sargas for some of his old war stories if she lived.

*   *   *   *   *   *

Two thunderous echoes caused the line to jump. The noise interrupted Duli's conversation with a young widow. She looked to the head of the line, even as she heard Shauna declare, "Got one!"

Duli could make out a dark form, crumpled half-hidden at the bend in the tunnel. A splash of blood on the wall marked the shot's impact after passing through the victim. The form still moved, raising an arm that was definitely human rather than dwarven. Hands reached out from the bend and pulled the victim from sight. Only the red stains on the wall and floor marked the first casualty claimed by the widows.

Duli stood motionless and dumbly stared at the spot. Her mind finally jolted her into the realization that Shauna and her partner likewise gaped down the hall. "Drop left and back! Go and load!"

She pulled Shauna out of line to get her friend moving. Her actions spurred the rest of the widows back to the continued danger. "Next two move up! Aim those muskets and claim another one!"

They didn't have to wait long. Within a few breaths, a head poked around the bend. Both widows fired. A cloud of smoke temporarily obscured their vision, though Duli believed they missed. She briefly heard the repetitive dings from a ricochet off the uneven mine wall, which thankfully didn't come back down the tunnel. It set her pulse racing even faster. The next two women stepped forward.

Her eyes stayed focused down the hall, as she wondered what the next move would be. The audacity of the next human surprised her. The human stepped out from the cover of the bend, wielding a short bow with the arrow drawn tight. He released it down the hall.

Just as quickly, he jumped back behind the bend. Only his head stuck out to witness the results of his shot. The two widows fired; both missed. The arrow arced too high and hit the ceiling.

Duli and the Tariykan came to the same realization: any bow shots would be difficult due to the low, dwarf-height ceiling. The next two widows took their place up front as the human head ducked back behind the bend. Several tense breaths went by as Duli waited to see what they would try next.

Two warriors, the biggest Duli had seen thus far, charged around the bend. They used both hands to bear large shields before them. The shields stretched wider than the humans and almost as tall. An eye-slit had been cut, allowing the shields to protect the heads while allowing some view in front of them. The shields obstructed most of the view, but as they bobbed along the dwarves could see the feet of several more humans charging behind. The shield-bearers hurried at a steady pace, trying to stay together.

One female voice spoke, "Their magic even sent those big things down the vents?"

Muskets started booming the moment they came around the bend. The widows fired fast, launching their single shots and ducking back to the rear. The shields proved to be thick: wooden center covered with metal bands. Duli watched round after round pound at them with no effect.

Luck intervened as another pair of widows readied their shot. One of the human shield-bearers banged against a support timber and it turned him and his shield sideways. Musket rounds slapped him to the ground. His shield dropped, leaving several humans exposed.

176

As the widows made room for the next pair, Duli aimed her musket at the first human attempting to recover the dropped shield. His light armor proved no match for Duli's shot. He fell on top of the shield.

The remaining shield-bearer stopped. He waited as others tried to get the second shield upright, but the widows thwarted every attempt. The widows moved fast, stepping up and firing before dropping back to reload. A number of bodies piled up around the dropped shield. Smoke from the muskets left the hallway partly obscured, but not enough to conceal the invaders.

Shauna's turn came around again. She took aim at the second shield-bearer. Since his shield rested on the ground, it left his head mostly exposed. Her shot blasted through his skull.

With both shields down, someone from the Tariykan line yelled an order in their foreign tongue. The remaining humans rushed forward. Widows kept up a steady fire. Not all the Tariykans followed through with the charge, but those who did met their death. Others ran back down the hall, seeking shelter. The thick smoke from the muskets covered the humans' retreat.

Duli knew they would come again. She grabbed the closest widows with empty muskets as they were heading back to reload. "With me, leave guns behind! Grab those shields!"

The group of seven widows ran into the smoky passage. Wounded humans were screaming just ahead of them, the sound echoing along the tunnel, only slightly muted through ears tortured by the repetition of gunshots in an enclosed area. Duli gambled that the Tariykans weren't hauling around too many of those large shields. "Once you grab one, run it back behind the lines. We don't want them using these again!"

The group of widows came under fire from bows as they reached the shields. One widow took a hit in the arm. The women quickly raised the shields for their own protection and ran back towards their line. Dry throats coughed out smoke. A few wounded Tariykans lying in the tunnel still moved. A couple of axe-wielding widows finished them off.

Once Duli resumed her spot and the other widows carried the shields to the back of the line, she looked back down the hall. It would be harder to charge over the bodies, but she suspected the Tariykans would attempt something more.

*   *   *   *   *   *

A dwarf woman ran up to Duli from behind, panting from the effort. "Fosha reports: they've started tangling with the humans. Nay problems yet."

Duli swept her arm to indicate the bodies in the hall. The dryness in her throat surprised her."We're holding strong too."

The dwarf sped away to rejoin Fosha's group. Duli sent a runner towards Leli. The runner returned to say Leli's group repelled a charge of humans.

"What was that? The light!" One of the front widows cried.

Duli turned to look down the hall. Before she could ask any questions, she watched one of the dwarven miracle-lights vanish into shadows. One moment it was lighting the smoky passage, the next there was only darkness in that area.

"Magic!" She cursed.

Another tunnel light winked out, then another. The humans' end of the tunnel became obscured by darkness. The magically-extinguished lights occurred closer and closer. The widows nervously shifted their hands and feet as their light retreated.

Duli heard movement down the tunnel: boot heels clicking stone, equipment rattling. A chill went down Duli's spine. Normally dwarves could see a good distance even without much light, but something about this magical darkness affected their vision. She suspected the humans could somehow see them just fine. As the front two widows fired shots into the darkness, Duli pulled them aside.

"Load these," she snapped, slapping paper tubes into their hands.

One asked, "Is this the scatter-shot you used in the wager?"

"Aye, remember how I demonstrated it for you. The rest of you, fire and stay here."

She did the same, firing a shot into the dark and loading from the paper tubes. Eight others loaded with Duli's scatter-shot rounds. She formed the first four widows into a line stretching across the hall. A second group of four moved into place as the light closest to their line went dim.

"Aim straight down the hall," Duli whispered. She turned to the remaining widows. "The rest of you, give ground. Run down the length of that last tunnel and reform yourselves there."

The majority of her command turned and ran down the hall. Within two breaths, another light went out. Duli's small group stood poised in the darkness. The lights at their backs barely illuminated anything.

Duli whispered, "Right after I give the command to fire, run as fast as you can back to the line and reload."

She strained her ears to listen for any sound. At the end of Duli's next breath, she heard a boot scuff against the floor.

178

"Fire!"

Nine muskets, Duli's included, briefly lit the tunnel as flames spit from the barrels. Only twenty feet away, invaders reeled from the volley. The brief scene left the impression several humans had been ready to fire bows at point-blank range. Instead, the tight formation of scatter-shot tore away limbs and shredded through bows and armor.

The widows bolted for safety. Pained cries echoed behind them as they fled into the light. Despite the disruption to the human advance, a pair of them still managed to fire arrows at the running dwarves. One arrow bounced off the metal portion of Duli's crafted armor. A second arrow pierced one of the other women in the back. She screamed and fell. The rest scooped her up with hardly a pause and snatched her weapon too.

They rounded the first bend of the tunnel. Just as quickly, they rounded another bend. As the tunnel straightened again they could see the remaining widows lined up a good distance down the hall.

Duli ushered the rest ahead. If a Tariykan arrow followed them down the tunnel, Duli would be the closest target. She thought, *Let an arrow strike me, as long as I go to my love.*

She followed the others, listening to the tunnel echoes. She could hear several boots running. It was impossible to tell if any were close behind them.

Duli's answer to that came as soon as she arrived at the first pair of loaded muskets. Both opened fire as soon as she was out of the way. Duli turned in time to see a pair of humans fall. The next two widows stepped up and sent another human staggering. The rest of the Tariykans turned and fled back to safety. Once the widows ran out of running targets, the next pair aimed their guns to finish off one of the wounded.

Once silence ruled the tunnel, Duli reloaded her musket. She started to use a solitary ball, then changed her mind and opted for more scatter-shot. She heard voices coming from down the hall, speaking in strange accents and syllables.

One of the dwarves whispered, "What if they dim the lights again?"

Duli didn't offer an answer. Without a priest, they had no defense against Tariykan mages. She thought about sending a runner to find Herothe, but she worried the priestess had enough on her mind. A couple dwarves were already helping the wounded ones depart.

One of the miners arrived, "The mines are clear. Get behind the drop block whenever you can."

Duli nodded, and he ran back towards Lower City. As she turned to glance down the hall, she noted the Tariykan magic at work again. Light after light winked out.

She whispered an order down the line, "Turn around and move back to the drop block. Move quietly. Hopefully the humans won't realize what we're doing."

The rearmost widows began to retreat. It took a minute before the line at the front moved. Duli noted the disappearance of more lights behind her.

Foreign shouts echoed from the darkness.

"Move!" Duli shouted. "Get to the intersection and we'll hand them a few volleys once we rejoin Fosha and Leli!"

They broke into a slow run. The passageway varied direction and width as they passed. Duli glanced back as she left a larger chamber, only to see shadows moving against the tunnel walls behind her. They came to the three-way intersection in time to mix with Fosha's and Leli's groups. Lagging behind, Duli and the widows closest to her slowed as the tunnels ahead became crowded. The three separate commands of widows began clogging the intersection as they all squeezed into the passage back to Lower City. Duli heard the stomping of boots approaching. She grabbed the closest widow and turned her to face the enemy.

"Katy, get ready to fire!"

Duli's voice was hoarse, and all their ears were sore, but they heard her. Katy and her partner turned and raised muskets. Humans rushed out from the last bend, barely thirty feet away. Their charge never slowed. Katy and her partner put shot through the humans at such close range that the dying Tariykans tumbled into their legs. Duli waited until the first ones fell before she fired at a third. The hail of small shot threw him backward.

"Don't step up! Keep moving down the hall."

The next two widows obeyed, firing down the passageway without moving forward from their spot. The musket blasts weren't far from Duli's head, and another ricochet bounced around the tunnel. She paid the sounds no mind as she worked to swivel her musket spike into position. It clicked into place even as another human bore down on them.

The human threw a dagger into the crowd of dwarves. The blade went over Duli's head. He brought his sword into play even as she set her feet for a thrust. Duli ducked low as she stabbed. The human's sword cut nothing except a support timber, even as Duli's spike drove into his torso. The victory proved costly: the human's weight wrenched the musket from her hands.

The remaining widows stood farther from her than the continuing charge of humans. Duli's right hand drew forth her long dagger, her left grabbed at her hatchet.

"As good a time as any to travel to Dorvanon." Duli thought as she stared down the approaching humans. *"Come forth, kill me."*

Duli planned to make them earn their victory. She predicted the next human's attack by the way he held a short, blade-tipped staff. She rolled past its thrust. Her axe ripped across his cheek, followed by a throat slash from the dagger. Her opponent fell mortally wounded.

180

Her voice spoke in a whisper as she set eyes on the next man. "Kill me."

They both swung weapons at the same time. The hatchet and sword sent sparks flying as they met. Before the human could retract his weapon for a second attack, Duli drew a cut down his swordarm. Momentum shifted to her as she attacked ferociously. The human suffered another cut to the arm, rending it useless. Hatchet and dagger brought forth more blood before he fell backward.

Duli stomped in his face as she stepped over the body. The widow locked eyes with the next Tariykan. Although he could not understand her words, she screamed her message from the depths of her heart.

"Kill me!"

Duli and the human collided as they fought. She could see the dim reflection off his blade as it slid against her shoulder. Duli simply pumped her arms repeatedly, driven by berserk anger. Neither saw the blood splotches hitting the floor between them. The human tried another swing of his sword, but close quarter combat favored Duli and her dagger. By the time they staggered apart, the human displayed weariness from many wounds. Such anger ruled Duli's emotions that she felt no wounds and didn't care whether any existed. She held her weapons wide, not noticing her right arm dipped lower than her left from the wound and the bruising from bracing her gun.

"KILL ME!"

The human could no longer threaten her. He stumbled one step, barely lifting his sword. Duli angrily chopped the hatchet across his skull. He fell aside without a sound.

Beyond him remained only one more Tariykan. This one refused to face her in close combat. He stood several steps away, fitting an arrow into his bow. At this range Duli would not be able to get to him with her weapons before he fired. If he possessed any skill, he would not miss her.

"End it! I won't move. Aim your shot well."

Even as Duli welcomed her demise, she vented a shout full of emotion. She stood unflinching, arms apart. The Tariykan bow steadied as his eyes promised death.

Thunder cracked next to Duli's head. The musket went off so close to her that Duli suffered pain and loud ringing in her ear. Seconds stretched to hours. She saw the Tariykan jerk even as he released his hold on the arrow. The arrow zipped towards her torso. Duli thought it would pierce her heart, but the path proved her wrong. She felt the arrow invade her gut. Time still moved slow as she watched the archer fall from the musket blast. Duli felt weak and her legs gave out. As she hit the ground, time resumed its normal pace. She saw Shauna standing over her with a smoking barrel.

Shauna gestured to some widows nearby. "Help me, before more come!"

Duli looked down at the arrow shaft. It protruded from her lower abdomen. Her hope of death was once again denied. She endured agony with every movement as Shauna and the others dragged her out of the tunnel. They set her on a cloak, pulling her along with more ease. Despite their care, Duli felt alone except for her pain. Her insides writhed as every movement jostled the sharp intruder. She believed Shauna spoke comforting words to her; Fosha's worried visage glanced down at her before disappearing. Everything dulled behind a fog of pain. One chant began to break through the pain, though Duli could not place the owner of the voice.

"Herothe! Summon her quickly. Herothe!"

The jarring movement ended as they set her upon the floor. Duli looked around the chamber. The familiarity of the vent flues and the large drop block pierced her recollection. Even as she looked upon the massive slab of stone, she heard a voice cry out.

"It's clear! Drop it!"

Several dwarves went to work closing the air flues. All activity paled compared to watching the massive block descend with increasing speed. The cavern shook when it slammed closed, sealing Duli's swiftest passage to Dorvanon.

CHAPTER 25

Screams echoed down cave walls. The noise pounded inside Duli's head, until she could no longer tell which screams were her own. Every breath caused the arrow to twist her guts. Keeping still brought anguish, yet every attempt to move invited torture. Duli's torment felt endless before hands touched near the wound. She flinched even as she slapped at the contact.

"Hold her!" shouted someone, but Duli could not match the voice to a face in her state of mind.

She weakly defended against the arms that restrained her. Duli cried out in pain and hopelessness as she heard more words spoken. Words meant nothing compared to the agony inside her.

"…our faith that Nandorrin cleanse your injuries and make them whole…"

Duli felt searing heat as the arrow in her gut turned to flame. Just as quickly, it disappeared. She felt a similar burn in her shoulder wound, which also faded immediately. The raging pain subsided. Gentle warmth, feeling as if snuggling near a campfire after a cold winter day, flooded through her body and washed away the pain. Duli opened her eyes.

"Herothe?

The dark-haired dwarf priestess nodded, "How do you feel? Try getting up…slowly."

Duli sat upright, noting only residual soreness in her abdomen and shoulder. The smell of gunpowder filled her nose. Black soot covered her wherever blood hadn't displaced it. How much blood was hers? Someone else's? She stuck a finger into the hole of her armor. She felt the wetness of her blood, but only a slight scar marred the skin. Duli moved her injured shoulder; stiff, but whole. She met Herothe's eyes. Duli found it remarkable that someone with Herothe's faith could channel the will of the gods. It seemed a joke that such a miracle would work so well on one who buried her faith in a grave.

She noted the concern on Herothe's features. "I'm alright. See to the others, please."

Duli could see and hear other widows suffering from wounds. Some still screamed from their soul as Duli had surely done moments ago. The sight of the fallen stone block brought her thoughts back to the moment. Miners finished turning the valves which cut all air to the mines below. Beyond that block, any humans or widows left alive would soon suffocate. As Herothe moved on, Duli turned to see Fosha kneeling beside her. The same mess of soot and blood painted years on the elder's face.

"How did they all fare?"

Fosha glanced around the widows in the room. "I know we lost a handful beyond the drop-block, all dead, but we couldn't get the bodies removed. Just about as many are dead or dying in here. I'd say just over a dozen others have smaller injuries that will be fine once the priests get to them all."

Duli recalled the number of humans claimed by her group. "Judging by how many we killed, I'd say we could have done worse."

Fosha nodded, "I got lucky. We defended the top of a sloped tunnel. By coincidence, there were barrels of miners' explosives nearby. We lit some and rolled them down to the humans. Blew the rest up as we left."

Fosha pointed towards some of the other wounded. "Leli's group suffered the worst."

Duli saw Leli kneeling between two widows: one talking, the other already still as the grave. She watched as the brigade officer comforted her friends.

"Hey," Shauna's voice grabbed Duli's attention, "I hope you weren't planning to leave this behind."

Shauna held forth Duli's musket. The spike still protruded, stained red. Duli stood and accepted it, touching the warm barrel. Shauna leaned forward and whispered, "Old Boreval will have a fit if he learned you left it where the humans could pick it up."

Duli let loose a snort. "Thank you, Shauna."

The widows' officers set about checking on their bloodied members. Herothe worked tirelessly mending the wounded. Two other priests joined her. Almost an hour passed before a dwarf messenger ran into the room.

"Captain Duli! Is Captain Duli here?"

Duli, Fosha and Leli turned stunned looks towards the approaching messenger. Fosha whispered, "Did he just call you a captain?"

The brigade leader ignored the question, waving to the messenger. "Over here."

The dwarf ran to their side, out of breath. He panted, "You are summoned with all haste to Top Plaza, at the entry gate to Staprel Gom. Have your brigade head there, but you are to run without delay. I'll show you to the spot."

184

Hoisting her musket sling higher on her shoulder, Duli asked, "Why am I heading there?"

"A war council, I know little else."

The messenger started to run regardless of whether Duli could follow. She called out as she tried to match his pace. "Who referred to me as a captain?"

"General Guffan," he replied, breaking into a sprint.

Duli hastened to catch up, throwing a disbelieving glance back at her officers. She barely heard Fosha's comment to an equally stunned Leli.

"I want to be the one to tell Popguv about this. I'd like to watch more of his hair fall out."

*   *   *   *   *   *

The messenger guided Duli to a chamber in Top Plaza. She entered and saw several high-ranked commanders of Tok-Maurron's army. King Harvagot Stonebrow sat at a table, surrounded by advisers pointing at various maps. General Guffan stood by the king's side as another dwarf delivered a report.

"...up from the pine woods. They headed straight for our main entrance. Our scouts spotted them early. By the time they even got close we had a line of shields and muskets stretched across Crosscut Trail."

As the dwarf paused, Guffan interjected, "How are they holding?"

"Well enough. We're outnumbered but we occupy the best terrain for defense. Murglor's ram riders circled around the human force. He's hitting them on the flanks and constantly moving ahead of their response."

The general nodded, "Tell them we'll have reinforcements as fast as they can march, but it may take half a candle notch."

The dwarf nodded and shouldered his way past Duli. As she stepped closer to the table, the general examined the blood splashed across her armor.

"We heard the mines were saved."

Duli nodded to Guffan. "We kept those humans on the wrong side of the drop-block. The miners got out."

The king studied her with impassive eyes, though Guffan did all the talking. "How bad are your losses?"

When Duli spoke, she noted Boreval in the back of the crowd. He didn't meet her eyes, but she would bet money he paid attention to every word. "A couple dozen dead or wounded…mostly wounded. The priests already have most of them in fighting shape."

Guffan kept a serious tone as he asked, "Do you feel they can handle another small assignment?"

She kept the grin off her face as she replied. "Of course!"

"I sent another company down to the mines to make sure the humans don't play any more tricks down there. The widows are to make their way to Ancestor's Vale so we can free up the company there. When you see Commander Mofren, tell him to get his men to the main gate and assist in that battle."

Duli recalled Ancestor's Vale. She never set hunting traps there since the rough terrain accommodated only the molber rams. The vale held the oldest entry into the passages of Tok-Maurron. The gate observed few travelers due to the uneven terrain and maze-like approach. There existed no short route between the two entrances to Tok-Maurron except through the city itself.

Guffan patiently awaited an answer. She didn't make him wait long. The widows were being sent to guard something minor in order for more males to join the fight. It wasn't what Duli had hoped, but at least it was an assignment. In dwarven traditions, any change took time.

"Thank you, we're honored."

The general dismissed her with a nod, while Boreval turned away.

* * * * * *

The widows marched out of Tok-Maurron's rear gate, emerging up into the sunlight and winds of Ancestor's Vale. Their course to the surface brought them past Commander Mofren and his men. Sentiments offered by the men, such as 'Enjoy the view, don't fall over the cliff' and 'Don't sleep through guard duty', were clear taunts to those whom the men felt were unfit to guard anything.

In the face of what the widows accomplished in the mines, such disdain was easily thrown aside. The women bore pride as a beacon; undiminished by the tongues of detractors. These men knew nothing of their feat in defending Tok-Maurron from below, but the women didn't feel the need to educate them. The widows knew their victory would soon be known all over Tok-Maurron.

186

Duli silently watched the last of the males disappear into the entry of the city. Once the widows were alone, she assigned several to ascend into the lookout portions of the battlements. The stonework defenses were not as good as the front entry, due to a lack of necessity. The trails approaching through Ancestor's Vale were steep and confusing for anyone unfamiliar with the terrain. The battlements offered a nearly unmatched view of the mountains behind Tok-Maurron. The lookouts would be able to spot any approach from below with ample warning.

Most of the widows were allowed to loaf around the beauty of that ridge. The battlements they defended had excellent cover over the lower trails. It was a perfect spot of tranquility for the widows to reflect on and chat about their recent fighting exploits. She saw Herothe pick a spot on the battlements where she could enjoy a clear view of the valley below. The priestess hadn't said anything, but Duli could tell the woman suffered more exhaustion than any of them. Miracles took their toll. Herothe pulled out a water skin and some food to replenish her strength.

She closed her eyes for a moment, enjoying the feel of the mountain winds on her face. If there was one thing Duli appreciated about her beardless condition, it was the feel of the air on her cheeks. She couldn't define the reason, since the surface world could be a scary place, lacking of the security of the dwarven tunnels. Was it something like freedom? The passage of something wild and unchained? Geordan's ghostly caress letting her know he still stood by her side?

A voice interrupted Duli's musings. "Are you proud, Duli?"

Duli glanced at Fosha. Her wish for the day would've been to die, but that was denied. However, she found her outlook bolstered by how well the women performed. Duli surprised herself with her introspection. "Aye. I'm very proud. I doubted our chances of fighting humans for the clan. We've accomplished as much as I'd ever hoped we would."

Fosha offered a grin. "That's two of us."

"I wonder how long it will take before the males accept us as equals."

"Not in our lifetime," Fosha quickly replied. At Duli's look, she added, "But it has been my honor to see more changes in a few years than I'd experienced over the rest of my life. Once the war is won they'll nay longer need us, and will surely overlook us. Until then, we can keep crafting a history to influence future generations."

As Duli silently considered Fosha's words, the elder waved a hand at Tok-Maurron. "Think on this. Those ancient dwarves who shaped the first tunnels of this city never lived to see how long their legacy would endure. Yet here we live in their accomplishment."

The leathercrafter considered those words as Fosha went to patrol the widows' position. As Duli stood there looking at the gates, she noticed some male dwarves exiting while pushing a cart. She recognized one from the mines.

She called out, "Fair day! What are you planning to do with the cart?"

The miner pointed to a covered tarp off to one side of the battlements. "There's blasting powder under those tarps. It's not safe on the surface while those humans are around. We're going to bring it into the city."

A few widows were surprised to find out they had been sitting on some crates containing explosives. They watched as the miner and his crew carefully moved the crates to the cart.

Duli asked, "Why were those out here?"

The miner pointed down the valley. "There is a rock wall just below the battlements that has a number of fractures. It's an avalanche waiting to happen; could block the main trail. The plan was to just blow it on our terms and use the gravel for some projects in the city. Better ask your company to give room. We have to take a lot of care in moving the stuff."

Widows quickly moved aside as the men set to work.

"Duuulliiiii!"

She looked around to see who was shouting her name. She spotted Shauna waving her hands from the battlements overlooking the road. From the tone of voice, her friend sounded very alarmed. Duli started to walk closer, soon breaking into a run as she noted more and more widows gathering at the edge and pointing down the vale.

Amidst the excitement of all the female voices, she heard Shauna shout, "They're coming! Nandorrin's anvil! How could they be assaulting from so many directions?"

Duli looked over the edge, her eyesight spanning the miles of Ancestor's Vale stretched out below. Widows stood packed together, shoulder-to-shoulder, sharing the view. She followed the pointing fingers to a splash of color moving slowly up the trail.

Although she couldn't make out individuals, the tightly packed rows of colors and pennants reminded her of the Tariykan army they encountered near the Steelfoot clan. Somehow human scouts, whether men or magical, discovered this entry. The dwarves stood entranced as more and more of the armored humans came into view.

"How many?" Someone voiced.

Duli tried to estimate the numbers, as difficult as that proved to be over such a distance. She counted the humans until it seemed they had as many members as the dwarves on the ridge. Soon the numbers swelled three times as many, and the humans kept marching into view. By the time the end of the line came into sight, Duli knew they were badly outnumbered.

"A thousand?" she asked Leli.

"Aye. I'm thinking you're right."

Duli glanced at the nearest widows, picking out one of the youngest ones. "Katy! Drop your musket and gear here. I need you to run to Staprel Gom. You will deliver a message."

Katy Dornan began shedding her gear next to the wall. She listened as Duli spoke. "Tell General Guffan and the king we have a thousand humans coming towards the back door of Tok-Maurron. It will take them some time to march up here, but we can't defend against a force that size. Ask them for advice. Go."

The widows continued to look at the advancing force with growing awe and dread. As Katy disappeared into the city, Duli found herself doubting the ability of her women to fight so many veteran warriors. Duli noticed Fosha and Leli standing on either side of her, watching the procession below.

"It will take them hours to ascend those rocky trails." Duli whispered. "We have time to prepare. Maybe Guffan can get help to us by then."

Fosha shook her head. "We just lost Commander Mofren because the fighting at the front is so fierce. Even taking the straightest route through Tok-Maurron, the front gate is miles away. Do we even know if they've still got other forces using magic to enter the city?"

Leli huffed, "The only reason we're here is because we already were their last resort."

Duli hid her emotions as she glanced back at the widows along the battlements. Her gaze slid back to the horde of humans marching up the vale.

Fosha put a hand on Duli's shoulder. "You know the truth of it. It's in your eyes, *Captain Duli*."

Duli stared at the elder.

"Any help we get will be too little or too late. You're in charge because you've done miracles bringing us this far. I have faith in you, and us."

CHAPTER 26

Sargas "Gun Hand" looked beyond the generals and Clan-Sires toward the widow entering the chamber. She attempted to speak to those lesser officers by the door, a look of urgency in her eyes, but she was pushed aside. Her apprehensive attempts to get someone's attention went unheeded as they discussed the fight at the Tok-Maurron's front entry. Sargas began to get an uneasy feeling. He asked himself why Duli would send a runner if everything remained fine at the rear entry.

Sargas called out, "Speak widow, what news do you bear?"

Katy replied in a wavering voice, "There are m-more humans coming up Ancestors' Vale. A…a thousand."

Several mouths suddenly went silent. The attention of everyone in the room shifted to the young woman. Sargas heard a creak of leather as King Harvagot sat forward in his chair.

Boreval responded first. "Are you sure about this? I don't think the humans have so many that they can sneak a force around us so easily. You aren't exaggerating are you?"

Katy stammered, "Well I saw…whether it's a thousand or several hundred, they still have us outnumbered."

General Guffan stared down at a map. Both Boreval and the king paused to hear his opinion. Guffan's face tilted to send his words to the king as he spoke. "I can recall Fornel's group. I might be able to get a runner to command Mofren's company back here, but they will likely be pulled from combat by that time."

While Guffan and the king conversed, Katy threw a sideways glance at Sargas. Sargas didn't know Katy well, but he helped her learn the ways of the musket during the widows' surface training. He nudged through the crowd to stand at her side.

He whispered, "What's on your mind?"

"I thought Fornel had given up the axe. Isn't he nearing a hundred and twenty?"

"More like a hundred and ten, and this morning he picked up axe and musket again because he felt nay other choice. He's heading a group of old timers, none of whom has likely fired their muskets in decades."

Gun Hand watched the expression on the young widow's face as she came to realize how desperately Tok-Maurron needed warriors. Both were drawn to a suggestion General Guffan made to King Harvagot.

"There is the option of leading them into Caravan Market. That cavern is large enough to accommodate several muskets, and we can station several good shooters on the higher levels. We can funnel them to enter through the relatively narrow West Arch. Once they charge in, we'll have muskets on the walkways and balconies overlooking the market. The widows, Fornel's group, and eventually Mofren's men can trap them there."

Boreval erupted in displeasure, "Inside Tok-Maurron? We need to hold the outer door, not turn Top Plaza into a battlefield!"

The general argued, "We can't give Duli enough reinforcements in time to hold those battlements. One way or another, they will get pushed back. This way, we can have the widows lead the humans to a narrow space in which we hold every advantage. I call it a 'weak leg' theory."

King Harvagot's low voice spoke over the volume of other chatter erupting in the room. "Describe this 'weak leg' theory." Upon hearing the king speak, all others quieted.

Guffan continued, "Imagine a wooden table – four legs. Each leg is part of the army. The enemy pushes against one of the legs. This becomes the 'weak leg', retreating back and allowing the enemy into the center. When they've overextended themselves, they now become surrounded by the other legs as we collapse the table onto them. The widows will act as the weak leg, leading the enemy into Caravan Market. From there, we'll have several avenues of attack, including the higher ground of the structures surrounding the market. Fornel, Mofren, and anyone else we can muster by then will hit them from every side."

A few other generals offered objections, but no one offered a better plan to deal with the Tariykans. Sargas listened along with the rest as the king approved Guffan's plan. He watched as Katy ran back to deliver the message to the Widows. Sargas approached a stack of muskets and powder along one wall. Resigned to the inevitable, he selected a musket and started loading it. For the first time in decades, he planned to fire at something other than target dummies.

*   *   *   *   *   *

Duli, shading her eyes from the sun, observed the work of the other miners as she spoke to their foreman, Faudlor. "I appreciate your decision to apply the explosives this way. It will be a better use for them."

The foreman nodded. "Truthfully, I started thinking up the same plan myself when you suggested it. I can't wait to see it go off."

Katy reappeared from the entryway into the mountain, running to Duli's side. She glanced at the miners perched around the rocky wall bordering the battlements, but didn't delay to ask about them. Duli, Faudlor and Leli swarmed around Katy as she discussed Guffan's strategy. Though Duli understood the necessity of the plan, she worried about allowing the battle to reach into the city.

"But what about the merchants and families? We've already had so many wounded from the mines!" Duli puzzled.

Faudlor spit, "Let them into the city? Are we not dwarves? Have they lost all sense of heritage? You never allow the enemy to walk into your home before putting up a true fight!"

Faudlor stormed away a few steps. The old miner pulled at his beard and muttered barely intelligible curses. Duli realized his frustration, but understood the logic behind the plan. The widow mused how she might share more of the miner's disgust if Tok-Maurron felt like her home.

She turned to Leli. "Let's talk to Fosha. We'll have to plan how to make this retreat work like Guffan wants."

Leli pointed, "Fosha's trying to get our attention."

The elder signaled them from the battlements, perched on the view of the open valley below. Once they rejoined her, she pointed over the battlements at the Tariykan force. "They aren't far away, but those fools are marching up Boklor's Folly."

Duli looked down and saw the line of oversized human pennants turning off the main trail and onto a smaller system of ledges. "Boklor's Folly?"

Fosha glanced over. "Boklor was a caravan master. He made numerous trips up this vale a century ago. From down there, that route looks like the quickest and easiest way up here. Instead, it dead-ends on that ledge there."

Fosha's pointing finger indicated a ledge running forty feet below the top of the battlements. The ledge looked wide enough for six large molber rams lined up horn-to-tail, but it was sandwiched between the stone battlements and a steep drop. If a person threw a rock off that ledge, it would drop hundreds of feet before hitting the valley slope.

192

"Boklor immortalized himself in shame after taking the wrong route too many times," Fosha grinned. "The humans are making the same mistake: ignoring the more-used trail in favor of the one that looks easiest."

Leli commented, "Thank the gods for that blessing. They'll realize their mistake when they're directly under our muskets. They'll backtrack to the main trail, but only after we rain down a few volleys."

Duli stared at the lower ledge for a few breaths. "What if they can't turn back?"

The brigade leader suddenly turned and ran to the miners, leaving Fosha and Leli straining to catch up. They arrived as Duli finished chatting with Faudlor. The miner stroked his beard in thoughtfulness.

Faudlor commented, "And if it doesn't work?"

Duli shrugged. "Then we haven't lost anything. We'll be forced to retreat as Guffan planned. But if we use the explosives this way, there might be a lot less humans invading Tok-Maurron."

The miner agreed.

*   *   *   *   *   *

Most of the widows kept their heads ducked out of sight as the Tariykan force marched to the ledge under the battlements. They sat in a long line, backs against battlements which snaked and turned. Around two hundred and fifty muskets stood upright and loaded, waiting for the moment they could spit fire. Only a few were allowed to peer over the edge, giving the humans the impression of a mostly unguarded entry. It bothered them that they were ordered not to fire before a signal was given. Unbeknownst to them, this also kept them safe from Tariykan mages lobbing spells at the battlements. Thus, they sat in small groups, forbidden to peek, allowed to pray, listening to the rhythmic approach of a thousand pairs of feet.

The humans marched on safely, until arriving at the dead end cliff underneath the widows. The human officers realized they were stuck between a steep dwarven-made wall and a deadly drop. Their leader only had a moment to wonder where they took a wrong turn before a voice called out in dwarven.

"Light it!" Duli shouted.

The miners set off the large supply of explosives in the unstable rock wall beyond the end of the battlements. Both dwarves and humans clapped hands over ears as tons of earth blew outward. A wave of boulders rumbled down over the main trail, as the dwarf planners originally feared it might, then continued to pile across the lower ledge. It caught the rearmost soldiers in the Tariykan army in its path. A number of widows couldn't resist peeking over the wall. They glimpsed humans breaking ranks and running, only to find there was nowhere to run in the press of bodies. A cloud of dust blew over the battlements, obstructing their view. For several long breaths, the only sense available to them came to their ears as a thunder of rolling rocks punctuated by shrill screams. Dust clogged their noses and caused the dwarves to cough. From the sounds below, the humans endured worse. The avalanche claimed over a hundred humans, burying them or sweeping them over the dropoff.

As the dust finally allowed some visibility, Duli and her officers called for the widows to rise up and fire. Masses of forms rose up on the walls. Despite the layer of dust, sunlight sparkled off the line of musket barrels as they pointed over the wall.

Fosha called out, "Remember: mages first, then officers, then bowmen!"

Duli watched the first volley tear into the Tariykan ranks with a thunder that rivaled the avalanche. She saw Shauna diverge from Fosha's priorities for understandable reasons. The fair-haired dwarf aimed at a human officer wearing such finery, surrounded by so many banners, Duli assumed he was someone of utmost importance. The humans lost their leader when Shauna's first shot took him from his horse.

Two widows next to Duli never finished reloading; a human magic-user sent forth a ball of fire to claim their lives. She felt a blast of heat, such as a forge, against one cheek. Duli took aim at the dangerous human and fired. As her musket smoke cleared, she saw the mage twitching in a pool of blood. It was only after her shot she heard the two burning widows still screaming as they died. It sent shivers into her soul. She looked over at the two women. The thrashing, blackened forms stayed in her mind long after she turned away.

Herothe Darkhair looked over the battlements with a special gift from Nandorrin's priesthood in her hands. She lit a fuse on a breakable container, which contained a mix of black powder blessed by the God of Fire. Calling out praises to her god, she threw it into the broken ranks below. It exploded into a hundred jagged fragments among the humans. Another mage attempted to blast the wall when Herothe ducked under cover. Her priestly miracles protected her; the mage proved to be less fortunate. Three muskets followed the spell's trail of smoke back to its source and put an end to the man.

An officer commanded the Tariykan archers to form a line. They made up a minority of the human force, since the invaders hoped to storm directly into the caverns. The archers had to fire nearly straight up to arc their missiles over the wall. They inflicted casualties, but for the most part the dwarves' armor and a protective cover on the battlements saved many from harm. The archers' commander, seeing the futility, ordered his men to try directly targeting dwarves as they popped up to fire. Moments later, the commander was dead from a dwarf that paid attention to where the shouted orders originated.

The majority of the Tariykan army, the footsoldiers, awaited orders on how to proceed. The wall proved too steep to climb, and large, loose rocks blocked the trail. Officers started to direct the movements of the foot soldiers, but as each one yelled orders he was singled out by a musket and killed. The next officer would realize he was in charge after much time wasted, only to die as he started yelling directions.

A few humans in the tail end of the line started ascending the rockslide without waiting for orders. They climbed amidst half-buried bodies of their countrymen. The first few were taken by surprise as dwarf miners with picks and knives jumped out from hiding.

Leli guided several widows into place near the miners, "Don't let them get up here! Keep firing!"

A barrage of musket fire cleared the rock slide of attackers. Leli joined in, shooting at a human crawling on hands and knees to reach the top. More humans started to climb and replace them. Some struggled to get to the top while wearing heavy armor. Widows reloaded and fired, punching holes through breastplates.

"Keep it up! Load as fast as Duli! Load like you're trying to put Boreval in his place!" Leli's voice ached from the dust and all her shouting.

Eventually, humans were trying to climb over bodies. Miners kept a firm line against a few that survived the climb.

"Hold strong! Keep the line intact!"

Duli looked over the ranks of humans, then glanced back at the widows. The battle began better than she dared hope. Unfortunately, she feared her widows would prove unable to hold the battlements. Spells blasted two or three widows at a time, and some of the human arrows were hitting their marks. The colored fletching of one arrow passed uncomfortably close to her eyes. Despite every human dropped, they swarmed the lower ledge while the widows were spread thinly on the wall.

Shauna and Katy crouched side-by-side as they reloaded and fired below. They fared better than a couple nearby widows who were self-bandaging wounds. Blood from one widow ran and pooled against the stone wall at Katy's feet. Katy called to Shauna when both were priming their muskets. "They don't seem to be returning fire as much."

Shauna's dusty face peeked over the wall. She lifted her gun as she spoke. "Think they've lost most of their mages and archers. Foot soldiers are running scared down there."

Her sentence punctuated by musket fire, she dropped back to reload.

Katy jumped up. She didn't want to hover as a target too long, in case any archers were left. She managed to steady her breath and fire a shot into the mass below.

Katy commented as she began reloading. "It is as if...imagine they are fish or something in a pond. Nay, a barrel! Helplessly trapped and we just poke our muskets over and shoot them."

As both women continued, Duli crept behind them and asked, "How are you doing?"

Shauna replied as she let loose another round, "Like shooting fish in a barrel!"

Duli grinned at that and moved further down the line. Katy frowned at Shauna. "You stole my words!"

"I improved them."

Unknown time dragged by as Duli repetitively loaded and fired. Heat from the gun barrel singed her fingers whenever she touched it. She felt drenched from sweat. The battlefield became choked with smoke from both muskets and spell fires. She couldn't see from one end of the battlements to the other. Loaded again, she prepared to rise up over the wall to shoot. She pushed away the fear of burning alive or taking another arrow to the gut. Duli took her time aiming over the wall at the disorganized humans below. She took her shot and watched another human drop. She couldn't even hear the sound of her musket over the constant din.

Herothe ran through the smoke towards her. One of the priestess' sleeves showed blood. If the injury had been hers, she must have used her prayers to heal it. Herothe appeared healthy but out-of-breath when she called to Duli. Duli couldn't hear the priestess at first. Herothe leaned over and shouted into her ear.

"Leli is asking for help by the rock slide. More humans are trying to climb up."

Duli nodded and grabbed a few widows from the wall. There weren't many manning that section, but the battlements seemed safe from any human climbers. She ran them to

196

where Leli and the miners struggled against the tide of humans. A few armored humans fought hand-to-hand against the defenders. Duli reached down and swiveled the spike on her gun forward. Herothe threw some type of bright flare into the attackers, blinding them for a few seconds. Duli and her reinforcements rushed into the fight.

After a timeless stretch, Duli looked up from her bloody spike. A number of bodies lay at her feet, dwarf and human, though one more enemy charged. Her eyes watched in amazement as Bandit leapt past and tore out the human's throat. She looked at him with astonishment, "How did you get out?"

The wolf's ability to escape their locked quarters barely surprised her anymore. Duli looked around as the wolf trotted to her side. The top was clear of humans, though more attempted to scale the loose rocks.

"Cover me for a second." Leli asked, cocking her hammer back.

Duli guarded the top of the rockslide. She saw a Tariykan officer standing near the bottom of the rocks. Apparently, some humans were trying to flee, but the officer threatened them with his sword and forced them to climb instead. Whoever he was, his inferiors didn't dare try to escape past him. Leli shot the officer. Duli saw the splash of blood as the man staggered backward. Once he fell, several other humans resumed their retreat back down the trail. Some still attempted to climb and fight the dwarves, but an increasing swarm of them took to flight.

"It's over," commented Faudlor, the miner.

Duli saw him point to a few enemy soldiers remaining on the lower ledge. The miner explained their actions.

"The warriors told me about this, but I never believed them. They say that often, when a fight is over and the humans lost, some survivors will kill themselves rather than go back to their army with the shame of defeat."

It reminded Duli of that scout she saw years back, who fell on his weapon rather than be taken prisoner. Many humans were committing suicide, falling upon their own swords. Others joined the stream of countrymen running back down the trail. Duli glanced down at the rockslide. Tariykan soldiers covered the rocks, with flesh or blood. The only noises from below were the wounded groaning or crying out in their strange language. Leli's company only fired scattered shots, aimed to hurry the retreating men.

Bandit bristled at the sight of the humans down the trail, but Duli reached over and stroked his fur. He calmed down and remained by her side. She glanced over her shoulder, but what she saw weighed heavily on her heart.

Across the battlements, more widows lay on the ground than those standing. Fires burned as funeral pyres for those killed by mages. While a few widows sent shots after the enemy, many turned to the task of binding wounds and checking for survivors. Most of the brigade took its toll at the top of the rock slide, fighting off the humans who got within the range of swords. The miners, as well as a small number of widows, set out down the rock slide to finish off the wounded humans. They bore only hatred in their hearts, and the knowledge that Tok-Maurron would shelter no human prisoners. Herothe turned to the task of trying to heal all the wounded. The priestess found herself overwhelmed by the number of voices calling out for her prayers.

Duli searched among the dead and wounded until one voice called out to her. Duli and the wolf hurried to the side of a pale widow. The brigade leader struggled for a moment to remember the woman's name.

"Maura? Hang on, I'll get help."

Maura shook her head. "Nay, just stay close."

Duli heard resignation in the woman's tone. Two arrow shafts, one broken, protruded from her torso. Duli knelt by the stricken widow, noting the blood pooled under her. The red liquid ran in small streams between her and nearby bodies, making it hard to tell where one started and the others' ended. Duli saw a familiar face nearby, a widow who stood healthy yet frozen by the scene of death around her.

"Katy. Katy!" Duli repeated until the young widow broke free of her distractions. "Run for assistance. Find priests! We need healers."

Katy Dornan nodded and ran back to Tok-Maurron. As she did, Duli saw someone exiting the city. Sargas Bristlebeard walked with a pair of old warriors, surveying the battlefield.

Maura's voice drifted to her ears. "I fulfilled my promise. I can die happy."

Anxious to keep the woman alert and talking until help arrived, Duli asked, "What promise?"

The widow pointed weakly towards the ledge covered by dead humans. "I killed one for every member of my family they took from me. Even when the first arrow hit, I just snapped it in rage and kept fighting. Three deaths avenged. I wanted to thank you, Duli, for giving me that chance."

Duli whispered, "Stay with me. You will have the chance to avenge them several times more."

Maura didn't reply, but offered a slight grin. Before more could be said, Sargas stood over both of them. His good eye swept the field as he commented to Duli.

"They sent me to find out what was going on. You were supposed to retreat so we could handle them."

The brigade leader looked up at him with steel in her eyes. "We found a way to win and we chanced it. We beat them back. You can tell General Guffan the 'weak leg' plan is still an option for later."

Sargas put a comforting hand on her shoulder. "You've every right to be proud. I wouldn't have believed this if I didn't see it for myself."

Sargas walked off to inspect the field, leaving Duli to concentrate on her fallen warrior. She noted Maura's eyes drifting closed.

"You've been with us from the start." Duli recalled. "You were one of the first ones who walked with us to the Steelfoot clan and endured the catapults."

Maura's eyes fluttered wider as she recalled some image in her head. "Aye. I stood firm. I'll stay by your side as long as I can."

Duli smiled, believing the woman would make it. The pale widow's next words stole the smile away.

"Stay by my side, Jaundar. I've been so cold without you. Your warmth feels good."

A breath let out, then another. When the third breath never came, Duli knew Maura's spirit had transcended to Dorvanon. She fought the sorrows that threatened to roll down her cheeks. Duli wasn't thinking of Maura so much as she missed Geordan.

"Guide her to a better home Jaundar," Duli prayed, "And tell Geordan he will have to wait a little longer for me."

She closed the dead woman's eyes and glanced around the battlements. *So many dead, yet here I live. Gods tell me, why am I kept alive when so many others are allowed to rejoin loved ones?"*

Bandit nudged her as she knelt. Duli gave the wolf a reassuring pat, noticing human blood stains on his muzzle. She stood and surveyed the bodies. Duli would have been willing to give everything to have been one of the ones who died quickly. Looking down the trail, she caught a glance of Fosha walking to her, one arm held tight against her side.

"Are you well?"

Fosha nodded towards her arm, "A burn from a cursed spell-hurler. Herothe took most of the sting out of it."

Fosha stood beside Duli in a moment of silence. Finally, the elder spoke. "I don't know how bad we're hurt yet. I know we lost more than a half."

"I'd say more than two-thirds fallen." Duli recalled they had two-hundred-and-sixty-seven when they rushed into the mines.

"Against a thousand or so humans, a good number of them dead."

"We stopped the humans. A good number of women got their revenge. Yet, at such cost of lives." Duli sighed. "Most of the brigade sleeps in Dorvanon now."

Duli and Fosha mourned the loss of so many as they shared their bitter victory.

* * * * * *

Duli dragged her feet down Nandorrin's Halls. She wasn't certain of the hour, only that the nighttime air on the surface reeked from the sheer mass of dead. Bandit never ran out of energy. He ran circles around her. Duli barely glanced at him through half-open eyes. Of all her adventures in Tok-Maurron, this day felt the longest. The dwarven city remained fully under their control. The humans of Tariyka were thrown back down the mountains.

Upon opening the door to her unlit quarters, Bandit jumped ahead with a growl. Never had she seen such a reaction from the wolf at her door. Bandit disappeared into the dark chamber in a rush of speed. His growl silenced. Although Duli couldn't see anything other than shapes in the darkness, she felt a presence.

Duli entered her chambers, keeping one hand on the door in case she might find the need to escape. She spoke a word of command, igniting the miraculous priest-crafted sconce on her wall. As soon as the light sprang forth, Duli let a gasp escape her lips.

Glaura sat on the edge of Duli's bed. In one hand she held a scissors, in the other, a clump of her reddish-brown beard. Clumps of cut hair sat in her lap and gathered around her feet. The woman's mutilated beard hung in uneven lengths, trimmed across jagged lines. Duli could see patches of skin exposed around the chin. She guessed that Glaura's eyes looked even more tired than her own. The sorrows were upon her friend's cheeks. Bandit stayed a respectful distance, sniffing the air.

Glaura's reddened eyes looked towards Duli. "I want to join the brigade. I want a gun."

Duli closed the door behind her as she slowly approached her friend. "Glaura…"

The fist holding the scissors shook as she demanded, "I want to join! Don't I qualify?! My husband is dead! My children are gone! I have naught left to me but vengeance!"

Duli had never heard such anguish from her friend. Even as Glaura blurted her words, Duli noticed the woman's shoulders shaking. She recalled her own pain upon knowing of Geordan's death, and how Glaura came to comfort her.

200

"If that is what you seek, I won't deny you," she said, moving slowly towards her friend.

She sat by Glaura's side. The former mother sank against her, and Duli put a comforting arm around her grieving friend. The brigade leader's words were firm.

"You'll stay here, with me, tonight." Duli embraced her trembling friend, as clumps of beard hair fell to the floor. "In the morning, if you still feel the same way, we'll find a musket for you."

CHAPTER 27

"Not bad for their first few shots," Duli observed as she watched Glaura and a dozen other new widows firing muskets in the Armory's training hall.

Fosha spared a glance at her. "Not one hit the heart cloth. I'd say only one-in-three shots even hit the target dummy."

Both women watched in silence as Leli, Shauna and Gun Hand trained the new Widow Brigade members. Duli smiled, "That's as good as any of us did when starting out."

A male rushed into the Armory and raced over to the pair. "I bear summons for an urgent Council meeting."

Fosha glanced at Duli. Duli nodded towards the door, "Go ahead. We'll be fine here."

The elder woman started for the exit, but the dwarf messenger held up a hand. "The invite was for Captain Duli."

Duli and Fosha traded glances in disbelief. Fosha, the respected elder, had been a participant in council meetings on behalf of the women for over a decade. Duli was embarrassed to be receiving more attention than her.

"Why me and not Fosha?"

"It's a war council. Representatives from other dwarven cities came to discuss the news of the war with the king and his generals. More than that I can't say, but you do lead a portion of Tok-Maurron's army."

She glanced at Fosha. Rather than showing signs of embarrassment, Fosha displayed a grin. Duli began to understand why her friend showed slight amusement. Fosha had watched the women treated unfairly in council meetings all her life. Now, Duli's efforts with the brigade had brought them new recognition.

Duli looked back at the male. "Am I allowed to bring one of my officers?"

"Of course. This way."

Duli shouted to Leli. "Fosha and I are being summoned. Keep training them hard."

Glaura looked up from her new musket long enough to meet Duli's eyes. Duli wondered what effect this war council would have on the brigade, and just as importantly, her dear friend.

Hours later, Duli and Fosha exited the meeting amidst groups of Tok-Maurron officers, nobility, and foreign envoys from the Silvermug clan. The two women sought an escape from the sea of grim faces. Duli wanted a chance to speak with Fosha, without the ears of others hanging on every word. Many dwarves erupted into heated discussions just outside the chamber.

Fosha led them to a smaller, unoccupied meeting chamber. Both women slipped inside and shut the door. For a moment, neither knew what to say. Fosha wore a troubled frown, and Duli felt too dumbstruck to know what to say first.

The elder blew out a tired sigh and met Duli's eyes. "I think everyone in that room felt like a hammer smacked them on the head."

Duli nodded, "That's a fair assessment. The first hour or so, they went on for so many introductions I felt like asking how you keep from sleeping through council meetings. And then…"

At her pause, Fosha nodded. "Just the thought of all those refugees trying to repopulate Silver Mountain, I never thought I'd hear of such a thing. Imagine the effort trying to bring the legendary city back to life."

"And they asked for me by name! Fosha, this means trade caravans havè been spreading word of Boreval's embarrassing loss to other cities!"

Fosha let loose a chuckle, releasing some of her tension, as Duli recalled the shock of the moment.

The chief envoy of the Silvermugs turned to the two female faces in the chamber. "I assume on of them is Duli?"

Duli's jaw nearly dropped in surprise. How did a recently-arrived foreigner know her name? "I am Duli."

He continued speaking with equal attention between her and Tok-Maurron's council. "When we visited Tok-Barollo, the traders there brought word of Duli's inventions. We were told of how she developed new ways to quickly fire a musket in close quarters." He turned to face her squarely. "Is it true you defeated four veteran shooters by reloading almost twice as fast, and destroying every target you hit?"

Duli couldn't resist glancing at Boreval before she spoke. The bald Clan-Sire reddened in the face and looked away.

Returning her eyes to the ambassador, she replied, "Aye. The Widow Brigade briefly used the same tactics against the humans when they invaded our mines. It saved lives."

Silently, Duli simmered towards Boreval. "Let your arrogance chew on that humble pie."

The envoy spoke to Boreval. "If we could be shown this technology, it would aid us greatly against the orc-kin and minotaurs inhabiting our lower halls."

Fosha interrupted her thoughts. "It seems your victory against Boreval sent echoes all the way across the mountains. They want us to train them? *Women* training *men?*"

Duli asked. "What do you know of Silver Mountain?"

Fosha rubbed her chin. "Before the Clan Wars, it was ancestral home to much of our race. The city was once the source of half the wealth of all our people. The Silvermugs may have kept the sacred hearthfires burning for all these centuries, but the city houses more invaders than dwarves, as they said."

"And they believe my methods will help them take back the mines and lower tunnels. My mind is too numb from the shock to accept it."

Fosha paced the room for a few silent breaths. "My thoughts are heavy with their warning."

Duli sighed. "Aye, that moment when we felt the hammer hit us…"

General Guffan bragged about their victory over the humans, "Now is not the time for us to loan you troops to retake that ancient city. It's more a crypt than a city by all reports. We are in our own war, and winning. We drove the humans from our doors and will harass them all the way back to their borders!"

The Silvermug envoys shared uneasy glances. The lead envoy finally found words. "You turned aside an expedition force. Our caravan has had scouts all over this region, contacting all the local clans. Many have already joined us, now that they realize the truth. You are hopelessly outnumbered."

The Silvermug dwarves revealed a map of the nearby hills and mountains. They began to describe the numbers and size of every element of the human army. Duli and Fosha knew Tok-Maurron boasted eight thousand dwarves, but after so many years of war relatively few were capable of holding a musket.

As the envoy placed markers and pointed at the map. A sensation of doom crept into the council room. The speaker revealed humans in such large numbers that most in the room found it hard to digest. Five thousand here, ten thousand there, another fifteen thousand besieging the nearby dwarf city Tok-Dahlbon. Duli had no concept of such numbers. As he continued to rattle off human armies and locations, the weight of a death sentence settled over the assembled dwarves. *What was once just a war now loomed as the widespread slaughter of their race.*

Even as Duli's head spun, the envoy paused and addressed King Harvagot. "You said they have already used magic to send men into your mines?"

The king nodded, his eyes never leaving their focus from the markers placed on the envoy's map.

"That won't be the worst thing they send down your vents." As he continued speaking, Duli recalled that moment when Glaura stumbled, bleeding, from the mines and away from the sight of her butchered family. *"Their evil magic is a frightening contrast to their warrior code. You will find more deadly surprises appearing in the midst of your cities, your crafters, your children...while at the same time they blanket the ground above and shove into your armies. Once they find our cities, we become just a rabbit in the hole for them. They have insidious ways of smoking us out."*

Her mind returned to the present, Fosha's eyes focusing aimlessly past her. The elder spoke, "And they throw us their one, simple solution: join them. Uproot the whole clan, and abandon Tok-Maurron. Create a new home with them and clear out the deep tunnels."

Duli shook her head. "Would we really consent to that? Regroup as a race, sealing ourselves into deep tunnels to recover? Is it even possible? Crafters...Deepmug's...Staprel Gom...Hearthden...the mines, all of it left behind?"

"I guess that's up to the council and the king. Will they consent to abandoning their home? Is our only other option death?"

Duli could see the extra worry lines on Fosha's brow. She tried to offer some comfort. "I left my home for Geordan."

Fosha nodded and turned to stare at a wall. Duli was glad that her eyes didn't betray her unspoken feeling. *"Since Geordan parted, I've never felt like I've been home."*

$$*\qquad*\qquad*\qquad*\qquad*\qquad*$$

Duli opened the door of her chambers. She glanced around the main room, looking unsuccessfully for Bandit. Once again, he seemed to have snuck out. Shrugging her tired shoulders she set down her pack and proceeded inside. Duli almost had the door closed when the wolf finally darted back inside.

"Aren't you always the sneaky bandit?" She spoke, though her voice held little humor.

She reached into her pack and unwrapped some strips of dried meat. Duli absently threw them over to the wolf's bed pile before starting to undress. Bandit set upon them instantly. Duli, in contrast, took her time throwing off some of her outer garments and sitting on the bed.

She glanced at the wolf as it tore through its meal. "The Silvermug caravan is already a week away, but the Clan Sires finally announced their decision. It took them long enough, yet maybe shorter than could be expected. Some of the insults they've thrown at each other these days rivaled some of the hateful words they've used on me in the past."

Duli let her attention drift from Bandit as he chewed. She stared across the room as she spoke. "We're all leaving. The whole city is going to pick up and just start over somewhere new." She turned back to the wolf. "I guess they'll *all* get a chance to be non-clan now."

Bandit didn't spare a glance at her. He swiveled his head back and forth, trying to tackle the last strings of meat.

"The humans didn't kill me quickly enough."

Duli threw her belt to the corner where the musket stood propped against the wall. Bandit stood, sniffed around for escaped morsels, and devoured them.

"I guess one city is as good as another for me. I always meant it when I said Tok-Maurron would never be my home."

Bandit wandered close to her. Duli reached out and pet him, even as he sniffed her for more treats.

"But…Geordan is my home. His body lies in the catacombs. How can I leave that behind?"

Duli reclined on the bed and drew over a blanket. As Bandit settled on his pile beside her, she reached over and pet him more. "I'm tempted to stay here. The humans will surely kill me, but my body will lie near his."

She glanced down at a pair of molber weave slippers: a gift from Herothe for all she had done for the widows. "Of course, they all expect me to go with them. I have a position of respect. They've stood by me, and I've stood by them. To some, it's like I'm a motherly figure."

Bandit snorted, even as he relaxed under Duli's gentle hands.

Duli offered a grim smile, "I agree. I seldom act in accordance with what others want."

Bandit curled into a comfortable sleeping position. Duli turned over and did likewise. She murmured, "What shall I do?"

Duli exited her room, carrying few possessions except a rolled blanket over one shoulder. Inside, all her things were packed and ready for the long trip, but it wasn't time to leave yet. Behind her, Bandit whimpered, but she ignored him. She closed the door and locked him in. A few steps into the hallway, Duli stopped and faced her chambers. She heard sniffing noises as the wolf's muzzle tried to sneak under the door.

As she patiently listened, she began hearing scratching sounds. Moments later, she heard the claws scraping higher, where the internal mechanism kept the wolf from opening the door. It proved to be only a minor difficulty to Bandit. Duli rolled her eyes as she saw it open and the wolf step out. He immediately lowered his head upon seeing his master standing there. Duli just shrugged her shoulders.

"Well, now I know how you're getting out. My luck to be stuck with the smart one of the litter. Come on."

Together they descended, following a route that went below Lower City, into an old mine shaft. Duli held aloft one of the priests' miracle sconces, commanding its light to illuminate the way. She barely paused at the statues of the gods standing sentry in front of Tok-Maurron's burial vault. Before going far she changed her mind, turned around, and strode back to the statue of Kelor, God of Luck. She spit upon his face and set off once again into the burial vault.

Duli and Bandit covered only a short distance before spotting another light source and hearing voices. Turning a corner, she discovered Shauna and Leli in conversation.

"…since my chambers are emptied anyway." Leli said, "All my lotions and poultices are stashed in the caravan. I can't believe this is our last night in Tok-Maurron."

Both noticed Duli and greeted her. Duli asked, "Paying last respects?"

Shauna nodded towards Duli's blanket. "Sleeping here, as you are."

Then Duli saw bedrolls at the feet of both women. She looked up in surprise. "I only mentioned it to Glaura."

Leli responded first. "And she told Shauna, who told me and Fosha, and then Herothe declared she would too. I think the whole brigade is down here."

After a bit of silence, Duli commented. "None of us will sleep well tonight."

Shauna shrugged. "Yet we wouldn't spend it any other way. Last night…and who knows if any of us will ever be able to come back."

All three women said their goodbyes, and each took their own path down the catacombs. Duli soon traveled alone again, down endless corridors lined with internment headstones. She passed by two more widows praying on blankets before the tombs of their husbands. One simply nodded in greeting as she went by, the widow's downcast face attempting to hide the sorrows on her cheeks. Duli found another widow already asleep, lying next to a small internment stone decorated with children's toys: a small hammer, a molber ram doll made from wool, a leather drum. She continued making her way down the maze where Geordan's ancestors rested. Bandit followed quietly, but she paid him no mind.

Duli dropped her blanket before Geordan's vault. She kneeled upon it, feeling Bandit sit against her. The wolf offered a warm and comforting weight, helping fend off the chills of the tomb. She set aside the priests' lamp, allowing it to continue letting off its miraculous light. Her fingers lightly traced the inscription of Geordan's name. The stone stole the warmth from her fingers.

"If only I had remained 'Duli the Leatherworker', I could have stayed behind and met my ending without anyone caring." Alone in that island of light, Duli let the sorrows fall from her eyes. The enormity of her fate felt too heavy to bear with dignity. "But now, they call me Captain Duli. I gave them a revolution, and we won. I avoided Mennurdan Guild, only to be trapped in a guild of my own making."

She steadied herself with a deep breath. "I have to get used to the idea that you aren't here. It's just a grave. Your soul is either in Dorvanon, or hovering by my side."

Duli closed her eyes and touched her forehead to the cold stone. "I'm going to Silver Mountain, and I'm taking you with me. There is only room in my heart for you. I ask that you carry me as well. Be close to my spirit until the day comes where I can make Dorvanon my home."

Duli curled up against the grave. Bandit snuggled closer, and she draped an arm around him. Like Duli, the rest of the brigade spent their last night in Tok-Maurron huddled beside the burial vaults of their loved ones.

CHAPTER 28

Duli faced death. She knew her time had arrived, though the means of her demise proved unexpected.

"Damn you to the shadows!" Duli raged as she swore at her murderer. "I hope you become some flea-bitten rug someday!"

And just as quickly, the ride ended. The molber ram carrying her stepped onto flat ground, allowing the woman to right herself in the saddle. Duli glanced back at the steep cliff behind them, wondering how the ram managed to get her down that slope without falling to their deaths. Moments later, Bandit ran down and also managed to stay on his feet.

She barely recovered two breaths before another musket blast echoed in the distance. Duli turned to find the source, but could see nothing past a small ridge covered with pines. She kicked her ram into motion again. "Move it you filthy beast! We're getting closer. Just don't kill me before we get there."

The ram jumped forward, the first two hoof beats coinciding with another two gunshots. Bandit chased along beside them, making the ram nervous and hard to control. Duli cast eyes left and right as she guided her mount through trees and rock formations. The wind went silent and still, but the rotten-egg smell of the gunpowder hung in the air. She knew she wasn't far from the source. She slowed the pace of the ram as she slipped her musket free of a leather sheath. She rested the butt on her hip, fighting the urge to set the hammer all the way back. New to ram-riding as she was, there might be a good chance she'd fire off her shot accidentally during a bounce in the saddle. Bandit sniffed the air and darted off. Duli trusted his instincts enough to let him lead, though the ram needed rough, strong urging to convince it to follow the wolf.

She came upon other ram-rider scouts, and together they found the source of the noise. Several widows milled about three human bodies. A widow with a dagger made sure the humans would never get back up. Duli spotted Glaura assisting another widow to bandage a bloody arm.

Duli worried mostly for her friend's health, but she picked her words so as not to ignore the other wounded widows. "What happened? Is anyone hurt badly?"

Glaura shrugged. "By the time I caught up to the action the ugly humans were already dead. I didn't even get to fire." Duli could see Glaura's fingers gripping her new gun tightly. "Two more humans were shot back that way. As for us, two will be limping for awhile."

Duli spotted Herothe as the priestess worked to heal an arrow wound in one of the widows. She turned in the saddle, trying to search their surroundings for signs of any more enemies. At any point, a few dozen dwarf patrols were riding out at the fringes of the slow-moving caravan. Tok-Maurron's refugees slowly crawled through the uneven mountain terrain, and patrols like this one helped obscure their people from the eyes of the human scouts. She wondered if it made any difference. Due to the constant fights between dwarf and human patrols, the humans had to have figured out the city's exodus. The trail of refuse and trampled grass left by the caravan would be easy to follow. At least, the dwarven patrols could keep the humans from getting close enough to the refugees to threaten their people.

It occurred to Duli how scary the surface world could be. In the tunnels, she knew her way and any danger could only come from a few routes. On the surface, the humans could be anywhere: past a veil of trees, behind a formation of rocks or swarming at the top of the next hill. The surface world made her feel vulnerable.

It relieved Duli that Glaura remained healthy. Duli nodded towards Glaura's musket. "Still haven't been able to repay the humans yet?"

Her friend always missed the skirmishes taking place on a daily basis. Glaura shrugged, "With the numbers of fights going on every day, I'm bound to get my turn soon."

"I'll have to report back, send a runner if anything else happens." Duli turned her ram and raced back towards Tok-Maurron's caravan. She tried to quell her fears about the dangers Glaura...and the rest of her friends...faced.

A moment later, her ram once again ascended the steep incline, with the wolf racing up a different route. She locked her hands to the saddlehorn with a death grip until they arrived at the flat top. Her path took her past the debris scattered in the wake of the long train of dwarves...fruit peels, discarded containers, even a broken mining cart someone had used for their own wagon. The ram threw mud over a fallen blanket. Duli turned her head to consider it as she passed. As her eyes scanned the abandoned stuff on the trail, her mind considered the great amount of treasures left abandoned in their old city. The debris along their route may have once seemed precious to whoever brought it. Now, the stuff discarded by thousands of people in flight over rough mountains only served to leave a clear trail to those who hunted them down.

Duli resumed her journey along the trail. She ran into General Guffan riding behind another ram patrol. Duli got the general's attention, though not in a favorable way. She wrestled with her reins and cussed at her mount as it barely missed ramming the general. Once she succeeded in bringing it to a stop, she noticed the amusement on Guffan's face. Duli spoke before the general could voice any comments.

"Another small patrol. Only a handful. They hurt some of the women but nay serious wounds."

"Not the only group out there either," he responded. They heard distant gunshots in a different direction. The general turned that way as he spoke. "Their armies are hovering over us, hoping to drain the mug in one attempt and leave none of us spilling past."

As General Guffan looked towards distant hills, Duli glanced around their immediate area at nearby dwarves. Many were around, but all were far enough way that it presented a rare moment to ask the general a question in relative privacy.

Duli spoke quietly, "General, why did you make me captain?"

Guffan barely turned his head, glancing at her out of the corner of his eyes. "Why didn't you go out and attack the humans by yourself?"

"I don't understand."

"Let me put it this way, how many times did you try to take your own life?"

Duli scowled at his rudeness, until she realized he wasn't trying to insult her. His eyes harbored no accusations. She found it hard to give him an honest answer, since she wasn't sure whether or not to count the many times she acted recklessly during battle. "A few times," Duli shrugged.

He prodded her further, "And did you hope the humans would do that favor for you?"

Duli didn't deny it. She nodded truthfully.

General Guffan swept his arm across the valleys behind them, "There are plenty of chances out there for you to get your wish. You could have walked off with just a knife at any time and they would have satisfied that desire. We left Tok-Maurron to the conquerors, and yet you are here, making your way deeper into the mountains with us."

He turned his ram so he could face her directly. His voice carried in a calm manner. "So why are you leading all these women? Why not just go off right now, fight your last battle, and be done with it?"

Duli had trouble finding an answer because her mind still grappled with that same question. Did she act to avoid death out of fear? She knew it wasn't that reason. Duli looked elsewhere for an answer, and her gaze brought her to Bandit. The wolf sat beside her ram, staring up at her. He waited expectantly for any sign from her, whether it would lead them to travel, eat, or camp. Bandit waited for her, because she was his pack leader. Duli felt an answer in her heart she never allowed herself to acknowledge before.

She looked straight at the general and declared, "They are my family."

Guffan gave a satisfied nod, "My only marriage in this world has been to the army, and every major decision I make focuses on them. The army has always been my first responsibility, as your family is to you." The general turned and rode away to meet with another scout riding towards him. He offered one last statement over his shoulder to Duli. "And that is why you are captain."

Within the next couple days, Duli witnessed twelve more skirmishes between humans and either her widows or male patrols nearby. She constantly rode between the retreating patrols and the long caravan of former Tok-Maurron residents. Every time Duli caught sight of the long line of wagons and refugees, it tugged her heart. Duli left her ancestral home for a man she loved; these dwarves were leaving everything they loved behind. After a particularly harrowing day of skirmishes, the caravan train pushed the limits of feet and mounts by continuing the march long after dark. Musket shots sounded frequently during the few hours spent in rest. Dawn barely broke the next day before a messenger arrived to summon Duli to an officers' meeting. The main body of Widow Brigade, few in number compared to the rest of the army, had the benefit of camping near the center of the caravan. King Harvagot and his highest officers usually camped in the vicinity of the widows. Duli kept wondering if it was from some outdated duty to shelter the women.

Duli and Fosha happened to run into Murglor "Half-Foot" as he rode towards the meeting. The famed ram rider arrived on a tired mount, appearing as if he'd spent the whole night in the saddle. The ram's flanks displayed splatters of fresh blood.

Duli called to him as soon as they were close. "Murglor, what news? The humans are pushing us hard from so many sides it feels like we're running through a narrowing tunnel."

Murglor glanced around before he answered. "If it's a cave-in, then it's already blocked the way we came in. The humans are on our backside as thick and repulsive as cave-mites."

The ram rider offered no more information for the two widows. It didn't take long for the three to arrive at the meeting. Duli glanced around, spotting King Harvagot, Boreval Stonebrow, General Guffan, Sargas Bristlebeard and numerous other officers. One thing that made the meeting unique, several non-military leaders of Tok-Maurron attended as well. Popguv Rockhand and several other guild leaders stood to one side. Several head priests

212

stood behind the king. A number of other elders, representing miners, engineers and other citizen groups hovered at the fringe of the meeting.

General Guffan wasted no time once he saw Murglor and Duli arrive. "I'll state this as fast as I can. The humans are upon us in so many numbers, we've been desperate to find a way to break free of them. Even if Silver Mountain stood a day's ride away, we'd dare not approach it for fear of leading the humans to that refuge." Even as he finished speaking, a number of distant musket shots echoed across the hills. A couple elders fidgeted, some stared at the ground.

The general pointed ahead. "We found a means to get them off our trail. There is a pass that cuts northwest through a high ridge. From what old maps show, this pass is the only passage through these mountains for days in either direction. Last night, a team started planting explosives in the rock walls on either side of the pass. Once we get the caravan up there, we can drop a rock slide on the humans and end the pursuit. We'll be at Silver Mountain before they can find us again. There is one problem. Murglor?"

Murglor took up the cue. "Across from the pass, to the south, is another steep ridge. The ridges don't connect, so the humans couldn't use it to get around us. Unfortunately, we scouted the area last night and ran into a second human force. It might be an extension of the army behind us, but either way, they got ahead and are moving to flank us. They'll soon occupy that southern ridge. We had to take a longer trail to get back here. The ridge itself is too steep to descend. Well, a ram could do it, but not one carrying a rider. One would have to throw down ropes and climb down to get to the start of the pass."

General Guffan spoke again. "The problem is that if left unchallenged the humans will be on that southern ridge before the whole caravan has gone by. They will have an excellent position to launch volleys or drop magic on us. They may not be able to attack down the steep cliff, but with ropes and spells the humans might accomplish some assault."

A number of dwarves mumbled amongst their friends. Popguv spoke for the guild leaders. "We could try to hurry our teams faster. Some could cut loose wagons."

The king shook his head. He answered before Guffan. "The pass is too narrow, and the caravan is too long. Nay matter how much we try to hurry, the humans have the advantage of time here. They could rain death upon half the city, even as we attempt to fend off the assault from behind at the same time."

Guffan took over, "Murglor tells me the edge of that southern ridge is a strong defensive position."

"For the humans if they get there," the ram rider agreed, "But if we get a company of fighters up there first, the humans will have a hard time getting past. A small group could delay them from setting up any ambush."

Sargas offered up a hand. "What about when the caravan heads up the pass? What happens to that company?"

"That's the problem," General Guffan admitted. "As the rear of the caravan gets to the pass, our rearguard will be fighting the main force right behind us. The company holding the southern ridge will have to join us by descending ropes down a steep cliff, undoubtedly with the second human force right behind them. If they attempt it too fast, the humans will hit the caravan with volleys from above; if they move too slowly, they will be trapped by the main human force down below."

Silence reigned for a few breaths as everyone present mulled over the situation. Sargas broke the silence. "You need a group willing to risk all their lives on this task."

General Guffan scanned the faces of his commanders before admitting, "I don't expect most of them to survive. The alternative is to let the humans have the southern ridge and allow the deaths of possibly thousands of citizens."

Most of the commanders stood as still as stone, though none met the eyes of the general. One shifted his weight between feet, stopping when he realized the sound overcame all the other noises. When no one immediately answered Guffan, he continued, "We don't have time to stand and think about it. We have to act soon."

Duli looked over the numerous captains and generals of the army. None looked eager to volunteer. They traded glances, each one hoping someone else would step forward. She realized she had to make the correct choice.

"The Widow Brigade volunteers for this task," Duli stated.

Out of the corner of her eyes, she noticed Fosha's head whip around in shock. Most of the other commanders looked equally surprised.

Boreval spoke up, "I protest…"

Duli interrupted him, "You always do."

"Duli, please reconsider," Guffan said.

She turned to face the general, "You asked for volunteers, are we not allowed?"

"Heed the words from your general. I may be asking a death sentence. I can't let the women take on this duty."

Murglor inquired, "How many widows are left?"

Duli glanced to Fosha. The elder woman offered a heated glare. Fosha answered through tight lips, "Eighty-seven. Two of whom are riding in wagons due to injuries."

"I can't believe less than a hundred can hold that ridge long enough to help," Murglor informed Guffan.

Duli didn't respond at first. She took two steps forward, placing herself in front of the other company commanders. Her stance gave her an unobstructed view of Boreval and

214

Popguv. "I am *Captain* Duli, as opposed to Crafter Duli, or Hunter Duli. Likewise, these are not just 'women', they are fighters. They are the Widow Brigade. They have been fighting long before we met the humans in battle. We had to fight our own clan just to be taken seriously."

She glared at Murglor, "We are tired of males telling us what we can't do."

General Guffan thundered, "You don't need to do this to prove yourselves. You earned your muskets."

Duli noted the king nodding at Guffan's words. She replied, "This is not an attempt to prove ourselves. This is simply…the right choice." Her pointing arm swung to encompass the captains behind her. "None of these men moved to volunteer. It is not fear of death that holds them back, but fear for family."

A number of dwarves nodded. Duli continued, "We're all brave enough to fight and save clan, but there is a big difference between these men and my widows. The widow ranks have nay husbands or children to leave behind. These men have families, or command those who do. They can't volunteer this sacrifice. We can. The Widow Brigade is the right choice for this task."

General Guffan held no response. He looked into the eyes of the other commanders. None argued Duli's words. King Harvagot stepped forward and addressed them all. "We have nay time for quarrels. If nay other commander will volunteer their men, then the widows have taken the honor upon themselves."

The king's challenge met silence. "Then let us undo a dishonor." He half-turned towards other dwarves gathered nearby. "Get me a priest. Better yet, an archbishop!"

Several church leaders stepped forward from those who were listening to the meeting. The king returned his gaze to Duli. His voice softened as much as Duli had ever witnessed. "Duli, it is not right that you continue to bear the distinction, and beardless condition, of non-clan. If you would permit it, I ask the priests to undo their miracle. You deserve to grow a beard and be among us, for you have surely proven yourself a member of Tok-Maurron."

Fosha gasped beside her. In all Duli's knowledge, the removal of the beard had never been reversed. She felt speechless, especially since none of the clergy appeared disagreeable to the king's action.

Duli thought about the duty ahead of the widows. With a humorless, helpless chuckle she said, "I may not survive to grow one."

The king didn't answer her comment. Duli took only a heartbeat before answering with her instincts.

"I am thankful, but I will pass on the offer. Take nay offense, I just…I'd miss the feel of the air upon my cheeks. The fact that you offered is honor enough. Let me be of Tok-Maurron, but without the beard."

King Harvagot nodded. He placed a firm hand on her shoulder. "Go with honor. Take with you the pride of representing Tok-Maurron as you wage battle."

CHAPTER 29

Duli turned away from the king and the generals, heading back to the widows to relay their assignment. Her swirl of thoughts left her too distracted to notice the tone of Fosha's heavy boot stomps catching up with her. As they passed through a relatively secluded area between two wagons, the older woman latched onto Duli's arm and spun her face-to-face. Duli opened her mouth to protest. She stopped short of speaking; noting the angry look Fosha threw her way. It was a look usually reserved for Mennurdan Guild leaders and humans.

"I have half a mind to slap you somewhere where it will leave a mark," hissed Fosha.

"What?" Duli couldn't suppress the shock from her face. "For doing the right thing?"

"The right thing for them? Or the right thing for you?"

When Duli didn't offer a fast response, Fosha continued. "Maybe more than anyone else, I've noted your suicidal urges. I'm not just talking about the hanging scar. You've been reckless every time we've gone into battle. I saw it in your eyes. Every single time, you approached it as your day to die. I thought you finally moved beyond it. I'm wrong."

Duli huffed back, "I didn't volunteer us to die. We're going to battle, same as we've done before."

The elder woman waved a hand back toward the officer assembly. "You heard them map out how dangerous this is. Even if we win, we're going to lose a lot of good souls."

"Exactly why *we* have to do it. Nay ties left to us, as I said. If any of those companies go, we'll have even more widows and fatherless children."

Fosha glanced around for eavesdroppers before leaning closer to Duli, "I've always known you to be smart Duli, but not coldly emotionless about your decisions. How badly are you hoping to be one of the ones not coming back?"

Duli felt ready to blow up at Fosha. She balled her fists and opened her mouth, only to be deflated by Fosha's next words.

"One of my widows told me she is considering leaving the brigade."

The surprise news shook the foundation from Duli's protest. "What? Why?"

"She thinks she is falling in love with someone."

Duli didn't know how to respond. The concept of a widow finding love again astonished her senses. She never expected to encounter such feelings among the women or herself.

Fosha elaborated, in a softer tone than before, "I asked her if she was sure. She said she knew the rules. She planned to quit the brigade if her passions were returned. After all, we can't have a Widow Brigade with married women, right? Some people get past their loss and create new lives. I'd hoped you were doing the same."

All the fire went out of Duli's response. She looked upon her friend. "What about you, Fosha?"

The elder raised her hands, "Oh, I'm too old for frolicking. I'm ready to face the end of my days, and will do so gladly. But I'll not hurry fate. Every day I live is another day to smite those who took my loved ones. My life defeats them more than my death."

Duli looked down, idly rolling a stone with her boot. "I can't take back my words to the king and council." She looked up to Fosha, whose face became unreadable. "What are you suggesting I do?"

Fosha sighed. "We don't have a choice. You already threw in the ante. All we can do now is play the hand."

"I can't force them to go. I'll ask for volunteers."

Fosha shook her head. "They've already followed you towards danger. They idolize you. You're their champion. None will step down at this point."

Finding nothing else to say, Duli led Fosha away from the wagons. Bandit trotted alongside her. Duli's mind swirled with burdens. She wondered if she could get the brigade through their challenge with no deaths. Duli led them this far, but where was she leading them? Duli envisioned an end to her road, but what of the others? Her mind weighed the thoughts of love after loss. As she reached down to pet Bandit's fur, she considered the possibility of losing her last bit of family.

"Duli! Wait up!"

Duli and Fosha slowed as Sargas huffed over to them.

"Come to offer a last piece of battle advice?" Duli forced a smile for her good friend. "Care to part with any other secrets of the black powder?"

Duli's comments fell flat. Sargas' good eye looked upon her with a serious nature. "I'm sorry to have to be the one to tell you this, Duli. I have to take your guns."

She reflexively clenched the musket...her husband's last legacy. A side glance at Fosha revealed the elder to be staring at Sargas the way she had at Duli a moment ago. "What?"

Sargas cast his eye down at the dirt. "I don't wish to be the one to ask you...all of you. You can't take the muskets on this task."

The realization slammed into Duli like a splash of freezing water. Dwarves don't take their muskets on dangerous missions. The widows volunteered for a very dangerous mission. They swore an oath to safeguard their muskets over their own lives. The very thing they fought so hard to earn would have to be forsaken during this desperate fight. Duli ran her hand over the carvings on Geordan's old musket.

Sargas looked ready to continue, but Duli interrupted him. She didn't want to hear him draw out the reasons. "You're right." Duli looked at Fosha. The elder stood tight-lipped, clenching her own gun. "We don't have much time. Assemble the brigade. Those who volunteer will deliver their muskets to Sargas."

Sargas moved away to make preparations. Fosha lingered until it was apparent Duli needed a moment alone. Once Fosha stepped away, Duli looked down at the designs on her musket. She ran her fingers over the notches carved by Geordan whenever he'd taken a human life. She turned it over and reexamined the designs on the opposite side. Beyond the barrel, Duli caught a glimpse of Bandit's eyes looking back at her.

"What have I done?" she whispered.

*   *   *   *   *   *

Sargas "Gun Hand" rolled the cage-like wagon into place near the gathered widows. He stepped down and walked past the bars of the wagon bed. The diminished numbers of the brigade formed a crescent around Duli's position. The old veteran barely glanced over, knowing that several women wouldn't be looking too kindly on him or the wagon at that moment. Duli gave a speech, expressing their odds in common terms and cautioning the women about the danger. Sargas half-listened as he took out a key and opened the barred door on the back. The wagon started the trip holding animals, but they had already been butchered for food. Now, it would serve as a means to lock up muskets, at least until they were needed again. Sargas found a bucket in the wagonbed and used it as a seat while he waited for Duli to finish.

"...only taking volunteers, since this will be dangerous. I've already told you why we must not take the guns with us. If you plan to join me, turn your musket and powder over to Sargas at the wagon. You can collect it once we rejoin the caravan. This is as important as any task I've ever laid before you. I'll go first."

Duli concluded her speech and walked toward the wagon. Sargas watched her approach. He could only describe her gaze as 'unfocused'. Her head may have been turned the right direction, but her eyes viewed something only she could see. Sargas could tell by her stride she was in no hurry to carry out the inevitable. The wolf walked alongside her as she stepped up to the wagon.

Even when Duli handed him her belts and pouches, she never looked Sargas in the eye. Her face remained a stoic mask, staring into his beard, as she gave away her inventions. He accepted her powder horn tipped with Deepmug's measuring spigot. Sargas set aside a bag which he knew contained several paper-wrapped scatter-shot rounds.

Duli paused before giving up her musket. Sargas thought he saw her lips moving, though whether from prayer or not he couldn't tell. She resumed looking into his beard when she pushed the musket firmly into his hands. From his close position, Sargas could barely make out the wetness in her green eyes. Her attempt to restrain the sorrows raised his admiration. The stoicism of their race would fool any non-dwarf who looked into her eyes at that moment.

She turned without a word. Resting one hand on the dagger at her belt, the other on her hatchet, she wandered to a lonely spot off to the side. Sargas glanced at the musket as he stored it. The weaponsmith recalled when Geordan died and the weapon came to the Armory. At that time, Geordan had carved eleven notches from kills. Today, Sargas counted twenty-seven. The gunsmith's thumbnail flicked away a stain of dried blood stubbornly clinging to the spike.

Fosha approached next. The elder handed Sargas her gun. She spoke in a scolding manner as she did, "Don't store it where it will get scuffed by anything." Without waiting for a response, she drew her late son's pickaxe from her belt and joined Duli.

The other officers, Herothe and Leli, followed. Herothe offered him a blessing as she handed over her gun. "May Nandorrin always favor your craft, Gun Hand."

Leli said nothing. The widow remained tight-lipped, staring into his beard as Duli had done, before walking away.

One by one the widows came forth as Sargas continued to pile muskets into the wagon. Several kept feelings hidden well. Shauna handed him her gun, her voice offered a light-hearted tone unshared by the steel in her eyes, "I carved the stock, read this spot here."

She walked away without another word, leaving Sargas to chuckle over the inventiveness of the curses she inscribed onto her muskets. Only after his mirth did he note Shauna's reputation as the widows' deadliest aim seemed well-deserved. She had almost as many notches on her gun as Duli, yet unlike Duli's musket, all these marks were Shauna's.

Some widows did not do so well at hiding the sorrows. Young Katy started to offer her musket, but pulled it back before Sargas could grab it. She paused only long enough to unbelt the gun sling from it. The sling, stitched with the name of her late husband, went over her shoulder as she again offered it back to Sargas. He had to gently pull it from her grasp before she turned away from him.

The widow behind her watched the exchange. She stopped to untie a child's toy from her sling.

Sargas noticed another widow exchange looks with one of the nearby male warriors. The gunsmith was not so old as to misread the look of longing that passed between them. Neither one said a thing. They passed an unspoken message with their eyes. The widow broke eye contact, handing Sargas her gun and powder.

When Glaura stepped up to the wagon, Sargas noted her sniffles and trembling lip. He recalled overhearing Glaura talking to one of the other widows the previous evening, commenting that she hadn't yet shot a human to repay them for her children. The weaponsmith wondered how many of the newer widows were handing over weapons untarnished by blood. Sargas took her musket, then stopped to examine her more closely.

"Glaura? Have you got a weapon to use?"

She shook her head.

An inspiration struck the old veteran. He reached to his side and pulled forth his old warhammer. "Once, this caved in the skulls of orcs and knocked the teeth from larger beasts. It's been too long since it saw proper use. Why don't you take it for now?"

Glaura's lips still trembled, yet forced a grin. "Thank you." She held it against her chest and walked over to join the growing crowd around Duli.

A crowd of male warriors overheard Sargas and began to make their own observations. Most of the widows joining Duli carried weapons sized for dead husbands, craft tools instead of proper weapons, or held no weapons at all. Those women showed their willingness to go into battle with sticks and stones, if necessary. Warriors and old veterans stepped forward, handing spare daggers, axes, and anything they could to widows who needed it. Sargas even saw Guffan grab a crossbow and hand it to Shauna. Several other crossbows migrated over to the women.

In the middle of the exchange of weapons stood a statue. Boreval stared ahead, chin lifted into the sky and above the display of clan generosity before him. At least one spare dagger sat in a sheath on his belt, but the elder Stonebrow did nothing. Sargas noticed him finally shift his stance. Boreval turned his back to the widows and casually walked away.

"We'll all live in Dorvanon someday," Sargas thought, "And when our male and female ancestors ask you what you gave for the clan today, I hope I'm there to watch you squirm."

Sargas turned to accept muskets from the remaining widows. Two remained, limping over from the wagon where priests had administered to them. Neither looked capable of fighting. "You two aren't fit to fight. Get your rest with the healers."

"You can't stop them from coming and I won't even try." Duli said.

Both leaned on their guns, using them as canes as they made their way to the wagon. Once their muskets were turned in, neither could leave the wagon until other dwarves gave them polearms to double as walking sticks.

He overheard Duli give an order, "Herothe, use your prayers to get their legs fit for running. Fosha, what's our count?"

"They're all here." She responded with confidence. "We aren't missing anyone."

Sargas watched from atop the wagon as Duli waved them forward. "Follow Murglor, he'll lead you up the trail. Hurry along now."

Leli stopped, "What are you doing, Duli?"

"I remembered one last thing I need to store on the wagon."

She recognized the trust in Bandit's eyes. Duli was both mother and pack-leader. She knew the wolf would follow her anywhere. Duli knew he didn't understand why she had tricked him into getting into the caged wagon, as she shut and locked the door.

Duli stared into those yellow eyes. The wolf began to paw the cage, testing it. He uttered a whine, though his tone turned angrier as he clawed at the cage bars.

She stared at her furry family member as she spoke over her shoulder, "Sargas?"

"Aye, Duli?"

"If I don't come back, don't let him out of this cage until the pass is collapsed, and there aren't any other dwarves around that might feel threatened and shoot him."

"Are you afraid for him?"

She nodded. "He doesn't stay out of fights, and if he gets on top of that cliff I can't get him down, out of trouble. I'll be trying to descend a rope with humans above and below me. How would he get down?"

Duli had to rub her eyes at that moment. She was compelled to do it before the dwarves nearby recognized the sorrows. "Cage is dirty," she commented.

Sargas spoke, "You act as if you already know you aren't coming back."

222

She laughed, but not out of amusement. A sad acceptance came over her, "I never expect to come back."

As her eyes remained locked on the wolf, Sargas changed subjects. "What if he tries to bite me when I let him out?"

Duli shook her head. "He'll be too eager to look for me. That's why you can't let him out until the pass is destroyed. He'll just end up dead in the middle of the humans otherwise."

She searched for more words, but Sargas spoke next. "The Silvermugs are planning on you teaching them your secrets with the scatter-shot."

"My secrets are there," Duli waved to indicate her bags. "You were at the wager; you know my tricks. You could teach them better than I could."

She wanted to add a few statements, but decided on simply saying, "Thank you…for a lot of things."

Duli hustled up the trail. As a group, the eighty-seven surviving widows raced to meet the enemy. She refused the temptation to look upon the wolf again. As she began to overtake the rearmost women, she tried to ignore his howls. Her ears would not close themselves any easier than her heart could.

CHAPTER 30

"This is the place." Murglor dismounted, limping on his maimed foot. "Who knows what this was long ago, but now it looks so old and weathered that it would appear natural. Only the even spacing of the pillars and openings giving any hint this was built, not formed naturally."

Duli glanced at the terrain. If there had once been a roof, it was long gone. Behind her, several of Murglor's riders continued building barricades between rough sections of raised stone pillars, some fallen. These formed the outer boundary of the ancient construction, the first wall the humans would have to breach. Murglor approached another such gap in a second wall of stone.

Murglor continued, "That outer ring of rocks is your only real first line of defense. There is some rough terrain beyond: creek bed, brush line, and more rock piles. It won't keep you hidden from their archers, so stay behind the stone, here, and let them try to get through the cracks. The humans will have to crowd together to get through those narrow gaps. And up ahead…"

She followed directly behind him as he squeezed through a crack in the stone. "…is where you can best protect your members as they descend the ropes. This inner ring is small, but very defensible."

Fosha, Herothe, and Leli followed as Duli surveyed the ledge. The inner ring of natural rocks, taller than dwarves, formed a very small space before the cliff edge dropped away to the valley. Broken scatterings of stone were all that remained of whatever altar or such thing once resided here. No construction blocked the view of the valley ahead. Those ancient builders probably savored the view too much. Duli estimated no more than twenty dwarves could even stand shoulder-to-shoulder in the space between the inner rocks. Ropes already lay fastened to old stumps and rock formations: coiled and ready to toss over when the widows began their retreat.

Murglor's next observation echoed Duli's thoughts. "The whole lot of you won't be able to take cover in here. If they start breaching the outer barrier, you'd best start sending warriors down the ropes. Otherwise, throw the humans back and scoot down during a break in the action."

From this vantage, Duli could plainly see the escape route north of them across the valley. Dwarven engineers worked in the pass, readying their explosives, though to Duli's eyes they were so far away they appeared small as ants. Below them, moving right under the ledge, Tok-Maurron's caravan tightened up to enter the narrow cut. Duli could not see the whole of the refugee caravan beyond the twisting valley floor, but she knew it extended for miles eastward.

Murglor awaited a response. Duli turned to him. "Thank you for preparing this place, Murglor. My women will take over. It's a fine spot to fight off the humans."

He replied, "Gods be with you. May we next see each other in Silver Mountain, rather than Dorvanon."

Duli found herself torn between different responses. She simply nodded and he took his leave. Leli got her attention. "His men told me they could hear sounds of the human army."

Even as she spoke, they heard Murglor calling for his men to mount up. The hoofbeats from his company's rams thundered away. Duli saw the eyes of other widows through the gap in the inner ring. Their faces reflected a dawning comprehension that they were truly on their own now.

Duli invented strategy even as she barked orders, "Leli and Herothe, you will split the front line, Leli on the left. Have the women continue to pile rocks and move brush to narrow down the lanes from which the humans can attack. Start placing your guns…"

In a moment of silence, Duli realized her slip of the lip. She corrected herself as her officers hid their emotions. "Place your warriors, go."

Leli and Herothe squeezed back through the gap and started shouting orders. Duli couldn't help reliving her earlier thoughts on the vulnerability of the surface world. The terrain should slow the humans, but what if their magic could help them climb or see past it?

"Fosha, your company will form around this inner ring. I'll need you to send reinforcements in wherever they may be needed."

"What about the crossbows? Shauna and the others?"

Duli glanced at the weathered stone wall. "Maybe we can get a few of them on top of this inner ring. Add a few on top of the outer stone pillars. I'm guessing we won't have as many bows at our command to trade open volleys with the humans, but they can get on some high ground and pick off mages and officers."

"Captain!" A wide-eyed widow stumbled into the ring of rocks. Her words betrayed a nervous tremble, "From Leli. She says we spotted some colors moving through an open area not far downhill. She can hear marching feet breaking twigs."

"Thanks. And look tough. We're about to get some revenge on those murderers."

The woman tightened her lower lip, nodded, and ran back to her spot. Duli cast a last glance over the edge of the cliff. The height became dizzying to her underground-attuned senses, and she had to look away. Ancestor's Vale had a much longer drop yet it never made her light-headed. Then again, she was never asked to descend a rope in combat down that valley.

She sought and found Shauna between the two rings of defenses. "I need you and the other crossbows to pick spots on the rock walls. We need you all to keep low, due to their archers. I only want you to risk yourselves firing at their mages or officers."

"I'll be there," Shauna pointed at a stone pedestal jutting out from the inner ring of rocks. "It will give me a good view of the center if they start breaking through. I'll be able to fire into some of the tight entries as well."

Duli nodded, wanting to say more but lacking the time to properly find the words. Shauna and the other crossbow-wielders fanned out and picked spots to defend. Duli saw Glaura squatting next to one of the gaps in the outer ring. Her friend gripped Sargas' warhammer close to her chest, biting her lip.

"How's the hammer feel?"

Glaura looked up. "A little heavy. I'll have to use both hands, but I'll be fine."

Duli gave Glaura a comforting squeeze on the shoulder as she continued down the line. Several women noticed Duli walking by, acknowledging her with a nod or a grim grin before resuming their preparations. She passed one widow kissing a lock of hair tied around her finger. Another widow paused in the act of burying a child's doll in a hand-dug pit. She noticed Duli and explained, "Nay human will be taking this prize back to his children."

Duli stopped beside Herothe, watching the priestess tuck away a holy symbol. "Did you say a prayer for us?" Duli asked.

"Already done," Herothe replied, keeping her eyes ahead towards her line of women. "Hopefully they'll hear us again like they did at Ancestor's Vale."

"We lost most of the brigade at Ancestor's Vale."

"And we won; a miracle." When Duli offered no further comment, Herothe asked, "What prayer may I offer on your behalf?"

Duli turned away from Herothe's eyes. "The gods know my prayer. They won't grant it."

226

Duli left Herothe's side before the priestess could say more. *"I should probably make some heartening comments before things get bloody. They could use a dose of courage."* Even as she thought about it, a hushed call declared the approach of the first humans. *"Well enough, I guess its past time for words."*

*   *   *   *   *   *

Shauna stared down the length of her crossbow past a thin veil of tall grass occupying her perch. Her bolt aligned with the gap in the stones, settling upon the lightly-armed human approaching it. From her angle, she could easily see the dwarves huddled with their weapons on either side of the gap. The women heard the sounds of the human approaching. They remained still and silent as they listened to his legs brushing past briars. The Tariykan scout approached nervously. She assumed he expected trouble. One hand clutched a strung bow; the other carried a bared knife. The human kicked at a pile of briars, placed by Murglor's riders.

He looked in Shauna's direction, and her breath caught. His eyes returned to the ground in front as his hand felt along the tight confines of rock. The grass, a scraggly brush which somehow flourished on the pedestal, had served its purpose of concealment. She watched him try to pick his way over the gnarled ground.

As the human scout emerged from the gap, he barely had time to gasp at seeing the huddled dwarves before Shauna's bolt flew free. Her shot struck his chest, throwing him back into the narrow passage. At the sound of her shot, other crossbows clicked on both sides.

Wounded cries let loose. A couple human voices screamed words in their language. The melee dwarves stood ready to repel a sudden rush, but the remaining humans were heard scampering away from the line.

Shauna didn't see anyone else attempting to help the stricken human. In another gap, she saw shadows in retreat. Shauna continued loading. Just below her position, Leli ran over to Duli. "Just scouts," Leli concluded, "Reporting back to let the rest know where we are."

Duli ran over to one of the gaps in the rock. Through a narrow field of vision, she saw the large pennants borne on the backs of their brightly colored warriors. The colors moved and weaved through some brush within throwing distance. Duli moved to another break in the rock wall and braved a glance. She saw a row their flag-tops, moments before each flag rose as the charging warriors ascended out of a runoff basin.

They had already seen Duli, she raised her weapons in challenge. Duli forced her legs to stand still and tall. The humans struggled through the brush between rocks to get to her. The first one dropped from a crossbow bolt. Duli felt pleasure in watching her first would-be attacker writhe on the ground. The next two rushed out unaware of the hidden widows on both sides of the gap. Curses assaulted them from both sides only half a breath before weapons did likewise. The next couple humans turned back to back to face the flanking attackers. She saw her chance and didn't hesitate. Duli, momentarily forgotten, charged in and embedded her hatchet blade into one. The other fell to numerous wounds within seconds.

As soon as the widows defending the gap crowded her out, Duli went down the line of defenders. She made sure no humans won their way past their defense. So far, the widows proved to have the upper hand in surprise and terrain.

An explosion thundered from the right end of the line. Duli, confused and worried as to the source, turned and ran that direction. The noise sounded more like gunpowder than any Tariykan spell. She arrived in time to see a flask with a fuse lobbed over the rocks. Herothe cackled in dreadful glee as another explosion pounded the humans on the other side.

Duli rushed over to the priestess amidst the sounds of more fighting nearby. "I can't believe you smuggled those here! They should have been left with the muskets!"

Herothe produced another flask, marked with Nandorrin's holy symbol, from her priest vestments.

"We can't let the Tariykans capture those!" Duli implored.

Herothe only laughed, "That's why I'm using these right away. This is the last one."

Herothe called upon the gods, using a miracle to ignite a flame from her fingers and light the fuse. Duli watched as Herothe threw the container over a low part of the rocks. She could only see the heads, shoulders, and back-pennants worn by the soldiers. Moments later, the blast blew everything apart, leaving a cloud of smoke in their place.

Herothe confided amidst more laughter, "If it's to be a proper fight, I had to sanctify it in Nandorrin's name."

A rush of humans charged one of the gaps in the rocks. They stumbled and cursed their way over brambles and a dead scout. Katy watched as one widow rose from hiding to send a throwing axe at the group. She heard human shouts but couldn't see if it hit its target. Katy mouthed a silent goodbye to her extended family from Deepmug's. She wanted to will a few last images of her husband to mind, but her thoughts were interrupted. The lead human stepped within the last few feet of brambles. Widows shouted war cries as they jumped up from hiding. Katy ran forward. As the humans shrieked their own war cries, Katy braced the end of her boar spear in the ground. Dwarves and humans clashed in a flurry of sharp metal and feral grunts.

One human leaped the remaining brambles only to fall upon her speartip. The shaft vibrated but held as the skewered human squirmed around the head. The strike would likely prove fatal, but landed too low to drop him immediately.

The human uttered high-pitched noises, when he found the voice to utter anything. Katy held firmly upon the spear as the man twisted against the lugs holding him upright. The human tried to strike her with his sword. His swings lacked strength and went wild. Despite this, Katy nearly panicked at their momentary impasse. She could do nothing but hold him in place, hoping for him to collapse or for one of the widows to finish him. Unfortunately, with battle raging around them, another human might just as easily finish her.

"Shauna!" She cried, knowing her friend's perch overlooked her position.

A reply followed, in the form of a crossbow bolt sprouting from the man's chest. His throat gurgled as he dropped to one side. Katy twisted her spear free and offered a nod to her friend. Shauna didn't respond, too intent on reloading quickly.

Katy thought, *"Still alive, at least for another few moments."* She changed the grip on her spear, feeling the sticky wetness of blood on the shaft as she did, and moved to help another widow.

Duli hurried along the line, watching all the gaps for problems. Fighting went on at each hole. So far, the widows held the advantage. The humans squeezed past obstacles, one at a time, only to face a ring of weapons. Duli glanced to her left. Fosha's widows huddled in groups, shifting their grips on their weapons, anxiously awaiting a call for support. Their task proved a difficult test of patience: waiting for friends and neighbors to be stricken before rushing ahead to take their spot.

Duli could empathize. On the move, she caught sight of women down on the ground. She pulled her vision away before allowing herself to recognize their forms. Her mind begged questions: *"Was that a neighbor or friend, dead or wounded? Do I need to send over another friend to take their place?"* Duli resisted, trying to shove such thoughts deep. She couldn't bear to recognize the death of someone close to her while dealing with all thoughts of battle.

Ahead, Duli saw an area where fighting along Leli's line spilled into the open area. She saw Leli and called to her. "How'd these humans get through?"

Her officer pointed, "They climbed over those low rocks there. We're handling it."

They didn't call for Fosha's support. Duli and Leli charged side-by-side, blindsiding a pair of humans. The men went down screaming. Enough widows surrounded the remaining humans that neither Duli nor Leli could get in another attack.

Aside from a few shouted foreign words from the other side of the rocks, the sounds of fighting diminished. Human warriors retreated back through the gaps.

Leli commented, "Looks like they need to catch their breath."

Duli, breathing heavily, nodded. She glanced at the blood on her hatchet. She tucked the handle into a ring at her belt without bothering to wipe it clean. "Give me a boost so I can see over the rocks."

After glancing at the rows of pennants in formation down the hill, Leli set her back down. "They have plenty of warriors left out there. I think they're starting to realize there's more of us than they figured, and that we're holding this spot instead of fighting a retreat action."

Leli glanced to the side, looking down the line of defense. "Looks a lot different than Ancestor's Vale."

Duli turned around. She could see all the way down to Herothe's end of the line, where the priestess administered her healing gift onto some wounded. Leli continued, "No smoke covering the field. My ears aren't ringing from muskets going off next to them."

Duli nodded, "Still have some familiar sounds: screams of the wounded." Even as she said it, she watched a nearby widow deliver a killing blow to a wounded human. "And the smells…the soiled odor signifying death."

Listening to the lull in the fighting, Duli glanced at the inner ring of stone. "I'm going to check the progress of the caravan."

She ran to the cliff and peered over. The caravan hurried along, but the end of it was barely in sight. The widows would have to hold out a lot longer. She did note a few empty wagons abandoned near the pass. Others moved as wagon masters shouted and cursed their mounts onward.

"They probably heard Herothe's surprises and know we're already fighting for time."

Duli rushed back to the line. She saw Glaura kneeling over a dead human. Squatting by her friend, she noticed the blood on the head of Sargas' hammer. Glaura realized she wasn't alone. She looked into Duli's eyes. Her eyes had a dull quality to them, as if something bright had gone out.

She spoke with a flat tone as she said, "My first kill. He wasn't even looking at me."

Duli whispered as she patted Glaura's shoulder. "Are you alright?"

Glaura nodded, and both stood.

230

"Take cover!" Someone shouted.

Duli and Glaura glanced around. She caught a glimpse of Shauna deliberately throwing herself down from her high perch and quickly rolling back against it. Before she could even see the threat, Glaura tackled Duli into the lee of a boulder. Duli looked out and saw scores of arrows dropping into the widow ranks.

CHAPTER 31

Noise filled her senses first. Widows yelling warnings, boots thumping along the ground, Glaura's tired breathing next to her own, and then the whistling of shafts in great numbers. Her eyes witnessed the results. Arrows feathered the scrub grasses between rings of stone. A couple sparked as they glanced off the tall stones, others splintered apart. Most dotted the dull grass like flowers opening for a sunny day. Duli heard a sharp intake of breath somewhere near, followed by a grunt of pain as a widow clamped a hand over her wound.

The rapid beat of falling death began to trickle to nothing. Glaura sat up and blew out a breath. "How many arrows did they bring?"

"It will be twice as many after the next volley hits," Duli said as she scrambled to her feet. She hauled Glaura upright and pushed her toward a larger face of stone. "Get better cover!"

Both heard the next round of whistling shafts as the women dove against their new shelter. Duli saw Herothe pulling a wounded woman to a better spot. Fosha yelled at her widows, "Keep down! Keep down!"

They watched the rain of colored shafts storm down again. Fletching of every color of the rainbow dotted the sky. Arrowheads chipped against rocks. Broken shafts tumbled over the women huddling behind boulders. One arrow stuck in the ground where Duli and Glaura previously sought cover. The dull thud of shafts sinking into grass contrasted with the sharper crack of steel heads clipping stone, combining to form a rapid beat of sounds.

A shriek from a wounded widow echoed down the line of rocks. The voice died under the new sound of a multitude of humans yelling their challenges across the field. Duli glanced through a gap in the stones. The sight of a wave of humans, distant but clambering over brush and the creek bed, confirmed her suspicions. She started yelling for the widows to regroup into their positions.

"Nay! Take cover again!" Fosha shouted.

As the humans walked forward, a third volley of arrows dropped down while widows ran back to their earlier spots. The first few shafts caught a couple out in the open. They screamed for aid as they dropped among the field of feathers. Shauna grabbed for the top of her perch, feet dangling a few feet over the grass, as an arrow clipped the stone near her face. Displaying her contempt for the God of Luck, she cursed, "Kelor's balls!"

Duli saw a widow rush to the aid of another. "Herothe! Get back to the stones!" Duli watched as an arrow stuck in the priestess' billowing sleeve. "Dorvanon take you! You're our only healer! Get back under cover!"

She jumped up to aid the priestess, only to be stopped by Glaura. "You can't go out there either! You're our leader!"

Glaura shoved Duli back against the rock and ran to help Herothe. Duli clenched her fists and hissed. Nearby widows echoed Glaura's comments. Reluctantly, Duli stayed and watched. She silently prayed more than she had in years. Glaura slid to the ground next to the two dwarves. They traded a few words before an arrow struck the priestess. Duli watched from behind as Herothe fell forward, the arrow centered in her upper back. Glaura and the other wounded widow both turned their attention to Herothe…all three women laying together in a field of deadly rain.

"Herothe! Herothe Darkhair!" Duli screamed. None of the women responded, and she couldn't hear their conversation. Her next words whispered a prayer more than a command, "Heal yourself and get over by the stones!"

Glaura helped the wounded widow to her feet, both looking upon the fallen priestess with sadness in their eyes. They limped to safety. Duli watched Herothe for some sign of life, despite what her heart already knew. Herothe lay unmoving in that field of fletchings. The sounds of falling arrows ceased, only to be replaced by the approaching war cries of the humans.

Duli couldn't get her muscles to cooperate, lest they betray the eyes that could only stay locked on her dead friend. She managed to get her voice to obey her wishes. "Fosha, take command of our right!"

"They're leading with shields!" Leli yelled, "Don't let them run over you! Trip them!"

Brightly colored shields, displaying artistry extravagant for their use, led the rush through the gaps. Humans slammed their way straight at the defending dwarves, attempting to open up room for their swordsmen. Leli's command barely left her lips and she followed her own advice. She charged in low at a human, tangling herself up in his legs as combatants from both sides piled next to them. A rolling mass of limbs thrashed, fingernails tearing at faces, teeth sinking into any flesh they could find. Swords and battleaxes, unwieldy in such quarters, caused wounds only when bodies rolled over the edges. Those few who could draw daggers stabbed their way to sunlight.

Amidst the fighting on the right-hand side of the dwarf line, Duli and Fosha started waving some of Fosha's waiting company into battle. Fosha grabbed Duli, "I can handle this. Check on Leli, her line is a mess."

Duli nodded. Before she could turn, she pointed at some humans climbing over the tall stone pillars. "Fosha! Their archers are taking the high ground."

"Trust in our crossbows to handle it. Send some of my women to help Leli!"

Duli glanced at Shauna, relieved to see the fair-haired dwarf firing her crossbow toward the new threat. Sweat obscured her eyes for a moment; she wiped it aside. The brigade leader ran down the line. "You there, follow me!"

A number of Fosha's anxious warriors gladly ran alongside Duli, eager to enter the battle at last. They started to fall behind her, only to form a wedge. With Duli at the lead, they sundered a line of humans. Widows stabbed and hacked away until they found themselves up against one of the gaps in the stone wall. Duli, catching her breath, feeling the pounding of her heart in her chest, turned around only to see a mass of confusion all about her. Enough humans managed to get past the gaps that the fighting rolled across the narrow, feathered field. She finally caught sight of Leli. The woman was alive, though her legs were buried in a pile of squirming bodies as her arms struggled to twist a trapped human's head off. Duli rallied the widows and charged to free her friend.

Glaura's hands felt cold and sweaty curled around Sargas' hammer. She attacked alongside a group of women trying to retake their position near one of the stone gaps. Bodies clashed in chaos. Glaura raised the hammer to strike at anything. A shield came right at her, slamming her down to the rocky ground. Her efforts to get back up were slowed as another body fell on top of her. Glaura wiggled free. She realized the other body was human and also very alive. Glaura brought the hammer down hard, once, twice, and a third for good measure. She forced her eyes away from the dented skull and got to her feet.

Due to where she had fallen, the humans coming out of the gap didn't see her. She had a view of their backs, but one in particular caught her eye. The human dressed differently than the armor of his companions. He didn't wear one of those flags on his back like the others. He wore numerous pouches on his belt instead of a weapon. The human dipped a hand into a pouch, and when he brought it out he threw fire at the nearest widows.

"A mage! I'm standing near a mage!"

Escape proved to be impossible, surrounded as she was, and it would be a matter of seconds before one of the humans would notice her. Glaura summoned up courage she didn't know she had. Hefting Sargas' hammer over her head, she ran up to the mage and gave him the hardest knock on the head she could. He dropped to his knees.

"For my babies!" Standing at his side, she took a horizontal swing which bashed in his face.

The humans turned on Glaura then, but at the same time a rush of widows from Fosha's reserve company arrived in support. One rushed forward despite flames licking at her own clothes. Glaura felt the sting as a sword cut across her side, but kept fighting.

Fosha watched her line breaking apart in several places. Women who she'd known since they were old enough to walk lay dead nearby. She turned toward the inner ring of rocks and her old company members. "Attack! Everyone attack! All of you move forward!"

The elder raised the pickaxe that once served one of her sons in battle. "You two, run with me!"

She attacked a group of men who were fighting their way past the widows. Fosha arrived too late to help stop a Tariykan blade striking down one of her old friends. Before its owner could retract the sword, she gave him the point of her pickaxe.

She angrily jerked it free in a spurt of blood as the other dwarves ran past, finding their own victims. Her gaze moved upward, noting several human archers on the outer rim of stones. Dwarven crossbows weren't killing them fast enough. One archer fired from his perch, and a widow near Fosha fell. A second one fired and Fosha felt the sting of the arrow strike through a breast.

After a moment in shock, Fosha tried to snap the shaft but the pain of doing so proved too much. She stayed on her feet, finding the will to keep going. With every breath, she felt the barbs of the arrowhead tearing at her lung.

Katy jabbed her dinner knife into a human's ribs. The knife finally broke after the fifth stab, leaving a deep cut on one finger, but the human no longer struggled. She tossed aside the broken weapon. It took a moment to untangle her legs from those of her opponent. The young widow looked about, trying to find where her boar spear fell. She spit out blood.

"I think I bit my tongue."

Sighting her spear, she ran over and picked it up in time to face another charging human. Kneeling as she was, Katy easily swung the spear into line and braced it against the ground. He skewered himself on the weapon. Eyes bulged out in a way that shocked Katy. She listened as awful gurgling sounds escaped his lips as he fell.

Her eyes went wide as she saw two more humans behind him, closing fast. Katy screamed between labored breaths as she tugged her spear free. Her arms trembled, making everything harder. "Shauna! A little help, please!"

Katy's voice carried to Shauna's high perch. Shauna lay on her back, crossbow at her side, with three Tariykan arrows in her body. Her ears could no longer hear, nor could her arms give aid. Blood marred her six golden braids. Shauna Horgar's glazed eyes faced skyward, her sight set on Dorvanon.

Duli brought her arm across her brow, removing more sweat from her eyes. Her hair felt like a greasy, tangled mess. Blood clung to her left hand; some of it coating a cut finger. She felt woozy from all her effort. She called out to nearby widows as she regained her breath.

"That gap! Hit them and drive them out!"

Two of her widows attacked another pair of humans. A few feet to their side, another human appeared in one of the other unguarded gaps. "With me!" She shouted, unsure if anyone else was close enough to hear.

A couple steps from the human, she reached down and picked up a discarded human shield. She threw it at his head, following with her dagger and hatchet. He went down and she jumped on top of him. Straddling his chest, she clumsily swung her tired arms. His face quickly became unrecognizable.

In the distance, she heard commands issued in the human tongue. She glanced up, noting several humans who were about to squeeze through the gap begin to back up instead. Off to one side, she glimpsed another human warrior limping back through the line of stones. Duli looked across the field and saw humans retreating. The Tariykan archers dropped out of sight.

She staggered to her feet. In her haste, her head started to swoon and she took several unsteady steps before righting herself. She glanced around.

236

Unmoving bodies lay everywhere. Several piled around the gaps in the rocks. A few draped over the stones of the outer ring. Some twitched, some moaned. Duli's mind couldn't believe her senses. Within a short span of time, everything went from chaos and confusion to deathly still silence. The prevailing sound in her ears came from her own rapid breaths. Once the humans vanished behind the rocks, hardly anyone remained who could sit or stand. She saw Fosha sitting in the grass, hand clutching an arrow in her armor. Katy dragged her legs out from under a human corpse. Even as Duli scanned the field, she saw another widow weaving a crooked path before dropping to the ground. She couldn't see more than a handful of widows upright.

Unlike the smoke-shrouded battle in Ancestor's Vale, one could clearly see the bodies of those slain across the width of the field. Dead, staring eyes could be seen in every direction. Sunlight sparkled across armor and dropped weapons. Trails of upturned earth snaked through crushed grass and broken arrows. Duli forced her gaze away from the scene. She saw enough dead friends lying near; she refused to focus on any more. Duli climbed a rock which offered a better view of the Tariykan forces.

Her heart dropped as she witnessed more ranks of human warriors arriving. New rows of flags reformed deeper lines. There were more humans across the field now than there had been earlier.

A voice called out behind her, "We've won. They've turned back."

Duli dropped to the ground. She forced her face into a mask of calm, hoping to avoid frightening the others by her expression. Duli turned toward Leli's voice. All of her stoic countenance crumbled as soon as she saw Leli's condition.

Leli stumbled forward, either heedless of her injuries or already resigned to her fate. Duli had no doubt that the blood staining Leli's face and side were mostly hers. She'd lost an arm to the battlefield. Duli rushed to her side as she saw the torn stump steadily pumping her life away.

Duli caught her friend and they fell, sitting, atop a corpse. She ripped the flag from the human body and wrapped Leli's arm. Despite her actions, she knew it was a losing battle.

"We have to get the others down the cliff." Leli said, her voice losing strength. "There's nay hurry, we beat them all."

Duli, hearing humans shouting commands, saw no need to break Leli's illusion. "We'll be fine. You need some rest."

Leli stared at the outer ring of stone. "Good ol' stone. Found a way to protect us here on the surface." Her eyes closed for a moment, but she blinked them open. "A rest sounds good, but we aren't finished. We have so much to do."

Perhaps Leli didn't notice, but Duli watched her lone arm slip from its grasp on Duli's armor. Leli couldn't keep her head up and focused. She allowed it to rest back against Duli's embrace. Duli abandoned her attempts to stem the flow from the torn limb. She wrapped both arms protectively around the other woman.

She recalled her friend's tragedy. Leli's husband survived battle with the humans only to succumb to a disease. If her husband had asked for help earlier, the priests likely could have cured it before it took away their child and him in his delirium.

"You don't have anything more to do." Duli whispered to Leli's half-lidded eyes. Her own eyes ran with the sorrows, dripping onto her shivering friend. "Rest now; don't fight it. You have a husband and child waiting for you. Sleep well, friend."

Duli knew she needed to keep moving. The dwarf caravan needed their defense and the humans were likely planning their next attack. Instead, Duli hugged Leli close. The world could spare a few moments for her to hold a dying friend.

CHAPTER 32

Duli wearily staggered into the inner ring of stones, where Murglor's men had secured their escape ropes. She heard the clash of battle somewhere below. She hoped it might be time for the widows to climb down ahead of the human army. Duli wanted to get away from the grief bled into this soil, even as she feared the descent. Dropping to her knees, she crawled to the cliff edge. With her injured hand she grabbed a coil of rope, ready to toss it down the cliff side. When Duli looked down into the valley, her shoulders slumped. Her breath choked on a defeated sigh. She closed her eyes and reopened them, but the truth of the scene below could not be ignored. Duli let the rope fall by her side. She allowed her body to collapse on the hard rocks, facing the others as they arrived. She wouldn't…couldn't…meet their eyes.

Katy supported Fosha into the inner ring. The younger widow looked fine despite her share of scratches. Fosha labored over shallow, rapid breaths. The elder's hand clenched around the arrow buried in one breast. Fosha's eyes squinted, masking the pain of her injury.

Glaura limped through another gap. Duli suffered at witnessing her friend's hardships. Glaura held one hand wrapped around a wound in her side. Ragged bunches of cloth stuffed the tear in her tunic, stains of blood betrayed their purpose.

Another widow arrived in the opposite side of the inner ring. This one had the arm of a companion draped over a shoulder. The wounded widow took no steps on her own, supported and dragged by the first. A third woman followed, exclaiming, "It's too late for her. She's passed. Look for yourself."

"By Taekbol's beard, she's alive! She's been speaking to me."

After a moment's argument, the lead widow relented and realized her wounded companion breathed no more. Both new arrivals set their friend down gently.

As more hearbeats went by, Duli awaited other survivors. None appeared. Fosha gasped, "Is it…time?"

Duli didn't answer. She counted the widows as some made their way to the cliff's edge. *"Six of us? Gods' poor humor! If the humans would have pushed their fight for another minute we'd all be dead. It would have been merciful."*

She glanced to the top of the tall stones guarding the inner circle. She spotted an unmistakable blond braid, splashed with blood. *"Dear Shauna, my good friend, your worries are over. You have left me behind and found your rest."*

Duli felt Fosha's stare, sitting a couple paces from her, as Katy peered over the cliff edge. One of the other widows next to Katy cursed, also looking over the edge. Duli watched as the scene below caused Katy to lose strength. The young widow bowed her head to the ground and said nothing. Glaura, also glancing over the side, allowed Sargas' hammer to fall from her hands and she collapsed to the ground.

By that time Duli raised her head and met Fosha's eyes. The elder understood, casting her glance downward. Duli realized her own hands were shaking. All the fire in her heart that had kept her fighting had gone out, letting the cold seep through her body. The aches and pains of accumulated injuries surfaced. Duli felt the sting of a cut in her back. Her left shoulder ached, perhaps from a muscle tear. The wound to her hand flared up and cracked the scab whenever she clenched it.

"All the humans down there," Glaura's voice whispered, "So now they have us."

Katy's voice shook, "We'll be buried up here."

Duli's reply cracked from a parched throat. "We'll bury as many of them as we can when they try to enter these stones."

Even as the words left her mouth, she knew she offered only false bravado. She recalled all the times she expected to die and lived. A truth took hold of her gut: she now lived in her last hour.

Katy's eyes remained on the scene below the cliff. "What is Murglor attempting?"

Curiosity got the better of Duli. She crawled on her hands and knees over to the cliff edge. Below their position, ranks of Tariykan swordsmen passed by heedless of the widows watching them from high above. Their lines stretched two hundred paces past where the widows had hoped to rappel down. The lead line of the human army, including groups of horsemen, wove right and left at the bottom of the pass chasing down dwarven ram riders. The pass itself stood nearly empty, with the exception of the refuse left behind by the refugee caravan. Duli could still make out the dust cloud of the trailing dwarf wagons at the top of the distant pass. The only force present harrying the front of the human advance consisted of a company of ram riders. She couldn't recognize any individuals from their height, but she knew it had to be Murglor's rear guard.

The widows watched as elements of Murglor's riders speared twice into the advancing forces, risking trapping themselves inside human lines. Both strikes occurred straight out from the widow's cliff vantage.

"He's trying to regain the ground below." Duli gasped. "The fool still hopes to save us."

Katy watched the latest dwarf charge turn into a retreat. "They're dying, and for what? They're only losing ground."

Duli shook her head. "They won't blow up the pass as long as they think they can save us. Madness! They're reforming again." Duli stood up. "We can't let this slaughter go on."

Duli ran out of the inner ring of stones. The other widows crawled to the edge and observed the fight, save Fosha. The elder struggled to breathe as she used one hand to begin searching her pack. Duli returned a minute later, her arms brimming with numerous Tariykan flags yanked free from the backs of the fallen. She started handing them to everyone.

"Wave these. Let our kin believe the humans already hold this ridge."

The first widow recoiled from the human marker, ever so briefly, before accepting it. Glaura hesitated, but changed her mind as they heard distant screams from the latest ram charge. The widows started waving the back-pennants vigorously. Katy waved one in each hand. Fosha grabbed a pennant. She waved it once, squinting in pain, and dropped it. They waved the banners until their arms were exhausted, hoping someone would see the display.

"I already heard you say you're ready to blow the thing. I may only have one eye but both ears work fine." Sargas scolded one of the miners. "I don't hold an army rank. I can't ask the riders to draw back."

One of the miners nodded his beard toward the pass below. "Someone comes."

A ram rider, awash in blood and sweat, urged his mount to the top of the pass. "We're retreating! Be ready with the explosives."

Sargas couldn't believe his ears. "The widows have been rescued?"

"Nay, none descended. Humans now hold that ridge."

The rider pointed, and everyone turned to look. None of them could make out the distant figures, but they could see the patches of bright color from Tariykan banners. Some humans, far off, were celebrating their victory over the widows.

Sargas felt his heart skip a beat. He blinked his good eye, hoping to see differently. Unfortunately, the vision held true. Distant human banners waved in the place where the widows fell to the last. The next words exchanged between the rider and the miners sounded distant in Sargas' ears. Even as the rider rode back down the slope, the aged dwarf fought the memories flooding his awareness. His thoughts could still envision Duli, grieving the recent loss of her husband, learning how to fire Geordan's musket in the training hall. In his own small way he had helped give birth to them. He trained them and defended them in front of clan leaders. A part of him felt dead and empty. Any pride he felt on behalf of his help withered under the tragedy of their destiny. He lost sight of the distant ridge as his vision blurred. He rubbed the sorrows away before others noticed.

"Make sure you let a lot of humans fill that pass before you collapse it on top of them," he whispered.

An angry ruckus pulled his attention. Numerous dwarves were cursing and stumbling to evade something. A dark shape raced between wagons, scaring rams as it weaved a path closer to Sargas. Bandit swerved near the old dwarf before launching past him faster than he could move.

"How did he get out?"

The wolf raced down the pass, heedless of the approaching ram riders. It skittered to one side and dove past the mass of hooves.

"Forgive me, Duli," Sargas implored. "I'm sorry."

The widows kept their eyes on the pass, discarded human flags draping the ground beside them, waiting for the miners to close the gap. They had the best spot to observe: almost a mile away and close to the elevation of the distant pass. The human ranks filled the valley as they followed the dwarven refugees, heedless of the danger. The widows watched the army climb higher, their own tension building as they imagined the destruction about to befall the humans. Without warning, rocks exploded on both sides of the high pass, on a scale much larger than the widows witnessed at Ancestor's Vale. The rock walls crumbled and collapsed, devouring the lead elements of the human army beneath them.

A breath later, the sound assailed their ears. All of them clapped their hands to their heads as the tremendous noise from the blast shook them. It thundered on for innumerable breaths. High-pitched screams of terror, a multitude of fear voiced by hundreds, carried along the wind. A wall of dust and rock rolled down the pass, swallowing up more of the human army. The widows saw the masses of men and animals panicking. Horses threw riders. Organized marching lines broke apart and stampeded from the collapse. Rocks slammed down faster than anyone could move, even on horseback. A cloud of earth rolled down the human army, obscuring and burying at the same time.

242

Duli knew the thunder of the collapsing pass became their death knell as well. She saw it in the eyes of the others. Their former escape route disappeared in the haze. "And so heralds the beginning of the end for us."

Despite the carnage, the dust stopped after covering only a small portion of Tariyka's forces. Duli and the widows could still see a long line of soldiers stretching to the limit of their vision in the valley below. For all the deaths the humans had suffered, there remained enough to still destroy Tok-Maurron. It would not happen this day, for the passage was blocked. As the sounds of the rock slide settled, Duli's ears caught a different sound from further down their own ridge. A set of axes could be heard chopping down trees.

"Idiot humans!" Duli muttered, "They're digging in because they know we're dug in. They don't realize they could just walk over us right now."

"Then we have time to share a drink." Fosha spoke as she drew a flask from her pack.

Duli worried anew for Fosha's injury. The bleeding on the outside had stopped, but what about her insides? The elder refused to let anyone touch the arrow. She spoke in clipped snippets, a few whispered words between each pained gasp of air stretching sentences out several breaths.

Fosha popped the cork. "Tok-Maurron is safe. The clan will be hidden beneath Silver Mountain within the next ten days. Their numbers will be bolstered by tens of thousands of our brothers and sisters. They will be hidden deep under the world by the time the humans circle around wide mountains just to find their way back to this spot."

The elder held out the flask for Duli. She accepted it, staring at it in her hand as the remaining widows sat around in a circle. Fosha offered, "Let us share a drink for those fallen."

Duli looked to the faces of those around her. She took most of her strength watching Fosha, witnessing the quiet dignity borne by the elder despite her injury. Duli raised the flask in the direction of Shauna's body. "I toast Shauna Horgar, bless her soul. She was the first one fighting by my side against humans the day I stole Geordan's musket. I wish I could have seen the day she stormed out of the Mennurdan Guild.

"Leli Gorm, who helped organize and lead the widows. She brought comfort to many through her lotions and oils; hopefully she has found comfort in Dorvanon.

"Herothe Darkhair. My one-time competitor, selling leather crafts together in Hearthden. Many of us can thank her healing miracles for our lives."

Duli paused, unsure how to best phrase her last toast. "And my love, Geordan. What would he say if he could see me now? I remember when he first brought me to Tok-Maurron. I was impressed and scared, smitten by the size of the city. I should have heeded more of the warning signs when they took away my beard. For all that, I was younger, and blind with love. Geordan comforted me beyond my worries. A toast to a husband who warded away all the other concerns of the world."

Duli drank and handed the flask to Katy Dornan. Katy offered her tribute. "I grew up in the family business, at Deepmug's. The tavern always seemed to be the center of everything in Lower City. I remember Fernon flirting with me until Loram threatened to cut off his drink supply. Then he got serious and proposed, and we wanted to have children right away. I never told anyone, but when he died, I thought I was with child."

The revelation shocked Duli. Now she understood why Katy had been so inconsolable during the funeral.

Katy continued, "It terrified me alongside my grief. Later I came to realize, despite my love of the brigade, I wish I had been carrying his child. I really wanted to be able to keep part of him with me. To my husband, Fernon."

Glaura took the flask after Katy's drink. While she composed her thoughts, Duli saw a slight laugh, barely a shake of the shoulders, at some memory. "I remember having nay interest in Tormero at first. I was trying to pair him with a friend, and events took a different turn. He gave me the two greatest gifts ever, Waurel and Feena." Her voice started to crack as she spoke the names, but Glaura recovered. "I appreciate how all of you hid your laughter when I showed up in the Hearthden after letting my children braid my beard. They made such an awful mess of it sometimes, but I treasured every mistake they ever made." She rubbed her beardless chin and drank.

Fosha accepted the bottle with a grimace. Her voice proved difficult to hear. Everyone patiently awaited every word as she struggled through her thoughts. "I was proud the day my sons followed in their father's footsteps. He was a veteran of a war with the goblin-kin who once claimed part of the present-day mines. Most of you were born around the time I stayed up late some nights, a babe on the breast, worrying if tonight was the night he wouldn't come home. I was honored to raise a family of warriors." Fosha struggled to take a sip, and set the flask in the hands of the next widow. "I wonder what they'd think of my joining the army…"

Her words drifted off. The others waited to make sure she was done before the next one started toasting dead friends and family. Duli's mind began to wander elsewhere as the last two widows offered their toasts. She turned her ears towards the human lines, listening for clues to their intent. The whistling of arrows could be heard, as another volley fell into the field between the rings of stone. None flew far enough to threaten the remaining widows.

The last widow, her toast done, overturned the flask to show it was empty.

"Well, it's time. I'm done waiting." Duli said as she got to her feet.

The others looked at her with wide eyes. Glaura asked, "What do you mean?"

Duli looked at her friend with softness in her eyes atypical of their stoic race. "Geordan's been waiting for years. The gods didn't let me die; I couldn't take my own life. Now the humans are right over on the other side of a field. All they're doing is lobbing arrows and delaying my death even further."

"Duli…" Glaura couldn't seem to find the words to argue more, though her concerns showed plain on her face.

"What? We're dead." Duli waved her hand from the cliff to the ring of stones. Her motion included the lone widow corpse in the inner ring. "They have us surrounded. It's just a question of time. We did our task for our people; all that remains is what we do for ourselves."

"What are you going to do?" asked Glaura.

Duli hitched her belt. She drew out her knife and hatchet. It proved hurtful to clench the hatchet with her injured hand, but she endured it. "Charge."

The words caused Katy to rock back, "Why?"

Glaura spoke, "You're trying to kill yourself again?"

Duli sighed, "This is different. I'm not running out there because I'm angry, or because I'm too scared to live. It's just…it's time. I'm ready. I'm at peace with it. I don't plan to keep Geordan waiting any longer."

Glaura looked down. She glanced over at Sargas' discarded hammer. Climbing to her feet, Glaura walked over and retrieved it. "Well then, as your friend, I'm not letting you charge alone."

Duli offered a grim smile. "I'm tempted to stop you, but our outcome will be the same whether we attack or not. It's good to face death on one's own terms."

Katy drew alongside, holding her boar spear. "I'll be at your side as well. This is likely the last charge of the brigade. I won't let it pass without joining in."

"We're all ready", one of the other widows said as they grabbed weapons and moved alongside Duli.

Duli patted Glaura's shoulder, offering a warm smile to the rest of them. She looked down, seeing Fosha still sitting and staring at the ground.

"How about you, Fosha?"

Fosha didn't move. She showed no hint of even listening to Duli's voice. Katy leaned over and touched Fosha's shoulder. The elder toppled over. Fosha's half-lidded eyes continued to stare straight ahead.

Katy gasped, "She…she's gone."

Duli's smile melted away. She stared at her friend, stricken by the quiet passing. It had been Fosha's brigade as much as her own. Herothe…Leli…Fosha…all those who helped shape the brigade as a fighting force were now gone, leaving her all alone.

The remaining widows all stood silently, incapable of turning their eyes away. The more she looked, the more she felt the moisture welling up in her eyes. Duli pushed away the sorrows the only way she could, with anger and determination.

"Feel proud!" She barked as an order. "Envy her silent farewell. She died among friends, sharing a drink."

Duli turned her head, glancing through a gap in the stones at the new feather shafts covering the field just outside.

"Such a peaceful death will not be our fate!"

CHAPTER 33

Duli stepped out from the inner ring of stones. The others followed, armored bodies scraping through the narrow opening. She paused, staring at the small field between the rows of stone. Over a hundred corpses of friend and foe alike lay contorted across the trampled meadow of arrows. Duli's gaze passed over the fallen widows. She no longer felt the compulsion to release the sorrows from her eyes, and she looked within herself for the reason.

"They have found their serenity in death. How can I grieve for their departure when I know my own is forthcoming? They have simply passed beyond my sight, waiting for me to join them. Maybe they're watching us now. Will they admire this final act?"

The remaining four widows formed a line on either side of her. Arms brushed against hers, a comforting touch to let her know she didn't stand alone. She listened to their silence, and felt their gazes on lost friends. She worried if their resolve would weaken at witnessing the macabre scene. Axes continued to chop into trees somewhere ahead, but the noise foremost in Duli's ears came from the barely audible breaths of those beside her.

"We can't charge like this. Not from loss. Not from grief. We need to ignite the spark in our spirits. We need to go forth with forge-fires bellowing from our lungs and vengeance assured in our eyes."

Duli cast a glance to her right. Katy stood by her side, another widow beyond her. She glanced at Katy's spear tip, held high and proud. Duli offered the woman a smile as she softly repeated the same advice she had once drilled into Katy's ears countless times training in Hearthden.

"Katy, keep your spear tip up."

Katy forced a smile in return. She repeated some of Duli's following advice from those days. "Stab for their hearts."

They nodded their determination. Duli looked left, seeing Glaura next to her and the last widow beyond. Glaura spoke first, hefting Sargas' hammer. "Forget about me aiming high. I want to crack their jewel-sacks!"

The tension broke as the widows let loose a wave of laughter. As the merriment began to fade, Duli knew they were almost in the right state of mind. She planted one foot forward, looking ready to run.

"For Geordan!" She shouted. Immediately after, she struck her hatchet blade down the length of her dagger. The sound echoed as a spark flew loose. Duli began stomping her lead foot into the ground as she shouted a cadence of names in the direction of the unseen enemy. "For Shauna! For Fosha…"

Katy began stomping a foot in tune, butting her spear against stone ground, shouting her own litany of names. "For Fernon! For Herothe…"

Glaura and the others joined in. "For Tormero! For Waurel! For Feena!"

They shouted louder, wanting every human to hear their grievances. Voices merged to one rhythm even though the names they shouted differed. They stomped the ground and clanged their weapons against any metal handy. Emboldened by their own actions, they fed and supplied greater levels of enthusiasm. The pace quickened as they roused their passions. Every voice cried out injustice. Every name released the hurt of their loss. Pain subsided; weariness succumbed to renewed feelings of energy. The stomping legs burned for the moment they could be set into motion towards the enemy. Their ears drowned in their own noise yet they hungered for more.

When Duli felt her intensity peaked, she changed her chant to repeat the same three words. "For the widows!"

All of them switched to echo Duli. 'For the widows' roared through burning throats. 'For the widows' rang across the field and beyond. 'For the widows' drove their stomping feet to send clods of earth scattering from divots in the ground. Duli felt their emotions build past the breaking point. She recalled images in her mind of the rockslides falling upon the humans. Duli imagined that first crack tearing across a cliff wall, with the humans standing in the path below.

Duli let loose the rock slide. "For the widows!"

She leaned her body and let her feet propel her forward. The chant screamed free of her lips between gritted teeth. Her arms pumped as she ran, fists clenched around her eager weapons, heedless of the blood on one hand, numb to any pain. She heard the widows surging forward, only a step behind. They scored the earth in their path. Grounded arrow shafts snapped and skittered away as they passed. Dwarven boots trampled fallen humans.

248

Grass tufts flew in their wake. 'For the widows' rolled forward like a tide, eager for the moment it would break against the humans.

An officer in the Tariykan army called upon the hundred archers in his company to ready arrows. Ahead of their position, two other ranks of soldiers formed around barely-constructed barricades, most no more than a single downed tree or an ankle-high pile of stones. Axes were dropped as men heard the orders to form lines and ran to form a defense. A heightened thrill of battle seized everyone from the moment dwarf voices could be heard shouting on the top of the rise. Everyone could hear the dwarves coming.

Archers formed behind the first few lines. Each quiver was a dozen arrows lighter than that morning, yet a dozen more arrows sat ready to launch at the dwarves. Ahead, the lines of defending swordsmen felt like a taut bowstring.

The first dwarf appeared, sand-colored hair trailing a solitary braid, brandishing a weapon in each hand, screaming loud enough to smite them by sound alone. Humans began to watch in wonder as a small line of dwarves followed her, all running through the same gap. The leader slowed her pace just enough for the others to form alongside her. The whole time, she never interrupted the death-promising stare aimed at the human lines. The sheer brazenness of her attitude counterbalanced the lack of blades at her side.

Soldier voices murmured as they watched the five dwarves make their suicidal approach. Human officers gave out commands, followed by the line of archers easing the tension off their bowstrings and lowered their weapons. Scores of swords raised in preparation for the clash. Soon, the archers in the back couldn't see the dwarves due to the tall humans ahead of them.

Duli's ears pounded with the noise of their battle cries, mixed with the tempo of pounding feet. The humans in their path stood ready. Tall and imposing, they held swords poised for a strike. Beyond them, Duli took note of a distant figure in the Tariykan lines. It had to be one of their officers, sitting tall and ornate on a horse's saddle.

"Do you have a blade that will strike true? Are you able to send me to Dorvanon?"

She flung herself forward, looking once again to the line of armed humans ahead. A voice of reason cracked through Duli's wall of rage. She realized such a straightforward charge would likely impale them whether or not they killed in return.

Duli noticed something about their back-pennants she could use for a plan. The humans straight ahead of them wore yellow pennants with a fish, while only a few paces to the right the line of banners turned green.

"At my command," she huffed between running breaths, "we'll turn a sharp right and charge into those green flags."

The widows roared in acknowledgment. Duli led the wedge without betraying her true target. They closed within fifteen paces...they could see the whites of the humans' eyes...

Ten paces...they could make out minor details in the etchings of the chest armor...

Five paces...muscles clenched and veins stood out as the men tensed to deliver a blow...

"Now! For the widows!"

She saw surprise in the eyes of their foes. The humans ahead of them were slow to strike as the widows turned just short of melee distance. The green-flagged humans, not expecting the sudden change in direction, didn't actually have their feet planted right or their arms in the right position.

On the edge of her sight, Duli saw Katy's speartip snake ahead and claim a hit. An instant later Duli launched into the air, hoping her target would expect her to go low instead. It worked. She brought her hatchet down hard on his weapon shoulder, and then momentum carried her dagger-first into his chest. Duli hoped her weight drove the blade past his light armor, but she had no time to look. She rolled to the ground with the human.

Feeling vulnerable, she tried to right herself and rise. Screams, grunts, metallic clangs carried to her ears, but most sounds felt rather hushed compared to the need to simply get up and look for danger. Someone's leather bag rolled past. Duli caught sight of a pair of human boots running toward her from the side. Instead of pushing up with her legs, she threw her weight to that side and launched out. The impact jarred her body as the human fell over her. Duli managed her senses first and crawled on top of the man. She alternated swings between dagger and hatchet, drawing blood.

Some hidden sense sent a warning to her thoughts. *"Get up! Keep moving!"* And so she did.

As she rose, she felt and saw a dagger fall free from a new wound in her leg. From the coating of blood it had sank in an inch deep. Duli pulled her eyes away from the morbid sight. She couldn't afford to give undue attention to it while caught in the chaos of battle.

She cast a glance to one side. An armored human faced off with Glaura. Glaura had her hammer ready but the human backed away to make use of his longer sword. His course brought him towards Duli. She chopped the hatchet against his back. It stopped the human, and Duli heard the meaty impact of the hammer from the other side.

Turning around, Duli flinched as the boar spear flashed by her face. Katy and a human both had hands on it, fighting for leverage. Blood scoured Katy's short hair. As the pair danced around, Duli's dagger slashed behind the human's leg. The human fell. Katy secured her grip on the spear and jabbed it into the man.

"Where are the other two widows?" she wondered.

Duli's injured leg stumbled, an act that saved her life. A Tariykan blade aimed for her back clipped a shoulder guard instead. A tangle of leather and cloth ripped away as Duli wheeled to face the newest threat. They locked weapons against each other. The human had the advantage and used his weight to bear Duli to the ground. His helmet clattered off her and rolled away. She struggled to keep his blade away from her face. She felt a burning pain in her shoulder where his earlier cut landed. Duli saw her green eyes reflected in the blade as it pushed steadily toward her neck.

One moment his face sneered over her, the next moment canine jaws clamped over his face as a mass of fur pushed him away. Duli got to her knees. Stunned, she watched her growling rescuer tear a chunk of flesh from the man.

"Bandit?!" In her astonishment, she ignored her pain as she sat up. "How do you always escape?"

Reinvigorated, she fell upon the man and stabbed him alongside her wolf companion. The man curled into a ball. Bandit forced openings and tore into the man. Duli struggled to her feet, blinking sweat from her eyes.

Bodies twitched around them. They left a sizable hole in the middle of the humans' front line. Humans from that endless line started to fan out in groups on either side of the surviving widows. Glaura and Katy continued fighting opponents. Duli looked ahead. The distant human officer still observed them. A second line of soldiers, thirty paces away, barred the route between her and him.

She pointed her dagger at the next line. "Onward! Cut to the heart of them!"

Without knowing if any of her friends were able to hear or obey, she charged again. Duli's wounded leg almost sent her toppling, but she readjusted and ran with a visible limp. As her hands pumped forward, she saw the bleeding had resumed on her injured hand.

Katy's speartip bobbed back into her field of view, on her right side. A glance left revealed Glaura catching up; her friend dealing with a limp of her own. The distance to the next line stretched on for endless breaths. Duli's concern narrowed to the weapons held by the second line. These humans bore arms to repel ram riders. Long spears bristled out from their position, forming a wall of sharp points. Duli began to regret her decision to charge, for surely they would only impale themselves. Resigned, she lowered her head and gritted her teeth.

In a rush of fur, Bandit darted forward between widows. The wolf ran unpredictably, trying to find his own route around the bristle of spears. He jumped to one side before changing his mind and darting several steps the other direction. As the wolf turned, some spears lowered and tried to keep track. As the wolf's charge crisscrossed before them, the spears lost their focus and began tangling themselves. No longer a cohesive wall, Bandit slipped under their points and drove his teeth into the mass of legs beyond.

Duli watched in amazement as men fell, cursing or screaming. The soldiers dropped spears or allowed them to swing randomly as they tried avoiding the crazy wolf. The widows exploited their disarray. Duli let loose another scream of rage at the moment when it was too late for the spearmen to stop her. Her body slipped through the disrupted barricade. She bowled into two men, pumping her weapons forward furiously as she strained her tired legs onward. She heard the impact on both sides of her as her two friends hit the line as well.

Individual noises became lost in the swirl of warfare's hurricane. Duli couldn't tell her own shouts from those around her. Her sight became a pattern of one frozen image after another…A hairy hand trying to push her shoulder away…Her dagger sinking into a man's armpit…A human falling down with his hands covering his face…Snapping her forehead into a yellowed, gap-toothed grimace…A broken spear shaft flung at someone off to her side. Through it all, she willed her legs to bull forward.

Her momentum came to an end when a heavy weight fell against one leg. On impulse, her left hand dropped to the side to steady herself. Her hand brushed against something. Wet fur. Sticky, wet fur. She kept her balance and brought her hand back up to her eyes. Short, gray wolf hairs stuck to new blood on her hand. She glanced down. Bandit sagged against her leg. The faintest of whimpers somehow could be heard over the storm of noise. She felt the tremble in the wolf's body as it sank down.

"Oh, my child. My family. I would have spared you this end."

Unable to move with the wolf's weight against her, Duli did something the dwarves called 'making one with the stone'. Her legs spread apart as best they could and locked into a stance. Through bleary, sorrows-filled eyes she could make out the tall shapes all around her.

"Come on then!" She cried. "Death is served here! Mine and yours! Come and share!"

Braced upon immobile legs, she swung her arms back and forth. She knew she couldn't defend herself. She struck at shapes and hoped to get lucky. There was a deep flash of pain, but she struck back. Duli began feeling disconnected from the aches of her body. She kept swinging her arms, finding no focus on the figures surrounding her. Her ears picked up only her own gasping breaths.

As if from a dream, one image became clear to her eyes. She saw him step from between the tall shadows. He smiled at her as he ran one hand down his thick beard. He looked exactly as she remembered him. Every perfect, beautiful detail of the man she loved emerged from the blur.

"Geordan?" Duli let the sorrows run unchecked down her face.

While everything else became a confused flickering of shadows, Geordan's comforting visage held firm. The clamor of battle began to fade. Her arms felt cold and tired, so Duli lowered them. Her voice cracked as she beseeched her love. "Take me home."

Duli never felt the blade that ended her life.

A timeless moment of silence and mist reigned, then she awoke as if from a dream. "Geordan?"

He stood before her again. His face was the same she had known and loved. He smiled through his beard, a warm look in his eyes. Geordan dressed as if for his own wedding, adorned armor mixed with fine garb.

"I'm here for you," he said, "I've always been near, awaiting the moment we could share our love again."

Duli became dimly aware that she stood somewhere new. Mountains ringed the meadow upon which they stood. The mountains themselves supported large, arched entrances and towers. A dwarf city encompassed the entire range, and Duli didn't have to ask the city's name. The gates, so clearly etched on Geordan's old gun, stood in front of one large entry. Duli smiled: the first true, genuine smile she'd enjoyed in years.

A weight she'd forgotten about lifted from her legs. She looked down. Bandit's mischievous eyes met hers. The wolf, healthy and whole, bounded away from her side and began to frolic in the meadow.

A blur of motion to her right caused her to glance to the side. Duli saw Katy, just as Katy had stood next to Duli in their last moments of life. Katy's garb had changed, a decorative and functional mix that would also be seen at a dwarf wedding. The woman, gazing across the meadow upon her own husband, became so overcome by emotions that she dropped to her knees. The sorrows came upon the younger widow, as she watched Fernon approach her with arms open.

"Waurel! Feena!"

Duli swung her head to the left, following the voice. Glaura sank to one knee in the grass, as her two bundles of joy ran to meet her. The boy and girl giggled as they ran, happy and playful as they were in life. The charge of the children knocked their mother into the grass, where she laughed aloud. Tormero followed a moment later, throwing a welcoming nod to Duli.

Then she was in Geordan's arms, staring up into his face. She touched his beard, and in return he reached a hand up and stroked her beardless cheek.

"You can dream it, and you'll have your own beard back."

Duli closed her eyes and lingered on the feel of his fingers sliding across her cheek. "I think I've grown to like this, if you don't mind."

He replied with a smile. Before Duli could go farther, she felt guilt welling up in her gut.

"Geordan, I… I tried to get to you sooner. I couldn't do it."

His arms held her tighter. A trace of sorrow passed across his eyes. "If you had taken your own life in a fit of rage or sadness, your soul would have never found its way to this peaceful place."

Duli's mind reeled at the folly she'd almost committed. As soon as she refocused on the present, she buried herself in his arms. Duli couldn't distract herself anymore from the reunion she'd envisioned for so long. She kissed him, she held him, and her arms promised to never let him go. Duli melted against him, the strength going from her legs to the firm embrace of her arms. He held her and whispered his eternal love into her ear.

On the mountain ridge behind him, the rest stood watching. Fosha stood next to her husband and lost boys. Shauna rested her head on her husband's shoulder. Leli once again held her young one in her arms as her husband stood with arm around her. Herothe and her man stood resplendent in their priestly vestments. The entire brigade and their loved ones stood together, cheering the last of their sisterhood to arrive in Dorvanon.

Duli and the widows were home.

About the Author

Douglas was born on Nov 28th, 1971 . He got to live many different places while growing up, courtesy of the assignments the US Army offered to his father. Too quiet and too shy for too long, there was always dreams of other worlds and places...and the desire to write about them.

He got into fantasy role-playing games in his mid-teens. The first such games played on a computer were offered by a Commodore 64. Often Douglas and his brother would create their own tabletop fantasy games and rules as well, all using very basic 6-sided die. Eventually, they also got into Dungeons and Dragons (©Wizards of the Coast LLC). As MMORPGs (Massively Multiplayer Online Role Playing Games) appeared, he tried a hand at several of them and made several new friends across the internet. To this day he has friends whom he meets in tabletop role-playing games, as well as online adventures. Many of his characters evolved in games, and each developed their own personality.

The Widow Brigade was the first novel planned after the lengthy completion of *The Earthrin Stones* series. The character Duli, like Doug's other characters, has lived online with other gamers, facing all sorts of challenges. From the start, however, Doug knew he had a special book destiny for this strong woman. The novel is set in the fantasy world of Dhea Loral...a world created for tabletop role-playing. Douglas continues to write novels and think up short stories, while pondering the changing world of print vs ebooks.

Douglas lives with his wife and two young children in Minnesota. He works in health care, serving people's healthcare needs in imaging. When most people see him, he is wearing scrubs. You can learn more at DheaLoral.com

About the Cover Artist

When Douglas searched for a cover artist for The Widow Brigade, he came across the website of Obsidian Abnormal. O Abnormal has a few YouTube tutorials on artwork. He currently runs a comic on his website with regular updates. He has a commision lineup for folks wanting artwork of characters or, in this case, cover art for a book.

Fans can support him through his Patreon page, and receieve special artwork and larger copies of his comic and wallpapers. His blog shares artwork, rants, The Bonebreakers, tutorials and more.

For more information, check out his website at www.theministryofabnormality.com

Made in the USA
San Bernardino, CA
29 May 2015